Serenity Bay

A NOVEL BY

BETTE NORDBERG

BETHANY HOUSE PUBLISHERS
Minneapolis, Minnesota

Published by Bethany House Publishers
A Ministry of Bethany Fellowship International
11400 Hampshire Avenue South
Minneapolis, Minnesota 55438
www.bethanyhouse.com

Printed in the United States of America by
Bethany Press International, Minneapolis, Minnesota 55438

Library of Congress Cataloging-in-Publication Data

Nordberg, Bette.
    Serenity Bay / by Bette Nordberg.
       p. cm.
    ISBN 0–7642–2396–8
    1. Puget Sound Region (Wash.)—Fiction. 2. Female friendship—Fiction.
3. Married women—Fiction. 4. Abused wives—Fiction. 5. Islands—Fiction.
I. Title.
PS3564.0553 S47   2000
813'.6—dc21
                                                       00–010526

BETTE NORDBERG graduated from the University of Washington as a physical therapist in 1977. In 1990 she turned from rehabilitation medicine to writing. Her first book, *Evangeline, Woman of Faith* (the biography of Evangeline McNeill), was published in 1996. She and her husband, Kim, recently helped plant Lighthouse Christian Center, a new church in the South Hill area of Puyallup, Washington, where Bette writes, directs drama, and plays keyboard. She has published numerous dramas, articles, and devotions. Married twenty-five years, Kim and Bette have four children, two in college and two at home.

The author may be contacted at her Web site: www.myfables.com.

One

STATIONERY, the color of pistachio ice cream, stared at me, blank and accusing. How could Susan ask me to write a letter no one will ever read? My left hand trembled slightly and I gripped the pen more fiercely, as a tear splashed onto the parchment. I tried to brush it away, but the paper bubbled, leaving a raised splotch in its place. What words could possibly express everything I feel?

"I can't do this. Not yet."

"You don't have to. I just thought it might help," Susan said. We sat quietly in her living room, each in our own swivel rocker, facing the ocean. Our day had been long, full of emotion, effort, and trauma, leaving us both drained and exhausted. "Someday, though," she said, "Leah might actually see it. Read it. You never know. Someday she may need to hear how you're feeling right now."

Obediently, I began writing *Dear Leah*. Tears blurred the words until I could no longer see. I dropped the pen into my lap. "I can't."

She nodded, stood, and came to my side, kneeling beside my chair. We stayed like that for a few minutes, me rocking and weeping, Susan lightly patting my shoulder. "What would I do without you?" I asked.

"I'm here, Patricia, because I want to be," she said softly. Reaching over to the table beside my chair, she lifted a box of tissue and offered it to me. "I wouldn't choose to be anywhere else." She pulled out a tissue and wiped her own nose vigorously. "I have the latte machine started," she whispered. "Would you like something hot to drink?"

I noded, afraid to trust my voice. With a long sigh Susan turned toward the kitchen.

Alone, I gazed out over the ocean.

Even in darkness I could clearly make out the bizarre triangular profiles of the trees. Here, on the west side of Cummins Island, relentless westerly winds buffet all the vegetation unfortunate enough to grow there. The trees that cannot withstand the assault of the wind do not survive. The ones that do are misshapen for life.

Just as the wind prunes trees, island life prunes people. Either they learn to grow under these conditions, or they leave. Though it seems an eternity, ten months ago I left.

Floating amid the inland water of Puget Sound, our island is shaped like a dinner roll with the first bite missing. A tiny harbor rests on the lee side. Tucked away from the wind, Serenity Bay provides protection for boats traveling through the San Juan Islands. Someone named our town for the peaceful, quiet waters of the bay; while I lived here, I never knew serenity.

Ours is a tiny village, complete with marina, hardware store, two-pump gas station, and a small grocery store. The ferry dock is here, along with moorage for the summer people. The rest of the village consists of tiny shops carved out of ancient wooden buildings with false fronts and wooden floors. In these shops the summer people buy ice cream, T-shirts, linen dresses, and paintings by local artists. From each storefront the scent of potpourri and bayberry candles waft into the summer air, mixing with the smell of saltwater tides and diesel fuel. This is our town, our community, and the place where I once lived.

Only the stoutest of humanity remain on Cummins Island over the winter. During those long bleak months, marina docks float under dark rainy skies. Glistening wooden planks empty both of people and boats. Raindrops bounce off waves in the harbor, and the ferry rocks in the wind, wrestling with its tie-down. The shops of the summer people close. The sidewalks empty of all but locals, who refuse to run through the rain to their cars.

All our shoes are waterproof, and our clothing is made of Gore-Tex. Winter rain is constant, varying from heavy falling dew to monsoonlike downpours. Fabric here never really dries but stays damp with ambient moisture—the same moisture that turns cedar siding green and feeds the moss growing on sidewalks, fences, and roof tiles. Winter nights begin shortly after the ringing of the afternoon school bell. The season lasts most of eight calendar months, fraying island nerves and testing tempers. Only the distant promise of warm temperatures and summer sunshine sustains the locals through the long bleak darkness.

Following the summer solstice, daytime temperatures soar to the midseventies, and the docks in Serenity Bay fill with boats—hundreds of them—all bobbing against their fenders, gently rocking in the swell. Some, with sleek black windows and startling whiteness, belong to company executives or chairmen of corporate boards. Next to these float the reconditioned wooden hulls of old tugs converted to cruisers for families—happy families—who spend their summers wandering from island to island on the glistening blue waters of Puget Sound.

From Memorial Day to Labor Day, summer people crowd the village sidewalks and wander from shop to shop, imagining what it would be like to live in this ideal setting. They imagine themselves buying groceries at the Stock 'n Save and think longingly of their children attending our six-room elementary school.

"We don't have swing sets in the city," they say. And they believe that our town is missing all the evils of big city life.

But they are wrong.

When I lived here, our home sat high on a cliff on the west side of Cummins Island. Facing brilliant sunsets and stunning seascapes, ours was some of the most valuable land on the island. Russell built a magnificent home for us there, large and impressive. With weathered cedar siding, he tucked it inconspicuously among the fir trees on the hill. He built an enviable house, but I loved it for a different reason. I loved it for the whales—orcas—beautiful black and white creatures who spent their summers playing in the broad protected harbor just north of our beach.

Our ten acres bordered a marine reserve. Inhospitable rocks hiding just under the surface of the water in the bay's entrance safeguarded the whales from the intrusion of whale-watching vessels. The whales found safety in the harbor, and every year they returned.

I knew when they arrived because I watched for them, waited for them, keeping the kitchen door open all through the early summer. With one ear I listened for their return. Crashing water told me they breached. Squeaks and squawks told me they were "taking roll." Whatever their cue, I knew they were back, and I dropped everything to run down a steep narrow pathway to the water's edge. There on dark rock ledges I sat, hugging my knees, listening to the powerful whoosh of air from their blowholes, watching their glistening black bodies roll and slap the water. I watched every bit of their play until at last they tired of me and swam away. Away from the cove. Away from the island.

At the same time, someone watched me. Without looking, I could feel Russell's telescope focused squarely on the center of my back. I watched the whales, and from the window of our living room, Russell watched me.

I shall always envy the whales. They left the island so easily.

———

Dr. Russell Koehler was just Russ when I first met him. A small-framed man, with gentle aqua eyes and light sandy hair. His eyelashes were so blond that they nearly disappeared above the blue of his eyes—until he glanced downward. That was the first thing I loved about him, his shy habit of looking down and hiding his eyes behind palm-branch eyelashes.

That was sixteen years ago.

Sally Rhone, my college roommate, had asked me to be the fourth member of a group going to a fraternity party at the Delta-Chi house. Initially, I refused. Generally I preferred to spend Friday nights in Travensky Hall with my friend Lynn, who played with me in the same university chamber orchestra. Neither Lynn nor I majored in music. Thus we'd been relegated to the remedial chamber group. Lynn, a stubborn woman, determined that we would work our way into the premiere orchestra. She'd set her heart on a European tour, courtesy of university coffers. Week after week we played the scales, études, and chamber pieces she believed would develop our full potential as cellists.

Over time, Lynn and I discovered that practice rooms were easier to get than dates, especially on Friday nights, and our private practice sessions soon developed into an entrenched habit. Week after week we labored toward the dream. Some weeks we spent entire evenings perfecting especially difficult four-measure passages. I hardly wanted to trade an evening of Schumann for the smell of beer and the deafening noise of bad speakers, even for Sally.

The particular event Sally had in mind was a costume affair, and it seemed that Ben, her boyfriend, had rustled up costumes for a foursome. Reportedly, Ben had a family friend in town and had begged Sally to find a willing fourth. At the last minute the woman backed out, leaving Sally desperate. So at three o'clock on Friday afternoon, she sat perched on the windowsill next to my desk, begging me to come along. Apparently I was just the right size for the costume in question.

I hated blind dates, not that I had mounds of experience. Still, it seemed to me that my failure rate remained extraordinarily high. I found these arrangements awkward and embarrassing. Worst of all, they seemed, without exception, to lead nowhere. None had ever developed into a second date. I couldn't explain this satisfactorily to Sally. I am hardly a candidate for the *Sports Illustrated* Swimsuit Edition—though I do not consider myself ugly. I found it much less painful to blame the dating system than myself.

Not only did Sally ask me to forgo an evening of music, but Monday marked the beginning of midterms. At the time, I anticipated a grueling exam in Microbiology 400. Though I struggled in the lab section, I fared better in the lectures. I believed my acceptance to nursing school might hinge on this particular test. Sally declared this small detail irrelevant. I needed a night off, she proclaimed, a chance to relax, to let my brain rejuvenate.

In truth, I didn't get out much. It felt nice to be wanted, even if only because I could squeeze into a size six. So I agreed to don the belly dancing costume and join Sally and Ben and his mysterious family friend.

Russell Koehler, my date, arrived looking like Peter O'Toole in *Lawrence of Arabia,* complete with turban. The picture of courtesy, he opened the car door for me and let me pass through doorways ahead of him. When we arrived at the party, he took my coat and brought me a drink. He found a place for us to sit. Like all frat parties, this one was noisy. Russ hovered attentively near me. I needn't have been afraid to go along. No one could be expected to hold an intelligent conversation in this environment anyway. Beer flowed freely among college students intent on having a good time. Over the loud music, our conversation was reduced to polite smiles and nods. Russ seemed nice enough.

Around eleven o'clock he took the beer glass from my hand, set it on the table, and pulled me off of the couch. "Let's get out of here," he shouted above the din. Still holding my hand, he led me to a porch off the back of the living room. Outside, we discovered a warm, quiet evening, unusual for late April.

"You don't belong in there," he said, gesturing toward the party behind us.

"What makes you think that?" I tried to sound coy, though I wondered if he were teasing me. Did he use this line on every woman he met?

"I can tell. You're a woman of purpose. Of quality. Not the kind who would sit around at a blaring party getting drunk."

He'd already taken off his turban, and in the light spilling from the French doors behind us, I saw his face clearly, in spite of the darkness. His eyes looked intense, yet gentle. Serious.

"Thank you. That was kind of you." I turned away, leaning against the railing. He followed my gaze, then, bending at the waist, rested his forearms on the banister. A light breeze stirred the air while I searched for another less personal subject. "Tell me, Russ. What are you studying?"

"Medicine," he answered. "I start my third year of med school next fall." I heard confidence in his voice, certainty.

"Oh, really. Where?" Medical students impressed me. In my first year in college, I noticed that nine out of ten freshmen called themselves premed students. Most never got closer than an average score on their Medical Aptitude Test. If they finished college at all, they graduated with degrees in biology or chemistry and ended up selling shoes. Some wisely switched to the more lucrative business market. Those who were accepted to med school had to be the best of the best.

In the course of our evening, I had noticed that Russell was quiet, not boastful, never demanding attention, not like the other medical students I'd met. I'd listened carefully on the way to the party. Though he added many quips to the conversation, he never dominated it. Russell hadn't engaged in Ben's verbal parrying.

"I'm at UCLA," he smiled at me in the dim light.

Curious, I probed. "Out of state?" Most students found out-of-state tuition an enormous burden.

"I have a scholarship. It doesn't cover everything, but it brings the cost down—almost the same as residential tuition."

"Good for you!" I said without thinking.

His lips turned up slightly at the corners, and his face softened. My outburst seemed to please him. "So what are you doing in Seattle?" I asked.

"Mother's birthday." He smiled in the half-light. "Dad wouldn't let me miss it. For that matter, my mother might disown me." He turned back to me, leaning on one elbow. "Whatever Mother wants, she generally gets." He grinned. "I don't mind too much, though. She's a good ol' gal."

When Ben's car came to a stop at our sorority, Russ jumped out and came around to open my door. "Let's give them a minute to say good-night," he whispered, nodding toward Sally and Ben. As we walked toward the front door, I felt his hand resting gently on the small of my back. We passed the double doors of the front entry, and I allowed him to guide me to the far end of the porch.

"I had a good time," he said, smiling. He glanced down at his shoes. Those eyelashes again.

"Me too. Thanks." Not the usual blind date, thank goodness. I would have to remember to thank Sally.

"Maybe we could do something again sometime. Can I call?"

"That'd be nice." *Not too eager*, a voice inside me coaxed. *Slow down, Patricia.*

He cupped my right hand in both of his and squeezed lightly. Leaning down, he brushed his lips gently against the side of my cheek. "Until later, then," he said quietly. Holding my eyes with his, he took a step back. Then he turned and walked briskly back to the car.

I don't know when I began breathing again. What an extraordinary man—not like anyone I'd ever known before. I took the house key from my purse and quietly let myself in the front door. I couldn't shake the feeling that something monumental had happened. Could one blind date change my life forever? I fervently hoped so.

Two

IT WOULD BE NEARLY THREE YEARS before I saw Russell Koehler again. And now, looking back, it seems funny to me that I find myself focusing on those three intervening years. In the wee hours of the night I comb through them, turning them over and over again in my mind, looking for clues. Now, when I wish more than anything to answer my own questions, I wonder if those years somehow hold the key. An explanation for the pain I have experienced. If the interpretation is there, I have yet to discover it.

Some of the intervening years are no more than photographs in my memory, pictures encapsulating the feelings and impressions left by important events. In my mind's eye I see myself holding the rejection letter from the university nursing school. I feel the shock of disbelief and the intense sting of failure. I vividly remember driving to Mom's apartment, knowing she would provide her usual dose of reassurance. After my father died, my mother had always been my biggest cheerleader. I remember spending the evening together—she full of encouragement, me full of doom and disappointment.

My carefully laid plans allowed for only one attempt at admission to nursing school. Mom wanted me to wait a year and try again. But I was too proud and money was too scarce. I needed to finish school and get a job.

By the spring of my second year I decided to finish my degree in biology and complete the requirements for a teaching certificate. This way, I could earn a living while I figured out if I wanted to return to the medical field. My third and fourth years of college remain a blur of cost-cutting images—opening a box of discount ice cream, wondering which flavor was really hidden inside; wearing corduroy pants until the wale in the knees vanished; combing the closets of my sorority sisters, looking for professional clothes for my first job interview.

During these last two years, my mom managed to find time and energy to encourage me along. She often invited me home for hot chocolate and a video. She sent chocolate chip cookies during finals week. I'd never have made it without her reassuring expressions of love.

Among my memories, I treasure the pride of landing my first teaching position, my first look at Johnson River, my first day of school at Clark's Creek Elementary.

Mostly when I think of my first year in the Grayson County School District, I can almost feel the fatigue, the overwhelming exhaustion of endless days spent decorating my classroom, planning lessons, working with young, anxious parents of brand-new kindergartners. I feel too the intense loneliness of being single in a new town. Of course I remember wonderful moments also, like the surprising joy in the face of a five-year-old the first time he associates the sound of a letter with its shape. His face lights up as though he has discovered nuclear energy. During my first year of teaching, there were many moments like that.

Other memories from those years are cinematic, playing in slow motion across the theater of my mind, each character delivering lines as deliberately as if scripted by Spielberg or Kubrick. Whenever I replay the film, the characters and words remain the same, archived without alteration, stored unchangeably in the synapse of my memory.

I remember my friend Annie, a second-grade teacher who became both my confidant and loving support over that long first winter. Both immersed in our jobs, our only regular pleasure was Friday night fish and chips at Sudsy's. More intermittent were Annie's schemes to find us each a soul mate.

I remember one plot in particular—her most farfetched, even for Annie. Washing paintbrushes after school one Wednesday afternoon, I looked up as she burst triumphantly into my classroom.

"Glad to find you here," she said, excited.

Ignoring her obvious animation, I handed her a bunch of long-handled brushes. "What did you need?" I asked. She grimaced and poured dish soap into the sink. "Stop splashing," I complained.

Turning off the water, she began dabbing brushes into the puddle of soap. "Beggars should not be picky," she began and held up her finger.

I didn't correct her. Annie frequently hacked up old expressions. It made her an enchanting friend—that and the fact that we were the picture of opposites. She stood five feet ten inches tall in stocking feet. I barely cleared sixty inches. Annie loved a crowd, while my shyness made parent-teacher conferences feel like a Broadway performance. Annie wore her straight blond hair in a shoulder-length bob. I kept mine as short as I could, budgeting carefully every trip to the hairdresser. After I washed it, I applied gel, effectively gluing the curls together into solid ringlets. Only gel kept my hair from looking like I sang backup for the Supremes.

"Look"—Annie's voice interrupted my thoughts—"a bunch of teachers are going up to Maple Lake State Park to camp next weekend."

"I hate camping." My disinterest would not dissuade Annie from her purpose.

"Well, not camping exactly. It's a research campground with cabins. The college is giving an outdoor education credit for a weekend class. How 'bout it?"

"I don't know." I looked up to find Annie distracted by a nearby picture book. She had given up on washing paintbrushes, and her hands dripped colored water on my new book. "Annie, put the book down," I commanded. Reluctantly, she turned her attention back to the sink. "When is the class?" I asked.

"The first weekend of November."

"Won't that be cold?" With a dirty look, I took her unwashed brushes and handed her an aluminum paint dish. "If you want to keep talking, you'd better keep washing."

She smirked. "Probably—cold, I mean—but what else can we do in the winter, especially on our salaries?" She paused and tipped her head at me. Her plans included more than she admitted.

"Okay, out with it. What else do you have up your sleeve?"

"I heard through the grapevine—" she paused again for dramatic effect—"that this class is a favorite of first-year male teachers. They say it's a real wilderness experience."

"Just what I want, a 'real wilderness experience.'"

"No, dear, what you want is to meet a man who is younger than your dear Mr. Brunner." Lars Brunner, my tightfisted, flannel-shirted, snowbirding landlord, could hardly be considered "dear."

"What makes you think I want to meet a man?" I objected.

"Oh, good friends know these things." She shook the dripping dish at me. "You've been holed up in that crazy place of yours all fall. The only place you ever go is Sudsy's. And I happen to know that you haven't dated since you moved here." Annie especially enjoyed the after-work group at Sudsy's on Fridays. "It's time you got out a little more."

I hated to admit it, but Annie was usually right. "Okay. If I did want to meet someone, why do I have to do it at a campground in the middle of the winter?"

"Because 'to have a friend, you must find one.'" She smiled to emphasize the appropriateness of her quote and handed the dish back to me. After rinsing her hands, she reached for a paper towel and continued. "I'll sign you up." With a wave she was out the door.

By November, winter had truly arrived. Lars and Elsie Brunner, the owners of the house where I rented a mother-in-law apartment, fled to sunny Arizona. I found myself alone in my little cliff-top apartment above the ocean.

Johnson River rarely experienced snow or prolonged cold, but that year nighttime temperatures dipped lower than normal. After nights without rain, we woke to the wonder of frost. Though it disappeared by eleven, the morning frost and continued cold reminded us of winter.

In preparation for our weekend class, I packed my warmest clothes, including long underwear and an electric heating pad. On a warm Friday afternoon, I met Annie at her apartment for the drive to Maple Lake Campground. Sunshine peeked through the trees over the highway as we drove through thick dark forests.

Dr. Noriyuki, a little man in an enormous down jacket, greeted us as we entered the parking area. He wore a wide smile full of large teeth and dark, heavy-framed glasses. "Welcome, ladies," he said, extending his hand through Annie's car window. "I have you assigned to cabin twelve. The last cabin on the right." To demonstrate, he turned away from us and gestured with his right hand.

I glanced at Annie. Did he think we were confused about right and left? She smiled.

"Dinner is served promptly at five," he said, his face nearly touching the window. "Be sure to dress warmly. We'll start right after dinner." He bowed and waved us off down the road. Annie giggled and drove off to find our "home away from home."

"Great resort," I said. The trees in the park grew so thick, they completely blocked the sky. Very little underbrush covered the ground. Moss and lichen clung to the branches like decorations from a Christmas tree. I found the effect both dark and eerie, like the setting for a murder mystery.

"Come on, Pat. It isn't that bad," Annie said. She pulled into a parking spot in front of a one-room cabin that reminded me of a child's playhouse. "Besides, don't be so grumpy. You'll have to apologize when I find you a new husband."

"What? You aren't happy with the one I have?"

"All right, Ms. English Professor. *If* I find you a husband."

"Correction noted, Miss Billington."

The enticing aroma of wet overcoats and pineapple sauce greeted us when we arrived in the cafeteria. After filling my plate with baked ham and scalloped potatoes, I scanned the dining room for a place to sit. I chose an empty table in the corner. Annie was right again. There were lots of men here. Unfortunately, most of them wore wedding rings.

Of course, this detail did not deter Annie. She sat down beside me, flashing a wide grin and a cheerful "hello" at every male stranger who wandered by. I felt a little embarrassed. To me, she looked desperate.

"Excuse me. Is this seat taken?"

Nice voice. I looked up from string beans.

"Of course not, please join us."

Too upbeat, Annie.

"Thank you." A tall fellow, the skinniest I had ever seen, with bright red hair curled in fluffy masses all over his head, pulled out the chair nearest Annie. He wore round wire-rimmed glasses and evidenced the kind of skin that only redheads are born with—nearly opaque with freckles.

Annie spoke. "And this is my friend, Patricia Morrow." I managed to nod on cue. He smiled. At least that part was normal. Annie continued. "We teach at Clark's Creek Elementary, in Johnson River. How about you?"

"Sheldon Graham," he answered politely. "I teach fifth graders at Minter Creek."

Just as I began to resent the intrusion of this stranger, I noticed something surprising. This gangling redhead had not taken his gaze off of my dear bubbling friend, Annie.

The rest of our weekend was a bust. Even Annie admitted it. Through constant rain and teeth-chattering cold, we dutifully constructed outdoor shelters of fir branches—ours leaked—made smoldering fires from wet wood, and cooked our own lukewarm meals. Annie and I got lost practicing compass navigation and would never have found our way back had it not been for the fully outfitted search and rescue conducted by Dr. Noriyuki. He didn't bow when he found us.

By the time we packed Annie's car, I was grateful to have been born in the twentieth century. I could hardly wait for a long hot bath and a good book. We drove home exhausted and hungry, both of us too tired to talk.

At Annie's apartment I helped carry her bags upstairs. While she unlocked her front door, I shivered. "Come in for some tea," she said. Ever cheerful Annie.

"Good idea. Might keep me from hypothermia until I get home."

"Well, at least now we know how to treat it," she giggled. The phone in her kitchen rang loudly. Throwing her keys on the couch, she hurried to answer.

"Oh, Sheldon," I heard her say politely, while she made a gagging motion with her free hand. I laughed out loud. She grimaced and turned away. Still chuckling, I sneaked out the front door and down the stairs. Served her right, the matchmaker.

And that was the pattern of my first year—work, Annie, children—at least until that spring, when things took a sudden and frightening turn.

In March, before the second half of parent conferences, my private world began to come apart. The first two days of meetings had gone well, and my confidence improved. I'd learned to converse intelligently with complete strangers.

On Thursday night I drove home around six in the evening. After a rainy winter I remember feeling delighted in the longer days of spring. I looked forward to a long walk on the beach.

As I turned into my driveway, I recognized my brother's Mazda parked in my space. Peculiar. He never came to visit without calling first.

I parked behind him and dragged myself, exhausted, from my little orange Subaru. Steve, already walking toward me, had both hands in his pockets, his head down. He never drove out to the coast. Why now?

"Hey, Steve. Good to see you!" He took my tote bag, and I wrapped my arms around his shoulders, giving him a warm and genuine hug. He squeezed back. Too long. Deep sigh. "What is it?" I asked.

Avoiding my eyes, he didn't answer. Silently he waited while I unlocked my apartment door. My heartbeat accelerated.

At last Steve settled into my only living room chair. "I'm so sorry to have to tell you this, Patty," he began. "But Mom called me this afternoon. She's been trying to call you all day." He paused. I took a long deliberate breath, willing my shoulders to relax. Steve never hurried.

"She went to the doctor today. She's sick, Patty." He blinked hard. "Real sick."

My mind flew from question to question, searching for answers, but I had no clues. Too many questions. "What . . ." I said weakly and closed my mouth, not knowing where to begin.

"Cancer." He held his lips tight, and his blue eyes fought tears gathering behind his dark lashes.

"Where?" I felt intense, unexplainable anger. "Don't tease me. Tell me everything."

"The pancreas, Patty."

"What does that mean?" I knew where the pancreas was and how it functioned, but I had no experience with this kind of cancer. "What does the doctor say?"

Steve launched into a long and halting explanation. For the past few months, Mom had experienced gnawing stomach discomfort, along with other vague symptoms. But two nights ago, excruciating pain and relentless vomiting forced her to call her neighbor across the hall. An ambulance took her to the hospital. Today, tests revealed pancreatic cancer.

"The doctor doesn't have much hope. She might survive as long as a year, or as little as three months." Steve broke down completely. I went to him and held his shoulders in my hands, leaning his head against me. We both cried.

"Isn't there anything they can do?"

He pulled away, gathering his dignity. "Nothing. The doctor told her there is nothing he can do. Not at this point."

"I can't believe that, not now. This is the era of cancer survivors. No one really dies anymore, do they?"

Steve leaned forward and buried his face in his hands. This was his answer.

"What do we do?" I asked.

"I don't know." He stood and walked to the window of my apartment. "There isn't anyone but you and me, Patty . . ." He paused, looking out. "I just don't know."

In his older brother role, Steve wouldn't leave until he was certain I would be all right. He'd always been the dutiful brother. Eventually, he drove back to the city—to his wife and children. I called Mom right away. Her neighbor and longtime friend answered the phone, and we cried together. I promised to visit after I finished my last conference on Friday afternoon.

During the long drive to Mom's, I wrestled with my own emotions, fear being the most prominent. Daddy died seven years ago, but I still missed him. Though Mom had tried, nothing could ever fill the void he left in my life.

In spite of being a self-sufficient adult, a voice warned that I would soon be an orphan. And the child who lived deep inside me fought with the fear of being left alone.

Gladys, our neighbor, opened Mom's door and let me in with a grateful hug. I tiptoed into Mom's bedroom. The familiar smell of White Ginger filled the darkened room. I found Mom asleep, her head turned away from me toward the wall.

"Mom," I whispered. She stirred but didn't wake.

"She's on some pretty heavy pain medicine," Gladys offered from the doorway. "I gave it to her about an hour ago—makes her sleepy."

I smiled my thanks and pulled a chair around her bed, close to Mother's sleeping face. "Gladys, if you need to run an errand or take care of something, I'll stay with her for a while." I took my mother's hand in both of mine.

"Well, I could start some dinner." She hesitated. "I'll just be across the hall if you need me." I heard the front door close.

Stroking Mom's thin fragile skin, I found myself thinking of all she meant to me. This woman carried me through Daddy's death, hiding her own grief in order to help me with mine. While I waited for her to wake, I let my eyes drift around her familiar and comforting bedroom. She kept it painted the same dark turquoise, with clean white enamel trim. Her treasures stood in exactly the same old places. My formal graduation portrait, in concert black, holding grandfather's cello. Ceramic handprints, all lined up—my row below my brother's—hung on the wall above her headboard. Tiny hand after tiny hand, all reminding her of our growth. As a joke, Steve and I made one last set of impressions during my senior year of high school. These last prints of fully grown hands still held their place of honor at the end of the line.

Pictures completely covered the top of her dresser, no two frames matching, scattered without order or reason. Her wedding picture. Steve and I as children. An anniversary picture. Daddy. The three of us at Daddy's funeral. Steve's wedding. My college graduation. Her grandchildren. Tacked to the mirror above the dresser hung the corsage she wore at Steve's wedding. My mother valued her memories. She considered her family her greatest treasure. And she was mine.

Next to her bed on the nightstand stood a water pitcher, a half-filled glass, and four prescription bottles. In the background rested her favorite crystal table lamp, covered with dust.

"Pet. You're home," her voice rasped, mostly air.

"Yes, Mamma. I wanted to come." I bent to kiss her pale cheek and squeezed her hand. "How are you feeling?"

"You didn't need to come. I'm fine, really."

Her eyes stayed half-closed, and I watched them drift shut at the end of every sentence. "You don't look 'fine,' Mamma. Steve came to see me. He told me everything."

Her eyes fluttered open again, but only briefly. "There isn't anything to tell. I'm just not well. The doctor says this is only a little episode. I'll feel better soon."

Her words confused me. Did she really believe that? Not knowing how to answer, I held her hand, gently stroking the pale skin. She drifted back to sleep.

For the rest of the spring I went home as often as I could. In a way, Mom was right. After that first episode drove her to the doctor, she rallied. Her pain became more manageable, and most of the time she cared for herself. During the week, when she needed someone, Gladys continued to meet her every need. Then every weekend I drove three hours to Mom's apartment and three hours back to Johnson River. The schedule left me exhausted, both from worry and work. But something inside refused to let Mom be alone.

By the first of June, I decided that I needed to move home. If this was to be my mother's last summer, I wanted to be with her. I wanted to spend it caring for her.

Though I hated to leave my life, my friends, my new community, I knew I had to be with Mom. So with some reluctance I let go of my apartment, packed my few household goods, resigned from Clark's Creek Elementary, and moved home.

Three

THAT SUMMER REMAINS A BLUR of images in my memory. Perhaps exhaustion or even grief shroud the pictures in my mind. Nevertheless, long days of sitting beside Mother's bed are cloaked with heaviness, with the smell of rubbing alcohol, with waiting for something I dreaded and yet anticipated with complete and absolute certainty. I sat there completely oblivious to the summer sunshine and the warm temperatures outside, hearing yet not registering the sounds of happy children playing in the courtyard below her window. Sometimes dozing, sometimes reading the newspaper out loud, I played make-believe with her—as though her illness were only temporary, as though Mom needed to keep up with events outside her singular world of pain and grief. We continued the ruse even as cancer drained her energy, stealing life from her bit by bit until at last my mother became a skeleton floating between her sheets, waiting patiently to be finished with life.

When death came, I felt ashamed to be relieved. Over the summer Mom's care had consumed me, like the cancer had consumed her, and now, at last, I could get on with life. I decided to stay in Seattle near Steve and his family. I found an inexpensive apartment in the city. Steve and I planned the funeral mass and buried Mom next to Dad in a cemetery north of town. The same priest who gave me my first communion also said the funeral mass for both my parents. I noticed that he cried during Mother's service.

During a week of hard work, we cleared out her apartment. Between feelings of grief and guilt, we disposed of most of her possessions. We packed box after box with her accumulated junk and hauled it to the Salvation Army. After all, what could we expect to accomplish with ten half-used skeins of acrylic yarn?

Steve and I rented a trailer and spent one entire day moving furniture and boxes of leftovers to my new place. The next day we cleaned and closed Mother's apartment. Steve stood in the parking lot beside the rear door of my Subaru shoving the last box into place. Then tugging on the handle, he closed the door with a shudder. He checked the lock and turned to me. "You look exhausted," he said.

"Great. Thanks for the compliment." I bent to lift the last box from the pavement. In spite of being wrapped in newspaper, the glass over mother's pictures clinked and rattled. Her dresser pictures were now mine except for those of Steve's family, which I had given to him.

"Here, I'll put those in your car," he said, taking the box from me. I followed him to the passenger door.

"Thanks, Steve. Thanks for everything." I reached up and hugged him, wanting to comfort us both.

"I should be thanking you." He slammed the car door, speaking as he did. "I really depended on your being here with Mom. I think it made the end easier for her. I know it was easier for me." He crossed his arms and leaned one hip against the car. "I've always known you two had something special—some mother-daughter thing." He smiled. "Is that a chauvinistic thing to say?"

I laughed. "No. Actually, it makes me feel better. I like to think that Mom loved me, that she needed me somehow." I turned back to look at the apartment building. Steve was right about my being tired. Ten weeks of caring for Mom left me exhausted, spent. In spite of our efforts to ease her pain, her last month had been excruciating. We had hospice nurses, though Mom felt more comfortable having me care for her. I supervised her medications, read to her, answered her telephone, bathed and dressed her. While she still ate, I cooked and fed her. I would spent the night on a cot in her room, and during her last days, I sat silently near her bed with my hand over hers, waiting for the end to come. As her body gave out, she refused both food and liquids, as if she recognized the end and wanted to hasten it along.

I did all I could for her and felt good about that, good about being there for her, as she had always been there for me.

In my own intellectual way, I believed that grief was easier for people who went through long illnesses. For that reason, when it was finally over, the intensity of my emotions surprised me. Certainly I loved her, and I knew I would miss her, but I felt something much heavier, much darker than ordinary grief. Part of me felt paralyzingly isolated. These thoughts haunted the drive to my new apartment.

With both Mom and Dad gone, I had only Steve. But Steve had family—a wife and two boys. I had no one. I couldn't quite kick the feeling that I could drive my little car off the Ballard Bridge and the rest of the world would not even notice. It was an eerie feeling. I tried to shake off that terrifying fear of being alone. I wondered if I would ever have a real family again.

My new place sat on top of Phinney Ridge. Rather than a traditional apartment, I chose to rent the top half of an old house. The three upstairs bedrooms had been renovated into a galley kitchen with a dining area, a living room, and a bedroom. It had an enormous bathroom—bigger than the whole kitchen in my last apartment—dominated by a massive forest green bathtub.

I'd chosen the place primarily because of the spectacular view. The dining room looked west and south over the waterway leading from Lake Union to Puget Sound. Every Friday a long line of pleasure boats paraded west toward the Ballard Locks. On Sunday afternoon the same line of boats returned to their berths in the city. I loved to watch them, imagining the families on board and the trips they enjoyed. Even better than the weekly boat procession were the daily sunsets. From my dining room table, I enjoyed an unobstructed view of the Olympic Mountains, backlit by flaming orange skies. Whenever I could, I spent the evening watching—though ostensibly doing some form of paper work—until afternoon sunlight gave way to darkness and city lights below.

The rent was perfect for a teacher without a job. But determined to rectify that small problem, I began interviewing immediately. By late August, most teaching positions had been filled. Under the enormous pressure of a shrinking calendar, I interviewed for a job at a nearby Catholic school, just walking distance from the house. At last, fortune seemed to be smiling.

The principal, Sister Mary Regina, turned out to be a gentle woman with an obvious love for children. The first time I saw her, on the day of my interview, she stood in the foyer of the fifty-year-old brick school building bent over a little boy, both of them gazing at a dead guppy floating upside down in a Dixie cup. While the child cried, Sister Mary Regina, draped in a heavy black and white nun's habit, tried gently to explain why she didn't think prayer would bring the guppy back.

"Peter," I overheard her say, "you know God cares as much about your guppy as you do." With her worn hand, she stroked his silky blond hair. "I think that God loved your guppy so much that He wanted him to have a better, bigger bowl to live in." Tears flowed down Peter's cheeks. "If we brought Gerald back to life, I think he'd be unhappy to leave heaven. You wouldn't want to make Gerald unhappy, would you?"

The little boy, in shorts and tennis shoes, rubbed his face with the palm of his hand. Tears smeared his dusty cheeks, leaving his small face splotched with mud. "I tell you what," she continued quietly. "I have a new teacher to interview, and as soon as I finish, I'll walk you over to Wilson's, and we'll pick out a new guppy. All right? My treat." He smiled. She turned him around at the shoulders and with a gentle pat sent him out the playground door. "Give me a half hour, will you, Peter?" she called after his retreating form. He turned to wave, water dripping from the cup as he walked away.

Our interview went well, and before I realized it, I found myself as completely in love with Sister Mary Regina as little Peter had been. She seemed thrilled to have an experienced teacher. "One year is perfect," she said, slapping the top of her desk with the palms of both hands. "Enough time to have a real feel for the battle and yet young enough for me to train correctly." She stood. "You shouldn't have developed any really bad habits—yet," she said, grinning broadly. "You're perfect for Saint Sebastian's, Patricia."

Embarrassed, I thanked her. I hoped that meant I'd won the job.

"All right, let me show you your new classroom," she said.

I did have a job! I followed her clicking rosary out of the office and down the hall. Around her legs, yards of shiny black fabric swirled above black athletic shoes and dark ankle socks.

"You know, when I first started teaching, I taught kindergartners too. I still love the little rascals." She nodded over her shoulder at me.

"Why did you quit teaching?" I hurried to catch up. Though she must be nearly sixty, she moved quickly.

"If it were up to me, I wouldn't have," she said as she unlocked the classroom door. "But the church is a demanding taskmaster. The diocese needed a principal, and I had the required education." She shrugged and gestured me inside. "There was no one else." Her smiling face reminded me of bread dough rising through a frame of black cardboard. I wondered why she chose to keep the old fashioned habit so few of her peers wore. But I would not ask. "Here we are," she stepped in and flipped on three switches that controlled the fluorescent classroom lights.

Though much smaller than my public classroom in Johnson River, this room was clean and cheerful, smelling of fresh wax and new paint. Windows lined the long wall. In one corner, an oak rocker rested along the edge of a large brown rag rug. In another, a handmade play kitchen stood next to long rows of children's picture books. Five artist's easels, each splattered with paint, lined the back wall, along with shelves of children's games and giant red cardboard blocks. From where we stood, I spotted a wooden trunk overflowing with what must be dress-up clothes.

"Now, there is one small peculiarity about this job, Patricia." Sister Mary Regina's sparkling eyes betrayed her humor. "I must insist that you allow me to come in once a week and read a story to your class. No excuses." She gestured with her index finger. "Will that be acceptable to you?"

"I can't think of anything more wonderful."

She wrapped one arm around my shoulder and hugged me. "Now, if you'll excuse me, I have a guppy to purchase. Why don't you take some time to explore your new room." She floated, a graceful black specter, toward the door. "Oh yes, here is the key." She handed me a single brass key. "Just lock up when you leave." She paused before turning back to the door "Our first teachers' meeting is August 30, at nine A.M. sharp. Be there!"

I would have walked to New York to attend a meeting with her.

In mid-September I ran into an old friend at the Safeway near my apartment. It was my first contact with anyone from my college days. "Now that you're back in town, you should be playing in the West Side Community Orchestra," Ryan said.

"I haven't played much over the last few years."

"The group is mostly volunteer, but generally they're pretty good, and it's fun." He leaned over the frozen food case and added, "It would be the perfect place to get back into orchestra music." He was right. I missed playing cello in an orchestra family. Maybe I would call for an audition.

Two weeks later I found myself sitting in front of the director. Henry Schroeder, a pasty-faced, dark-haired man, appeared nearly thirty. "And how long have you played?" He nodded at my cello and looked down at his paper work.

"Since I was twelve." His brusque impersonal manner made me nervous. I wiped dampness from my hands onto the lap of my chino pants. I noticed that he noticed, and I wished I'd behaved more professionally.

"And what are you playing for us today?" he said without looking up. There was no "us" in the room.

"The Prelude in G Major from Suite No. 1 by J. S. Bach." I paused.

No response. I settled into the chair and took a deep breath. Closing my eyes, I willed myself to relax, set the bow, and envisioned the sheet music. As I began to move the bow, the music took over my body. As always, it came alive in the strings, in the bow, in my hands. Grandfather's cello sang. The music swelled and filled the tiny studio. I felt it. When the music came alive, so did I.

With the last note dying away I lifted the bow from the strings and looked up to find him staring at me, his elbows sitting on the desk. His chin rested on his thumbs, long fingers laced together. With a deep sigh, he pushed his glasses up the bridge of his nose. "That, Ms. Morrow, was lovely. Thank you." He stood and walked toward me, offering his hand. "I'll be calling soon. If you have the time, we would be honored to have you in our orchestra."

A new job and a new orchestra family, all in the same season! Things were definitely looking up.

Saint Sebastian's turned out to be everything I'd hoped. As always, my kindergartners were delightful, and the other teachers—a mix of lay teachers and nuns—became a constant source of amusement and support. Though this year would be my second year of teaching, work began to fall into a routine of sorts. I even allowed myself to take on a few private cello students.

Of course I had no dating life. What should I expect teaching with a building full of nuns. Regardless, we became good friends, and I found them to be caring professionals. There were men in the orchestra, though most of them were married. Our rehearsals demanded so much attention that we didn't get to know one another as people, but rather by instrument—"She's the one with the English cello"—by our musical style, and by our professionalism.

Our winter concert schedule included four performances for season ticket holders. We also performed for community events and festivals, and of course during the Christmas season we played somewhere nearly every week. I found the orchestra to be a satisfying group, and they gave me new reason to practice. If only Lynn, my old practice partner, could see me now. I worked on concert music an hour every day—much more on weekends.

My only real disappointment that year came when my brother, Steve, chose Christmas to announce his transfer to Grand Forks, North Dakota. His company, which produced farm chemicals, needed a plant manager. The move represented a promotion for him, but for me it represented an enormous loss. They needed him to take over in January. How I hated to have him leave.

Winter in the Northwest is a long, dark affair. Gray skies often obscure sunshine for seven straight months. Between the clouds and the rain, my job and orchestra rehearsals, I struggled with loneliness. I wanted something more, or perhaps more accurately, something different than a professional life. I wanted family. Every day, with the ringing of the afternoon bell, I walked my students to the parking lot where we met their car pools. I envied those joyous reunions between mothers and children. In the midst of so much hugging and hoopla over their daily work, I wondered if any child would ever light up that way for me.

I thought often about Annie's proclamation, "I want everything, the husband, the kids, the house, the dog, the white picket fence. . . ." Annie got what she wanted. She married Sheldon and moved to Spokane.

Me too. I wanted everything too. The realization that I might never marry weighed heavily on me. In spite of my desire to find a mate, my life seemed destined to singleness. I found few opportunities to meet available men. And though I might reconcile myself to never marry, the possibility of being forever childless brought even greater sadness.

Sister Mary Regina, who had grown from employer to mentor, sensed my restlessness, and more than once tried to comfort me. One morning in the audiovisual room, as I fiddled with the focus on an antique opaque projector, she cornered me. "You need to become a nun," she said without introduction.

"Thank you. I take that as a compliment."

"Our order is desperate for gifted teachers."

"But, Sister," I said patiently, though indeed I wanted to pummel the projector. "There's a small problem with your plan. I want my own children. Dozens and dozens of them. I think the convent might have a problem with that."

"Well, at least if you won't become a nun, you'd have children like a good Catholic." She chortled and reached over to adjust the machine. As if by magic, the lid fell into place. She shrugged.

"Though you would make an excellent nun." She shrugged again, smiling at her own joke. Without another word, she turned to leave.

"Sister Mary Regina," I called after her. "Wait!" I hurried out the door and fell into step beside her. "Can I ask a personal question?" She gave me a curious glance and nodded. I continued. "Do you ever regret not marrying and having children of your own?"

She stopped walking and thoughtfully placed her two forearms inside her billowing black sleeves. Her pale blue eyes looked deep into mine. "I never regret it, my dear. I have two hundred and forty-three children. More than you will ever have." She gazed thoughtfully for a moment, then patted my shoulder. "No, I've never regretted it. God has a much better way."

Oh, how I hoped she was right.

That spring our school decided to celebrate St. Patrick's Day with a roller skating party. Sister Mary Regina put me in charge of snacks. Along with the help of our first-grade teacher, I managed to bake three hundred cupcakes—all from a mix, of course. Early Saturday morning I carted boxes of treats and gallon jars of juice into the lobby of the roller rink. Three of us set up the snack area, hanging green and orange crepe paper streamers across the ceiling. My students—most only five years old—were delighted to have an excuse to skate together, and I expected every one of them to attend. I looked forward to the party.

"Miss Morrow?" A dark-eyed beauty from my afternoon class tugged at the bottom of my cardigan sweater. "Are you going to skate today?"

I climbed down from my step stool and bent to speak with her. "Of course I'm planning to skate, Bethany."

"Would you skate with me?" Her voice carried a little whine.

"I'd love to."

"That's good," she said, her ponytail nodding with her head, " 'Cuz my mommy can't come today, and I don't really know how to skate."

I tried not to smile. "Well, if you promise not to tell anyone, I don't know how to skate very well either. So maybe, if you'll help me, we can figure it out together. Okay?"

Enormously relieved, she grinned. "All right. My big sister is going to help me put on skates," she said, pointing to the rental counter. "Then I'll come get you." Without looking back, she walked toward the wooden benches of the lobby, her ponytail swinging behind her.

I hurried to finish decorating. As children arrived, the staff helped them put on their skates. I tied hundreds of long brown bootlaces.

With everyone ready, I put on my own skates. Though I hadn't worn roller skates since my own childhood, these felt familiar, almost comfortable. I looked forward to a turn around the rink. Little Bethany, in pink leggings and a gray sweat shirt, came tiptoeing delicately across the carpet. "Are you ready?"

"Let me at it." I grasped her five-year-old hand in mine, and we walked gingerly toward the wood floor, something like old people on an icy sidewalk. Students and parents crowded the rink, all moving slowly in a large counterclockwise circle. The loudspeakers played a fuzzy version of the latest hits, which blended with the clank and noise of skate wheels into a deafening roar. Bethany and I moved carefully inside, away from the other skaters, and slowly progressed around the two turns at one end of the large rink. As we cleared the second turn, an overweight third-grader lost control and fell toward us from the wrong direction. Letting go, I heard Bethany squeal as she hit the floor.

Oh boy. I lost her. The crowd surged forward and carried me away from my young protégée. Cautiously, I stepped to the edge of the flowing students and turned back to help Bethany.

Somehow my right skate became tangled in the wheels of my left, which stopped the skate quite suddenly. Though my feet no longer moved, my upper body continued rotating. I don't know quite how, but without warning I fell toward the floor, twisting desperately to catch myself. At that same instant, even before I even hit the ground, I both heard and felt the snap in my right ankle.

The pain was the worst I'd ever experienced, and for a minute the other skaters changed direction only slightly as they swarmed by. Overcome by the searing agony in my ankle, I bit violently into my lower lip. Just my luck. I managed to say something very inappropriate for a parochial school. Tears rolled down the sides of my face and onto the wooden floor.

Sister Margaret, the second-grade teacher, noticed something amiss. Turning around, she knelt down beside me.

"What is it, Patricia?"

"My ankle. It's broken." I breathed hard. "I heard it break."

"All right. Let me help." She began to unlace my boot.

"No, not the skate. Don't take off the skate!" I tried not to yell at her, but my voice rose, even in the roar of skates and music.

"I have to, dear." Though Sister Margaret was herself no more than forty, she managed to mother everyone on the teaching staff.

"Please don't."

Ignoring my plea, she removed the skate and peeled the sock from my right foot. I tried to sit up. My ankle had already turned an angry black and blue.

"Can you walk?" she asked.

"No. I can't move."

"Can you wiggle your toes?"

"No!" I shouted. " Please don't touch me." I gave up and sank back onto my elbows and from there to the floor.

"I think we'd better call an ambulance."

The owner of the rink knelt beside me and placed a homemade ice pack on the outside of my ankle. I struggled to keep from crying out. "I think we need an ambulance," he agreed. "Sister," he said to Margaret, "go call 9–1–1." I moaned.

While we waited for the ambulance, the entire party came to an abrupt and unfortunate end. My students cried noisily. Sister Mary Regina, in long black habit and brown skates, announced it was time for treats, leaving me alone with the owner of the rink to wait for the ambulance. What a wonderful party! Bethany and I hadn't even made it all the way around the rink.

The ambulance crew, who turned out to be the most handsome collection of men I had ever seen in one place, came in to assess my injury. I felt completely humiliated, embarrassed to be coddled and cared for by these burly, gorgeous members of the opposite sex. They wrapped my ankle in chemical ice packs and placed my leg into a two-board splint, which they secured with yellow webbing and metal buckles. My hair was a mess, and I groaned in pain. How I wished the floor would swallow me alive. In spite of it all, I managed to smile at the kids as they wheeled me through the lobby on a secretarial chair, which the rink owner kept for just these kinds of occasions, to the waiting vehicle outside. I hated for my accident to ruin their party.

On that particular weekend afternoon, of course, patients swamped the emergency room. The triage nurse left me in a wheelchair, my feet elevated on swaying leg rests, in front of a television. My handsome attendants disappeared. I expected one of my fellow teachers to appear, but no one came. The splint and ice combined to immobilize and numb my ankle. Together, they greatly reduced the pain. However, two hours later I found my teeth chattering and my body shivering from neck to ankles with cold.

"Excuse me," I called through clenched teeth to a passing nurse. "How much longer?"

She took the registration slip from my lap and checked her watch. "I can't guarantee. But it shouldn't be too much longer." She started away.

The shivers felt violent. "I'm so cold. Could you put me someplace warmer?" Mentally, I blamed the air conditioning for my discomfort.

For the first time, she took a serious look at my leg, including the ice and the splint. Her eyebrows furrowed before a moment of recognition came over her face. "Ice-induced hypothermia," she stated, as if I'd understand. "I'll get a blanket."

She returned quickly with a warm flannel blanket. "Fresh out of the oven," she confided, wrapping it around my shoulders. "That should help. I'll see if I can get you in to see the doctor now."

I shivered, too cold to care. The blanket felt heavenly.

Moments later she returned to wheel me behind the front desk, twice bumping my extended leg into the wall before we safely found the exam room. Extremely grateful we didn't have further to go, I chose not to complain. Somehow she managed to help me from the chair to the exam table. She asked the usual questions and began to remove the splint. Then, with the largest shears I had ever seen, she cut the right leg off my favorite jeans.

"There. This will keep you from having to slide them down over your ankle. The doctor will be able to take a good look now." She began to cut up the left side seam. I wished I'd shaved my legs.

"Wait. Do I have time to go to the bathroom? It's been hours."

She hesitated, checked her watch. "I guess so. The doctor should be here in just another minute." She opened the exam room door. "It's that door across the hall."

I looked at her and back at the great distance across the hall, perhaps ten feet to the bathroom door. Suddenly she understood and offered me her arm. Leaning on her, I hobbled across the hall to the bathroom. Hopping was hard work, and I sweated from pain in spite of my shivering cold. Together, we managed to position me in front of the toilet with what was left of my pants dropped down around my ankles. I balanced carefully on my left leg while she held the right one out in front of me. Slowly, holding onto the bars on both sides of the toilet, I lowered myself onto the seat.

"I'll leave you alone for a minute," she said, closing the bathroom door. Good decision. This was one performance I didn't wish to give with an audience.

When I finished, I realized to my embarrassment that I couldn't stand up by myself. Under ordinary circumstances I should have been able to lift myself using the bars beside the toilet. But I could not manage both the bars and my foot at the same time. I could not tell which hurt more, the foot hanging down below my knee or the sudden motion of trying to stand. I looked around the tiny bathroom for a call button. Though I spotted one, I could not reach it. The string to the call button had been tied to a light switch beyond it. I tried to stand. No luck. Intense pain. Perhaps if I rocked forward and threw myself up, I might reach the call button. In spite of the pain, I tried again. Almost. I collapsed back onto the toilet seat. Searing pain shot through my ankle.

By now, tears rolled down my cheeks, and I brushed them away. Looking at my stained palms, I realized I'd managed to wipe mascara all over my face. Great. Now I had raccoon eyes. I called out, "Nurse, help." My own weak, soundless voice echoed back in the tiny room. "Please. Help!"

No response. Where on earth had that nurse gone? I wondered if other patients had decomposed right here on this same toilet seat. Well, I had to try to stand by myself. Either I would make it, or I would crawl across the linoleum to the door.

I placed my right leg far out in front of me and rocked—forward and back, forward and back. "One, two, three . . ." Holding on to the bars, I threw myself forward and up. Nearly vertical, I lost my balance and began to fall backwards. On the way down I made a desperate lunge, grabbing at the cord hanging from the call button. Got it. From inside the bathroom, I heard the bell announcing my distress throughout the emergency area. I managed to land curled up on the floor, my face facing away from the toilet. Just behind the odor of antiseptic cleaning solutions, I smelled the smells of bathrooms everywhere. My body screamed with pain. I refused to move.

Well, she deserved it, going off like that to leave me. Here I lay on the floor in a heap with my underwear and what was left of my jeans caught around my ankles.

Eventually, years later it seemed, the hall door opened slightly, and I heard a male voice say, "Miss Morrow, are you all right in here?"

Of course I'm not all right, you idiot. "I could use some help," I answered meekly. I'd managed to wait by turning fully onto my left side, hanging my right ankle forward. From this frozen position, I could barely see the person speaking. I arched my back and turned my face upward to look. I fully intended to give that nurse a piece of my mind!

Then the bathroom door opened further. There in the shadow of the fluorescent hallway light, I recognized Russell Koehler, my blind date of three years earlier. Only this time, he was all dressed up like a doctor.

Four

THANKS TO THE HELP OF A NURSE, an orderly, and a wheelchair, I did eventually get off the bathroom floor. Of course, by then the bathroom was too full to shut the door, and everyone walking by stopped to watch. Most of them remembered not to giggle. Eventually, they returned me safely to the exam table, where I waited, covered by a paper tablecloth the texture of coarse sandpaper. Already exhausted, I'd yet to see a doctor. Then, to make matters worse, I clearly recognized the voices of two fellow teachers above surrounding hospital noises, followed by a soft knock at the door.

"Come in," I called. Sister Thomas, a chubby woman with wiry white hair and soft fleshy cheeks landed heavily in the chair nearest me, the daily newspaper tucked under one arm. "So what's wrong with you?" she asked matter-of-factly.

"I'm not sure yet. I haven't seen the doctor."

She gave a small throaty noise, unquestionably the sound of disapproval, and opened her paper.

Sister Claire stepped in breathlessly, holding her chest with one hand. "We thought we'd never find you," she said, panting. "Where have you been?"

Sister Claire was as thin as Sister Thomas was fat, but her concern was genuine, and I felt relieved to have her with me. Still, I refused to share my humiliating bathroom experience with a couple of nuns. "I've spent the better part of today freezing to death in a wheelchair out there," I said, pointing to the waiting room.

"We were so worried!" Sister Claire interrupted, flapping her hands in the air. "We had to wait until all the parents came for the children, and then we had to clean the whole place up before we could come to the hospital." Her high-pitched, breathy voice bordered on irritating. "The problem was, we didn't know where the firemen took you."

"They weren't firemen," Sister Thomas corrected.

"Well, whatever they were," she whined, "they spirited poor Patricia away before we could ask any questions. I had to make a bunch of phone calls to find you." Abruptly, she landed her thin frame on the doctor's stool, which nearly rolled out from under her. "Do you realize there are five hospitals near the skating rink?"

"Four," Sister Thomas said sternly, her voice coming from deep within the local section of the paper.

"Five, including the children's hospital."

"They wouldn't take her to the children's hospital," Sister Thomas chided, without looking up from the paper. "She isn't a child, Claire."

"They might. You never know. She's young." She paused, adding with emphasis, "Much younger than you."

The corner of the newspaper folded down, and the older sister scowled over it. "Anyway," she said firmly, "We're here, and that's all that counts." The paper slid back into place.

Right. Wasn't I lucky?

Thankfully, the doctor who examined me was not Russell. Instead, an elderly man with eyebrows bushier than my feather duster poked and prodded at me. He looked like he might be a patient himself, his back bent nearly in half from some infirmity of his own. I responded to his terse questions. Wasting no energy on bedside manner, he nodded, grunting an occasional "Hmm." His behavior suggested that my condition defied medical explanation. He ordered X rays.

The technician turned out to be a man near my own age. He stretched me into awkward, painful positions and insisted that I hold perfectly still while he left the room and walked—by way of Milwaukee, I think—to the control panel.

Schunk, bleep. A high-pitched noise came from deep within the machine. The technician returned, folding me into yet another pose. *Schunk, bleep.* Another picture. I tried to pretend that I was fully clothed, with all my dignity firmly intact, but my inadequate imagination would not cooperate.

Back in the exam room, the elderly doctor declared my right fibula broken—though not displaced—in two places. I requested an English translation.

"You've broken the small outer bone in your ankle," he explained as though to a child. "It should be completely healed in about six to eight weeks. In the meantime, we'll have to keep it immobile."

"Will I be able to walk on it?"

He tolerated my ignorance. "Not for the first week or so." He returned his appreciative gaze to the X ray hanging on the light box. "Of course, you'll have to see an orthopedist. After a week, I suspect he'll give you a boot that you can walk with."

"Now, don't worry, dear," Sister Claire crooned. "We'll take care of everything. You just leave the details to us." She patted my shoulder.

"Oh, leave her alone, Claire. She's a grown woman. Don't treat her like a child." Sister Thomas crossed her legs and turned to the business section. "No matter how much younger she is."

The ministrations of the two women amused the physician. Chuckling, he said, "Well, I'll just have my nurse come in and make a temporary cast for you. Then, with some pain medication, you can go home." He made scratchy, illegible notes on a prescription pad and handed the slip of paper to Claire. "She should be babied for a few days. There will be quite a bit of pain." Sister Claire clucked with pleasure. "And you should expect both bruising and swelling. I want her to keep the foot elevated and use lots of ice."

Claire smirked over at Mary Thomas and folded the prescription into precise fourths before tucking it carefully into her skirt pocket.

At home on the couch, with my right leg resting high on pillows, I slept peacefully. Suddenly the doorbell rang. So sleepy. Must be the medication. I nestled deeper into my pillows. Sister Claire, heating tomato soup in the kitchen, bustled out to answer the door. Sister Thomas, who sat fully reclined in my mother's old chair, looked up from her paper and grimaced.

"Well, now, look what we have here." Claire's voice roused me from a lovely dream. She entered the living room carrying a crystal vase that overflowed with champagne-colored long-stemmed roses. She tried to place the vase on the end table near my feet. However, the stems of these particular roses were so long that they knocked the lampshade off the lamp and onto the floor. As she bent over to pick up the shade, Claire's backside clipped the pile of pillows under my leg, dropping my cast onto the couch. "Oh, sorry, dear," she apologized, thrusting my foot back onto the pillows. I bit my lip.

"So how are you feeling?" a deep male voice asked. My nurse's antics had so preoccupied me that I jumped at the words. Someone had followed Sister Claire into the apartment. I looked up to find Russell Koehler staring down at me.

He wore a dark gray sports coat flecked with tiny bits of blue and rust. A striped tie accented his blue chambray shirt. Below this, he wore faded blue jeans. What a marvelous surprise! In spite of sleepiness, my heart began beating very fast.

"Oh, Russ. I didn't expect you." Not in a million years. "I'm afraid I'm a little drowsy from pain medicine."

"Don't worry about that. I just dropped by to check on you." He stood away from the couch, in the middle of my little living room, with hands stuffed comfortably in his jeans pockets. "And to bring flowers."

"How thoughtful of you." I smiled, trying to appear the most gracious hostess—not easy to do while sprawled on the couch in pajama bottoms and a faded green T-shirt. I felt as though someone had hung me from the ceiling by my cast. Some hostess.

An awkward silence followed. Sister Claire found a spot for the flowers on the coffee table and returned to the kitchen. Russell pulled his hands from his pockets and walked around the table.

"Mind if I sit down?" His eyebrows danced upward.

"Oh no, of course not," I said helplessly. Sister Thomas sat in my only chair, which left Russell the coffee table. "I mean if you can find a place, please, sit down." He perched cautiously on the edge. From my position on the couch, I saw Claire standing guard just inside the kitchen door.

"I hope you don't mind that I didn't see you in the emergency room. I didn't want to embarrass you." He grinned the same old disarming smile that I remembered. I'd forgotten how lovely his aqua eyes were, glancing down behind those thick eyelashes.

"Thanks. It was pretty embarrassing as it was." Mortifying, actually.

"Besides, to be perfectly truthful, I had an ulterior motive." He'd grown a mustache since I last saw him, and I couldn't help thinking how handsome it was. He looked older, more "doctorly."

"An ulterior motive? What do you mean?"

"I wanted you to see Dr. McLean because I didn't want you to be my patient."

"Oh?"

Sister Claire leaned forward in the doorway and Sister Mary Thomas edged her newspaper downward ever so slightly. My security guards paid close attention.

"You see, it isn't ethical to fraternize with a patient." He had the most remarkable smile. "However, if you aren't my patient, I can fraternize as much as I like."

My drowsiness vanished. "Dr. Koehler, are you telling me that you have a plot that includes fraternization?" I tried hard to sound shocked, but I hadn't flirted in so long, I wasn't sure I remembered how.

"That's the plan, Miss Morrow." He nodded his head with mock seriousness. "Lots and lots of fraternization."

Sister Claire, leaning forward on her tiptoes in the doorway, suddenly lost her balance and nearly fell into the living room. Russell laughed out loud.

The newspaper came down in a huff. "Claire, I should think you would try to be more discreet."

"Seems about time for visiting hours to end," Russell said, rubbing his mustache to cover a smile. "Anyway, I need to be going. Can I call later?"

I'd heard that line before. "That would be nice."

Russ called Sunday afternoon from the hospital, Monday morning from his apartment, and Tuesday from the phone in his car. Wednesday, I received a delivery of exotic tropical flowers from a Pike Place Market florist. The card read, *To replace wilting roses. How is the new cast? Save Friday evening. Russell*

Friday, precisely at six, my doorbell rang and Russell appeared, dressed in a black suit and purple silk tie. I leaned precariously on crutches.

"Why didn't you tell me you were going to dress like something from *Gentleman's Quarterly*?" I moaned. "Look at me!" I'd chosen a denim jumper and tights—the only thing which fit over my new pink cast.

"You'd look beautiful in a bathrobe." His voice had a gentle, soothing quality to it. "Besides, I dressed for you, not the restaurant. I don't care what you wear, as long as you're comfortable."

"Nothing is comfortable with crutches. You should see the skin under my arms." I balanced on one leg, trying to hold the crutches away from my chest.

Wrapping his fingers around my shoulders, he kissed me lightly. "I expected that, so I brought you something." He handed me a small brown paper bag. "It's just the stuff. All my patients swear by it."

Inside, I discovered Udder Cream in a plastic tube, decorated in a Guernsey motif. " 'Guaranteed to soothe chafed, irritated skin,' " I read out loud. "Well, that's me."

"Why don't you give it a try? I'll wait." He crossed the room and meticulously pulled the creases of his suit pants up as he lowered himself into the recliner. Something about the gesture reminded me of my father—I pictured him sitting that same way. My mother once told me that Dad did it to keep his pants from wrinkling. I put the tube in my mouth and hobbled into my bedroom. The cream would make a great excuse to change into a real dress.

The cream felt great, and when we arrived at the front entrance of the Canlis restaurant, I was very glad I made time to change. A uniformed valet met us under a covered drive. Russell gave him the keys and hurried around the back of the car. By the time he got to my door, Russell pushed a Cadillac style wheelchair.

"Hop in," he commanded. "Your chariot awaits."

"I don't need a wheelchair," I objected. "I can walk."

"I know you don't need it. But at one week, all my fracture patients have such sore arms that I knew you'd appreciate it." He unfolded the seat and shoved the leg rests out of the way. "Come, now. Put away your pride."

Standing, I pivoted slowly and dropped into the waiting chair. He lifted my feet onto the rests, gently elevating my cast.

"See? Being pampered isn't all bad." He patted my shoulder as he wheeled me through the door held open by the host.

Russell excelled at pampering. We were led to a corner table, which overlooked a gorgeous view of Lake Union. Twinkling lights reflected off the water below. Awaiting our arrival, a bottle of wine stood chilling. Russell had even ordered dinner ahead. "I want every minute here completely to ourselves, with no interruptions," he explained.

Even Cinderella would have envied this night.

Five

OUR FIRST DATE took place the Friday after St. Patrick's Day. For the rest of spring, Russell showered me with attention in spite of being in the midst of his second year of family practice residency. Russell had transferred to the University of Washington Medical School during his third year, when his mother fell ill with a bout of high blood pressure.

His training demanded all the energy he had, yet almost every week he managed to find time for a wonderful fairy-tale date. We wandered through the Pike Place Market, ate the three-hour breakfast at Snoqualmie Falls, and rowed a two-person kayak through the Mountlake Cut. We took pictures of rhododendron blossoms at the arboretum and rode the dinner train to the Chateau St. Michelle Winery.

One of the things I loved best about Russell was his ability to engage in conversation. I soon discovered that Russell came from a very wealthy Seattle family. His father managed a large and successful development company—the family business—and I recognized many of the projects they constructed all over the Pacific Northwest. Russell's parents lived on an old estate overlooking Lake Washington, near the university.

Once during the first week in May, Russell picked me up in a long dark chauffeured limousine.

"What's this?" I asked, hobbling to the curb in front of my apartment.

"We're going someplace special today," Russell answered, opening the door.

Though I no longer needed crutches, I still sported a nylon-webbed orthopedic boot. Its rocker bottom made me walk like an eighty-year-old lady. I eased myself onto the leather seat.

"Where?" I asked. Russell lived a flamboyant life. Though ceaselessly entertaining, I still had difficulty getting used to it all.

"It's a surprise."

"Where did you get this thing?" I snuggled closer to him in the soft bench seat.

He took my hand and squeezed lightly. "It's my mother's."

"You never told me your mother had a chauffeured limousine!"

"You never asked." He gazed out the window, watching the scenery go by. "Actually, my father bought it for her last birthday, and the chauffeur came with it. City traffic tires Mother."

"Some people take the bus."

"Not Mother."

"When do I get to meet this remarkable mother of yours?"

"Later," he chuckled, "when I'm certain you are so fond of me that Mother cannot possibly scare you away."

We traveled east through the university district, down the hill to Mountlake Boulevard, and soon crossed Lake Washington via the floating bridge. "Where are we going?" I asked again. When he called, Russell had instructed me to wear jeans and bring a warm coat.

"You'll see," he answered, patting the back of my hand, seeming to take pleasure in the mystery.

To my surprise, we eventually arrived at an eastside marina. Tall masts of graceful sailboats punctured the perfect blue of northwest skies. A gentle breeze blew from the south, and the spring air was cool. I zipped up my jacket. What had Russell planned this time?

The limousine slid away, and Russ took my hand, leading me toward the docks.

"This way, Pet," he said. I limped along behind him. In his eagerness, Russ moved too fast for me, but I didn't want to spoil his fun. When we arrived at the end of the pier, he stopped to let me enjoy the view.

I gasped. I'd never seen so many huge, beautiful, expensive boats in one place. In the distance, rows of boathouses protected the largest yachts. Hundreds more, tied to the docks, bobbed in the water. Such a picture! Mount Rainier held court in the southern sky just above the lake and all of these magnificent boats. I didn't want to move.

Russell grew impatient and pulled me away from the rail toward a long narrow ramp leading down to the docks.

"I can't walk down that thing. . . ." Without a word, he scooped me into his arms and started down the ramp. I giggled, both embarrassed and delighted. Reaching the dock, he set me down, grinning.

"Now hurry. We're behind schedule."

"Schedule? What schedule?"

"You'll see. Let's go." As I followed him through the maze of swaying docks, we traveled farther and farther from the pier. At last he stopped, but in my concentration to avoid tripping, I nearly ran into him.

"Okay, this is it."

"What?" I questioned.

"The boat. This is our date today. Let's get on board."

Russell stepped onto the boarding platform of a large, beautiful yacht. I stood gaping at him from the dock below. I knew the Koehlers had money, but this? He opened the deck gate and extended his hand to me. "Just one big step. Put your good foot up on the deck, and I'll lift you on board."

The boat rocked heavily in the water, and though boarding with one foot frightened me, the idea of such luxury prodded me on board. The spacious afterdeck held several pieces of full-sized outdoor furniture, including recliners and a small table. We passed through sliding glass doors into the salon where I found a leather wraparound couch. Moving toward the bow, I discovered a small kitchen-dining area. Steep stairs exited toward the front. Russell led the way up narrow oak steps, emerging onto an upper piloting area, complete with gauges and gizmos, lights and switches. Pulling myself heavily by the handrail, I followed him upstairs. There, Russell turned a single key and powerful engines turned over.

"Now, you sit here while I cast off." He disappeared back down the stairs. "I'll be right back." Moments later I saw him on the dock untying large ropes and tossing them onto the boat. He jumped back on the afterdeck and soon stood beside me again at the wheel.

"This is amazing."

"I know. My folks have had the boat for years, but I still get a thrill every time I pull out." He moved the right lever forward and turned the wheel. Slowly we left the dock behind. I noticed No Wake signs along the shore. Moving out into the lake, I found myself entranced by views of mansions and yachts and houses and businesses. Eventually we passed under the Mountlake Bridge. I looked up through the bridge deck to see cars passing over us, hearing the whine of tires mingle with the roar of traffic on the grating. The sun shone brightly, and a cold breeze blew through my hair. It was invigorating, and for a moment I imagined being rich enough to own all this.

About an hour later, Russell slowed to approach another smaller dock. Carefully he brought the boat in and tied up.

"What's next?" I asked over the rail.

"Next I dazzle you with my culinary skills." He smiled. "But I can't cook and pilot at the same time. Meet me in the galley."

Clearly Russ spent many hours getting ready for our trip. He pulled containers of precut vegetables and marinating meat from the refrigerator. He lit a propane grill mounted on the railing of the afterdeck and returned to stab meat and vegetables onto kabob skewers. He finished by tossing a Caesar salad and covering it with croutons.

"Can I help?"

"Absolutely not. You are my guest this afternoon." He turned on a CD player and whistled to classical music while he worked. I noticed that Russell whistled off-key. I sat at a barstool and watched with fascination.

Outside, he set a table with a linen cloth, candles in hurricane glasses, and china plates. The sky took on the presunset glow of late afternoon. The air grew still as the wind died down.

He pulled a chair away from the table. "Now sit and enjoy."

We indulged in a delicious meal. But even more wonderful was the deep apricot of the western sky. In contrast, the Seattle skyline took on a midnight silhouette. I couldn't take my eyes away from the changing horizon. "It is magnificent," I breathed.

"I knew you'd like it. This is my favorite place to watch the sun go down."

These were the kinds of dates that we enjoyed. I knew, long before I admitted it, that I loved Russell Koehler. And I believed that he loved me. Though we never spoke of long-range plans, I knew I had become very important to him.

One week before Saint Sebastian's recessed for the summer holiday, Russell won an appointment as the senior advisor of his program. In celebration his mother threw a glittering party at the family home. She hired caterers, decorators, servers, and even a valet to park her guests' cars. I was the only one at the party without a diamond tennis bracelet. That was the first time I met Russell's family.

Russell's mother clearly didn't like me, though I could not have said how exactly I came to be certain of this bit of information. It might have been the condescension I heard in her voice or her obvious disapproval when she observed my clothes. Perhaps I disliked the way she spoke to Russell around me—as though I weren't really present. But, too awed by my surroundings and too captivated by Russell, I did not resent his mother. She could look at my dress and wrinkle her nose as much as she liked.

On July 1, Dr. Russell Koehler began his last year in the family practice rotation. It had been a long haul, four years of medical school and two full years of ninety-hour workweeks. Though proud of his determination and perseverance, I knew his schedule left little time for courtship. I felt guilty about the hours we spent together. He should have been sleeping, and I knew it.

One hot August afternoon, I decided to cool off by taking a late afternoon shower. Before I could dress, my doorbell rang. Expecting Russell, I answered the door in my terrycloth bathrobe. Instead, a rather embarrassed Henry Schroeder stood waiting for me.

"Henry, what are you doing here?" I pulled the robe tighter around my waist and retied the belt. The orchestra conductor had never visited my home before.

"I'm sorry to come without calling, Patricia," he said, backing away from my screen door. "But I had to speak with you. I don't know what else to do." He looked miserable.

"Of course. Come in, Henry." I opened the door and let him squeeze into the narrow hallway. Upstairs, he paced back and forth across my living room floor.

"Sit down, Henry. You're wearing a path in the carpet." I gestured to the only chair and sat opposite him on the couch.

"Thank you, Patricia." He sat and buried his face in his hands. "I'm just so surprised, that's all. I knew you would help me."

"Why don't you start from the beginning," I urged gently.

"All right. Today I got a phone call from Andrew Carpenter. He's quitting the symphony orchestra." Henry spread his hands in front of him.

"You're kidding. Andrew? Why?"

"He says he has been offered a position in the Seattle Symphony. Paid, of course." Henry sighed. "He can't refuse. It is a huge opportunity for him."

"I see." Andrew, our principal cellist, held a paid position. He ran cello rehearsals, fielded complaints, and because he had been with our orchestra longer than anyone, Andrew functioned as Henry's right-hand man. Losing Andrew was clearly a blow.

"I came to ask if you would take his place."

"Me? Why me?" Astonished, I pulled the robe tighter around my neck.

"Because you play beautifully. I knew you could do it from the day you auditioned." He stood, pacing again.

Again the doorbell rang. Still stunned by Henry's news, I hurried downstairs to answer. Without thinking, I threw open the front door. Russell peered at me from behind the screen door. "Ah, Russell. I didn't expect you."

"I know," he grinned. "I got off early this afternoon. I thought we could go have dinner at the waterfront. How 'bout Ivar's?"

"Ah," I hesitated, glancing upstairs. An awkward situation.

"Don't worry. I'll give you time to change." He pulled open the door and walked in. I followed, still trying to find a way to explain.

"Russell, this isn't exactly a good time . . ." He entered my apartment through the door at the top of the stairs and disappeared into the living room before I could stop him. Russell nearly ran into Henry, who still paced vigorously in worry and frustration.

"Who are you?" Russell demanded.

"Russell Koehler, this is Henry Schroeder, my symphony conductor." I sighed, realizing what it must look like. "Henry, this is Dr. Russell Koehler, my friend."

Henry smiled congenially and offered Russ his hand. Russell stared hard at him and suddenly turned away, striding toward my hall door. I hurried after him.

"Wait, Russell! It isn't what you think," I called out. He ran down the stairs, skipping stairs in his haste. I followed helplessly. "Wait! Let me explain!"

On the porch, he turned suddenly to face me, his features tight with rage. "Patty, I thought we had something special. And now I find you here—with him—like this." He looked down at my bare throat.

"It isn't what you think, Russell. I was taking a shower."

Russell turned abruptly and walked quickly to his car.

"Russell, he just showed up," I shouted after him. Without looking back, he slammed the car door and drove away.

What a mess. Henry left after I promised to consider taking the cello position. I dressed hurriedly and then began my own pacing, back and forth in front of my kitchen telephone. Surely Russell would call. Certainly he wouldn't let something this foolish destroy everything. But the phone didn't ring.

I spent the night asleep in the chair nearest the phone, waiting for it to ring.

The next day I stayed in the apartment, afraid to miss his call. The phone never rang. By evening I'd grown frantic. I couldn't risk losing someone as wonderful as Russell over such a silly incident. At seven, I drove to his apartment.

He answered the door in running shorts and a muscle shirt, sweat dripping down his chest. I noticed again how the years had changed his physique. No longer a marathoner, Russell Koehler now resembled a gymnast. I looked away, embarrassed.

"Russell, I'm so sorry about yesterday," I said, staring at the floor.

"Who was he, Pat?" Looking up, I noticed his eyes were hard and angry.

"No one. I mean ... really ... he is my conductor," I stammered.

"What was he doing at your apartment?" Russ put his hands on his hips, still breathing heavily.

I sensed his softening. He would understand. I knew he would. "Our principal cellist quit. He came to offer the job to me." Still standing in the hallway, I wondered how many of his neighbors stood listening just inside their own doors. "Please, Russell, can I come in? Let me explain."

Reluctantly, he let go of the front door, swinging it open to let me pass. In his living room I chose a wing chair, marveling again at how meticulously he kept his apartment. He sat stiffly opposite me.

"Truly, I was taking a shower when Henry came. I answered the door, thinking it might be you." I took a deep breath. "He looked so upset, and I know him so well. I just didn't think. I asked him upstairs. That was when you came."

Russell's body relaxed visibly into the back of his chair. He smiled slightly. "So you're telling me that this whole thing is all perfectly innocent."

"Of course it is. I'm hardly the runaround type. You know that. I love you, Russ." There. It was out. I'd said it.

He stood quickly, came to my chair, and lifted me gently. Wrapping both arms around me, he said, "Oh, Patty. Let's not have another misunderstanding like this."

"I'm so sorry, Russ."

He kissed me. "Me too. Why don't we make sure it never happens again."

"What?" I pulled away, looking up into his eyes.

"Marry me," he said simply.

Six

RUSSELL'S FACE could not have conveyed greater surprise. His mouth dropped open, and his eyes opened wide. He looked as if I had slapped him. I can't explain why I refused his proposal. I only knew that something deep inside suddenly felt very unsure. Of course I loved him. Who wouldn't? Being with Russ was a never-ending fairy tale. Every date motion-picture perfect. Completely romantic. He exuded kindness and consideration, as affectionate as a golden retriever. Why on earth had I said no?

He stared back at me, his aqua blue eyes filling with tears. "So you don't want me, then?"

"No, Russell, that's not it at all."

"Then why won't you marry me? We're perfect for each other." He stepped back, holding my shoulders at arm's length. "You complete me, Patricia. I love everything about you. I love the way you fit perfectly under my arm. I love your curly hair. I love your gentle brown eyes. I know I can't live without you, Patty." He held me close again.

"I love you too, Russell," I whispered into his shoulder. "It's just too sudden. That's all." I tried to sound both gentle and firm. "It's just too sudden," I repeated as I pulled away and sat down. The seconds ticked away in silence. I ran both hands through my hair, straining to come up with the right words. "We've only been together since last spring. You have your training left to finish."

"I need you, Patty. I can't finish anything without knowing for sure that you are mine." Kneeling in front of my knees, he slipped one hand under my chin and lifted my face to his. "Patty, look at me. You saw how crazy I was yesterday. I'm crazy without you."

"I don't know, Russ. Give me a chance to think."

Russell didn't mention marriage again for a long time, but not a moment passed without some reminder of his love. He sent flowers to my classroom. He called from the hospital. Once, during lunch recess, he even sent a singing telegram to the teachers' lounge.

On a Friday in early October, Russ arranged to pick me up after school. "I'm bringing bikes," he said. "We're going to bike the Burke-Gillman Trail. And, Patty, please try not to let one of those mothers corner you in the parking lot." I heard him laugh. "It gets dark early these days."

When all my students were safely headed home, I went to the school office intending to check my mailbox. As I came around the front counter, I discovered Russell emerging from Sister Mary Regina's office. She held her head bent toward him, ear tipped, as if to catch every word. Her right arm encircled his, escorting him forward. In her intensity she nearly bumped into me.

"Oh, Patricia," her eyes twinkled in conspiracy, "I was just getting to know your friend Russell. A wonderful man, Patricia." She looked at Russell, and I actually saw her wink at him. Ludicrous. Sister Mary Regina—winking at a man?

Russell had that effect on people, leaving them enamored, trusting him simply by the gentle, direct way he had with everyone. I felt proud to be chosen by such a quality man.

We biked for nearly an hour, then stopped at a small park near the edge of Lake Washington. Over the rear tire, Russ's bike frame carried saddlebags, which he had packed with a blanket and a picnic dinner. In the warm late-afternoon sunshine, mottled by birch trees, we stretched out on a blanket to watch the ducks glide over the water of a small inlet. Soon the clouds turned pink. The temperature dropped. We both knew it was time to go. Still, we lingered. Russ took off his hooded sweatshirt and draped it over my shoulders.

"Getting cold?" he asked.

"A little." A shiver betrayed me.

"Better go, then," he replied. Reluctantly we packed the left-overs, and I stood to fold the blanket together.

"Patricia, before we go," he said, catching my hand, "I want to say something."

Still holding the corner of our quilt, I looked up at him. He grasped my arms in both his hands and pulled me toward him. "I need to say it—just this once." He seemed to look through my eyes to the very core of me. "I won't give up, Patricia. I will win you." He pulled me closer. "I'll wait you out—however long it takes. I will have you for my wife."

I shivered, suddenly aware of how early the sun set in early fall. Soon it would be dark. "You're cold," he said. "We need to get back." We peddled back to his car. As twilight turned to evening, a gentle breeze stirred the air. I continued to shiver. Was it the cold— or something else? We drove home in silence.

Fall gave way to winter. Gentle, warm raindrops turned to blowing, stinging needle pricks. Heavy wind and winter storms brought down the rest of the leaves. Darkness arrived earlier every day. Still, I taught and Russell worked. He spent his winter rotation at Harborview, a county hospital where government funding and university staff cared for the least of Seattle's natives. The Family Medicine department referred to Russell's patients as "under-served." On good days everyone else referred to them as indigent. On bad days the comments of the staff could not be repeated. These patients were neither educated nor compliant when it came to medical care. Russ found himself continually frustrated by his work. I sensed it in the tension he displayed when we were together.

"I tell you, Patty, there is nothing so irritating as caring for the same patient three weekends in a row, knowing that they can't pay for anything and knowing at the same time that they'll be back to their old activities by Monday." It was true. Many of Russell's patients were addicts, dealers, street people, and full-time criminals.

Few ever filled his prescriptions. Even fewer followed his instructions or kept return appointments. "Last weekend two of my gunshot patients were repeaters."

"Repeaters?"

"We saw them earlier this month for some other assault. Why should I take care of these guys? So they can let someone else shoot them?"

"I'm sorry, Russ."

"I tell you, I'm practicing 'drive-thru' medicine. This isn't the reason I became a doctor."

In spite of his frustration, I found myself the singular focus of his attention during nonclinic hours. He loved to have unusual gifts delivered to the school. This habit brought him fame among my fellow teachers. The sisters knew him by first name and regularly questioned me about our wedding date. Everyone on the staff felt certain that Russell was perfect for me.

That Christmas Russell's mother invited me to a family party at her home. It would be a formal affair, and Russell told me that I should choose something both sophisticated and elegant to wear. As private school teachers rarely use the adjectives "sophisticated and elegant" to describe their wardrobes, I grappled with his instruction.

"Now, where do you expect me to come up with something sophisticated?"

"I'll help you find something."

"Not in my closet, you won't."

"So we'll go shopping." Russ had an answer for everything. We scheduled a day for shopping, starting off at an exclusive dress shop on Fifth Avenue where a curvaceous blonde greeted Russell by name.

"How do you know her?" I whispered after we were seated in the waiting area.

"She takes care of my mother."

Somehow the blonde's voice betrayed more than professional interest in Russell.

When she returned, she carried an armload of evening dresses.

"Allow me to show you a few things in your size, Patricia." I heard a distinct tone of patronization.

She began by showing me gaudy, overdone gowns, either laden with beads or dripping with lace. I lacked the self-confidence to reject her choices. After all, she was Russell's friend. Just as I began to squirm, Russell interrupted her presentation.

"No, no. These aren't right for Patty. She is much too tiny for this frilly nonsense." He stood, picked up the gowns by the hangers and handed them back to her. "Find us something sumptuous—yet classic. And be sure that it isn't black. Professional musicians wear black to work." He winked at me and continued, "And this event is pure pleasure."

The blonde obediently took the dresses into the back room. I sighed with relief. Russell understood so much about me. I trusted him to help me find the perfect outfit.

She returned with far more appropriate selections. This time she chose deep, rich colors—burgundy and sapphire—in fabrics of velvet and satin.

Russell selected three, and I tried them on. He enjoyed the fashion show, sitting on the round white couch, leaning back with crossed legs, arms stretched out on either side. He had me walk, turn, and sit in each dress and finally pronounced the sapphire velvet the dress of choice.

"It makes your hair look like midnight, and it fits your body like it was made for you. In fact, you will make my mother's Christmas decorations look drab by comparison."

Staring into the mirror, the transformation I observed startled me. The dress's narrow silhouette fit perfectly. The cut velvet bodice had a sweetheart neckline, attractively shaped yet modest. I felt like a princess. When I emerged from the dressing room, Russell waited at the front counter, a dress bag draped over his arm.

"You didn't pay for the dress."

"Of course I did. I don't expect a schoolteacher to buy a dress just for my mother's frivolous party." He grinned and tucked my arm through his. "Besides, I'm the one who gets to look at you in it. Don't you think I should have to pay the price for such beauty?"

As I passed through the door, I looked over my shoulder to see the saleswoman shake her head in disbelief. Something in me wanted to be angry at her obvious disapproval. But I refused to let her envy rob me of my own deep pleasure. Being with Russell, being showered with his attention and appreciation, was a wonderful experience.

Then we went to the Satin Foot, where in a tiny showroom customers sat in velvet club chairs trying on shoes. The salesman wore a rose boutonniere on his three-piece wool suit. After measuring my feet, he asked what we were looking for.

"Actually, I'd like to have something dyed," Russell responded, as though he dressed women every day.

"Of course, and what fabric are we matching?" The salesman asked, nonplused.

"This evening gown." Russ held the dress bag out, opening the zipper to reveal the sapphire velvet.

"What style were you considering?"

"Something classic, sleek."

The man stood and walked to a display. He returned with three different evening shoes. "These can all be custom dyed. Elegant. Any of them would be an excellent choice for this dress."

Russell chose a suede pump, and the salesman brought it to me in my size. "You are fortunate. Few stores carry these small sizes."

I tried on both of the shoes and declared them a perfect fit. Russell paid for the shoes and left the dress with the salesman for a custom match. Cinderella had new slippers.

We stopped for lunch in a Pike Place Market restaurant, which overlooked Elliot Bay. Through open windows we caught the smell of saltwater mixed with old pilings and winter dampness. Russell and I ordered clam chowder served in bowls formed of freshly baked French bread. We held hands under the table and talked about the fun of shopping together. We lingered over the steaming soup, crunching crisp bread crust. Suddenly looking at his watch, Russell said, "Oh, we need to hurry. We have an appointment."

"What? Where are we going?"

"Finish up, Pet. It's a surprise."

We walked up the hill against a hard chilling wind, and I clutched my coat high around my neck. The streets of Seattle glowed with Christmas decorations. Tiny bulbs hung from bare limbs of city trees. Russ wrapped his arm protectively around me, and I snuggled into his warm wool coat. As we crossed the street, I looked up at the Rainier Tower building and marveled again at its construction. The structure looked like a seventy-story pencil standing on its point. How could the thing possibly stay up?

My gazing distracted me until Russell opened the glass door of Fox's Gems. Something deep inside panicked, and I caught my breath.

I must have balked slightly because Russell noticed. "Relax, honey, it's not what you think," he whispered as he held the door. I took a deep breath and stepped inside.

"Mr. Stendler, here we are," Russell said aloud. Another salesman, this one in a dark gray suit, stepped forward with his arm outstretched.

"Dr. Koehler, so good to see you again." He led us to an oak jewelry case, gleaming with inlaid brass trim. The wool carpet was butter yellow, so deep that my shoes sank into it with every step. We sat in thickly padded barrel chairs while Mr. Stendler took his seat behind the case. Discreetly, he unlocked sliding doors.

"As you requested, Dr. Koehler, I have three especially beautiful pieces chosen for this occasion." He lifted three black velvet boxes from the back of the case.

"All fourteen carat, of course. This—" he paused, opening the first box—"is three-quarter carat total weight." He slid the box toward us, opening it as he did so. Inside gleamed a golden heart pendant, with square cut diamonds framing the right half of the heart. "And this," he continued, "is a one carat stone." He opened a second box to reveal a silver twisted loop hanging from a delicate chain. The base of the loop held a single round diamond. In the last box lay a third necklace, where three perfectly matched diamonds rested, framed on each side by a single golden rod.

One at a time, Russell lifted each box, carefully examining the stones and settings. "What do you think?" He looked at me with the intensity of a surgical consultation.

"I'm uh . . ." I hesitated, glancing up at the salesman. I didn't know what to say. I couldn't believe that his dressing me for his mother's party included buying extravagant jewelry. I had gone too far in accepting Russell's lavish gifts.

"Won't you excuse us, please, Mr. Stendler?" Russell asked politely.

The man nodded silently and rose from his chair.

When he was out of hearing, Russell asked, "Patricia, what are you thinking?"

"I'm thinking that this is too much. I can't accept this, Russell."

"Of course you can. The party is my mother's idea. The dress is for her party. But the pendant—that is for you, Pet. After all, it is Christmas. Shouldn't I buy you a gift?" He reached over and squeezed my hand lightly. "If it were up to me, I'd be choosing an engagement ring. But you won't let me do that." He smiled. "You will completely crush my self-esteem unless you let me spoil you with something. Just this one little thing? Please, Patricia?"

The whole situation overwhelmed me. Though I felt treasured, my instinct told me not to accept such an extravagant gift. The diamonds twinkled up at me from inside their boxes, and I hesitated a moment longer. Then, looking back at Russell, I sighed. "All right. I would love to have a pendant." He smiled his most broad, triumphant smile. "But, Russ, I don't know anything about jewelry. Please don't make me choose."

He nodded, glowing with his own success.

We left with the single diamond dangling at the bottom of the white gold loop. A shopping day I would never forget.

The Koehlers held their party on a Saturday evening two weeks before Christmas. Russell picked me up in his car, and we arrived fashionably late. As Russell walked around to open my door, I tried to take in the enormity of the occasion.

The Koehler home could more accurately be called a mansion, fashioned of large cream-colored stones. Light spilled out of every window, sending a warm and inviting glow onto the grounds. Christmas lights twinkled elegantly from perfectly landscaped flower beds. Torches, flames swaying gently in the winter air, lined the pathway to the front door. Near the entry, water spouted from an imp in the center of a small fountain. Other guests arrived as well. Women in long evening gowns and wrapped in furs emerged gracefully from chauffeured limousines. Men in tuxedos and expensive overcoats greeted one another effusively. Suddenly I felt out of place, frightened. This was not the three-bedroom track house I grew up in. How could I ever fit into this family?

As we entered the house, a butler took our coats. "Welcome, Dr. Koehler. Your parents are in the music room." Russell thanked him and guided me to the right, into the formal living room. An enormous noble fir, spouting the tiniest clear Christmas lights, filled the window toward the street. Perfectly matching golden globes hung beneath garlands of twisted chiffon ribbon. Glass angels hung from every limb.

The guests, holding crystal champagne glasses, mingled in small groups. Light conversation and gentle laughter floated through every corner of the room.

Mrs. Koehler had hired maids who dressed like extras from a Broadway musical. In formal black and white, they moved silently among the guests, carrying trays of drinks and elaborately prepared appetizers.

I slipped my arm through Russell's as we moved though the room. He patted my hand reassuringly. Greeting his parents' friends by name, Russell graciously introduced me to more guests than I would ever remember. He made small talk with confidence and seemed proud to have me hanging on his arm. In a room toward the back of the house, a small group played dance music, and a few couples waltzed across a gleaming wooden floor.

I smiled on cue, shook hands when offered, and did my best to look as though I traveled in these circles regularly. In truth, I felt horribly out of place, like Cinderella at the ball. I couldn't have spoken, because fear had stuck my tongue firmly to the roof of my mouth.

"Such a pleasure to meet you."

"Thank you. A lovely party, isn't it?"

"A beautiful girl you've discovered, Russell."

More smiling. More nodding. Polite laughter. *How soon can we leave?*

Russell and I went through the buffet line in the formal dining room, where we found the table covered from end to end with silver chafing dishes. In the center of the table, on a giant ice oyster shell, hung layer after layer of fresh shrimp. "Flown in from Mexico," Russell said, gesturing to it. "But the sauce is good, if you like that kind of thing."

We ate with our plates balanced carefully on our knees in a corner of the dining room. Russell ate heartily. I nibbled. "Better dig in," he winked. "We riffraff never know where our next meal may come from."

I tried to eat but couldn't and satisfied myself that I had tasted everything. Content to observe, I watched other guests proceed through the line. Some I recognized from pictures I'd seen in the newspaper. One was the owner of Seattle's pro baseball team. Another I recognized as one of the county's most successful software executives. Eventually, Russell guided me to the dance floor, where the band began a slow waltz.

We were the only dancers without silver hair, and I felt the eyes of everyone in the room. It made me nervous. I hated attention, and I think I nearly trampled Russ's dress shoes. "Please, Russ. This is so uncomfortable. People are staring at us."

"They are just jealous." He smiled tenderly.

"I think they wonder how anyone with such little feet can have so much trouble controlling them."

Russell laughed out loud and pulled me closer. "Let 'em wonder."

The music ended with polite applause, and we moved to wicker furniture behind potted palms.

"Excuse me."

I looked up to find a silver-haired gentleman in a tuxedo bending toward Russell. His eyes sparkled with friendly recognition.

"Oh, Uncle William." Russell rose, shaking hands. "This is Patricia Morrow, my date. Patricia, this is William, my father's oldest brother."

Bowing slightly, he asked, "May I join you?" Russell rolled his eyes at me, and I bit my lip to suppress a giggle. William had striking dark eyes, considering his age, which I guessed to be nearly eighty. He seated himself near me on the love seat. "So what brings you to a Koehler gathering?"

"Russell's mother invited me." I smiled, trying to appear pleased to speak with him. Something about his manner made me feel as though I were under a microscope. I wondered if my dinner were hanging off my nose. Had I held a napkin, I would have wiped my face.

Russ gracefully excused himself. "Well, William, they expect me at the hospital early tomorrow. I must give my thanks to Mother." He strode away before I could stop him.

"I hear you teach school," William said with a touch of disapproval.

"Yes, I have kindergartners." I watched Russell bounce up the stairs at the end of the room.

"Really?"

No, I'm really a Soviet spy. "Yes, I've been teaching for a few years now, and I love it." Certainly he did not mean to sound like an interrogator. I decided to turn the focus to him. "Tell me, Mr. Koehler, what do you do for a living?"

"Please. Call me William." He took a long drink from his glass. "I'm retired now. But I used to be part of the Koehler construction firm."

"Oh, how nice." William Koehler did not make conversation easy. The silence between us lengthened, and William seemed content to stare at me while he drank. Really, kindergartners were much easier to entertain. Where had Russell disappeared to? I smiled and nodded weakly. I'd just begun to wish that I were a drinking woman when one of the tuxedoed waiters approached.

"Mr. Koehler," he said with a small bow of deference, "you're wanted on the telephone." The old gentleman stood and excused himself.

"So nice to visit with you," he said.

"Yes, charming," I lied.

With Uncle William out of the way, I determined to find Russ before some other relative found me. He had to be here somewhere. I wound my way through the milling, drinking, dancing crowd, wandering through the waitresses, looking for Russ. He was not in the music room. I searched the living area and checked the dining room again. He seemed to have disappeared.

I asked the butler stationed at the front door.

"He came through asking for his parents, miss," he replied with restrained politeness.

I watched as other guests, followed by penguin waiters, wandered up the large circular stairway to the second floor. Glancing around, I lifted my skirt and started up. At the top of the stairs, I found a long hallway. Double doors on the left revealed a large library, surrounded on every wall with books. Genuine leather-covered volumes lined the shelves from floor to ceiling, and a fully lighted globe stood on the floor near the front window. Blue smoke floated in the air, and older men sat on leather furniture engaged in intense discussion. Russell was not here. The conversation stopped suddenly, and too late I realized that they stared blankly at me. Their expressions varied from disinterest to resentment.

"Excuse me, I was just looking for Russell."

One white-haired gentleman, whose tummy rested squarely and completely on his thighs, grunted, "Not here." I tried to exit soundlessly, closing the double doors behind me.

I tiptoed along the wide carpeted corridor, looking from door to door. Some were closed. I didn't open them. A group of three women exited from a door on the right, through which I glimpsed a full wall of theater mirrors. A dusty pink glow escaped, and I saw dressing table chairs sitting against a pink marble counter. From the doorway, I heard a toilet flush. Clearly, a restroom for the ladies.

I continued, still looking, and was suddenly arrested by what seemed to be Russell's voice coming in an angry staccato from behind a partially closed door. Other voices joined in angrily. From the hallway, I viewed dark wallpaper above wooden paneling. His father's study? Just as I began to push open the door, Russ's voice returned loudly.

"How dare you talk about her that way!"

I froze, listening intently.

"We're just trying to protect you." Russ's mother spoke in a controlled tone. "She just isn't the right woman for you. You know that."

"After all, where does she come from? Who are her people?" Russell's father spoke in a deep, controlled voice. "You are two entirely different people. If you marry her, it will be nothing but trouble, Russell. I'm warning you now."

"She loves me, and I love her. What could be more important than that? We'll make our own life." Russell's anger rose, spilling over.

"Of course she loves you, dear. Who wouldn't?" I leaned forward, unable to resist listening to this very private conversation. His mother's voice continued. "You dress her in designer fashions. You buy her expensive jewelry. You take her on the yacht." Her voice dripped with disgust. "It is in her best interest to love you. She would love Hitler under these conditions."

"No," Russell snapped. "No. She isn't like that." He shouted, "You'll see. Both of you. You'll see."

I heard movement and backed quickly away from the door. Suddenly it swung away from me, and Russell burst into the hallway. I saw hurt mingled with surprise on his face. His eyes glistened with tears.

"I'm sorry," he said simply. "Let's go."

At the bottom of the stairs, he accosted the butler who greeted guests. "Our coats, please. *Now!*"

Russell stood fuming, then pacing, until the gentleman arrived carrying our coats. Without a word Russell took them both and left. I blinked awkwardly. "Thank you," I offered, embarrassed, then hurried outside to catch Russell.

The evening turned out to be like something from a cheap formula novel. If I hadn't been so embarrassed, so mortified, I might have laughed. The words coming from the upstairs room seemed scripted on a twenty-year-old typewriter.

But we rode home in silence. Somewhere between Russell's parents' and the Mountlake Bridge, my embarrassment and faint amusement transformed itself into boiling anger. How dare they decide I was not good enough for their son? What did they really know about me? We'd barely spoken. In truth, I possessed no pedigree. As Russell cooled off, my pride heated up. It made for a dangerous combination.

Somewhere between the bridge and my apartment, on a tiny pull-off along Lake Washington, I agreed to become Mrs. Russell Koehler.

Seven

FROM THE MOMENT I AGREED to marry Russell, he became a different man. He whistled constantly and walked with a
peculiar lilt, which reminded me of a man walking on the moon,
bouncing with every step.

Of course our engagement devastated Russell's family. They
tried to talk him out of it. When he refused, they begged him to
wait until after he finished his residency. He would not be dis-
suaded. They upped the ante and revoked his financial subsidy. Un-
moved by the sudden loss of resources, Russell's state of ecstasy continued.

Though I felt sorry to be the source of this family feud, I refused
to dwell on it. Russell's love, expressed by his constant attention and
generosity, made me feel deeply treasured. From that winter, I de-
rive some of my happiest memories.

We did all the things that engaged couples do. We chose a ring,
looked at apartments, and agreed on a dinnerware pattern. We
planned color schemes for the master bedroom and the bath. We
chose stainless, then decided to forgo both crystal and china for the
time being. Together we bubbled from store to store, signing up for
every bridal registry in town.

With newly limited finances, we changed our dating pattern. We
took long romantic walks and substituted picnics for dinners out.
We learned in-line skating on Rollerblades we bought at a sports

reseller and danced for free every Friday night at Big Band Night at the Seattle Center.

All the while, we planned our wedding. Because of my mother's death, we had to forgo many normal wedding traditions. Russell sensed my grief and decided to help me shop for a wedding gown. He had impeccable taste, and I couldn't refuse him this simple pleasure. Though we shopped, we never purchased. We couldn't afford the lovely gowns we found, and I secretly wondered if Russell simply enjoyed seeing me in elaborate, beautiful clothes. We dreamed about everything. Buying a house. Taking vacations. Starting a practice. Having children. Growing old.

We spent precious hours discussing our future family. We considered names and wondered if our children would arrive with dark curly hair like mine or have Russell's fair straight hair. Should we have three children or four? How far apart should the births be?

On weekend afternoons we drove through city neighborhoods looking at houses, trying to imagine the kind of house we might someday own. We giggled. We dreamed. We talked. We kissed.

Finances—or I should say the lack of them—persisted as our only source of prolonged difficulty. Though I continued to teach, Saint Sebastian's provided only a very small salary. Even though we practiced great frugality, we had difficulty saving money. We had nothing extra, even for a small wedding. Russell's token salary as a medical resident barely covered his rent. Together, we decided to save every penny, hoping somehow to have enough money by spring to marry.

Russell continued to be attentive and loving, but the edge on his attention vanished. He seemed satisfied, at last content. Our relationship grew more relaxed, more comfortable. We moved from silk to denim, and I liked things much better that way.

Russell settled into his position at the top of the residency totem pole. Responsibility for the younger residents and occasional opportunities to teach seemed to please him. Though he still looked forward to having his own private office, he managed to survive the horrid schedule, the nights on call, the ruthless supervisors, and the retaliatory nursing staff. He slept when he could and managed to keep a sense of detachment about his work. Even his professional tension seemed to ease.

One Friday night in early March, Russ called from the hospital.

"Pet, guess what?" Dispensing with formality, Russell had adopted my grandfather's abbreviation of Patricia.

"Hello to you too, sweetheart." I yawned. Struggling to sit up, I squinted at the numbers on my bedside clock. "Russ, it's after two-thirty in the morning. How can I possibly win a guessing game at this hour?"

"I know, and I only have a minute." I heard excitement in his voice. "I have a lady in Ultrasound, so I have to get back to the floor."

"Okay, so what is it? What happened?"

"My grandmother died."

"Oh, Russell, I'm sorry."

"Don't be—she was really old." In spite of myself, I giggled.

"That didn't come out the way I meant it to." He covered the phone, and I heard muffled voices in the background. "I'm really sorry to lose her. She was a good old dame. What I called about is that she left me the island place."

"The island place? What are you talking about?"

"After my grandpa retired, they bought twenty acres on the west side of Cummins Island. Up in the San Juan Islands."

"I didn't know you had family there."

"I don't really. It was their summer place when Gramps was alive. We went up to visit when I was a kid."

"Where is Cummins Island?" Still trying to wake, I had trouble following him. Though I could barely keep my eyes open, my ex-cited fiancé had worked all day and long into the night. Amazing. I yawned again.

"You have to take a ferry to get there," he said. Again muffled conversation filled the background. I waited patiently. "Anyway." His voice grew intense, urgent. "After Grandpa died, Nana moved up to the island for good. She loved it there. She stayed until she couldn't keep the place by herself, and Mom moved her back to the city."

"To the Norse Home."

"Right. We visited her there."

Actually, we'd joined the family for dinner at the retirement home on Nana's birthday. But I didn't want to interrupt him now. Because of Russell's obvious hurry and excitement, I feared that he might miss telling me something important.

"Well, this week I had a phone call from my dad—"

"Your dad?" I interrupted him. "That's wonderful, honey."

"Right, yeah, well he couldn't avoid me this time. Anyway, he called, but I didn't get back to him until this afternoon. He told me Grandmother died on Monday, and the service is tomorrow."

"Oh, Russell." Wide-awake, I sat up in bed.

"Patty, I don't mean to sound callous, but I've got to hurry. Don't you see?"

"See what?"

"Now we can get married."

"How?"

"Dad says she left the whole island property to me. I can sell it, and we can use the money to get married. We'll even be able to have a little honeymoon."

"Oh," I said breathlessly. Such a wonderful, sudden, unexpected gift. I felt guilty being happy about his grandmother's death.

"I have to go, Pet." I heard background voices again. "I'll call tomorrow when I get a minute."

He hung up before I could ask about the service. Apparently Russell didn't plan to attend.

The next weekend, Russell's first break from the hospital in weeks, we decided to drive from the city to Cummins Island to inspect the property—our new property. I packed a picnic basket, and we loaded the car with blankets, coats, and umbrellas. In the Northwest, beautiful spring weather can be followed in minutes by snow. We prepared for any eventuality.

I didn't know it then, but that happy excursion brought me to the place that eventually became my home. Though I grew up only ninety miles south of the San Juan Islands, I'd never visited the area before. From the moment we boarded the interisland ferry, I sensed some special mystery, a refuge of sorts. Nothing prepared me for its breathtaking beauty. On this particularly clear, sunny weekend, the enormity of Nana's gift struck me deeply.

Glossy and deep green, the interisland water reflected the lush, dark undergrowth that covers the islands around it. As the ferry plied the water, we caught surprising views of harbor seals floating on their backs. Slapping the water with their fins, they rolled and slipped beneath the surface, leaving no ripple, no trace of their presence.

Bright spring leaves hung on deciduous trees lining island shores. I admired madroños hanging far out over the banks, peeling red bark while clinging to sheer sandy cliffs. Round, smooth gray rocks covered the beaches. Everywhere fir trees, thousands of them, punctured the blue sky from hilly island summits.

The ferry seemed to stop at every little harbor village as the loudspeaker announced names I remembered vaguely from my days in elementary school. These places were real, not dots on a Washington map. Tiny communities, surrounded by densely forested hills, had been hidden away from the hustle of the city. I felt happy contentment watching calm water lapping at the edge of lovely islands as the ferry floated by. I could love this place.

We left the ferry at a village called Serenity Bay. True to its name, the harbor was calm, the docks deserted, the streets peaceful.

"I'm hungry," Russell declared as our car pulled out of ferry traffic and onto the village streets. "Want something to eat?"

I was too enamored to eat, but wanting to make the trip last as long as possible, I agreed. "Russ, what about the picnic?"

"No problem. We'll eat that later. Maybe on the way home." He scanned the sidewalks, looking for a restaurant. "I'm in the mood for French dip."

We found a little café sitting on a corner across from a sporting goods store and looked for a place to park. Apparently everyone in this town walked, as parking spaces seemed nonexistent. Eventually we left the car in a lot below the restaurant and hiked up the steep hill to the corner. The hike left me a little breathless.

As we stepped into the café, time seemed to move backward. An antique cash register rested above a worn wooden display cabinet that held fresh homemade pies. The waitress, whose nametag read *Sylvia*, reminded me of an *Andy Griffith Show* rerun. She wore a starched short-sleeved pink dress with white cuffs turned back into perfect points. The dining room held mismatched tables, dressed in red-and-white checkered cloths, on dark wooden floors. Two enormous fans hanging from a twenty-foot ceiling circled high above the dining room.

Sylvia led us to a small table and gave us both menus covered in yellowing plastic. I smelled coffee brewing and something else—disinfectant? Clear plastic protected the checked tablecloth, and resting my hands on top of it, I found it still damp with the same disinfectant I smelled.

I relished the room, the floors, the atmosphere—all of it—and we enjoyed a leisurely lunch, though I picked at my vegetable soup. An hour later, with Sylvia's instructions penciled on the back of a paper napkin, we wound our way along a fir-draped country road toward the property.

"Oh yes, I remember that old farmhouse." Russell pointed down a grassy lane to a home in a clearing. Fresh laundry, hanging from a clothesline beside the house, fluttered in the wind.

"How long has it been?"

"Since I've been here? I've been trying to figure that out." Russ scratched at his cheek while mentally calculating. "Nana moved to the Norse Home when I was in junior high. So I don't think I've spent the summer up here since then. I guess that makes it about twelve years."

"Have things changed much?"

"Oh yes," he chuckled. "Used to be there wasn't any choice about which road to take out of town. They only had one." He slowed the car to manage a particularly sharp turn. "Nowdays, though, with people working from home and the big back-to-nature movement, things have really grown here."

We passed through acres of fenced pasture, cows on the left, horses on the right. I watched the farms flow by the car windows. "How many people live on the island?"

"I couldn't be sure, maybe five thousand on the whole island."
He turned the car off the pavement onto a gravel lane. Completely
covered by brush, the driveway opening resembled the mouth of a
cave. Our car straddled a grassy center strip, with puddles on either
side splashing muck onto Russell's car.

Trees dripped water onto the windshield, and sunlight sparkled
in the raindrops on the leaves beside the car. Branches scratched at
our car as we drove down the long, tortuous driveway. Just as I
began to wonder how far back the house sat, we emerged into a
clearing completely surrounded by enormous rhododendrons.
Crimson blossoms, as big as basketballs, hung from nearly every
limb. Each bloom played host to a myriad of fat, noisy bumblebees.
I heard myself gasp.

Russ laughed. "I guess it's pretty spectacular for a city girl."

"I've never seen anything so beautiful."

"Wait till you see the view from the back porch."

"I can hardly see the house."

"Oh, it's back there, all right. But these stupid plants grow like
weeds here. I suppose they haven't been cut back since Grandpa
died." He opened the car door and climbed out.

As I watched, Russell disappeared through a barely perceptible
hole in the rhododendrons. I hurried to follow him. Behind the
blossoms stood an untrimmed rose arbor, whose leaves were just
starting to show. Its branches hung low over the stone path. In an
effort to avoid thorns, we walked sideways through the roses. Still,
they tore at my jeans. As I pulled away, I looked up to catch my first
glimpse of the old house.

The two-story Tudor was grand in every way, though very old.
Wide wooden steps led to a covered porch, which ran along the
entire front of the house. Large identical windows graced both sides
of the single mahogany entry. The stucco, framed in dark wood,
had been painted a soft beige. At the end of the front porch hung
a wooden porch swing.

"Oh, Russell, look. Isn't it beautiful? I've always wanted a porch
with a swing." I decided to try it out.

"You're an incurable romantic," Russell said as he wiggled his key into the front door.

"I know. Romantics make great musicians," I said from my position on the slatted seat. My feet barely reached the wooden porch floor. I slid forward and, with clumsy effort, managed to get the swing moving. "You should join me. It's perfect," I coaxed.

He held the door open. "Do you want to see this or not?"

Of course I did. I dismounted the swing just in time to follow him through the front door. The house was dark inside, rich with the smell of dust. Russell slid his hands along the wall, looking for the light switch. "Must be here somewhere," he said. "Nana always used to stand on the porch waving when we came. I never had to use this switch." I reached for the slatted window shades next to the front door. Feeling my way down the center post, I found the handle. With a simple twist, light flooded the entry. Moments later Russ found the switch.

I turned to face a beautiful wooden stairway covered in what looked to be an antique oriental runner. Brass rails held the runner in place. Cobwebs draped deeply textured plaster walls. Dark wood trimmed both the floor and walls.

We turned left into what must have been the living room and found it filled with furniture. White cotton dust covers rested over every piece. Someone had gone to a lot of trouble to close up this house. I lifted one of the sheets and discovered underneath a magnificent Victorian sofa, covered in rich burgundy velvet.

"Nana loved her old furniture." Russell barely stopped to look. Instead, he moved to the window, throwing open heavy damask draperies.

Under another sheet I found the glossy dark wood of a lamp table. Even from under the dust cover, I noticed the tabletop was in perfect condition, supported by highly carved legs. I wanted to enjoy every detail.

"Oh, Russell. Everything is so beautiful."

In the living room, the intricate patterns of a Persian rug in navy and red covered dark wooden floors. The smooth plaster ceiling had no corners, but instead, at the juncture where the walls and ceiling met, the plaster had been completely rounded, softened. The effect was that of a white balloon hanging suspended over the walls. I'd never seen anything so elegant.

I followed Russ to heavily paneled double doors leading out of the living room. Nearly nine feet high, the doors slid open into pockets hidden in the walls. When opened, the two rooms merged into one elegant space.

We found an enormous old table and eight—no, ten—ornately carved high-back chairs in the center of the dining room. Just as I reached out to lift the drape from the table, Russell cleared his throat.

"Honey, we only have today. We need to see the whole property today."

"You're right. I am behaving like a tourist in a castle." I smiled. "But it's a beautiful castle. You must admit it."

"Come on. Let's get this over with." He pushed open the swinging door on the opposite side of the room and disappeared.

Reluctantly, I followed. We entered a small room with counters on every wall, cupboards above and below, and a small window separating this room from the formal dining area. Painted a garish green, white floor tiles brightened the room only slightly. "It's the butler's pantry," Russell said, barely pausing before he pushed open the next door.

From the pantry we stepped into the most immense old kitchen I had ever seen. Soft yellow walls magnified the sunlight that bathed the room, spilling through narrow back windows onto huge rectangles on tiled floor. Surrounded by six wooden chairs, a worn table rested in one corner. With an unfinished surface—like butcher block—its deep marring hinted at an elaborate history. I imagined hundreds of meals prepared and served on its maple surface. Closing my eyes, I envisioned Russell's Nana sitting at the table, snapping fresh beans into a ceramic bowl while a canning kettle bubbled on the old stove behind her chair.

This was a kitchen for families, for making memories. A room which held deep and lasting love in every detail. From the enormous stainless steel sink to granite counters and glass cabinet doors, it was a room full of life and warmth. I felt it, and I loved it instantly.

This room's only concession to modern life was a very large re-frigerator immediately to the left of the swinging door. It stood si-lently now, propped open by an old towel. Suddenly I saw myself coming down in the middle of the night for a glass of milk and a cookie. Opening that door. Sitting at that old table.

I wanted to see the view from the rectangular windows. Squeez-ing behind the table and chairs, I pulled back sheer café curtains. As I pressed my nose into the antique glass, my breath caught in my throat. "Oh, Russell, why didn't you tell me?"

He laughed. "How could I tell you about that?"

"You're right. No one could prepare me for this." I squinted, trying to bring the blurry landscape into focus, but rippled antique glass made it impossible. Details disappeared in the wavering bub-bled surface.

"It's fantastic," I whispered again. "I've never seen anything like it. Which way are we facing?"

"Here," he said. "It's much easier to see from the porch. Come on out." He fiddled with the lock on the back door and passed through an old screen, which slammed shut behind him with a bang.

More than twelve feet wide, the completely covered porch ran the entire length of the house. Several windows opened from the house on to the porch along its length. Enclosed on the seaward side by a partial stucco wall, framed screens rested above the wall. Though securely enclosed, fresh air and sunlight filled the space. I imagined children playing here. In my mind I heard the sound of Matchbox cars, of Tonka toys, and a toddler's tricycle.

Adirondack chairs with matching footstools sat scattered in groups along this porch. For some reason, this furniture had not been stored or covered. The wood had long since faded to silver gray, rough with the raised grain of moisture and old age.

Russell was right. From here a spectacular view stretched unbro-ken before me. I saw only the unending blue of the Puget Sound sparkling in the afternoon sunlight. I made out the soft gray of land blending into a hazy horizon in the distance. To the right I saw the deep blue green of a nearby island. "Which one is that?"

"Orcas, I think." Russell stood beside me. "But I really can't remember much. When I was a kid, I used to paddle around out there in Nana's little rowboat. I knew every nook and cranny of every island around here. But not anymore." He turned toward me. "Want to look around upstairs?"

"Of course." I wrapped my arms around his neck and kissed him warmly. He liked it, I could tell. "You are an amazing man, Dr. Koehler. And now that I see this, I understand more than ever."

After we wandered through the upper floors, we decided to share tea on the screened porch. The porch faced west, and on this early spring day the afternoon sun filled the space with light and warmth. We boiled water on the old stove and brought our mugs out to the chairs.

"Russell, are you sure you want to sell this place?" I wrapped the string of the tea bag around my spoon, tightening gently. "It's so beautiful. So homey."

"But look at the view, Pat. Think of the money." Russ had launched his Jack Benny imitation.

"I know. But have you ever wondered . . ." I stirred my tea, thinking, hoping. "What about starting a practice up here? This'd be a great place to raise a family."

"I don't know. What kind of medical community is this? I'd have to do all my consulting with the veterinarian in East Sound."

"That's not fair. We aren't exactly talking about a third-world country here."

"No." He stood, still holding his mug, and walked to the screen, listening, thinking. "I guess not."

"We could keep part of the property for us. Sell part of it for now." I put down my own cup and joined him at the window. I noticed tiny specks of white out on the water and guessed that they meant the wind had picked up. Gulls floated in currents of sea air. "We could pull together enough to get married and start a practice at the same time."

"Patricia, you don't have any idea how many doctors are on this island."

"No, but neither do you."

"Well," he turned and looked into my eyes. "Okay. I tell you what. I'll consider it. But only because you seem to think this hair-brained scheme of yours will work. And only because I love you more than life."

I wrapped both arms around his neck and hugged him happily. "I can see that I'm not going to be the only romantic in our family."

"I suppose I can live anywhere, as long as you're happy."

"I could be happy here." I snuggled up to his chest, tucking myself under his arm. He wrapped both arms around my shoulders.

"Being with you makes me happy," he said simply.

Eight

IT BECAME OUR DREAM to open a family medicine practice on Cummins Island. Through a local real estate agent, we managed to sell half of Nana's property, leaving the old house and ten acres for ourselves. With the cash from the sale, we paid off Russell's car, some of his education debt, and put the rest away as a cushion for the years until the practice had a positive cash flow.

I became Mrs. Russell Koehler on June 23 in a small ceremony in the Parish Hall at Saint Sebastian's. With linoleum floors and bare walls, the room itself felt as warm and inviting as frozen meat. Poor Father McRae fought with his own voice, which bounced back at us from gray gymnasium walls. He sounded a little like a car horn in a tunnel.

No music warmed our ceremony—we could not afford to hire musicians. Though I begged, Russell refused to let me play. How would it look, he wondered, to have the bride straddling a cello? I asked if we could have a string quartet from the orchestra. They would love to give us the gift of wedding music. Russell wouldn't hear of it. Sometimes Russell was too proud for his own good.

In spite of our poverty, I was deliriously happy marrying Russell.

Though Russell's parents chose not to attend, friends, teachers from my school, and some of the medical staff who worked with Russell surrounded us as we exchanged our vows. My brother, Steve, flew into town with his wife and my two nephews. Annie stood with me, and another resident stood with Russell. I chose a classic suit in pale blue linen, something I hoped to wear again. Gone were the days of dyed-to-match leather and solitaire diamonds. The ceremony transformed me into the happy wife of an impoverished medical resident.

We spent our honeymoon at the old house on Cummins Island where we enjoyed a warm, beautiful week. We made breakfast together, walked the beach, and lounged on the covered porch, reading books. In the evenings, with firelight dancing on the plaster walls, we celebrated our love in front of enormous fires in the old living room. Russell seemed as contented as I.

With all three years of his residency completed, Russell won a fellowship for further study. His responsibilities included supervision of new residents, as well as bits of teaching at the medical school. Because all residents begin new assignments on the first of July, we enjoyed only four short days of honeymoon. The staff needed Russell in Seattle to set the pace for the new doctors. Reluctantly we packed the car to return to the city.

"Is that everything?" Russell said, bending over the trunk of the car, arranging bags.

"I think so. Shall I take another look around?"

"Yeah. No telling how long it will be before we get back up here."

I turned and ran up the old porch steps. In the darkened living room, the covered furniture and closed drapes contributed to my own sadness. How I hated to leave this beautiful home empty. This place should be lived in, enjoyed. I went up the stairway to find everything as it should be. We'd left no trace of our stay in paradise. The bed in the master bedroom had been stripped, the bathroom sparkled.

"Patricia. Come down here, please." Russell's voice interrupted my musing. Curious, I started down the stairs, heading toward the back of the house where I found Russell on the screen porch staring at the wooden chair in the farthest corner.

"What'd you find?" I thought I'd removed all our things from the porch.

"You know what I found." I heard anger in his voice and saw a strange new tightness in the features of his face.

"No, Russell, I don't. I wouldn't ask if I already knew."

He turned to face me. "Patricia, when did you buy this?" He dangled a coffee mug in the air, pinching the handle between his thumb and index finger. His features betrayed disgust.

"Oh, that. I bought it this week in town."

"When?"

"I don't know. Sunday, I think," I said lightly, thinking how silly his display seemed to me. "The day we went in for groceries."

"Patricia, you were with me the whole time. When did you sneak away to buy this?"

"Sneak away? I didn't sneak away. I found it in the tourist section of the Stock 'n Save. I put it in the grocery cart with everything else. You must have missed it."

"Missed it? I didn't know I needed to supervise you like a child."

His last comment hurt, but I tried to ignore it and maintain my composure. Russell, normally so generous, had never behaved this way.

"I just wanted a little something to remember our honeymoon. It cost three and a half dollars, for goodness' sake—on sale."

His disgust returned to anger. I remember that I watched the shift and noted the moment the change occurred. His eyes opened very wide, and his eyebrows rose to a peculiar position on his forehead. There they were—the eyebrows up, the eyes like fried eggs.

"Patricia, is this the way things are going to be? Are you going to waste money all the time like this?"

"Russell, I'm sorry. I didn't know it would upset you so much."

His face tightened. "I wouldn't be upset—not if I could trust you."

"Of course you can trust me, Russell. This is just a misunderstanding. You're right. I should have mentioned it. I just didn't think about it."

Russell stormed off the porch and headed back toward the kitchen. As he passed by me, he turned sideways, his shoulder forcefully shoving me out of the way. The screen door slammed behind him as he entered the kitchen. Too stunned to follow, I stood shaking my head. All of this for a coffee mug? No mug could possibly be worth this kind of grief.

I heard him start the car and shift into gear. What now? I hurried out to the front steps, just in time to see the car roll away from the house.

"Russ, wait! Really, Russ." Waving my hands, I stumbled down the stairs and across the little yard. When I emerged from the rhododendrons, frantic and tearful, he slammed on the brakes, and I got in. Russell drove into town, careening his little car around every turn, pushing both the speed limit and my own tolerance for terror. We arrived at the ferry terminal just as the 4:15 ferry pulled away from the dock. In cold, awkward silence, we waited for the next boat.

Somewhere out on the Sound, halfway between Serenity Bay and Twalleson, I decided. Enough. "Russ, I'm sorry about all of this. I didn't mean to upset you. You were right, I should have checked with you. I know things are tight."

His teeth clenched. He glanced out the car window to the car deck. No response.

I sighed. "If I'd known it would upset you, I wouldn't have done it. Really. I just thought our honeymoon had been so wonderful, so inexpensive, that you wouldn't mind."

His face softened. I saw him reconsider.

"Please don't stay mad at me. I hate to have you angry. You know that." I reached out and took his hand in mine, gently rubbing the back of it. He responded with the tiniest of squeezes.

"I don't like to be angry either, Pet." His eyes glistened.

"So then, it's over?"

"What's over?"

"The fight?"

"Who could stay mad at those beautiful brown eyes?"

"Good. Then we can start making up. I hear that's the best part." I wrapped both arms around his neck and drew his lips to mine. When we docked at Twalleson, the lot attendant knocked on the window.

"Time to break it up, folks." He walked away from the car laughing. I climbed out of Russell's lap while he started the engine, put the car in gear, and drove up the ramp.

And so our first year of marriage began.

———

We decided to keep my apartment on Phinney Ridge, which was cheaper than Russ's place and close enough to Saint Sebastian's that I could walk to school. Russell closed his apartment, and we moved his things to my place. Russ had much nicer furniture than mine, so gradually we gave away or sold most of my old stuff. Cleaning, sorting, and nesting occupied most of the rest of our summer.

During our engagement, Russell's apartment always looked like an ad in a decorating magazine. He liked antiseptic, while I preferred tidy clutter. Light dusting satisfied me. Russell cleaned until he could declare his apartment a "sterile field." I expected conflict about our dissimilarities and worked hard to keep the house up to his standard.

The accumulation involved in blending two households really bothered Russ. He seemed driven to get rid of the extra junk, especially the tacky and worn-out accumulations of my mother. Though I felt selfish, it hurt to throw away my mother's treasures. Many, like the crocheted tablecloth I kept on my dining room table, showed unmistakable signs of age. It had stains and holes, but my grandmother made it, using the same pineapple pattern she used for everything she crocheted. This tablecloth had adorned the dining room table in my mother's home from the day Grandmother made it all through my childhood years. Russell couldn't understand that these things were all that remained of my youth.

In the end, I gave in. One hot August day, I watched while Russell packed most of what remained into boxes and took it to the Salvation Army. Then, alone in the silence of our tiny apartment, I cried.

Late in August while I washed dinner dishes, Russell came in

with the newspaper folded open to the want ads. "I've been thinking, Pet."

"About what?" I handed him a towel.

He frowned, reluctantly accepting the towel. "About your car."

"What about it?"

"Do you know how much it costs to insure two cars in the city?"

"No, I just got married." I smiled charmingly while handing
him a plate. "Until now I only had one car."

"Well, it's a bundle, I tell you. I think we should sell your car
and keep mine. We'd save about four hundred a year."

I rinsed a frying pan. "What would I drive?"

"We live close enough to the school that you could walk."

"I do walk."

"I mean, all the time. When it rains, I could drop you off on my
way to the hospital."

"I don't know, Russ. I hate to give up my car. Wouldn't it be
cheaper yet to sell yours?" He scowled and took a glass from the
drying rack. I added, "Surely a new Avalon is more expensive to
insure than a ten-year-old Subaru."

"You're right. But mine is paid for and much more reliable than
your old rattletrap. When you need to run errands and buy groceries, I'd take the bus to the hospital. I'd feel safer if you drove a
newer car around town."

As always, my logical bridegroom made perfect sense, but something about this conversation felt wrong. I struggled to control
growing anger. "Russ, I don't want to be stuck without a car. Didn't
we make enough selling the property to pay for my insurance? I
mean, we still have my salary, and we kept the cheaper apartment.
Don't you think—"

"Patricia, you weren't listening. I explained that I have already
thought about this. I know whether we can make it or not."

Blinking back tears, I tried again. "In a year, you'll be working.
You'll have a salary."

"Patricia, you can't possibly understand the financial obligation
of finishing school and starting a practice."

"Russ, you don't have to start your own practice. You could join an established group."

"Aren't you entertaining?" he sneered. "Just this spring you wanted me to start a practice up on the island, and now, when it costs you to see your dream come true, you bail out. So is this how things are going to be? You want the moon, but you want me to pay for it?"

"That's not what I'm saying, Russ." I put my dishcloth down and turned to face him, trying not to cry. "I just don't see you making the same kind of sacrifices."

"How dare you say that? I spend ninety hours a week at the hospital breaking my backside so that you can have your perfect little dream life up there on the island. Beat that for sacrifice."

"I didn't mean it that way, you know I—"

"Patricia, I don't think you know what you want."

"Of course I do. I want you to be happy." I turned to lean against the counter. "I just hate to sell my car, that's all. Let me think—"

"There isn't anything to think about. I already put the ad in the paper." Russell folded his dishtowel in perfect quarters and hung it on the rack. He stared into my eyes for a long moment and then walked deliberately from the room. As the dining room door slammed, a long-stemmed wineglass fell from the dish rack and shattered into a thousand tiny pieces.

———

Russell stopped speaking to me, and for three long days we rattled around our tiny apartment like a pair of pouting children. He spent his nights on the couch and ate his meals at the hospital. Gradually, I realized Russell would not give in. People called about my car, but no buyer appeared. Secretly, I hoped it wouldn't sell. Then perhaps Russell would have to change his mind.

My anger burned itself out, but Russell's became a bush fire with no end in sight. My mother used to tell me that women had to be willows because men were oaks. *"In order to have a good marriage, a woman must be flexible,"* she had told me. Perhaps this was what she meant.

This miserable cold war needed to come to an end, and clearly I had to take the first step. I apologized to Russell, and he sold my car the next afternoon.

Things went along that way for most of the fall. He demanded. I resisted. We fought. Eventually, after long painful silences, I asked forgiveness and we made up. I fought my own battle with depression and discouragement. I couldn't understand what happened to the attentive, loving man I had married.

I rationalized that the pressure of his work caused his irrational behavior. After all, with only a degree in education, what could I possibly understand about the pressure of medical school and residency?

I played cello in the orchestra that fall, though between school and Russell, I found myself far too busy to teach private lessons. At least I played. I gave up my position as principal chair. The new lead cellist moved to Seattle from Connecticut. We played a full fall season.

Near Halloween, I felt another pressure of my own. I missed my second menstrual period. I certainly couldn't be pregnant. We had been very careful—taken every precaution. I convinced myself that this interruption was simply my body's response to a new and somewhat difficult marriage. I continued to assuage my fear until the first week of November, when I began every day by hanging my head over the toilet in our bright green bathroom. It was not like any other stress I'd experienced.

The over-the-counter pregnancy test confirmed my worst fear.

I kept the discovery to myself for some weeks. Russell did not notice my fatigue or loss of appetite. Actually, just as I wondered how to tell him, the whole thing sort of told itself.

On a Friday night, Russell came home from the hospital tired but happy. "I have good news!"

"What are you so happy about?" I glanced up from student papers spread across my desk.

"My teaching review came back today. I received an 'excellent' rating."

"Wonderful. I'm happy for you." I put down my pen and rubbed tired eyes. These days, I rarely found Russell in a playful mood. His happiness genuinely pleased me.

"Look, you finish whatever it is you are doing, and I'll cook." He grinned. "I brought home a surprise for dinner." He waved at me with a large paper bag and disappeared into the kitchen.

In the midst of overwhelming fatigue, progress reports for conferences loomed high on my list of responsibilities. Beginning Monday, I faced appointments with thirty-eight sets of parents anxious to hear every detail of their children's academic progress. I tried again to focus on the forms in front of me. I heard Russell humming to himself in the kitchen, banging pots and pans, and running water in the sink. Eventually the air turned heavy with steam. Delightful smells floated into the living room.

"Are you almost ready in there?" I called through the kitchen door. "Because I'm so hungry I can't wait much longer. I'll have to get a snack."

"No way," he retorted. "This dinner was much too expensive to ruin your appetite with a snack. You'll just have to wait."

Minutes passed. I tried to be patient, but my hunger grew to nausea. *Oh, please, God, let him serve dinner soon.* Just then Russell came through the door, wearing a red barbecue apron and a kitchen towel folded and draped over his right forearm.

"Madame would like to be seated now?"

"Absolutely. Madame is starving."

"Well, then, follow me, my most beautiful Madame." He turned back and, with a flashy little saunter, led me to the dinner table. Candles glowed from crystal holders. Two china plates, the only ones we owned, gleamed in readiness.

"Oh, Russ, everything looks beautiful." I sat in the chair he held for me. "This is so sweet of you."

He took the seat across from me, grinning mischievously through the candle glow.

"Please, can we eat? I'm excruciatingly hungry."

"Oh, of course. Here you are." He served salad from a mixing bowl. Russ had cut the vegetables with the precision of a surgeon, celery in exactly matching angles. Unwilling to waste more time on observation, I dug in with my fork, stopping only to tear and butter a whole-wheat roll.

"Patricia, slow down. You need to be more careful. How can you keep that dainty little figure if you continue to eat like this?"

Frankly, Russ, I'm not planning to keep this dainty figure much longer. "I guess I missed lunch. Sorry." I deliberately tried to slow down. My stomach began to roll. *Give me something real to eat.* I downed more of the roll. Russell opened a bottle of Chardonnay.

"Mind if I just have water?" Pregnant women shouldn't drink.

He shrugged and stood to bring water from the kitchen, all the while rambling on about his success with his new supervisor. "It isn't easy to please a woman," he said. "Especially one who thinks she's God's gift to medicine. But this lady really likes me, I can tell. She said I have a way with the students."

"Great." I smiled. *Bring on the food.*

"She says that most of the new residents get so caught up in the H and P—I mean history and physical—that they forget they're talking to real people. She says I've really helped our residents improve."

"You've always been good at relating to everyone." *Where is dinner?*

"Anyway, she's recommending me for a teaching award."

"Wonderful, Russ." I took another gulp of water. My nausea grew exponentially. "I'm sorry to disturb your story. But could we eat dinner? Then I think I could listen a little better."

His smile drooped a bit, but he responded quickly. "Sure. I'll get the main course." While putting on thickly padded potholders, he moved to the stove. From there, he retrieved a gleaming stainless kettle and placed it on a folded towel between our plates. With a flourish, he removed the lid.

Oh no. The smell.

He fished into the depths of the kettle with a long pair of tongs.

Without warning, he placed an enormous lobster in the center of my plate.

Raising my hand to my mouth, I threw up all over it.

Russell found me hugging the toilet with both arms, my head drooping just above the water line. He carried a bowl of warm water and a clean kitchen towel. "Here," he said, handing the towel to me. "It always feels better if you can kind of clean up after." He placed a bath towel under my arms.

"Thanks," I breathed and curled up on the bathroom floor.

"I'll go open up the bed. You'll feel better lying down."

I didn't bother to explain. Not now. Not like this. This wasn't the way he was supposed to find out. Later. I'd have to explain later.

Around ten o'clock, I woke up on the bathroom floor, covered in a down blanket, my stomach settled. I brushed my teeth and dressed for bed. While I performed this bedtime ritual, I wrestled with the task ahead. I had to tell him. This was as bad a time as any.

"Russ, honey, I need to talk to you." I entered our little living room to find Russ sitting in a club chair under a pedestal lamp, focused on a medical journal.

"You should be going to bed," he said without looking up from his article.

"Not really, Russ." I walked closer. "I'm not sick."

That got his attention. "Well, for not being sick, you sure made a mess out of a very expensive lobster dinner." He looked puzzled. "Would you mind telling me what is going on here?"

"Russell, you're the doctor. You tell me. My cycle is two months late. I'm sick every morning. I'm too tired to climb the stairs at night." I paused, smiling. "I think it's a pretty easy diagnosis, don't you?"

He stared hard at me. His mouth became a straight line. "What exactly are you saying, Patricia?"

"We're going to have a baby, Russ." I moved toward him, wanting to give him a hug. "I'm pregnant." His shoulders went very stiff. I let go, searching his eyes.

"How could you do this to me?" His voice became a threatening whisper. "How could you let this happen?"

"Russ, I didn't do it to you." I nearly giggled, emphasizing the words. I'd expected him to be frustrated, but his response surprised me. With my most charming voice, I continued, nearly pleading, "We did it together. That is how it's done, you know—together." I smiled into his face. Without seeing me, Russ withdrew. I felt him grow more distant, more cold. I struggled to bring him back. "Our first baby, Russell," I implored. "It's unexpected. Inconvenient. But for heaven's sake, this isn't the end of the world. We'll just have to do the best we can."

"I didn't do this. You did." He growled. "I don't have to make the best of anything. I want you to have an abortion."

His cruel words kicked me, and I felt the air go out of my lungs like a prizefighter toppling over backwards. "No, Russ. Never." I stood, backing away. "I could never have an abortion. Don't ask me to do that."

"I'm not asking," he yelled. He stood and moved toward the doorway. Just before he left the room, he turned back. "I'm telling you. You will have an abortion."

I clenched my fist and gave in to weeping. "I would never kill a baby," I screamed through my sobs. "I will leave you," I cried, "but I will never, ever have an abortion."

Russell stepped toward me, and I expected him to reach out to comfort me. Instead, I looked up just in time to see his open hand come at me from high over his head. Slapping me square on the cheek, the force of his blow knocked me onto the floor. Without another word, he left the room. I heard the front door slam and his feet pound down the inside stairway.

Still crying, I stood and walked to the corner of the room. Leaning my forearms on the wall, I dropped my head onto my hands, sobbing with shame and disbelief. What had just happened? Though my cheek stung and my head ached from the force of the blow, some part of me argued that I'd imagined the entire episode. Russell did not really hit me. But the image of his hand coming toward my face played over and over again, and each time my mind saw it, my body flinched and ducked—in spite of Russell's absence.

I paced some, hugging myself with my arms, struggling with the memory of the evening. Eventually exhausted, I turned off the lights in our apartment and went to sit on the floor of the living room. From there I gazed out the front window over the street below. Glowing in the phosphorescence of a streetlight, I focused on the empty spot where Russell parked his car. The more I thought about the incident, the more I realized how much was my fault. Russell worked more than ninety hours every week. Life and death decisions comprised his daily responsibilities. Today he'd come home exhausted, at the end of a long and challenging week, to share good news with me.

I'd spoiled more than his celebratory dinner. My news threatened to spoil his success. I wished I'd waited for a better time to tell him about the baby. He would have taken the surprise better. I waited there by the window, hoping for Russell's return. He did not come home.

Eventually the evening chill, or something much deeper, left me shivering there in the dark. I could do no more. I got up and went to bed. Alone.

That was the first time Russell ever hit me.

Nine

THE NEXT MORNING I WOKE to Russell's gentle touch. "Morning, Pet."

Rolling over, I rubbed my eyes. He sat on the edge of the bed, wearing Calvin Klein jeans and a UCLA sweat shirt. "How you feeling this morning?"

"A little queasy." I scooted up the bed, hugging the blankets close.

"Well, my patients tell me they feel better if they get a little something in their stomachs before they try to get up." He leaned over and lifted a tray from the floor. Next to a rose in a tiny bud vase, buttered toast rested on a salad plate. "Why don't you try this? Maybe it will settle your stomach a bit."

"Thanks, Russ." He adjusted the pillows behind me, plumping one lengthwise over another, so I could sit more comfortably. "I must look a mess," I said, trying to smooth my wild hair.

"You look beautiful."

A long awkward silence followed while I nibbled at the first piece of toast. Russell watched me intently. Normally, I never eat in bed. I don't like to sleep with crumbs. But this morning, of all mornings, I wanted to cooperate. More than anything, I wanted to make last night go away, to exorcise the memory. Clearly, Russ felt as badly as I did about it all. In his own way, he was trying to make it up to me.

"I'll start your bath water," he said.

"You don't have to."

"I know, but you deserve a little extra pampering this morning."

"That's very kind of you, Russ."

Before he left the room, he kissed me tenderly, in precisely the same place his hand struck the night before. I wondered. Did he place the kiss deliberately—as though the touch of his lips could wipe away the blow?

The bathroom mirror betrayed no trace of last night's conflict. Only severely swollen eyelids exposed the flood of my tears. In warm scented water I wrestled with the truth. Something had changed.

No. Russell never meant for things to go that far. Anyone trying to cope with the responsibility and pressure of new residents might make the same mistake. The man who struck me was not Russell. This man—this kind, thoughtful husband—this was the Russell I married.

Long before I resolved the conflict, my bath water cooled. Russell's intense, loving attention continued for the entire weekend and most of the next week. On Wednesday evening, he brought flowers. On Thursday, he surprised me with gourmet coffee ground in a specialty shop near the hospital.

"Russell, you don't have to bring me gifts. Remember us? We're broke," I teased.

He looked hurt. "Pet, there is no gift big enough to tell you how much you mean to me."

"Really? How nice of you to say." I wrapped my arms around his shoulders. We kissed.

"In fact, I've been thinking." He drew his face away.

"Oh?"

"Yes. I do think, you know." He smiled, aqua eyes sparkling with mischief. "What do you think about a date night?"

"A date night?"

"Yes, an unbreakable, absolute commitment to be together at least once every week. Of course, we'll have to schedule it around my call nights." He brushed hair from my forehead. "But we could do it. After all, with a baby coming so soon, we need to spend as much time together as we can—before diapers and nursing and croup take over our lives."

"But, Russ, we can't afford to go out every week."

"We don't have to go out, really." He wrapped his arms around my waist pulling me closer. "There are lots of ways to spend time together without spending money." An impish smile betrayed his thoughts. "We just need to focus on each other more often."

"I think one night together every week would be wonderful," I answered sincerely. We kissed again. "How 'bout we start tonight?"

We never did eat dinner.

———

Most of the winter passed pleasantly. In February, I resigned from the community orchestra. Though I could still hold my cello comfortably, my tummy bulged beyond the limit of my performance "blacks." I knew Russ would not approve of spending money for formal maternity clothes. I decided that I would play only for myself.

For the first time in my life, I allowed myself time to practice and to play for the sheer pleasure of music. With no deadlines or concert dates, I focused on the challenge of learning and conquering new pieces. I tried new styles, new composers. I even began some simple compositions of my own. Nothing publishable, but the joy of the new life growing inside me spilled over onto the strings of my cello.

I played for the children at school. I played for the nuns at lunchtime. I even performed for the opening of a newly remodeled hardware store in Freemont, owned by a Saint Sebastian's parishioner.

Russell spent the spring preparing to take his last licensing exam. He became nervous and short-tempered. On top of nearly ninety hours every week caring for patients and supervising staff, he spent every spare minute studying and reviewing for his test. At the same time, because of his seniority, he regularly prepared case presentations for the residents on his specialty team.

I sensed his increasing tension in our relationship as well. One Saturday afternoon in late March, I went to the grocery store by myself. Russ, on call at the hospital, didn't expect to come home until Sunday afternoon. Left with the weekend to myself, I took my time with shopping. Afterwards, I went next door for a latte and to read the Saturday paper. Later, I wandered happily from shop to shop in the surrounding antique stores, scouting for baby things and admiring lovely old pieces I could never afford to purchase. I rarely allowed myself this pleasure, and I relished the quiet time alone.

In one little shop I stumbled across an old-fashioned baby buggy. It had a large comfortable mattress in a bed suspended nearly waist high. The entire frame rolled on four ten-inch wire wheels. Though I admit I'm no mechanic, the whole thing seemed in reasonably good condition. I decided to check it out.

"May I look at the carriage?" I asked.

The salesman, an older man with half glasses perched at the end of a huge fleshy nose, barely looked up from his newspaper. "Sure." He did not move from his barstool.

So much for service. By myself, I carefully backed the carriage out from behind an antique dresser and maneuvered it toward the shop windows, where late afternoon sunlight filtered through dusty windows. The bare mattress needed sheets, but I could make those. The canvas sides were remarkably clean. I tried to put up the frame for the sunshade, but it refused to unfold. As I struggled, the buggy slid away from me and the handle crashed into an antique hall tree. The proprietor looked up with pronounced irritation. Appraising the size of my belly and my interest in the buggy, he folded his newspaper and reluctantly rose from his stool.

"Here, lady. Let me help you with that," he said.

"I'm sorry. The frame seems stuck." I let go of the handle. "I can't seem to get the sunshade up."

He looked at me with reproach and moved the buggy carefully away from his expensive antique furniture. "Let's see what I can do." He crouched at the frame, nodding to himself and mumbling.

"I see," he said. "Just needs a bolt here in this little hole. Then the whole thing will pivot up—like this. See?"

I didn't see and must have looked completely blank. Sighing, he stood up. "I have some tools. I'll see what I can do." The role of "damsel in distress" definitely had advantages.

He disappeared through a narrow doorway behind a striped gauze curtain. I heard the rattle of tools. When he came back, he carried pliers and wore a leather carpenter's belt. Various screws, or perhaps they were bolts, protruded from his fat lips. He spit them into his hand and squatted again by the buggy. "One of these should do."

I watched for a few moments, then turned to look through the shop. I found myself rubbing my nose with my index finger. The dust and smell of moldy books made my nose itch. Disorganization characterized this store, and I wondered how the old man ever remembered what he had to sell.

In a corner near the back of the store, I discovered an old wooden violin case. I carefully lifted the lid and pulled the antique instrument from its case, holding it toward the light, checking the varnish for signs of repair. The E string was missing, and the bridge needed to be replaced. The baby inside me kicked, and I smiled. Someday, I would teach my own child to play. Together, we would play the most wonderful pieces of music. *Someday*, I thought, and sneezed abruptly. No Kleenex.

"Gesundheit," the shop owner answered from beside the buggy. "There. It goes up good as new." He stood, pulling the stiff gray canvas over the sun frame.

In spite of mildly stained fabric, I tried to imagine the buggy smelling clean and fresh, holding a beautiful newborn. The old man gently turned the handle toward me and rolled it across the floor. The wheels squeaked noisily.

"That won't do," he said, smiling. He disappeared again through the curtain and returned with a can of lubricant. "Nothin' like a little WD–40." He sprayed oil onto the wheels and tightened screws. He rolled it again. "There, quiet as a mouse. Can't have squeaky wheels wakin' the baby, can we?"

"How much?" His repair work might have raised the price.

"Thirty dollars even."

A good buy, I thought. A buggy could serve as both bed and stroller. More importantly, Russ and I could put off buying a crib, at least until we had a real income. "I'll take it," I agreed. "Can I write a check?"

"Sorry, lady. I don't take no checks." He seemed disappointed to have to say it. "Been shorted too many times in this neighborhood. Didn't used to be that way, though." He reached into his back pocket and pulled out a stained cotton handkerchief. With the sound of migrating geese, he blew his nose. "When I first started here, I could leave the door unlocked and go have coffee." He shook his head sadly, stuffing the cloth back into his pocket. "No more, though." He snorted. "Nope, I take cash. Just plain old cash."

I looked at my watch. His shop would close soon. "I don't have any cash with me. Would you hold the buggy until Monday afternoon? I'll go to the bank right after school and come buy it."

"You a teacher?"

I nodded. He seemed to consider my proposition. I worried. A long pause followed.

"Sorry, lady. A fine buggy like this . . . well, I just can't hold it." He shrugged and went back behind the counter. Sliding his glasses on, he picked up his newspaper.

"Okay. Okay." I followed him to the counter. "If I go down to the cash machine, could you hold it until I get back?"

He glanced at an old mantel clock sitting beside his cash register. Rubbing his day-old beard, he shrugged again. "Well, I guess so, lady. My wife is wantin' me home on time, though. You hurry and get your cash. I'll wait for you."

By the time I closed the shop door, the old man was deep into the sports section.

An hour later I managed to get the buggy out of Russell's car and onto the sidewalk outside our apartment. After another fifteen minutes, I had unfolded it. With some anxiety, I wondered how I could possibly get it all the way upstairs to our apartment by myself.

I glanced up, thinking again how very far up our front door seemed. I noticed lights glimmering through our front windows. Had I left lights on?

I managed to get the buggy through the front door with little trouble. Fortunately it was not horribly heavy. However, I was getting to be—heavy, I mean—and hauling myself up the stairs had grown more difficult every day. *Slowly,* I told myself, panting. *Take your time.*

The problem with antiques is that they are old. And, in the old days lightweight alloys and plastics hadn't been invented yet. So somewhere between the front door and the first landing, my buggy transformed itself into a Model T Ford. It made a horrible racket, bumping wheels against every stair, squeaking in rebellion against the motion. My back ached, and I gasped for air. I developed a simple system. Stepping backwards, it went like this: Step, step. Drag, pull. When the rear wheels rested upon the next step, I paused and panted. And panted. And panted. Slowly, we made it to the middle of the stairs.

I needed a break. Shoving my hip into the handle, I pressed the buggy against the wall while I tried to catch my breath. My back cramped, and I straightened up to ease the pain. Just as I did, the wheels gave way, and the entire buggy began a remarkably rapid descent to the front door. "No! You stupid thing," I shouted. With a crash, my new antique slammed into the screen door at the bottom of the stairs. I sat down in frustration, looking up just in time to see the right front wheel fall off the axle. The buggy tipped sideways precariously.

"What's going on out here?" Russ burst through the door at the top of the stairs.

"Oh, nothing." Suddenly the whole episode took on a humorous slant, like the kind of story that ends up in a baby book years later. I started to giggle.

He came out onto the landing. "Where have you been all afternoon?"

"Me?" I stood up, rubbing sore palms on my hips. "Oh, I got

groceries, and then I did a little shopping." I pointed down at the buggy.

"What on earth is that?" He started down the stairs, his face showing disgust.

"It's a baby buggy, Russ. Isn't it sweet?" Why do I say things like that? Sometimes I sound like a child. He passed my stair without so much as a greeting.

"Where on earth did you get this piece of junk?" He held the broken wheel as if it were diseased. "It's filthy."

"At an antique store in Wallingford." I waddled back downstairs to join him. "The old guy made sure the frame works, and he oiled the springs." I had no plans to tell Russ about the cash.

"Patty, why would you decide to buy something like this without checking with me first?"

"I'm sorry, Russ. The guy said he wouldn't hold it. I figure it's in great shape—for only thirty dollars—and we won't have to buy a bed or a stroller until you are working." I demonstrated the sunshade. "Don't you think it's a great idea?"

Anyone could clearly see Russell did not think the buggy was a great idea. "Go upstairs, Patricia." His face froze.

I'd been sent to my room. "I'll help you carry it upstairs."

"No!" His curt, cold tone made it clear that I had crossed the line. Meekly, I led the way upstairs. He followed, carrying the buggy behind me. The hall door had no more than closed before he started yelling.

"Patricia, where have you been all afternoon?"

"Russell, I told you. I bought groceries, and then I went shopping."

"I heard what you said. But if you went shopping, where are the groceries?"

"In the car. I didn't know you were home. The old guy put the buggy on top of the bags, and I decided to carry it up first." I took off my jacket and dropped it over a kitchen chair. With exaggerated frustration, Russell picked it up and hung it up in our closet. Trying to remain calm, I poured myself a glass of water.

He went down to the car. When he returned, he carried four

plastic bags. I followed him to the kitchen and started putting things away.

"Patty, I'd appreciate it if you would tell me the truth."

"The truth? What are you talking about?" I spun around. "I did tell the truth."

He held the grocery store receipt in his hand. "This receipt says you bought groceries at 1:47 P.M."

"So?"

"So it's after six o'clock." He looked at his watch and then glared at me. "That was more than four hours ago. Where have you been since then?"

"I told you. I went shopping."

"For four hours?"

"No. Not all of it." I fought rising anger. He doubted my word. Still, I could not guess what he believed I had been doing all afternoon. I turned away and opened the cupboard.

"What do you mean, not all of it? I want the truth, Patty." He reached over my shoulder and slammed the cupboard door.

"Come on, Russell. I don't have to explain every minute of my day, do I?"

"Why not? Do you have something to hide?"

"Oh, please." In spite of myself, I rolled my eyes at him. "This is completely ridiculous. I don't ask you for a record of your day."

"I'm not asking for a record. I just want the truth." His anger electrified the air.

"Okay, here it is." I slammed a box of cereal onto the counter. "I bought groceries. Then I had a latte and read the newspaper. Then I went shopping. Then I found the buggy, which the old guy fixed. Then I went to the cash machine—there is probably a record of that somewhere. You can check it if you don't believe me." I rubbed my forehead. Wanting to calm things down, I deliberately lowered my voice. "I bought the buggy, and I came home. There." I reached up to put the cereal away, quietly closing a cupboard door. "Does that satisfy you? Or do you want to know that I also went to the bathroom once at the grocery store and twice at the latte shop?"

"Don't you talk to me that way." He took a menacing step forward.

"Me?" I straightened myself to my full five feet, refusing to back down. "You are the one being silly here. I should think you'd want to apologize to me." I turned to leave the kitchen, but with one side step he blocked my path to the door. "Russell, please. Go cool off."

His eyes widened and his eyebrows rose. At the same moment, closing his fist, he swung for my head. I raised my hand to protect myself and ducked at the same time. He missed. Exponentially, his anger grew, and he growled as he stepped toward me.

"You disrespectful witch." His closed fist met my cheekbone, and I went down. I rolled away just as his foot came toward me. With a primitive scream, he kicked me in the side. "How dare you!" His tirade continued. "You go out and spend my hard-earned money without so much as even asking. You are gone for hours without letting me know where you are, and now you tell me to 'cool off'?" He stood back, panting.

Russell had become a madman. Where had all this rage and anger come from? What had I done? Though I clearly heard and understood them, I could not believe his words. Then, as suddenly as he began, he finished. He left the room, and I heard him go down the stairs. The car started, and he was gone.

———

I spent Sunday indoors. His fist left a raised blue lump on my cheekbone, and the eye above it swelled maliciously. But Russell's words had done a great deal more damage. Remarkably, those were the wounds I could not see in the bathroom mirror. The pain his words inflicted left me aching all day.

Late Sunday afternoon, I called Sister Mary Regina to explain that I would not be teaching on Monday.

"Are you terribly ill?" she asked gently.

"Not really," I reassured her. "Just not feeling well."

"Is Russell working? Do you need me to come check on you?"

"Oh no, Sister. Really, Russell is pampering me to death." I lied. "That won't be necessary."

She agreed to find a substitute for my classroom. "And I'll light a candle for your health at morning mass."

It would take more than a candle to make me well.

Monday morning I wandered restlessly through our apartment. Russell did not return, and I wondered why. Was it the fight? Or his schedule? His absence frightened me and calmed me at the same time. Would he ever come home again? Did I want him to come home? I tried to keep ice on my bruised face.

My restlessness increased. I needed to do something, to talk to someone. But who? How do you tell someone that your husband has hit you? Besides, no one could possibly understand. This angry man did not resemble the true Russell Koehler I'd fallen in love with. I had done something to him. He never lost his temper with anyone else. Why me? What had I done wrong?

I found the city phone book and turned to the yellow pages. I looked up counselors. There were pages of listings. Family Therapists. Rape Counselors. Crisis Centers. Psychologists. I couldn't face a stranger with my problems. I closed the book and paced the apartment. I settled into my favorite chair and picked up the Sunday paper. An ad, tucked in the women's section, caught my eye. *Domestic Violence Hotline.* Something inside responded, and I dialed the number.

"Hello. Domestic Violence Crisis line, Debbie speaking." A long pause. "Hello, is anyone there?" Another pause. "This is the Domestic Violence Crisis line. May I help you?" Another pause. I gathered my courage.

"Yes. I . . . I just need to talk to someone," I whispered.

"That's why I'm here. What would you like to talk about?"

"Um, I . . . well, I don't know. I shouldn't have called." I wanted to hang up.

"Wait." Her voice sounded urgent and soft at the same time. "Are you safe now? Is someone assaulting you right now?"

"No. It isn't like that." Trembling, I took a deep breath. "I mean, well, yes, I'm safe."

"Okay. Then let's just talk. I don't have anything else I need to do right now. Okay?" She gave the slightest hint of a laugh, and I found myself imagining her smile. "Tell me what's going on in your life."

"Uh, my husband, he . . . well," I heard myself whisper the words, "sometimes, when he is really angry, he . . ."

"He hits you?" She was not impatient, nor was she surprised. It seemed as though she said it all the time.

"Only twice. Only when he's . . ." I began to cry softly, feeling deeply ashamed.

"Believe me, honey," she said, "I've heard it all. Go ahead and talk about it. When did he hit you last?"

"Last night."

"Do you need to see a doctor?" she asked gently.

"No, I'm fine, really."

"If you were really fine, you wouldn't be calling," she prodded. "You can keep him away. You can get a protective order. Do you want to talk about that?"

"Oh no. No. I wouldn't do that." I dabbed at my face with a tissue, touching the bruise. "I couldn't do that."

More gently. "What is your first name?"

"Patricia. Patty, really."

"Well, Patty, what is it you want?" She waited quietly until the silence threatened to swallow us both.

"I want him to stop hitting me."

"No one can make him stop," she said. "He has to do that himself." She let that sink in. "The only thing you can do is protect yourself and give him a reason to stop."

"What do you mean?" Such confusing words.

"Look, I talk to women like you every day. Believe me, these guys are more alike than different. It won't stop, Patty. The truth is, it's likely to get worse."

"No, you don't understand. Russ isn't like that. It's just that he's under so much pressure right now. I don't want him to leave. I love him. Really, I love him."

"Of course you do. I understand." How could this woman possibly understand?

"And he loves me. I just don't know why I make him so angry."

"It isn't you, Patty. You don't make him do these things."

"But he doesn't get mad at anyone else," I argued. "It must be me. There must be something I do that makes him so crazy."

"No, Patty. You're wrong. You aren't the reason he loses his temper. He won't change if you assume responsibility for his behavior. You have to . . ."

Abruptly, I hung up the phone. This woman didn't understand at all. How could she? Russell was my husband, and I didn't understand him myself.

Ten

LEAH ALICE KOEHLER, whose middle name represented Russell's last attempt at reconciliation with his mother, joined us early on the morning of June 8. The delivery room nurses declared her a perfect replica of her mother. Dark curly hair covered her tiny head, exactly like the images in my own baby pictures. Russell loved her completely from her first moments in the delivery room.

Watching him cuddle Leah's bare body in his arms, cooing and smiling at her, I knew the woman at the crisis clinic was wrong. Things would not get worse. Russell made mistakes, but he was not a monster. This man—this educated, loving husband and father—had a beautiful new reason to leave violence behind.

I called Annie, my teaching friend, just moments after Leah was born. "I can't let you be alone," she declared emphatically over the phone. "You need me to be your mom for a while, until you're on your feet." Though Annie and Sheldon now taught in a school three hundred miles away, she came to spend a week with me. Annie always liked playing mother.

During that week she taught me everything she knew about caring for a newborn, proclaiming herself an expert, as her firstborn had just celebrated his first birthday. Annie's supportive friendship turned out to be the most precious baby gift we received.

Leah, a lovely, healthy baby, whose blue eyes turned deep brown by Independence Day, had nearly doubled her birth weight by the end of July. At her eight-week checkup, our pediatrician declared that my breast milk must be made of pure cream. Leah smiled easily and began to laugh out loud. I slid into motherhood as easily as water down a drain. Leah became the center of my life.

Every afternoon she and I buggied around the neighborhood. On calm, warm evenings we repeated our trek in reverse. Leah loved her world in a predictable schedule. I could order my day by the regularity of her calls for attention, eating every four hours, a morning nap of one and a half hours, followed by a two-hour playtime. Who needs a Day-Timer? I had Leah.

While I basked in motherhood, Russell finished his fellowship. After much preparation, he took his family practice specialty boards. While I nursed our new daughter, changed diapers, and washed clothes, Russell worried about his test results.

We planned to move to Cummins Island in late August. As the date approached, Russell spent most of his time up at the island. We took out a small business loan, which Russ used to get his office space in Serenity Bay ready for business. Just off Front Street in the back corner of a little strip mall, Russ rented a thousand square feet. We hoped both local residents and summer visitors would be able to find the clinic easily. Russell cleaned and painted and, with the help of a retired boatbuilder, installed prefab cabinets in all three exam rooms. Somehow he found time to research computer systems and medical billing software and to purchase equipment for the office. The preparations left him haggard, and when he returned to Seattle, he fell into bed exhausted.

For the first half of August, Leah and I traveled back and forth from Seattle to Nana's island house, cleaning and painting, getting the house ready. Actually, I painted and Leah, perched in the antique buggy, gurgled and cooed while she supervised my work. I played the radio for company, introducing Leah to my favorite classics. More than once, Leah napped in the buggy with her skin dotted with paint from the walls. I never quite figured out how to nurse without getting paint from my clothes smudged all over my hungry infant.

Nana's house, old and charming, echoed with the sounds of our

preparations. We sold most of Nana's furniture to an estate liqui-
dator, who gave us a sizable lump sum. This cash delighted Russell.
He'd never really liked the dark old stuff anyway, and he immediately used most of the check as payment toward his school loan.
Though we were cash poor, we had reduced our debt, which felt
very gratifying. It would be a long time before we could afford to
purchase our own furnishings. Though the old house stood largely
unadorned, at least it was bathed in light colors and fresh paint.

Early on the morning of August 20, I pulled Russell's car door
closed and started the engine, beginning our final move to the island. Sister Claire, who had insisted on helping, waved at me from
the curb.

"Be careful," she said through my open window. Then clasping
her fingers over her lips, she began to cry. "I'll miss you, dear," she
whispered.

I waved back, laughing at her through my own tears, and rolled
up the window. Dear, tenderhearted Claire.

Russell, parked just in front of me, drove a midsize Budget
rental truck. I planned to follow him north to Twalleson, where we
would all board an early morning ferry to Cummins Island. He put
his blinker on and pulled away from the sidewalk.

Leah's baby seat sat firmly strapped in the backseat. Lampshades
rested on the floor in front of her, and sleeves of shirts, wrapped
snugly in extra sheets, stuck out from their bundles around her. I
smiled as bravely as I could and drove out into the street. "So here
we go, honey. A brand-new life."

She responded by screwing up her tiny face and beginning to
cry. Unfortunately, I joined her. Six months ago, leaving the city for
the relative quiet of island life seemed like a great idea. No more
traffic. No violence. Nothing but a safe, tranquil island life. Now I
felt far less certain. What on earth made me think this would be a
great idea?

From 45th Street, I glanced down the hill to Saint Sebastian's.
My mind wandered. If I weren't leaving, I'd be there today, getting
my classroom ready for the new school year. Sister Mary Regina had
offered to let me share a full-time teaching position. "Can't afford

to lose my best teacher," she had declared.

Through tears, I saw the bell tower above the sanctuary and the chain link fence surrounding the schoolyard. Had we made a terrible mistake?

The trip proved to be a terrible intrusion in Leah's schedule, and she screamed her objection all the way to the ferry terminal. By the time we parked in the loading lot, I felt like a nervous wreck. Moving my seat back, I nursed her from behind the steering wheel, speaking gently and rubbing her tiny head. I tried as much to calm her as to quiet my own fear. Russ brought me a cup of coffee from the restaurant.

"Here," he said, passing it through the car window. "It's going to be a long day." He started to walk away but turned back, "Wait. I forgot." He took a few steps back to the car window. "I bought you some bottled water." He pulled a container from his coat pocket. "Thought you needed some extra fluids." He winked. "Nursing mother, you know."

"Thanks." I said, taking the bottle. "You're right. I didn't drink anything before we left." Thirst, my constant companion since Leah's birth, left my mouth perpetually dry. How like Russell to think of me.

Leah slept through the entire ferry ride, and exhaustion kept me dozing in the driver's seat. I wanted to remember the move, to keep it forever treasured in the scrapbook in my memory. Instead, I dragged my way through it like a patient waking from general anesthesia.

After we docked, I followed Russell from the ferry terminal to the house. We had not arranged for anyone to help us there, so we spent the afternoon carrying boxes inside. By late afternoon, we'd grown too tired to continue. We managed to drag our bed upstairs, one piece at a time. While Russ put the pieces together, I dragged the little buggy upstairs, banging it against my newly painted wall with surprising regularity. Crawling over the stuff remaining in the rental truck, I found clean sheets, stashed in a box near the front. Upstairs, I made our beds. We ate a dinner of peanut butter and jelly sandwiches and fell into bed before dark. Even Leah was worn out, and sleep came immediately for all of us.

We could not call ourselves unpacked for nearly a week, due in part to the amount of time Russell spent every day at the office. He continued, in spite of exhaustion, to work long hours before and after seeing patients. He installed equipment, organized a record-keeping system, and ordered supplies. He hired an island woman, an R.N., whose children now attended high school in Twalleson. She became his "Girl Friday," answering phones, billing patients—of whom he saw only ten in the first week of September—and helping with clinical procedures. At night Russell filled out his own insurance forms, and every morning he dropped off a claim envelope at the village post office. Russ tried to help at home, but fatigue often rendered him unconscious in a living room chair long before bedtime. Unsuccessfully, I tried to convince him to stop pushing himself so hard. But he would not hear of it. Life had become a matter of priorities—business first—or we would soon stop eating.

With sadness I watched the first day of school come and go without being a part of it. I missed my students. I tried to rationalize that parenting was as important as teaching, that now more than ever, Leah needed me. But I missed the smiling, eager faces and laughing voices of kindergartners.

Summer warmth gave way to fall rain, and little by little the island began to feel like home. I bought groceries at the Stock 'n Save and tools at the hardware store. I noticed other parents waiting with their students for the island school bus, and I longed for the kind of companionship they obviously shared with one another. I wished for a sense of belonging, though I knew it would take time. Russell's constant absence made my loneliness worse.

At first I felt frustrated spending my days with no car on the west side of the island. In the city, I used to take the bus downtown or push Leah's buggy around our little route. But I soon discovered the danger of buggy rides on narrow, winding two-lane highways, though I only tried it once. Once was more than enough. First I dragged Leah in the antique contraption all the way from the house down the gravel lane to the highway. Then, because the highway had no shoulder, I spent the entire walk dodging speeding cars. I did not find this exercise rewarding and vowed never to try it again.

In my loneliness I turned again to long walks on the beach. There, in the cold breeze, the smell of saltwater, and the calling of seagulls, I again found comfort.

With Leah nestled in a denim front pack, we walked the beach below the property together. It fascinated me, this island beach, so very different from the ocean in Johnson River. Here lay billions of smooth round rocks and lapping waves, so unlike the sandy beach and four-foot breakers of Grayson County. Tidal pools filled with starfish, sea cucumbers, tiny crabs, and miniature fish riveted my imagination. Before long, I brought home books on tidal life and learned much about the tiny creatures who lived sequestered lives in the bottom of sea puddles.

As fall deepened, Russell continued to struggle with his business, or lack of it. We discovered how difficult it is to start a medical practice in such a tiny community. The residents of Serenity Bay did not freely share their trust. Holding fast to their own traditions, people seemed reluctant to try the new "young fella" on Front Street. Though the last doctor on Cummins Island retired nearly four years before our arrival, villagers felt no need to place their confidence in Russell.

We opened the business at a difficult time of year. Every fall the summer people made an abrupt and complete exodus from the San Juan Islands to the city. Unfortunately, the summer people were the only ones who might have trusted Russell. But they disappeared long before we started scheduling patients, leaving Serenity Bay looking much like a ghost town.

By Thanksgiving Russell had grown so concerned about finances that he decided to take a weekend job in the emergency room at the Twalleson Community Hospital. The moonlighting position paid three hundred dollars a day, enough in one month to cover the rent on his office space and some of our business loans as well.

"Don't worry, the business will take off soon," he tried to comfort me. "But until then, we have to do something."

Every Friday afternoon Russell took the two o'clock ferry into

Twalleson. There he worked a forty-eight hour shift. Then, in the wee hours of Monday morning, he returned to the island. He made up an extra bed on the cot in the spare room, and when I questioned him about it, he said, "I don't want to wake you or the baby at three in the morning." With a small squeeze around my shoulders, he added, "It won't last forever, Pet."

But it did. Or at least it seemed to. Winter turned cold and bleak. I had not yet met anyone—other than the locals who owned or operated the town's businesses—and I began to wonder if the world of diapers had become my lifelong prison. I played my cello for long hours while Leah napped, missing the companionship and challenge of fellow musicians. With Russell absent so much of the time, I had little real housekeeping to do. I struggled to stay occupied and found some solace in the books I checked out from the bookmobile, whose visit to the Stock 'n Save became the highlight of my week. I wished I had taken longer painting the old house. At least I would still have something to do.

One day, as I struggled to hold a wiggling baby on her changing table, I had a marvelous idea. Though I'd painted Leah's room that summer, I had never really decorated it. It needed something more. Perhaps I could stencil the walls of her bedroom?

I knew of only one complication. I had no idea how to do it. I considered that to be both good and bad. At least the undertaking could be prolonged while I learned. With any luck, I could drag the project out for a long time, perhaps until summer sunshine again filled our breakfast nook.

With this plan in mind, I put Leah in her car seat and drove Russell to work. Then I stopped at the hardware store in town, where I had seen displays of stencils, brushes, and sponges. Perhaps I could buy a book and figure it out as I went along. We parked in the lot beside the store.

Inside, I discovered my error. The hardware store did not carry instruction books, and the salesman, a fortyish man with a bald spot that began just above his ears confessed, "To tell the truth, miss, I don't have the foggiest idea how it's done."

He folded his arms across his chest, and the pause that followed grew heavy. Leah chose precisely that moment to fill her diaper. Frowning, he shrugged and walked away. From behind, I noticed the hair below his bald spot had been gathered into a long ponytail.

I felt dampness oozing out the side of Leah's sleeper, her legs already slick with the stuff, and I bent to lower her onto the floor. Like all moms, I carried wipes in my purse. Truthfully, I planned only to clean my own hands. Leah was more in need of a garden hose than a damp towel. However, just as I leaned forward, another woman tried to slide behind us. My rear end smacked squarely into hers, knocking her into the paint rollers. I heard her make a peculiar whimper as she tried to avoid collapsing onto the display. Mortified, I tried to apologize.

"Oh no. Don't worry," she responded with a chuckle. "Either I'm too wide or these aisles are too narrow." She stuck out her right hand, "Hi, I'm Susan. Susan Addison. You're new here."

Without thinking, I reached toward her with my soggy hand. Too late. We shook diaper hands. She felt the wetness and glanced down at her own hand, grimacing.

"Oh, I'm so sorry." I wanted the floor to swallow me. "The baby just—and I was going to—oh . . ." My cheeks burned. "Here, I have some wipes." I handed her the package I'd dug out of my bag.

"Hey, it's motherhood, you know?" She shrugged and smiled again, accepting my offer of relief. We opened the foil envelopes together. "Actually, I think I'm still wearing Brittany's breakfast. I kind of need a bath—you know?" She dabbed at the front of her sweat shirt.

"I can't tell you how embarrassed I am."

"Well, get over it." She handed me her dirty wipe, which I accepted obediently. "You still haven't told me your name." She smiled again. A crash sounded nearby. "Oh no." She scanned the floor. "Brit?"

She turned abruptly, in spite of her size, and followed the sound. "Brittany Anne Addison, where are you?" Unfolding a baby blanket, I scooped Leah off the floor, taking care to protect my clothing, and followed Susan. Another crash, smaller this time. The bald man came around the other end of the aisle just as we discovered Susan's missing toddler.

"What is going on?" Clearly the bald guy preferred children to stay out of his store.

A freckled, redheaded baby girl sat grinning happily on the floor. With both hands, she threw tiny objects into the air, littering the floor around her plump legs with screws and bolts and fasteners. Her happy kicking sent bursts of hardware rolling under nearby display shelves.

"Brittany Anne Addison." Susan picked her up. "What do you think you're doing? You know you are to stay with Mommy," she scolded the unaffected baby. "Don't you wander off without me." Susan punctuated her correction with pointed emphasis on every other word. Brittany lifted a screw-filled fist to her mouth. "No!" Susan went fishing in the depths of the baby's mouth with her index finger. "We don't eat hardware." Susan sighed. "Motherhood. Nothing like it. You know what I'm sayin'?"

With an indignant grunt, Ponytail Man began picking up plastic drawers. In spite of myself, I giggled. Brittany had single-handedly opened, emptied, and blended the contents of seven carefully labeled drawers.

Susan recovered quickly. "Sorry about this, Jim. I promise not to bring her back till she turns sixteen."

Jim, perturbed but determined to be polite, held his lips firmly together and gave no response.

Throwing Brittany over one hip, Susan turned to me. "How 'bout we go find some coffee?" she whispered, nodding her head in Ponytail Man's direction. Her face said urgently, "Let's get out of here!"

"Great. I'd love to."

"First, though"—she pointed to the diaper bag dangling from my shoulder—"let's take care of that hazardous chemical spill you're carrying around."

We spent the rest of the morning in the old café on Front Street, drinking coffee and visiting. Outside the café windows, gray clouds drizzled a cold, reluctant rain. Inside, I discovered sunshine.

Susan shared a cinnamon roll with Brittany while I nursed Leah.

I knew immediately what a rare and delightful friend Susan Addison might become. But to discover her here, in the middle of my winter loneliness, made her all the more precious. Just three years older than I, Susan already had a five-year-old. She told me her husband, David, worked on a tugboat crew, which frequently kept him away from home.

These trips required Susan to become a jack-of-all-trades—even those traditionally considered unfeminine. Just this morning, she reported triumphantly, she had changed the oil in her Volvo and replaced the filter.

Tall by my standards, nearly five feet eight inches, Susan sported a more moderate version of the same freckles I first noticed in her daughter. I liked the way her freckles seemed to smile with her. As we visited, I discovered that Susan loved baking and specialized, she told me, in anything whose primary ingredient was sugar. Over coffee, she kept a running commentary on the relative merits of the various desserts featured at the Island Café.

"So what were you doing at the hardware store?" she asked as we closed the café door behind us. "Neither of us ever bought anything." She laughed lightly. "Though I guess Brittany sort of closed that opportunity, didn't she?"

"Oh, I was looking for a 'how-to' book." I pulled the baby blanket over Leah's face, trying to shield her from the cold drizzle. "But they didn't have one."

"Okay," she said slowly. "I don't know how they do it in the city, but here on the island, we get hardware in the hardware store and books in a bookstore."

Susan reached down to lift Brittany, but the toddler objected loudly, insisting on walking down the old cement steps under her own power. Susan rolled her eyes and offered a hand instead, muttering, "She gets all of her stubbornness from her father."

"Touché—I mean about the books." I bent to take the toddler's other hand. "What I was looking for was a book about stenciling. You know, that stuff people do for borders on walls?"

Brittany stumbled unsteadily onto the sidewalk, and when I felt certain she was safe, I let go. "Anyway, by the time we bumped into each other, I figured out that they don't carry any—books, I mean." I turned up the collar of my coat, silently vowing never to leave the house without an umbrella.

"Of course not. For that kind of thing, you need a professional."

"I didn't think it was that hard to do," I said, disappointed. "Oh well, then I guess I'll have to forget the whole thing." We walked to the parking lot together. "I can't afford to hire someone. Russ would kill me."

"Oh, I didn't say you need to hire someone. I just said you need a professional." Susan's freckles moved into smile position, and the lines at the corners of her green eyes deepened.

"Okay. I'll bite. How do you get professional help without paying for it?"

"You ask me. I do stenciling all the time." She unlocked the rear door of her gray Volvo and tucked Brittany into the car seat. "After all, we mothers have to help one another out, you know?"

"You're kidding. You stencil?"

"Sure. Just give me a call." With a wave, Susan slid into the driver's seat and pulled away.

Susan Addison became my first friend on Cummins Island, but not my last. Growing up in Twalleson, Susan considered herself a local, and as such, she knew and was accepted by everyone. Soon, because of our friendship, I had been promoted to the rank of "insider" and was included in many island activities. We shopped together, went to the park together, and before long, Susan invited me to join a small group of women who met in town every day to walk.

"I can't," I objected. "I don't have a car."

"No problem. We all drive to the development to walk. It's the only place on the island with sidewalks. Otherwise we'd never be able to push a stroller around on this island."

How well I knew. "But that doesn't take care of my car," I persisted. Frequently in our conversations, I had to work to keep Susan with me.

"What I am saying is—" she paused, and with a tiny sigh expressed her exasperation—"that I will pick you up every morning." She emphasized the word *I*, clearly indicating her patience with my stupidity.

Our daily walk developed into a routine of its own. We dropped Taylor—Susan's daughter—off at preschool and proceeded to the loop where the women met. The five ladies who comprised our group each pushed a stroller, and I of course pushed the antique buggy. Then we marched five abreast for two breathless miles.

I admit that the whole plan didn't seem ecologically sound— driving into town so that I could go walking—but I found the women wonderful company, and walking every day helped to pass the long hours without Russell.

These women were all old friends of Susan's, having been part of the same church for years. They accepted me as though I'd spent my entire life on the island. They kept no secrets, pulled no punches, and shared every aspect of their daily lives with one another. Theirs was a kind of intimacy I had never experienced.

Emotions, raw as sewage, were part of our daily fare. Whatever joy or sorrow they experienced, they shared. Sometimes we laughed until we had to stop for air. Sometimes we cried. For the most part, I joined in. Except for my one dark secret, which I would not trust to anyone, these women knew and accepted me completely. I found our relationships both wonderful and slightly frightening at the same time. Trust is expensive, and I found myself as hesitant as the islanders to give it away.

Occasionally these women prayed over whatever traumas they happened to be grappling with. Though I appeared to participate by bowing my head and lowering my eyes, I never spoke in prayer, nor did I request their intercession on my behalf. I marveled at their apparent intimacy with God. Theirs was not the same religion I'd grown up with. I knew only a formal, standoffish God, one of memorized prayers who could not be bothered with the difficulties of potty training or putting reluctant children to bed. It frightened me that these women spoke to God with such familiarity. Would lightning strike as we prayed?

One day, after praying over a broken washing machine, Gail, the oldest of our group, turned to me and said, "So, Patty, where do you go to church?"

"I, uh . . . well, I'm Catholic," I said, feeling my face burn. Did she suspect something? Had my behavior during prayer betrayed my ignorance of spiritual things?

"I didn't know that," she replied.

"So you attend mass here on the island?" another woman asked.

"Uh, no, not exactly," I stammered.

Another joined in immediately. "You're sure welcome to visit our church. We have a great pastor and a wonderful children's program."

Just as I stumbled through a reluctant thank-you, Susan stepped in to rescue me.

"She just moved here, guys," Susan said, laughing. "Give her a chance to unpack her suitcase before you drag her to church." She threw one arm around my shoulder and winked conspiratorially. "Our pastor is teaching on evangelism this month. You'll have to excuse them if they act like sharks." She grinned at her friends and led me away to the car.

By spring I'd grown to love island life. With Susan's encouragement, I volunteered at the island school, where on Thursdays I worked in the library after our walk. While Leah took her morning nap, I assisted the librarian who was in the middle of changing over to a computerized system. I helped students find books and read to the classes who visited the library. While I kept things moving efficiently out front, the librarian, an elderly woman, occupied a back office where she fought with a new computer she nicknamed "Lucifer."

True to her word, Susan helped me stencil Leah's room, though it nearly took two weeks to finish three days of work. Susan managed to squeeze the sharing of her artistic talent between Bible study, choir practice, children's programs, cookie baking, shopping, and the various crises of her many friends. Because Susan's life seemed to revolve around the needs of her church and her friends, she had difficulty finding time to paint.

Of course we worked only during nap times, so on appointed days, Susan arrived at my house just after lunch, laden with brushes, paints, stencils, and a diaper bag. Our work routine always remained the same. After three trips from her car to the house, we spent an hour getting the girls to bed, after which we recuperated by drinking coffee and tasting Susan's latest cookie recipe. As the volunteer editor for her church cookbook, Susan took it upon herself to test every cookie recipe submitted. She designated March as bars and squares month. Susan loved to bake, and her figure was as generous as her disposition.

Through our efforts we managed to grow a trellis of roses, matching those flourishing in our front hedge, around the upper third of the walls in Leah's bedroom. I found the effect stunning. Susan did meticulous work, and while we scrubbed, taped, dappled, and visited, more than roses bloomed. Ours grew into a delightful and nurturing friendship.

We finished on a Thursday afternoon. Because of his weekend work, Russell did not view the results until the following Tuesday when he tucked Leah into bed.

Entering the kitchen, he demanded, "What have you done to her room?" I stood at the sink, drying the last of the dinner dishes. He opened the cupboard for a mug.

"We stenciled. Do you like it?"

"Who? Who did it?" He poured the last of the dinner coffee into his cup and leaned against the counter.

"I did." I felt my stomach turn over. "Well, really, my new friend and I did."

"What new friend?" The intensity in his voice frightened me.

"Susan. I've told you about her." I hung up the kitchen towel, trying hard to sound light and relaxed. "She lives on West Ridge Road."

"What did that mess upstairs cost me?" He gestured upstairs.

"Almost nothing," I minimized. "The stencils were Susan's. We bought the paint with her discount at the craft store in Twalleson." Why did his inquisitions always make me feel like a child?

"What do you mean, *her* discount?"

"She has a business license." I took a deep breath and swallowed my fear, trying desperately to slow things down. "She does decorating as a side business and gets a professional discount for supplies." I reached behind the sink to the windowsill and took down a jar of hand cream. With deliberate calmness, I put on the cream, rubbing my hands slowly, methodically. I gazed out the window at tiny specks of white water on the strait. Out on the sound, a storm brewed.

"Patricia. I should think I could trust you by now." Roughly, he took my shoulder, turning me toward him.

"Trust? What on earth do you mean—trust?" I bit my lip, dragging at calm. I must stay calm.

"I mean, here I am slaving away every day at work, working the emergency room, and you blow money on finger painting."

"Russell, please. I don't understand how spending ten dollars on paint is such a big deal."

"If you don't earn it, it isn't." His pupils shrunk to pin dots. His face grew hard, as if it had been sculpted from marble, his voice flat. Though I knew what was coming, I tried to deny it. We left Russell's anger on the mainland.

Hadn't we?

With his left hand he brought the mug into the air and swung at me. I ducked, and at the last moment, his hand passed above my face. The mug smashed against the cabinet over the sink. Still angrier, he threw the handle.

"I can't trust you. You have no sense," he seethed. "You spend my hard-earned money as if it came from the kitchen faucet."

"Russ, I'm sorry." Try as I might, I could not keep the fear down. It slipped into my voice. "It won't happen again." I tried to step away. His body pinned mine against the sink, the counter digging into the small of my back.

"You're right, it won't." His voice suddenly slowed, as though speaking to a very young child. "Because I'm going to make sure it won't. I'm going to close the checking account. From now on, all you get is what I give you."

"Russ, don't be silly. It was a mistake. That's all." I slid out from under his hips and turned to leave the kitchen. He stepped into my path.

"You'll leave when I tell you." He grabbed my shoulder, squeezing hard.

"Russ, please. Don't do this!" I pulled away. "Control yourself!"

My words broke the dam of his control, and his anger spilled over, pouring, flushing, destroying everything in its path. My own words marked the beginning of my first beating on the island.

How wrong I was—his anger had followed us. As deliberately as an enemy agent, it traced us, tracked us down. And now it was going to destroy us.

————

After that incident, Russell began to close the circle around me. Though I didn't understand it at the time, Russell wanted complete and absolute, unequivocal control. He started with money. He regulated my spending by controlling how much he gave me. Then he demanded receipts. Finally, he began patrolling my time. He monitored where I went and with whom. He knew how long every trip should take and began calling home at unexpected times during the day to assure himself that I had not left.

Then he began to narrow my connections with people. He insisted that I reduce the number of phone calls I made to Annie and the nuns at Saint Sebastian's. He discouraged the calls to my island friends. He even complained about the cost of calling Steve.

In one of his repentant stages, Russell bought me a used car. But swinging again toward control, he limited the amount of gas he put in the tank. Russell cloaked his control in expressions of concern for our family, for our welfare. Within two years of the first island beating, he succeeded in dominating every part of my life.

Russell no longer needed to hit me. His anger, his words, his silence—all frightened me as much as his fists. Whenever I could, I cooperated. More than anything, I wanted peace, whatever the cost. In the pursuit of peace, I built an elaborate dreamworld. I made excuses for Russell and then accepted his apologies, his explanations.

Our life became a bizarre fantasy. His reality. My fairy tale.

One hot afternoon just after Leah turned three, Russell came home late for dinner. "Tomorrow, Patricia, I think you ought to put an ad in the paper."

"What ad?" I sat in a club chair, glancing through a mail-order catalog.

"Looking for day care." He turned away, putting his coat in the hall closet.

"Day care? I don't know what you're talking about." I closed the magazine cover.

"You don't think you can bring the baby to the office every day, do you?"

"Of course not. What is going on here? Why would I be coming to the office?"

"Patty, it's very simple. Hiring help is the most expensive part of my overhead. Now that my practice has grown, I have to use my nurse for nursing, not billing. I have to have you come work for me. It's the only way."

"Russ, we didn't talk about that. I never agreed to work for you at the office."

"I don't expect you to agree." He turned and walked from the room. "I expect you to be there. Monday."

How dare Russell decide I work in his office! How dare he decide that someone else should care for our baby! Incensed, I followed him to the stereo, where he turned on the receiver.

"What do you mean? I'm not coming to work for you." Leah, playing house in the same room, pushed a tiny baby stroller across the wood floor. "I couldn't think of giving Leah to a sitter. No, Russell. That's it. No."

Leah stopped playing and looked up, an expression of surprise on her innocent face.

"I am not giving you an option," he said. Hate was back again. "You will be at the office on Monday. I don't care what you have to do with her."

"I will not." I screamed the words, my resentment pouring out in both pitch and volume. Leah began to cry.

"You will do exactly as I say." He stepped toward me and struck me in the face, slamming me backward into the stereo cabinet. My elbow broke the glass in the door, and I slumped to the floor. Leah screamed, running toward me.

Staring at each other, frozen, I from the floor, he over me, the doorbell suddenly rang. Leah dropped into my lap crying. He glanced at the door and back at me. Having no escape, he swore fiercely, walked past the front door, and up the stairs.

From the floor, I could not see through the side windows in the entry hall. Our surprise visitor now pounded fiercely on the door, ringing the bell again and again. Undoubtedly hearing Leah's mournful sobbing, this guest had grown concerned for her safety. I could not pretend to be absent. Whoever rang our bell must have seen Russ walk by the window and up the stairs, must have heard Leah, perhaps even heard the arguing and the breaking glass. I had to do something before the visitor broke down the front door.

I smoothed my hair and brushed tears from my cheeks. Standing, I crossed the room to the entry hall. I drew deep breaths, trying desperately to calm myself. I thought frantically for an excuse. How would I explain? I opened the door.

There, on our porch, stood Susan. From her hurt, pained expression and from the tears gathering in her eyes, I knew. Susan understood everything.

Eleven

SUSAN'S TEARS SPILLED OVER, running freely down her cheeks. "I didn't know," she said, pulling me into her embrace. "I just didn't know." She patted my shoulder like a mother consoling an injured child. In spite of deep shame, I accepted her expression of sorrow. At last she knew my secret.

"I'd better get Leah." I broke away, wiping tears from my cheeks.

"I heard glass."

I nodded, took her arm, and brought her into the house. Leah continued to whimper, still sitting in the corner where I had fallen. I picked her up and sat holding her in the rocking chair. "There, sweetie. It's all over." I rocked and soothed. "Everything is fine now."

Susan glanced around the room, surveying damage. Then she went to the kitchen for a broom. By the time Leah settled down with her thumb, Susan had removed the glass, brought me a glass of water, and made an ice pack for my face. In spite of the cold, I felt a swelling on my cheekbone. Susan sat opposite me with a Diet Coke.

The phone rang, but neither of us moved to answer it. On the third ring, I heard Russ cross the floor above us and answer the hall phone. With detached professionalism, he came down the stairs pulling on a sport coat. Without speaking, he walked out the front door. Just as if nothing had happened.

An emergency call. I felt relief in his leaving the house.

Susan and I talked long into the evening. Somehow having a real confidant almost made the ache in my bruised cheek worthwhile. After all these years, someone finally knew what life was like for me. Someone understood. Someone cared.

Susan cared.

She asked how long the violence had been going on, how much damage Russell had done. Had he ever hurt Leah? Had I been hospitalized?

She listened, tears rolling down her cheeks, while I talked about Russell and about how deeply I loved him. Susan did not judge. She did not assign blame or condemnation. She did not even appear to hate Russell. Her response surprised me. I expected a raging, angry friend. Instead, I think her quiet tears made it easier for me to tell the truth—all of it. I found her listening ear cleansing to my soul. I was no longer alone. At last Susan knew, and she believed me.

———

But Susan's knowing didn't save me from Russell's behavior. Life on Cummins Island continued as before. Russell and I continued to experience occasional rough spells, interspersed with long periods of relative peace. I always knew when Russell's anger was about to explode. The tension built between us until it seemed almost visible. During those periods, everything I did seemed to escalate his agitation. No matter how I tried to appease him, over time the pressure built to its inevitable conclusion—anything from a simple slap to a violent beating, always accompanied by angry, hurtful words.

In the meantime I did go to work in Russell's office, where I learned to manage the telephones and to schedule appointments. Instinctively, I knew that money was not the true reason Russell wanted me working there. It didn't take a certified public accountant to understand that I could make more as a teacher than I saved Russell by working at his minimum-wage office job.

Clearly Russell wanted to keep an eye on me, and how better to accomplish this goal than by having me right under his nose? Being in the office daily, I worked under Russ's watchful eye. And he watched my every move. At the same time, long office hours effectively extinguished my exposure to the outside world. No longer able to walk with my friends, I found our relationships began to drift. I believe that Russell hoped, over time, to completely eliminate my friendships with Susan and the others who formed my only contact with a healthy world.

In spite of work I found Susan's friendship to be immutable, and I valued it more than any earthly treasure. Only occasionally did we speak of my continuing difficulty with Russell, most often after a violent outbreak. She never suggested I leave him, though I know she feared for my safety. I saw it in her eyes, in the tense muscles of her face. After every explosion, in spite of her own emotion, Susan listened to me with patience, helping me sort through my widely oscillating feelings and fears. She promised undying loyalty and whatever help I requested. She told me that she prayed frequently for me, and for Russell, and somehow knowing that gave me courage.

Ironically, going to work for Russell became part of the web which tied Susan and me more closely together. One afternoon she called me at the office in tears to explain that her husband, David, had fallen from the roof of the new house they were framing.

"Bring him right in," I instructed her calmly. "Park in the handicapped spot by the back door. I'll have a room ready and waiting for you when you get here."

"Thanks." The phone went dead.

If Susan had told David anything about Russell, he betrayed no hint of his knowledge. Though he was hurting, David managed to stay alert during the exam and the X rays of his shoulder and ribs. Susan, however, did not do so well. She came out of the exam room crying, her face white with fear. David leaned heavily on her shoulder. Russell escorted them to their car, opening doors along the way.

"What is it?" I asked when he returned.

"A dislocated shoulder, two broken ribs, and a bad ankle

sprain," Russell said, standing at the counter over my desk, writing in David's chart. "Lucky, though. Could have been killed. Get the pharmacy on the phone, will you?"

After work I stopped by Susan's. In the family room, David, encased in ice, lay sound asleep on the couch. Taylor and Brittany watched TV stretched out on beanbags. Strains of "Heigh-Ho, Heigh-Ho" drifted from an old Disney film.

"How's he doing?" I whispered.

"Hurting."

"How about you?"

"Hurting," she answered and smiled weakly. "I hate it when he's sick."

"You aren't telling me everything."

"Miss Perceptive, aren't you?" Susan wiped her eyes with her hand and sniffed.

"I've known you too long. Don't think you can keep me in the dark."

She gestured with her finger and led me into the kitchen. "David's crew is scheduled to go to Alaska this week." She sighed. "Obviously, he won't be going, maybe not for a long time."

"But you're insured, right?"

"Right. Health insurance. But it takes time to get coverage for lost wages. We've just started the house. We have subcontractors to pay." She took another deep breath and gestured toward her sleeping husband with her thumb. "It just isn't the best time for him to dally around at home without pay." I recognized concern in her eyes.

"I just wish there was something I could do to help." I began to chew on my own index finger. "I'd give you money if I could."

"I know you would." She waved a vacant hand toward me. "Actually, I've been thinking about taking in a few kids for baby-sitting." She opened her cookie jar and absently began munching on a homemade gingersnap. "I could do that without leaving him alone, and it wouldn't disturb our own family too much. What do you think?"

"What do I think?" I laughed, taking the cookie she offered. "I think you'd have six extra kids in a heartbeat." She poured two glasses of milk and handed me the larger. "After all, who else is willing to do day care on the island?" I continued, "Every working mom on Cummins Island drags her kids to the six A.M. ferry and drops them at a Kindercare in Twalleson." I took a drink of cold milk. In spite of continuous warnings by health professionals, Susan preferred whole milk with her cookies. I had to admit she was right. Whole milk tasted much better than skim.

"That's what I thought," she agreed. "But I don't have any idea how much to charge."

"I can help with that," I answered, bitterness creeping into my voice. "I've been paying that old . . ." I took another bite of cookie. "Wait! Wait just a minute." I nearly choked on the crumbs. Why had I been so slow in coming to this? "What about Leah? If you're going to do day care, would you take Leah?"

She laughed. "I wondered if you'd get the hint."

And so we came to an arrangement of mutual benefit. After all, who could I trust more than Susan to care for Leah in my place? For the first time, instead of resentment, I felt good about leaving Leah in the morning. I could concentrate at work. Trusting Susan with Leah was the highest honor I could give any friend.

When I wasn't working, we did what good friends do. We visited. We went shopping on the mainland. We gossiped some and laughed constantly. No matter what the occasion, Susan found some offbeat viewpoint to laugh about. It was impossible to attend a wedding with Susan. Her irreverence for things formal or serious was unavoidably catchy. More than once I found myself choking down inappropriate chuckles on some particularly silent and somber occasion.

"Remind me never to wear a print that large," she would whisper. Or "I wonder where he found that suit? I thought polyester was extinct."

Russell's business continued to struggle. Though island people respected him professionally—he joined the Rotary Club and became chairman of the "Harbor Days" committee—Russell had yet to make any close friends. He resented the easy way the community accepted me while they treated him with respectful distance. He seemed destined to struggle for a way to become an "islander."

In the two years after I began working at the office, his violence took yet another turn. It started when he lost a patient, Don Chambers. Don, only forty-seven years old, died suddenly of massive heart failure just four weeks after passing his company physical with flying colors. Russell, of course, had given the physical.

On the night Don passed away, Russell came home from the Twalleson hospital in the most despondent mood I had ever witnessed. I never knew whether he blamed himself for missing the impending heart problem or whether he feared the islanders' condemnation for the death. Either way, I paid for his frustration.

The next morning, I called Susan to tell her I wouldn't be dropping Leah off. I could not go to work. She suspected the truth immediately and rang our doorbell only moments after Russell left for the office. She found my eyes swollen, my body bruised, and my spirit in critical condition. This time no matter how hard I tried, I could not blame myself for Russell's behavior. He had simply expelled his rage on my body. For the first time, I saw that Russell's problem was entirely separate from me. I couldn't fix it.

"You need help," Susan said simply. "More help than I know how to give." She wrapped an ice pack in a kitchen towel and laid it gently against the bruise on my upper arm.

"Please, Susan," I said. "Don't start now. I can't talk about all of this now. I hurt everywhere. I just need to sleep."

"Okay," she agreed. "You sleep, and I'll stay here with the kids until you feel like getting up." She picked Leah's sleeper off the living room floor while she talked. "I just want to say one thing." She turned to me with a piercing stare. After a long moment she said, "I love you. I can't stand by without saying anything and watch him kill you. There has to be an answer. Somewhere, there has to be an answer."

I nodded, too tired to disagree.

"Have you thought about church? Maybe you guys could get some help at church." She put an armload of toys into the laundry basket. "We have a great Young Married's Sunday school class at

our church. The guy who teaches it has a degree in counseling."
Her voice pleaded with me. "Could you get Russ to consider going
to Sunday school?"

I stood slowly, carefully trying to hold the ice pack without putting pressure on the bruise. "Maybe," I said weakly, though I didn't
believe her plan would work. "Maybe. I'll try to talk to him." I went
up to bed.

As usual, Russell showered me with attention and love after the
episode, while never really admitting that the violence took place.
He came home with tickets for a vacation. "We need to get away,"
he said, holding me in his arms. "Too much pressure around here.
Our marriage will do better if we make more time together. Come
away with me, Pet."

Many of our vacations followed a violent episode. This one took
us to the tip of the Baja Peninsula. While Susan kept Leah, we spent
a week in the tiny resort community of Cabo San Lucas. There, in
the white-hot sun, Russell was the attentive, loving man I knew from
our dating days.

We had a wonderful week, sleeping long hours, floating in a
warm aqua swimming pool. We ate sumptuous buffet dinners and
danced outdoors in the warm evening air until midnight. We con-
nected again, and I hoped beyond hope that Russell was right. If we
took frequent time away from the pressure, our relationship would
prosper. It certainly flourished in the luxuriant heat of the tropics.

In Cabo, while lying on a pebbly ocean beach together, I
broached the idea Susan had suggested. "Russell," I began, lying
on my tummy with my head on my forearms. I spoke cautiously into
the space below my elbow. "I've been wondering . . . what do you
think about us going to church together?"

Stretched out on his back next to me with a towel draped across
his face, he answered, "What do you mean, church?"

"Well, I've been thinking that maybe we should go to church.
You know, maybe we could take a class or something." I rolled onto
my side, trying to look casual, as though the idea had just recently
popped into my head. "You know, maybe study is what makes a marriage work."

He pulled the towel from his face. "What gave you an idea like that? You know I'm not Catholic." He laughed. "Besides, what would a priest know about marriage?"

"I wasn't thinking about a priest."

"No? Who then?"

"The community church has a Sunday school class about marriage."

"Sunday is my only day to sleep in."

"I know. Mine too. But it would be good for Leah to get some kind of religious education." I rolled onto my back. I'd already gone too far. I knew better than to sound as though this idea were important to me. If I ever hoped for Russell to consider it, it had to be his idea. "Never mind. You're right. It'd never work."

"Hmm," he murmured absently, settling back down on the beach.

"Besides, with all those islanders there every Sunday, you'd probably be besieged by the locals—you know, asking for free advice and everything."

He didn't respond, but I believed I scored a hit. While I feigned sleep, Russell sat up and walked thoughtfully to the ocean for a long swim.

———

Returning to the Pacific Northwest, things did not change.

After dinner one evening as Russ read through the day's mail, I brought him a cup of herbal tea. "Remember dancing on the patio in Cabo?" I asked absently.

"Sure."

"Wasn't it wonderful?" I sat beside his chair, with my feet tucked under me, while strains of a Beethoven symphony floated from the CD player.

"Patty, it was nice. But it was a vacation."

"I know." I hesitated. "Have you thought any more about my idea?"

"What idea?" He'd obviously completely forgotten.

"You know," I prompted. "Church. We talked about a marriage class in a church."

"Patty, listen," he said, clearly irritated. "I'm too old to go to Sunday school. I work hard all week, and I'm not going to spend my Sunday morning in church."

"What about Leah?" I fought to contain my disappointment. "She ought to have some religious training."

With frustration, he slapped an envelope onto his thigh. "Look, I'm not going to discuss this any further. If you want Leah in Sunday school, that's one thing. But don't ask me to go." He stood up to leave the room. "It's not going to happen," he said with emphasis.

The next Sunday I got up to take Leah to church. If Russell wouldn't come, I would go by myself. When I walked into the kitchen, he sat at the kitchen table reading the Sunday paper, drinking his morning coffee. "What are you doing?" he asked, as if he had no idea.

"I'm taking Leah to church."

"Great. I'll ride into town with you." He closed the paper and stood up. "We can have breakfast at the café and pick her up when it's over."

Russell's words surprised me, but I knew better than to argue. How like Russ to make sure that I wouldn't go to church without him. By taking me to breakfast, he kept me out of church and saved his island reputation at the same time.

If Susan hadn't been Leah's Sunday school teacher, I would have been mortified dropping her off at class every Sunday, only to go out to breakfast. But Susan encouraged me, saying, "Who knows? Maybe something about her going to church will entice him to try it. Don't give up." She hugged me. "He loves Leah, and if she likes church, maybe he'll come for her sake."

He didn't. Whenever her class performed at a service, he sat proudly in the front row of the sanctuary. But he never went on any other occasion. He explained his own decision saying, "I don't have time to go to church. Besides, it's good for people who need that sort of thing but not for me. I don't need it."

Our roller-coaster marriage continued. Russell did well financially—though not with local patients. He worked fifteen-hour days during the summer, caring for the boaters who invaded Serenity Bay. Summer days were filled with wrapping sprained ankles and bruised bones and pulling fishing hooks from tender fingers. The summer people paid Russell's prices without flinching, happy to find a physician who could fit them into his schedule.

As things improved financially, Russell decided to build a new house. Determined to look successful in every way, he had an architect design a modern building, full of angles and windows, overlooking Angler's Pass. He chose the piece of Nana's land furthest north and west, abutting the Marine Park on its northern border. Russell delighted in the building process—the planning, working with the subcontractors, even getting the permits.

As with most of our marriage, building the house became his project. He did not consult me on any detail, and he never understood why I lacked his enthusiasm. I found myself alternating between resignation and anger, one moment glad to be excused from the details, the next, angry that he built kitchen cupboards too high for me to reach.

The house took ten full months from start to finish, and I admit I enjoyed having Russell so preoccupied. With Russell distracted, I found myself far less likely to feel his wrath.

With great sadness I moved from Nana's old place to the new house. Immediately, I missed the old garden, the roses, the apple trees, and the stenciling that Susan and I had done. I missed the screen porch and the old yellow kitchen with glass cupboards. Our new house sat out on a cliff, taking the brunt of the west wind, begging to be assaulted by every storm which passed. I wondered if the new dwelling better represented our stormy and dangerous relationship.

Even after we moved, Susan continued to look for ways to get me out of the house, to enlarge my world. She determined to help me find and keep a circle of close and reliable friends. Almost as if part of an unspoken tug of war, Russell went out of his way to thwart her plans. One year she enlisted my help her with her church's Christmas boutique. The next summer, she and I cooked meals at a children's summer camp held at the state campground south of Serenity Bay.

Susan stubbornly refused to let me wallow in the sadness and frustration of a life controlled by Russell. She could not control his behavior. Nor did she try to influence my decisions about my own future. She did what she could. Her stubborn determination led to her most outlandishly wonderful scheme. I heard about it one morning as I dropped Leah off before work.

"Patty, I've got a great idea!" she greeted me at her front door.

"When do you ever run out of ideas?"

"No, this one is the kicker. Honest." She swung open the door and took a very sleepy Leah out of my embrace.

"I'll bet." I followed her inside.

"Wait. You haven't even heard it yet."

"I don't have time, Susan." I put Leah's backpack on the kitchen counter. "I'm supposed to start the billing cycle on the office computer this morning."

"All right. Be that way." She deposited Leah in David's enormous recliner. "You can spend your entire day stewing over what crazy and wonderful thing I have cooked up now." Her eyes sparkled, and her smile betrayed mischief.

"I won't be able to get another thing done," I said, turning to leave. Eight-thirty was far too early for Susan's enthusiasm.

Her eyes twinkled as she led me to the front door. "Don't blame me," she teased. "I tried to let you in on it. Now you'll just have to wait. Bye!" She shut the door in my face.

Susan knew me far too well. Curiosity bugged me all day long.

Hers turned out to be a thoroughly outlandish idea. The most ridiculously wonderful idea she'd ever come up with. Susan arranged with the principal of the island school to start a student orchestra. Of course, Susan planned for me to be responsible for directing and teaching. She promised to take care of development and organization. At first I objected. My training was with kindergartners, not music students.

"Oh, come on. It can't be that difficult," she said, perturbed at my reluctance. "I've heard you play. We aren't expecting you to teach them Beethoven. You only need to get them started on string instruments. They can take lessons from a real teacher when they get into junior high."

"Thanks."

"Oh, you know what I mean." She sipped from a mug of steaming hot chocolate.

"But I can't teach that many kids by myself." I thought of the tuning of instruments, teaching note reading, the individual help students would need.

"I know. I've found the perfect helper."

"Who?" Would she never run out of objections?

"Me."

I laughed. "You? What do you know about music?"

"I'll have you know, I used to sing in college. In fact, when we first married, I used to sing at funerals to bring in extra money."

This fact my friend had wisely kept from me. Somehow the idea of Susan, hiding behind a privacy screen, singing at some stranger's funeral struck me as terribly funny.

"Don't laugh. I made twenty-five dollars for every funeral. Cash!" she concluded, pointing a cookie at me for emphasis.

"I'm sorry. I shouldn't have laughed," I said and collapsed into giggles again.

"There were times we would've starved to death if people hadn't kept dying."

Susan won. Our class began in late October, with twenty-two third- and fourth-grade students. We met at eight o'clock on Wednesday and Friday mornings, which allowed me to teach before I started at Russell's office. In January, we gave our first concert, which included such famous pieces as "Hot Cross Buns" and "Good King Wenceslaus." We received rave reviews and were even mentioned in the "What's Happening" column of the Serenity Bay *Bugler*.

Russell hated to share me with the community, but nearly every day at least one of his patients mentioned our work with the students. They all expressed such gratitude that he soon realized he had no plausible way to restrain me without coming across as the ultimate spoilsport. His reputation soared on the coattail of our musical success.

Late in the summer after Leah's second-grade year, I had another serious shock. I discovered that I was again pregnant. My mother-heart thrilled at the idea of another baby, but I felt anxious about the future. How could I bring another child into this unstable world of ours? Things between Russell and me gravitated between happiness and devastation. Leah had learned to cope by disappearing at the moment of crisis. She became an expert at hiding in her bedroom. I did not live the "happily ever after" I'd hoped for. Part of me felt very guilty for being pregnant. Another part hoped that new life might bring change.

Again, morning sickness assaulted me, and I woke every morning to an abrupt and violent trip to the bathroom. After my stomach settled I often hiked down the steep trail to the beach below our new house. Depression and indecision threatened to engulf me. In those early hours, I climbed onto the rocks, let myself breathe the cool morning air, smelled the salt, and walked until exhaustion overtook me. It was in this state, this confused, half-sad, half-delighted state, that I first discovered the orcas. From Nana's house, tucked back in the trees, I'd never noticed them. I'd never climbed down to the little inlet where they played. But now that we lived further north, out on the edge of the cliff, I discovered the glistening black occupants of interisland waters. The whales. Singing, rolling, playing, slapping the water endlessly.

Their celebration of life made my decision for me. In the end, I refused to plan my way out of this pregnancy. With a new baby on the way and a daughter beginning the third grade, I convinced myself that I had much to look forward to. Leah would start music lessons this fall. The baby would arrive before spring. Things had to be improving. If orcas could survive the harsh, formidable life they faced, so could I. Russell's behavior was difficult, but not impossible. No matter how he responded to this pregnancy, I would survive.

On the last Saturday morning in August, I prepared Russell's favorite breakfast. Over buttermilk waffles slathered in strawberry compote, I announced my pregnancy. Firmly and calmly I explained how happy I felt about another baby. I tried to leave Russell no options, no opportunity for rage.

His response completely surprised me. Pulling me onto his lap, he kissed me warmly. "I'm so happy, Pet," he said. "Leah needs a baby brother, don't you think?"

I snuggled into his embrace, my cheek on his shoulder, relieved by his reaction. Perhaps at long last we could become the family I longed for.

Twelve

BY THE TIME SCHOOL STARTED in September, my nausea had subsided. Again Susan and I led an elementary orchestra. Because some of our students had advanced, we expanded to two groups. The more experienced players came on Thursday mornings and progressed quickly to such difficult works as "Zum Golly" and "Jolly Sailor." Our new students played together on Tuesdays. Leah, at last old enough to join us, felt overwhelmed by the size of a cello—even a half-sized one. Always her own person, Leah decided to try the violin.

Leah loved orchestra class. Because she was the smallest third grader in the island school, we rented a half-sized violin from a Twalleson music store and faithfully paid the monthly rental fee. At some moments I felt guilty using household money for instrument rental, but I tried to ignore those feelings.

Susan enjoyed our stint as "music professors," and truthfully, she turned out to be very good help. With a surprisingly accurate ear for pitch, she picked up tuning very quickly. Susan read music in both bass and treble clef, which qualified her to teach note reading. While I led the group from the front of the class, Susan walked among students, listening to individual instruments, giving encouragement here, spotting incorrect techniques there, always watching to be certain the students understood the skill at hand. We both considered our orchestra project to be great fun.

Leah progressed quickly, thrilled to participate with her mom in musical things. Eventually, we approached Russell with the idea of purchasing her own instrument. Though reluctant, he agreed, and I spent the months of January and February combing want ads and music stores in search of the perfect student violin. After a few false starts, I found it in a small city north of Twalleson where a school district advertised a disposal sale of its rental inventory. Early in March we purchased a three-quarter-sized, hand-carved copy of a Stradivarius. We brought it home, polished it, and put on new strings. Leah planned a surprise celebration for her new instrument, which she considered now a member of the family.

On the appointed day Leah spent the last hour before dinner decorating the dining room table. I helped her press a tablecloth and set the table. Leah still had difficulty putting silverware in its proper place. "Forks on the left," I reminded her.

"I want everything perfect when we introduce Daddy to Ariel," she said.

"Ariel?"

"Yes, Ariel," she answered firmly. "Susan told me that I should name my new instrument. So I've decided to name my violin Ariel, because she will be a beautiful singer when she grows up."

I kept my chuckles to myself. Leah watched Disney movies over and over. It seemed appropriate for her to choose a Disney name for the new violin.

Later, while I made salad, Leah came through the kitchen door with an armful of early wildflowers she'd chosen from the meadow above the house. Laboriously, she wove them into a garland and strung them around the center of our round oak table. She folded matching napkins and put candles in the center of the table.

I couldn't help but share her excitement. I remembered the day my grandfather gave me my cello. After blowing out twelve candles on my cake, Grandfather escorted me to our living room, where he parked me in his antique picnic chair. That was exciting enough. The grandchildren were never allowed to sit on his picnic chair. From the tiny wooden chair, Grandfather played his cello for the family. *"The perfect height,"* he would say. *"What would I do if you broke my chair? There is no other chair like it."*

Sitting on his little chair, I obediently held my hands over my eyes while he went to fetch my birthday gift. I can remember clearly the excitement and pride I felt when he presented his instrument to me. I remember the wonder of plucking the strings and holding the bow for the first time. *"It was meant to be yours, Patricia,"* he said. *"My hands are old, and they refuse to make music any longer. Now it is up to you, my Pet. Your hands are young and strong. There is music in your heart and soon it will come from your hands."*

Unlike Leah's violin, my cello was very old. During the Second World War, Grandfather fled Czechoslovakia. Only days before the borders were closed to Jews, Grandfather and his beloved cello escaped the hands of Hitler. Alone, he journeyed to Paris, crossed the Atlantic, and entered New York City. With only his cello and bow and the clothes on his back, he made his way to Chicago. There he met and married my grandmother Marta.

Eventually, poverty and pneumonia forced Grandfather to trade the cello for antibiotics. In spite of Marta's illness, fortune smiled on Grandfather. The pharmacist who took the cello as a trade recognized its beauty. He knew Grandfather would come back for the cello, keeping the instrument safely stored behind his private office. By working two jobs and saving every penny he could, Grandfather eventually redeemed his beloved friend.

Over time, Grandfather's cello became my friend as well. With his help and encouragement, I learned to coax music from her strings. A bit smaller than modern instruments, her tone was warm and true. I played her through high school and college.

The orchestra became my home away from home. Musicians became my family. The world of melody, emotion, and tone was a world I wanted to give to Leah. I wanted her to know the beauty of music. Someday, the two of us would play duets together, mother and daughter entwined in the mystery of music.

To celebrate, I made lasagna—Russ's favorite—and baked homemade bread. I wanted everything to go perfectly for Leah's sake. After much preparation, we sat down in the living room to wait for Russ.

By six-thirty he had not come. At seven, with Leah too hungry to wait any longer, I fed her dinner and let her watch a video in the family room. I continued to wait for Russ, but an uneasy feeling grew in my stomach. Just pregnancy, I told myself and chewed a few antacids. Another hour passed before we heard his car in the driveway.

I recognized tension immediately in the tight features of his face. He responded to my greetings with one-word answers, short and clipped. Not a good day to talk about Leah's violin. Though the lasagna was dry and overcooked, I put dinner for two on the table. I poured ice water and relit the candles.

"What's this?" He gestured to Leah's decorations.

"We were planning a surprise for you," I said quietly. "I guess this isn't the perfect day for it."

"Darn right," he snapped. "Nothing went right today. And I don't need a party—tonight of all nights—in my own home." He sat in his usual place, still wearing his tie and suit pants.

He reached for the lasagna dish but seeing its contents, slammed it down near his plate. "What did you do to this?" Disgust dripped from his words.

"I'm sorry, Russ. It's a little overcooked. We expected you hours ago." My stomach tightened.

"I'll bet you did. Like I work at McDonald's. What do you think I do? Sit around all day, doing nothing, waiting to come home to you?" He put both arms on the table, his perfectly groomed fingers tapping the tablecloth.

"No, honey. It really was Leah's idea. She had something—"

Leah bounced into the dining room to give her Daddy a hug. "Daddy, you're home," she squealed, throwing her arms around his neck. Reluctantly, he patted her back. "Wait till you see what Mommy bought me today!" She turned and ran from the room.

"So you spent more of my money today."

"We talked about it, Russ. It isn't a surprise."

"Sure. What is it this time—more clothes? A new bedroom set?"

"Please, Russ, just wait. Try to let Leah have her fun." I sighed and rubbed my forehead. *Please, let my intuition be wrong.* But something inside knew what was coming. *Not today, please, Russ.*

"Oh yeah. You two can have fun while I work all day to pay for it. My only purpose in life is to eat this stinking overcooked meal and be happy with what I get."

Before I could reply, Leah bounced through the door, carrying the tiny case with her. "See, Daddy? It's my new violin!" She opened the case and lifted the instrument from its blue velvet nesting place. "Her name is Ariel. Isn't she beautiful?"

"So how much was that?" He directed the question to me, ignoring Leah's glimmering eyes.

"A little over a hundred. It's a three-quarter size. I had it appraised by the music dealer in the city. He said it was a great buy—small sizes are hard to find."

I heard a defensive, pleading sound in my own voice and recognized the sound of fear. I did not want this evening to turn out like so many other evenings. Not again. Not for me, and especially not for Leah. I wanted today to be a treasured memory for her—like the day Grandfather gave me my cello. I couldn't allow Russ's anger to destroy the memory for Leah.

Leah sensed our tension and glanced back and forth between us. "Daddy, I said, 'Isn't she beautiful?' Don't you love it?" She placed the tiny instrument on her shoulder and took the bow from its case. The twinkle in her brown eyes reflected the warm glossy finish on the instrument.

"Only a hundred? Is that all? Do you know how long it takes me to clear one hundred dollars?" His voice rose to a yell, and I knew we had crossed some magic, invisible line. I also knew that there was nothing I could do that would change the outcome.

"Leah, honey, take the violin to your room and stay there." I kept my voice low and calm, deliberate.

Leah looked questioningly at me, then glanced back to her father, her face a portrait of disappointment. She turned, still holding the instrument, and left the dining room.

From behind I saw her shoulders sag. Suddenly I felt very sad and very tired. "Why couldn't you just act excited, Russ? Just once, why couldn't you be happy for someone besides yourself?" Instinctively, I realized my own danger but refused to let the moment go. "This is such an important day for her. Why can't you just once be a kind person? A good father?"

In the living room, Leah began to saw away on the violin. A sick, harsh sound came from the new instrument. He looked at me with hard, cold eyes. "How dare you tell me how to behave? I make a living caring for other people. I spend every minute of every day taking care of other people. And now, when I finally get home, all you can do is criticize my parenting skills?" The screeching in the living room continued. He stopped and glanced toward the dining room door.

"Not only that, but you turn my peaceful home into a noisy, unbearable place with that stupid instrument. Then you accuse me of not caring for my own child. That takes a lot of nerve, Patty."

He rose to his feet and stood so near the side of my chair that his knees rested above my right thigh. "Tell me, Patty. Is she my child? How do I even know?" He whispered, low and threatening, full of evil. "This all started years ago, didn't it, Patty? I was slaving away in medical school and suddenly you get pregnant. Tell me, Patricia, how did that happen?"

"Russ, please get ahold of yourself," I implored. "Look at her. She looks just like you. Of course she's yours." I took a deep breath and ran my hand through my hair. I tried to control the trembling that threatened to engulf my voice. "Russ, I'm only asking you to be a little understanding. That's all." I couldn't bear to look at him, didn't want to face the cold hatred in his eyes. The screeching continued from the living room. Through that long instant, my thoughts danced and skipped, searching desperately for some magic phrase that would placate his anger. What could I say? What could I do? Nothing came to me.

He turned suddenly and almost ran to the doorway, toward Leah and her instrument. "Stop that," he shouted. "Stop that, I say."

I untangled my feet from the legs of the chair and ran behind Russell into the living room. Leah stood frozen in place, staring at her father with an expression of surprise and disbelief on her tiny face. The violin still rested on her shoulder, the bow moving across the strings. He reached her just as she lifted the bow into the air.

"No, Daddy, don't!" she screamed, clutching the body of the violin to her chest.

Russell grabbed the instrument. "Don't you tell me no!" he shrieked. He wrestled the violin from her grip. "I want peace in my house, not this horrid screeching." Taking the bow from her other hand, he turned toward the end post of the stairway and held her tiny violin high over his head. As he posed there, threatening to destroy the instrument, he bellowed, "I'll teach you . . ."

Filled with anger that bubbled over and spilled out, I forgot myself. "No, don't!"

With one hand he slammed the bow across the railing, splitting it into two pieces held together only by the horsehair.

"Please. No!" I cried again, rushing toward him, but the tiny instrument had already begun its downward arc over the post. With a sick *twang* the violin body slammed down. Wooden pieces flew outward from the impact. At the same moment, a horrified cry came from Leah, and she lunged at her father to recover her beloved violin. Just as she reached his side, he turned and, with a grunt, heaved her out of his way. Her sixty-pound body offered no resistance, and she flew toward the stairwell like a damp towel. With a distinct snap, I heard the bone in her forearm give way as it slammed against the railing. Down the stairs her limp body tumbled.

The sound of the breaking bone resounded in my head, and I came after Russell like a she-bear. Screeching, I raised my hands, wanting to pummel him with my fists. All of my anger, all of my resentment, all of the buried emotion of our disastrous marriage was suddenly available to me as raw, angry energy. For once, I fought back. I wanted to kill him. If I'd been strong enough, I would have.

Before I could inflict damage, he grabbed my wrists. Twisting both of them, he stomped on my right foot. I bent in half from the pain. Letting go, he began to pound at my head with both of his fists. As I sank to the floor, he began kicking my stomach with his feet. The baby. All my anger turned instantly to self-preservation. To protect my innocent unborn child, I rolled onto my hands and knees and curled into a ball covering my head with my arms. The blows continued—on my back, my shoulders, my arms, my head. Except for the side of my pregnant belly, his feet could not reach the baby.

All the while, Russ continued to scream. He accused me of infidelity. He called me horrible sexual names. He ridiculed my appearance, my pregnant body, my motherhood. He assured me that no one else would ever want me, could ever want me.

While his heavy wing tips delivered blow after blow to my body, his hate-filled heart delivered blow after blow to my soul. *Hang on,* I told myself. *Live through it. For Leah. For the baby. Live through this.*

Suddenly the kicking stopped, and Russell walked away, breathing heavily, still swearing. For a moment I lay motionless, waiting. Had he stopped? Was he gone?

I heard Leah whimpering and gasping for air at the bottom of the stairs. *Help her—I must help Leah.* The pain in my right shoulder was so severe that I was sick to my stomach. After throwing up on the living room carpet, I crawled on both knees and one hand toward the stairs to Leah.

"Leah, honey, Mommy's here." I tried to reassure her, tried to sound light, cheerful. But my voice emerged in a rasping whisper. I paused to swallow stomach acid and retched again. "I'm coming, honey. It's over." I rose to my knees and dragged myself to a stand so that I could descend the stairs. Blood dripped from Leah's lower lip, and leaning against the wall, she cradled her left arm in her right, hugging her chest. Tears streamed down her cheeks, and she trembled in terror. Blood trickled from a small gash above her left eye. I moved slowly, painfully down the stairs. "Honey, it's me, Mommy." Another step. "It's okay. We're okay now." I sat down on the step above her and pulled her head into my lap, trying to soothe her, stroking her hair. I murmured reassurances while my head pounded and my body screamed.

Minutes later I realized that Leah had difficulty breathing. Something was seriously wrong. I tried to pick her up, but her cry of pain so startled me that I did not. For a moment I forgot my shoulder and started to panic. What should I do with an injured child here on this desolate island?

"Not so fast." Russell's voice came low and hard from the top of the stairs. "I'm not finished with you yet."

I looked from Leah to Russ, struggling to think clearly. *We're not safe. This is not over yet. Think*, I screamed at myself. *She needs you now.* I looked up again and saw that Russell held my cello out in front of his body.

"She's hurt, Russ. We need to go to the hospital." I fought to keep panic from my voice. Russell thrived on my fear. "Please!" He held the cello in front of him, hesitating.

"Enough," I said firmly, feigning confidence. "Leah needs more doctoring than you can do here. This isn't like the other times, Russell. Please." I swallowed again, on the edge of vomiting. "Help me take her to the hospital."

"Not until I'm through with you." With the decision made, his voice became calm, cold, and frightening. For a single moment I understood—this would be my last day on earth. But it was not my body Russell wanted to destroy. He put the cello on the floor at the top of the stairs and posed there, his right foot just above the strings. Holding my gaze with his own, he brought his foot down violently over the bridge. In an instant my grandfather's precious instrument was gone. The strings gave way with a low haunting ring, the bridge collapsing into the sound hole. Again and again he stomped, venting his rage and frustration. All the while his cold hard eyes stared into my fear. When there was nothing left of the cello, he spoke.

"Don't you ever forget," he said, his voice cold and terrifying, "I can do the same thing to you." With one mighty kick, he sent what was left of my cello tumbling over the edge of the stairway. It rolled once, twice, and came to rest on the step above me. He turned toward the entry hall and left the house, the front door standing wide open behind him.

A soft knocking roused me from sleep. I must have dozed off. My left hand tingled from sleeping on my elbow, and I felt the indentation of my wedding ring on my cheek. The edge of the wooden chair had transformed both my legs into sleeping stumps. I looked up to see the curtains part and deep green eyes peer at me from a face suspended between fabric panels.

"Mrs. Koehler?" A woman's body materialized through the curtain. "I'm Andrea Larson, the hospital social worker. May I come in?"

While I slept, the room had filled with light. But the hospital seemed surprisingly quiet. Must be early. I glanced at Leah, who slept peacefully in the bed next to my chair. I felt confused, disoriented. What did this woman want? Why had she come?

She parted the curtain and stepped into the sanctuary of our hospital room. "Dr. Nickleson, the emergency room doctor, asked me to visit you." She smiled from over a clipboard she hugged to her chest.

"Oh yes. Well, then, have a seat." Rubbing my face, my mind continued to struggle. *Wake up, Patricia. Think. What did we tell the doctor?* Dazed from sleep as much as exhaustion and fear, I struggled to clear my thoughts. The woman pulled a wooden chair close to the other side of Leah's bed. We stared at each other over Leah's sleeping body.

"This must be so frightening for you," she began gently, nearly whispering. "The nurses tell me that Leah is going to be fine, though."

"Yes," I agreed. My lip started to tremble, and I put my fingers to my face trying to stop the motion.

"Tell me what happened yesterday," she said quietly.

I tried to remember the story. Something about a beach and a fall. What if I made a mistake? At this point, they might take Leah from me. *Think*, I told myself. *Think.*

"It was such a long day," I began. "I told the doctor yesterday. I don't really have anything more to tell you. . . ." I hesitated, watching Leah breathe peacefully. "It was an accident." Leah stirred.

"I'm sure it was, Mrs. Koehler. No good mother ever wants to hurt her own child. You can trust me. Tell me what really happened." She sat back, waiting patiently, a tiny encouraging smile playing at her lips.

"Umm, well, Leah and I went to the beach yesterday evening—to look for crabs. And she was climbing on the rocks and strained her ankle." I turned away from Andrea's gaze. It was difficult to lie to such intense, caring eyes. "She refused to walk back to the house by herself. So I tried to carry her."

"That must have been difficult, considering your pregnancy. Where was your husband, Mrs. Koehler?" She did not shift her position in the chair, her green eyes fixed steadily on my face.

I glanced at the eyes and away again. "He had an emergency at the clinic."

"So you carried your daughter back to the house?"

"Yes, well, I started back up the path, and it had been raining. The rocks were slippery, and I must have started to slide. I don't really remember how it happened. We just tumbled over the side of the path and rolled down the hill. The next thing I knew, Leah was crying, and we were both stuck on the side of the hill in the thickets."

"That must be why she needed stitches on her face," she suggested.

"Yes, the woods are very thick on the side of the hill toward the beach." I looked directly into her green eyes, daring her to disbelieve. She returned my gaze without flinching.

"You know, Mrs. Koehler, we see a lot of women in this hospital who have been hurt—badly hurt—by the very men who claim to love them. You can see why I need to ask these painful questions." She looked at me for a long while, then brought out the clipboard and began to write. Looking away, I let her write in silence. What could this beautiful, gentle woman understand about my world, about my life with Russell? I blinked back tears.

"Well, I guess that's everything." She put her pen into her jacket pocket and stood to leave. "You know, Mrs. Koehler, women don't have to be afraid of being beaten. Many women decide to leave. They begin again. It is possible."

"Yes, I understand." I deserved an Oscar. "But this wasn't like that. My husband is a wonderful man." I smiled into her eyes, hoping to appear the picture of confidence.

"I'm sure he is," she said quietly. She looked at me another long minute and reached into the pocket of her suit coat. "I always give this to everyone I speak with. My number is on the bottom. And an emergency number is written there in ink." She pointed to the top of the card. "If you ever need someone to help you, someone to talk to, you can call that number anytime—day or night."

She stepped toward me and held out her hand. "Well, then, I guess I'll be going."

I shook her hand reluctantly. Before she turned away, we heard another knock. Susan pulled the curtain back and the sun rose in the tiny hospital room. Shocked to find someone with me, Susan stopped suddenly. "Oh, excuse me. I didn't know you had a visitor."

"No, Susan, Ms. Larson was just leaving. Please come in."

Andrea Larson nodded to Susan and left the room as silently as she had come.

"So who was that?" Susan jerked her thumb toward the doorway.

"A social worker. The emergency room doctor thinks that Russell beat Leah—or worse yet—that I beat her."

Susan threw her coat over the back of the empty chair and dragged it closer to mine. "I imagine they've seen just about everything down there," she said. I distinctly heard sorrow in her voice. She sat down heavily.

My hand rested on Leah's ankle, rubbing along her shin. She shifted and moaned softly. I sat down again and leaned back into my chair, leaving my hand on the bed. "If they really believed that one of us did this, they'd take the children away." Tears spilled down my cheeks.

"Maybe. I don't know."

"She said women do get away."

"I think it's possible."

"But I don't have anywhere safe to run. Russ would never let us leave. He's told me he would kill me if I try."

Susan reached across the bed and gently placed her hand on top of mine. I turned to see her staring into my eyes. "I saw the cello, Patricia," she whispered. "You have to do something. It's time."

Thirteen

ON THURSDAY EVENING DR. BECKER, Leah's ortho-
pedic surgeon, came into our hospital room to find Leah sitting up,
drinking a milk shake. I sat cuddled beside her reading a children's
book that Susan brought, subtitled *The Book of Jonah in Rhyme*. Poem
after poem told the story of Jonah's journey into the belly of the
whale. The book enthralled Leah, but frankly, the story was lost on
me. Happy to be interrupted, I closed the cover and turned my
attention to Dr. Becker.

"And how is our Miss Leah this afternoon?" He held an aluminum chart casually under one elbow.

She looked at him shyly, and I nudged her. "Okay," she whispered.

"I think she's feeling much better," I volunteered, wanting to
fill in the silence. "When can I take her home?"

"Well, let's talk about that. Why don't you come down the hall
with me? We have a lounge where we can sit more comfortably." He
took a step back and held the door open with one arm. "Leah, can
I borrow your mom for a minute? I'll bring her right back." Dr.
Becker winked and smiled, and Leah reluctantly nodded her permission. I gave her the book and rolled my bulky body over the side
of the hospital bed. The baby inside my belly kicked his objection
to the motion. Sliding off, I slipped on my shoes, smoothed my

rumpled clothes, and stopped to grab my purse. Dr. Becker followed me from the room.

"Isn't she doing well?" I asked as we walked. He smiled down at me but didn't answer. We passed the nurses' station, which bustled with activity. Several staff members nodded acknowledgment, though I had the strange, guilty feeling of being called to the principal's office. The lounge door stood open just beyond the nurses' station. We entered, and he directed me toward two low vinyl-covered chairs near the windows.

Dr. Becker cleared his throat and sat down, carefully placing Leah's chart on the table beside him. "Well, I'll tell you, Mrs. Koehler, normally I would have discharged Leah as soon as she was out of anesthesia." He crossed his legs and fiddled with the top of his pen. "But in this case, to tell you the truth, I'm not really sure." Leaning his chin on his hand, he fingered his upper lip while he gazed out the window. It seemed to me that he deliberately let my anxiety grow.

"What's wrong? I thought she was doing better."

"No, Leah is fine—this time." He looked directly at me, his brown eyes forming a piercing stare. "What worries me is this: What happens the next time?" His gaze never wavered, and I felt as though it might bore through my face.

"It was an accident. There won't be a 'next time.' " Refusing to stare back, I focused on a place just behind his shoulder.

"Really, Mrs. Koehler, there is only one way to be sure that there isn't a 'next time.' " Again there was a long silence. I grew more uncomfortable, more fearful, the pain in my stomach a reliable measure of my fear. Where was he going with all this?

"When you came to the emergency room," he continued, "Dr. Nickleson noticed that Leah wasn't the only one injured. Yet you didn't ask anyone to examine you. That made him suspicious." Putting the pen into his breast pocket, Dr. Becker went on. "He had the nurse listen to your baby's heartbeat—as a precaution." I glanced at his face and found the intensity still there. He leaned forward in the chair, nearly over his knees. "He told me she found bruises." He pulled dark square-framed glasses from his face and pointed the earpieces at me. "That's why Andrea came to speak to you."

He paused again. "I can't force you to do anything, Mrs. Koehler. But I can tell you this. I won't allow a child to stay in a dangerous home. Normally, with these suspicions, I am required to report this kind of incident. However, because I work with Russ and know him so well, I can't bring myself to start that procedure. What I need is this: I need your assurance—your absolute guarantee— that nothing of this nature will ever happen again." He drew a deep breath, leaned back, and rubbed his face with immaculate, soft hands. In that moment, he looked very tired. He wore the same olive green slacks and plaid shirt he'd worn into the emergency room the night before.

I tried to put on a confident face. If nothing else, this event had forced me to become the consummate actress. "I understand what you're saying, Doctor. But you're wrong. We're perfectly safe. Leah is the most important person in my life. I would never allow any- thing or anyone to hurt her." I smiled as bravely as I could.

My speech did little to satisfy him, but with nothing left to say, he sighed and got to his feet. When I stood, I found myself looking directly into his soft round belly. "All right, then," he said with res- ignation. "I'll take you at your word. As soon as I check on Leah, you may take her home." Without another word, he walked out of the room.

I nearly fell into the vinyl chair. He knew. My thoughts tumbled back and forth. I'd given my word, a promise far easier for him to extract than for me to keep.

How could I keep my pledge? What could I do about Russ?

Until this week it had never occurred to me to leave. Russ often threatened to kill me if I left. And I believed that he would. In leav- ing, I had too much to lose and far too little to gain. Russ had never seriously hurt me before. I excused every angry outburst with my own imaginative justifications.

But this event changed everything. Now, suddenly, I needed to protect Leah and the baby. And someone else knew, someone who could take the children from me. I could think of only one way to keep both my children and my promise to Dr. Becker. If I chose to make that final decision, I would need time, resources, and a plan. I sat in the cold little lounge for a long time after the doctor left, twisting my wedding ring around my finger, thinking. There, alone, pushed to the edge by this stranger and a new concern for the children, I made my decision.

Long after the dinner trays were collected, while Leah and I watched *Gilligan's Island* reruns, the door to Leah's room opened again. In walked the largest bouquet of long-stemmed roses I had ever seen. Fragrance filled the room. Somewhere behind the flowers stood Russ, holding a giant stuffed giraffe under his other arm. He crossed quickly to Leah, tucking the toy into bed beside her and kissing her lightly on the forehead.

"So here you are. I understand that I get to take my favorite girl home tonight."

"Yes, Daddy," she said quietly, hesitantly.

"Wonderful. I was just coming through the lobby of the hospital when this giraffe jumped into my arms and said, 'Take me to Leah!' What could I say? I just had to bring him along." The giraffe was taller than Leah, golden yellow with caramel spots, made of deliciously soft fur. Leah caressed it with her good hand.

"Thank you, Daddy."

"And for the most beautiful woman in the world, flowers." He came around the bed to give me the vase. As I took the roses from him, he pulled me toward him, kissing my lips. "I would have brought more, but these were all the red ones in Twalleson. They will have to do." I felt myself stiffen. I'd been here before, through this very exercise.

"Thank you, Russell." Smiling sweetly, I turned to find a place for the flowers. Dr. Becker had made my decision for me. I could not let Russell's contrition keep me from my path. My only hope was to play along, to let Russell believe that this event was no different from all the others. I took a slow, deep breath, an unsuccessful attempt to calm my racing heart.

He seemed not to notice. "I brought the Jag," he announced to Leah. "How would you like to sit up front with Daddy? Huh, baby?"

She smiled, but only slightly. "Okay." Neither her voice nor her manner held enthusiasm. The event on the island had broken more than her forearm. Russell's anger had crushed her spirit.

"Well, we should pack up, then. We need to catch the eight-thirty ferry home." He looked around the room, as if to assess the volume of packing to be done. "I thought we could stop by Baskin-Robbins on the way. How 'bout it?"

"Russ, I don't think we need to stop for ice cream."

"Why not?" I felt his tension rise.

"Well, Susan came by this afternoon and brought Leah a milk shake. I don't think she needs anything else."

"Susan? She was here?" He let anger flicker across his face but hid it quickly. "Well, there's always room for ice cream—right, baby?"

I glanced at Leah, who looked at me pleadingly. "Well," I said, telegraphing a raised eyebrow to her. "I suppose I could help you finish some." *Please go along, Leah. Don't upset him. Don't upset Daddy.*

Checking out of the hospital took another forty minutes. Russell, the picture of a perfect husband and caring father, made several trips to the car. Between these, he chatted with the nurse and offered whatever help I needed.

"I don't want you to hurt yourself, Patricia. Let me carry that." He took the vase of flowers.

"Such a gentleman," the nurse said, smiling after his retreating form. We continued with the check-out procedure. "Now, we want you to keep the cast dry. Use a grocery or trash bag when she showers. And here is an appointment card from Dr. Becker. He wants to see her in four weeks." As she explained each procedure, the nurse made precise little check marks in the appropriate boxes on her form. "Then he'll take an X ray and decide how the healing is coming along. The stitches on her forehead come out in four days. Of course, I expect Dr. Koehler will want to take those out. It will save you a ferry trip." She paused to make a note, check off more items, and then continued. "I'd like you to take Leah's temperature every day and call Dr. Becker's nurse if it goes higher than one hundred degrees." Check. "Now, some swelling in her hand is normal. But elevating her arm should eliminate most of it. Watch her fingers. They should be warm and pink." Check. "Oh, Dr. Koehler"—her voice took on a sugary tone—"there you are!" Russell, back from a trip to the car, stopped to see what she wanted. "Why don't you just sign here for me?" She offered him her pen.

He smiled broadly and, with a Shakespearean flourish, signed his name to the form. Though I had suffered through her endless list of instructions, the nurse asked Russell to sign the form. Embarrassed, I stood and dug into my purse. I needed an antacid. Russell had that effect on people. Leah sat patiently on the edge of her unmade bed, her eyes still focused on the television.

In the parking lot Russell opened the car doors for us, and I slipped into the backseat. Leah rode shotgun. While Russ walked around to the driver's side, Leah turned questioning eyes to me. I smiled, hoping to reassure her. "Everything will be fine, honey," I said quietly. In truth, I felt as frightened as she.

By the time we pulled into the driveway, it was nearly nine-thirty. While we waited patiently for Russ to unlock the front door, I leaned against the roof post, my body aching, exhausted. The nightmare of the past twenty-four hours seemed to have taken weeks of energy. My bones hurt. My head ached. My heart felt broken beyond repair.

For the first time I noticed the darkness in our driveway. The wind in the trees drew my thoughts in a new direction. Suddenly I realized how very isolated we were in our house over the cliff. Our nearest neighbors, renters in Nana's old house, lived just over a mile away. No one would ever hear anything from our home. The thought made me shiver.

"Welcome home, you two," Russell said with annoying enthusiasm. He held the screen door with his back and threw open the front door. In the living room stood a brand-new bicycle with mountain bike tires and bright yellow paint, an expensive adult-style bike, created in miniature for Leah.

"It's beautiful, Daddy," she whispered. She stood beside it, stroking the soft padded seat.

"I'm glad you like it," he said, clearly pleased with his choice.

"It should help you get the strength back in your arm."

She looked back at us with a peculiar, blank expression on her face. The life had gone from her eyes, and I felt a moment of unutterable sadness.

"I want to go to bed now," she said. "Is that all right?"

"Of course. You're tired." I stepped toward her and reached out to stroke her hair. "You go on downstairs, and I'll come later to check your teeth." Silently, Leah left the room.

"She didn't even say good-night." Russell seemed genuinely surprised.

I didn't respond. My nerves felt raw, and my stomach held an undercurrent of fear that I could not calm. Herbal tea seemed like the right move. I needed to get away from him. "I'm going to make some tea," I said and left for the kitchen.

The house was dark, and as I passed through the dining room, I slapped the dimmer switch lightly without turning the knob to brighten the room. Russ followed me into the kitchen. "Well, what do you think?"

"What do I think of what?"

"The gift."

"I think she's a little young for that kind of bike."

He sighed loudly. "Not the bike, Patricia."

"I have no idea what you are talking about." I filled the teakettle, taking refuge in my evening ritual. I felt him come up behind me, and the tingling on my skin seemed almost audible.

He reached over my shoulder and pried the kettle from my hand. Then he pulled me back toward the dining room. Water continued to run in the sink. "Cover your eyes. It's a surprise." I closed my eyes tightly, obediently covering them with my free hand. His hand over my wrist made me shudder involuntarily.

"Okay. Now." I opened my eyes. There, on the dining room table, a new cello rested inside a wheeled case. Price tags hung from both the cello and the case.

"Well, what do you think?"

"I don't know what to say." Seeing the cello brought fresh tears, though not of gratitude or joy. Russell's face shone bright with pride and enthusiasm.

"You don't have to say anything. I called the violin maker in Seattle—the German guy who used to fix that old thing of your grandpa's. He picked it out and sent it up on the interisland flight this afternoon." Russ went to the case and lifted the instrument from the velvet. "I was afraid it might not get here. But it did. I had Belinda drive down to the harbor dock to pick it up." He held the instrument out toward me. I had no option but to take it. "I'm sorry your old instrument was broken," he continued cheerfully, "but I've always thought you deserve something better. You play so beautifully. So I bought the best instrument the old guy had." He stroked the strings. "It cost a fortune, but you're worth every penny."

Suddenly, without explanation, something inside of me flamed up. Whether through anger or recognition, for the first time in all these years, I heard the true Russell Koehler speaking. Some part of me had finally detached itself from my own desire, my own yearning for love. And in becoming detached, I finally saw the pattern. So this was my life. This penitent, attentive man only appeared after some horrible display of anger and violence. I saw that the peace of his repentance lasted only until the next escalation of tension. Eventually, anger would express its deadly venom. Then I would hear these same sorrowful words from this same proud man. *Okay,* I said to myself. *I can play along. Dear God, let the honeymoon last.*

"Play it for me?" Russell held my elbows gently.

I shook my head. "I couldn't." Music was dead to me. Russell killed it.

"Patty, nothing pleases me more than to hear you play." He guided me to the picnic chair in the living room. Obediently, I sat. Empty. Sad. Hopeless.

He returned to the dining room for the cello. Then he pulled out the end pin and stood the cello between my knees. I grasped the instrument, the ribs of the cello pushing into the bruise on my right thigh. Russ handed me my old bow.

I can do this. I have to do this. I took the bow from his hand and turned the screw, tightening the horsehair. Gently I tuned the strings, then closing my eyes, I began a painful, tortured melody in a minor key. Mechanically, habitually, I played. It was all that my dead heart could manage. My lifeless soul would never play real music again.

"That was beautiful," he breathed. There in the dark we sat for a moment or two longer. "Come, Patricia. Let's go down to bed."

———

"Susan, I'm going to ask something. Something very important," I said. On a warm afternoon in early spring, the ocean below the house shimmered bright silver.

Susan sat in a lounge chair on our deck with a coffee mug in one hand and her latest cookie in the other. "Sure, anything. You know that." She sipped the last of her coffee.

"I need your help."

She nearly spit out her coffee. "How?"

"I'm going to run. I'm going to take Leah and the baby. I'm getting out."

"You're sure? You've thought this through?"

"Absolutely. I know that Russell isn't going to change. His violence gets worse with every episode. This last time I was certain he would kill me. I don't know why he didn't. He's told me he would never let me leave. Not ever."

Visibly frightened, Susan shivered. "So how are you going to do it?"

"I'm not completely sure yet. But I can't do it by myself."

"What can I do?"

"I need money."

Tears glistened in her eyes. "I don't have any." She put her cup down on the table and scooted forward in her chair. "I'd give you everything I have, you know that. I just don't have any." Her eyes seemed suddenly very large, alert—no, terrified.

I couldn't resist squeezing her forearm. "I know you would, Susan. That's not what I meant." I lowered my voice, even though I knew Russ was in his office seeing patients. "I've been thinking about it for days now. I can't get at our own money. Russell only gives me enough for groceries and occasional shopping. Every day when I come home, he checks my receipts." Susan looked horrified. I'd never admitted this much before. I paused, took a deep breath, and continued. I couldn't turn back now. I had to tell her everything. "Susan, I know that if I tried to get cash from the bank, somehow he'd find out. The community is too small here, and everyone respects him."

"But you can't run without money." She brought her feet over the side of the lounge chair to face me.

"I know. What I need you to do . . ." I paused, "is to be my errand woman."

"Errand woman?"

"Yes. I can only think of one way to get enough money to get out of here." I paused again, breaking a cookie and throwing crumbs to the sparrows. Susan was my closest friend, and I trusted her more than I'd ever trusted anyone. Now I trusted her with my life. "I've gone through everything. I have jewelry—lots of it. I have clothes and gifts from Russell that still have the price tags attached. All I need you to do is to go into Twalleson and return the items—"

"And give the money to you."

"No, not quite. I need you to keep it . . . until I need it."

"When? When will you leave?" Her voice no longer held excitement, only a tone of unbearable sadness.

"Not until after the baby is born. I have to know that the baby is safe and that Leah's arm is healed enough. We have a checkup in four weeks. Then, if I am strong enough, I will leave."

"Patty, what about your car? It isn't safe enough to get away."

Susan knew my secondhand car had more than 150,000 miles on it. She called it my rattletrap. "It will do," I reassured her. "I'll have to make it do."

"What if I drove you?"

"You can't. I can't put you in that kind of danger. I don't know what Russell might do if we got caught. And then after . . . maybe his attorney . . . I can't let you."

"Then take our car."

"I can't do that. You need it."

"I can come get it later, after you've settled." She must have seen me hesitate because she continued with a new enthusiasm. "You know, it's really the wisest thing. No one will notice you in my car. You can get as far away as you need to, then David and I will come get it when you let us know where you are. Think about it?"

I loved Susan, and I didn't want her involved in my plans any more than I could help. But her offer of a car seemed like an answer from heaven. "All right. I'll think about it."

"What about until then? Will you be safe until you leave?"

"I think so. Russell is in a different phase now." How could I explain his bizarre behavior to someone who had never witnessed it? "When he is violent, it's like he purges himself for a while. He's sorry, at least it seems like he is. Right now, Russ is all gifts and attention. He's so polite, you'd think we were strangers. But he never admits that anything really happened. Sometimes I think I'm going crazy. I mean, how could this wonderful man do anything like what I remember?"

"You aren't crazy. I took you to the hospital. I know what he did." Because of the sunshine, Susan squinted, and her freckles blended together into a warm bronze cast on her ivory skin.

"I'll never forget." We sat quietly for a while. The baby rolled like a whale in my tummy. I wondered for the thousandth time how I could ever leave this friend, this wonderful, honest, faithful friend. "I think I'm safe for a while because Russell is still courting me. As long as the gifts keep coming, I'm safe."

Susan's face was damp, the cookie uneaten on her plate. "You are my dearest friend," she said. "I don't think I can bear to let you leave." She wiped her tears away and cleared her throat. "But I understand. You have to."

"Then you'll help? There's no one else I can trust."

"You know I will."

"Thank you."

When Susan drove away, her van carried everything I could safely unload. Together we'd chosen things we thought Russell would never miss.

As I watched her van disappear down our driveway, I wished that I could sell the new cello. But Russell would notice the missing cello.

No, that wasn't true. Actually, I wished that I could burn the cello. I'd use it to roast marshmallows.

———

Leaving Russell meant we had to go into hiding. To be completely safe, I had to end my relationships with everyone I loved. Only by severing every connection could I hope to keep him from tracking us. Most of my ties held me to Cummins Island, but there was one other. Not only would I lose my island friends, I would have to separate myself from my brother as well. Though he no longer lived nearby, we tried hard to stay in touch.

On a sunny afternoon three days after I gave Susan the job of selling my things, I let Leah watch a video while I sat down to compose a letter to Steve. I brewed myself some raspberry tea and pulled out my stationery and address book. Sitting at the kitchen table, I wondered where to begin. Should I tell him everything? Why had I held back until now? I felt such shame over my situation that I blushed even before I began to write. I chewed on the end of my pen, staring at the paper, wondering what to do. Steve and I had been trained from our childhood that divorce was wrong. I believed that. How could Steve possibly understand what I'd been through?

I weighed every option and decided on honesty. *Dear Steve,* I wrote carefully, meticulously. *I have decided to leave Russell. I know this will come as a shock to you. Please believe that I have no other choice. I've tried to make things better, but I cannot. Until now, I've purposely kept the truth from you. And even today I can't explain everything. Please be sure . . .*

The doorbell rang. Who would come to visit us now—in the afternoon? Music from the television drifted up into the kitchen. Leah had not heard the bell. I looked down at the words on the paper. Hating to quit before I'd finished, I stood to answer the door. As I approached the front door, I glanced through the entry hall windows and saw Joe West, Susan's pastor, standing on my front porch.

"Hello, Mrs. Koehler," he said, cheerfully extending his hand into the small space between the door and the frame. I did not shake it.

"Hello," I said without opening the door further. I thought only of the unfinished note on my kitchen table, not wanting anyone to see it. I needed to finish the letter. I could not ask him into the house.

He hesitated, clearing his throat. A moment passed. "Um, well, I heard that Leah had an accident. I came to visit her and see how she's feeling." He stuck his hand into his jeans pocket. What did he know? Had Susan said something to him?

"She's doing much better."

"Great." Another pause. He smiled, adding sheepishly, "Could I say hello? To Leah, I mean?"

"She's watching a video," I said, by way of excusing her.

"I won't stay," he said, smiling. He wore a cotton turtleneck sweater, baggy jeans, and canvas tennis shoes. His dark hair grew wild, and he had the beginnings of an afternoon shadow on his face. He was not like any of the priests I'd ever known. Clearly this man intended to see Leah. All right. I could handle this.

"Why don't I take you around to the deck, and you and Leah can visit there?"

His eyebrows rose a bit, and I wondered if I'd surprised him. "Sure. That'd be great," he said. I came through the front door and led him around the house to the deck. I gestured to the lawn furniture, and he sat obediently. "What a breathtaking view you have here. I'd have never known it was this beautiful from the highway." He swept his hand toward the water. "So many trees between here and the road, you'd never know what the water looks like."

"Thank you," I answered. What had happened to me? Why did I feel so threatened? "I'll just go tell Leah you're here," I said, backing away.

In the kitchen I went straight to the table and carefully folded my letter to Steve. I slipped it into the pocket of my jeans. I would finish it later and mail it tomorrow in town. "Leah," I called, "Pastor Joe is here to see you!"

She bounced up the stairs to the kitchen. "Where, Mom?" she said. "Where is he?" Her face beamed. I hadn't seen her this animated since our trip to the hospital.

"Out on the deck." I caught her elbow just as she started for the door. "Listen, Leah, I need to tell you something." I knelt down so that my eyes looked directly into hers. "Honey, remember when we went to the hospital?"

She nodded, her eyes growing large and serious.

"Remember when I told you that we needed to keep Daddy's temper a secret?" She nodded again. "Honey, this is important to Mommy. Please, honey, don't tell Pastor Joe anything about how you broke your arm, okay?"

"Why, Mom? He's nice."

"I know, Leah. But we can't tell anyone what happened. Not even Pastor Joe. Bad things could happen if we tell." Her face grew frightened for a minute, and I wished I hadn't said anything. Perhaps I shouldn't have. "Don't worry, Leah. You just have to be very careful not to tell anyone about Daddy."

She nodded very slowly. "All right."

"Now go visit with Pastor Joe."

She ran out the back door, slamming the screen behind her. "Pastor Joe!"

I stayed behind, making a tray of lemonade and cookies and watching the two of them through the kitchen windows. Joe smiled and Leah laughed. The two of them, sitting there in the sunshine, looked completely comfortable with each other. Just as I finished the tray, Leah came back into the kitchen.

"Mom, where is the pen?"

"What pen?"

"My cast pen."

"In the top drawer by the phone." She dug through the drawer, leaving it as though it had been attacked by an eggbeater. "Come on out, Mom. You'll really like Pastor Joe."

I smiled, watching again as she ran to him with the pen. He bent over her, carefully placing her arm on the picnic table, and began to draw on the plaster cast. By the time I joined them, he'd finished his artwork. Leah proudly showed me the new addition to her friends' signatures and decorations. Joe had drawn a remarkably touching face of a man, complete with beard and long hair. "Who is that?" I asked, knowing the answer before she spoke.

"It's Jesus," she answered happily. "Now I can see that Jesus is with me always."

Fourteen

TENSION AND WILD ANXIETY filled the weeks that passed between my visit with Susan and the appointed day of my escape. I made as many plans as I could, trying always to cover my true intentions. Susan and I took extra precautions about our conversations, speaking of my plans only when we were alone and out of earshot of children or strangers.

Of course, there must have been wonderful moments as well. But looking back, even those, like the birth of our baby, are colored with fear. Russell James, named for his daddy, was born on a Saturday morning just two weeks after Leah and I came home from the Twalleson hospital. Fortunately, intense labor began immediately with RJ, and when we checked into the maternity ward, I had no opportunity to remember the hospital from my previous visit. Surviving the intense and frequent pain of each contraction became my only concern. I have pictures, though, of Russell's model behavior as a cooperative labor coach and loving husband. In spite of my aversion toward him, I allowed him to touch me, stroking my back during the contractions, and to fawn over me as though he cared. I exclaimed over the beauty of the roses he brought to my room and gratefully accepted his gifts for our baby.

I had to speak to myself over and over about Russell's behavior. *Peace is only temporary*, I reminded myself. *He will change again, as soon as he feels comfortable. This is only a prelude to the next episode. It will come. Like winter rain, the violence will return.*

Four long and frightening weeks after the baby's birth, the day of our escape finally arrived. On Tuesday of the third week in April, I feigned sleep while Russell got ready for work. As soon as I heard the garage door close, I rolled out of bed, checking the bedside clock. It read 5:20 A.M. I pulled on the clothes I'd hidden in the back of our closet. Every step carefully planned, I ran to the storage room to get suitcases, nearly tripping in my haste. Back in the bedroom, I threw clothes at the open bags lying on the bed, including only those things I knew I must have. *No time for emotion,* I kept telling myself. *Escape. Escape!*

Packing didn't take long. I had stashed the children's things in neat stacks in the laundry room, where I hoped Russ wouldn't notice. Over the last two days I'd been consumed with making lists in my head. What did we absolutely need? What could I safely leave behind? I thought of little else.

Five thirty-seven. I needed strength. My legs trembled and my stomach growled. I tried to force down some breakfast but couldn't swallow. Everything tasted sour. I put scrambled eggs down the disposal and poured a full cup of dark coffee. Exhausted—I hadn't slept—but edgy at the same time, I thought perhaps the coffee ritual would be good for me, would settle my emotions. The sun rose behind our house while I sat in the living room looking out over the water. The sky blossomed in glorious pink—the color of raspberry sherbet. Spots of clouds streaking tiny patterns across the sky reflected the glory of the new day. Though I saw it, I did not allow myself to feel it. This would be my last sunrise from my favorite chair.

The minutes crawled by. Only 5:50. More than three hours to go. Still too early to wake the kids. I promised myself I would not deviate from my carefully outlined plan. They needed their rest. Besides, why wake them? I didn't want to entertain them until time to leave.

Anxious, I found myself wandering from room to room. Though I would take nothing more than I could carry, my heart grieved to leave the little things behind. Russ's only concession to my personhood was expressed by his willingness to let me keep reminders of special people and special times. These treasures had to stay behind, but part of my heart stayed with them. I checked the clock again—6:18.

In the living room, I caressed the delicately carved ironwood statue I brought home from our first trip to Cabo San Lucas. I'd purchased a dolphin rising from the water in a lovely leap of freedom. In our bedroom, I touched a watercolor painted by a friend in town, a gift for my last birthday. The sunrise colors in her painting reminded me of the rising promise of our friendship. The painting blurred before me, and I wiped tears from my cheeks.

I couldn't carry a painting along. *How silly*, I scolded myself. Escape was a matter of life and death, not art.

I realized that I needed to say good-bye to one other thing. In doing so, I hoped to gather enough strength to finish what I'd begun. I knelt on the floor beside our bed and lifted the dust ruffle. From the darkness underneath, I pulled my old cello case out into the light. I sat back on my heels, unfastened the hinges, and opened the cover. After I returned from the hospital, I'd placed the instrument back in the case, unwilling to part with it. I found the shattered pieces of my grandfather's cello just as I had left them, surrounded by the musty smell of velvet, of wood and rosin. Strings still hung from the pegs; splinters of rich hand-carved maple projected themselves up through the spaces between them. Lovingly and full of grief, I fingered the ebony tailpiece. How could anyone destroy something so precious? Beyond repair, the cello had become nothing more than firewood. I knew I must leave the instrument behind. The splintered wood had its desired effect. In the midst of deep sorrow, anger rose to give me strength. The anger would hold fear away—long enough for us to escape. I reached in and lifted the peg box, tugging the C peg out of its hole. After unwinding the string, I slipped the smooth wood piece into my pocket. Gently, I replaced the cello. Tears began again. This time, I cried for myself.

The baby's fussing called me back to the present. I needed to nurse him, pack the car, and catch the ferry. I reminded myself of my own danger, of the sights and sounds of the hospital. Our lives depended on getting out, on getting away. I would not allow myself to lose any more precious time savoring the emotions of leaving this life behind.

By eight o'clock I'd dressed the children and backed the car into the garage. Closing the garage door completely, I loaded the trunk. I couldn't risk being seen by someone who might call Russ. At that moment, I don't know whether I was more afraid of his violence or of his ability to sweet-talk me out of leaving. It didn't matter; the suitcases were in the trunk.

On my way through the laundry room, I heard Leah's voice speaking quietly, deliberately. I glanced at my watch—8:10. I did not recognize the usual sound of play and went to investigate. I found Leah sitting on the bed in her room with all of her favorite dolls carefully leaned against her pillows, propped in an attentive position. She spoke to the dolls as I entered the room.

"Leah, honey, what are you doing?" I felt the moments ticking away. The 9:15 ferry would not wait for a mother-daughter moment.

"I'm saying good-bye," she explained matter-of-factly. "I don't want them to think I'm leaving forever. It's only for a little while, isn't it, Mommy?" She looked up hopefully.

"Oh, Leah. You'll have your dolls again. We just don't have room for everything today." I sat beside her and gave her an enormous hug, for both of us. 8:13.

"Leah, we have to go now. The ferry won't wait." I cupped her shoulders between my hands and scooted her off of her bed. "When things are settled, I'll get your dolls for you. I promise." I guided her toward the hallway. "Now can you find your backpack and bring it to the garage for me? I'll put the baby in the car seat."

She nodded with great seriousness and walked toward the family room. From behind, I saw her trying to scratch into the depths of her latest cast.

We drove out of the garage at 8:20. Susan's house, only three miles from ours, stood just off the road into town. Turning into her driveway, I saw her new minivan waiting for us. I found the keys she'd hidden under a rock beside the front porch, just as she'd promised. Leah helped me transfer our things into Susan's car. On the steering wheel, I found a note. *I am praying for you. I love you. Please let me know where you are.* She'd hidden money in an envelope under the floor mat, exactly as we arranged. I tucked it beside me on the passenger seat.

No Kleenex. I rubbed my dripping nose and blinked good-bye to Susan's house. Starting the car, I backed carefully out of her driveway. The ferry landing, and freedom, waited only five miles away. In town I turned left onto Madrona and drove three blocks south of Front Street. When I had safely passed Russ's office, I turned back onto Main and drove through town toward the terminal.

At the dock, cars filled the parking lot. The attendant directed me to the fourth traffic lane, near the middle of the lot. I checked my watch—8:45. By my calculations, I had just missed the ferry to British Columbia. Why were so many cars waiting for a late morning ferry to the mainland?

"Leah, watch the baby for me," I said, unbuckling my seat belt.

"Where are you going?" Her voice rose, the pitch disclosing her fear. She didn't want me to leave. After all she'd been through, everything frightened her. She reached over from the passenger seat to clutch my right hand fiercely.

My heart softened. "I'm just going over to talk to that man in the orange vest." I pointed. "You'll be able to see me the whole time I'm gone. All right, sweetie?" She reluctantly nodded her consent.

As I opened the car door, a beeping sound made us both jump. I struggled with the keys and finally pulled them from the ignition. "I want to ask him about the ferry schedule." I stroked her hair. "Here. I'll lock the car, and when I come back, you can push this button to let me in. Okay?" I tried to sound calm and confident, but my stomach felt like an overfilled water balloon being squeezed by a giant hand.

She looked back at her baby brother, who slept, contentedly sucking his pacifier. She must have felt safe enough to let me go, for she gave me a very grown-up nod and let go of my hand. "Hurry back, Mama," she said. Through the windshield, I saw her rub the skin on her forehead over her scar.

I glanced over the parking lot. Things seemed safe. Thankfully, I recognized no one. This saved me the trouble of explaining Susan's car. I turned up the collar on my coat and began walking as confidently as I could toward the college student who worked as a lot attendant.

"Good morning." I smiled. "I'd hoped to catch the 9:15 to the mainland." I gestured at the other cars. "Seems like a lot of cars to get on an interisland ferry. Is everything on schedule?"

Without looking up, he waved a gray pickup into the next position in line. "Nope. The Kaleetan is out of service today. This here's the British Columbia crowd. Everything's way behind."

I felt the giant hand tighten its hold. "So how long is the delay?"

"Can't say. They have two little boats doing the run into the city, but the morning commuters ain't even off the island yet. It'll be a while, I guess."

His hands signaled "stop," and without looking back, he walked up the hill toward oncoming traffic. He had nothing more to say.

I wanted to scream, *Not late. Not today. You can't leave me here today.* My teeth chattered, though I did not feel cold. I took a deep breath and clenched my teeth to stop the noise. Everything depended on our catching the 9:15 ferry to the city. I felt like the proverbial sitting duck, waiting in a parking lot with my children. If anyone should recognize us and call Russ . . .

My hands began to tremble, and I stuffed them deep into my coat pockets and clung to the pocket lining. Determined to stay calm, I bit my lower lip. Only a delay, I told myself. Nothing could keep us from getting away. Nothing.

Back in the front seat I waited as patiently as I could in the little white minivan. Leah and I took turns reading a Richard Scarry book about planes and cars. My attention wandered, and I found myself glancing repeatedly toward the opening of the inlet where ferries entered the bay. Was it here yet?

"Mommy, why do you keep looking out the window?" Leah,

long since out of her seat, stood with one hand on the dashboard, peering out at the empty water.

"Oh, honey, I'm just watching for the ferry. When it comes, it will come in right between those two rocks there." I pointed toward the harbor entrance.

"When will it come?"

"Soon, Leah. Mamma hopes it will come very soon."

At the same time, I kept a close eye on my rearview mirror. Approaching the dock, four lanes of traffic covered a gentle hill the size of a football field. Our car sat parked at a slight downhill angle, and in my mirror I could see with perfect clarity the top of the hill behind the ferry landing. I don't know what I expected to see there, but fear, and the painful rolling in my stomach, kept dragging my eyes back to the mirror. So far, the coast was clear.

The ferry to British Columbia arrived, and cars streamed off of the deck, up the hill, and past the ticket booth. The service-minded college student busied himself directing traffic. After Leah and I finished a page about delivery trucks, the baby's gentle fussing grew into hungry cries. I took him out of his car seat and settled him on my lap while I opened the snap on my nursing bra. RJ had the peculiar habit of eating several closely spaced meals every morning. Hungry again, his tiny mouth searched eagerly among my clothes.

Leah moved to the backseat where she began "reading" Susan's book in her most motherly voice. Just as RJ's mouth found my breast, I glanced again to the mirror. A flashing light reflecting off a parked car riveted my attention. The baby latched on, milk began to flow, and my stomach rolled over. A sheriff's car rolled into view at the top of the hill.

The traffic off-loading the ferry blocked the police cruiser from entering the dock area. It rolled to a stop just behind the ticket booth. My tongue stuck to the roof of my mouth as Sheriff Scott Anderson emerged from his car. He lifted his sunglasses and scanned the cars in the lot carefully.

Don't panic, I told myself. *Maybe he's come to meet guests at the ferry.* But I knew better, and I spoke gently, urgently to Leah. "You know, honey. I think maybe we'll just get on this ferry. What do you think?" I swallowed deliberately. My stomach threatened to crawl into my throat.

While RJ continued to nurse, blissfully unaware of our danger, I stared into the mirror. I saw Russ's silver Jaguar pull up beside the sheriff's car. Russ jumped from the driver's seat and ran over to Scott, moving quickly with agitated, giant gestures. I watched the two men scan the parking lot. Silently, I thanked God that I had traded cars with Susan. We were safe. For now.

Traffic changed direction, and the lot attendant began loading the ferry. The line of crawling trucks and recreational vehicles kept Russ and Scott from the car lot. Eventually the traffic slowed, and both Russ and Scott managed to cross the traffic lane and get to the ticket booth. The agent must not have remembered me, because they did not come straight to Susan's car. Another break. So many mainland kids took jobs with the ferry system. Fortunately this one had never seen me before. Russ and Scott separated and began moving from car to car.

However rash, I knew I had to make a move. Scott Anderson, a good family man, would never believe the truth about Russ. If someone forced me to return home, I knew with certainty that Russ would make sure that I never lived to try again. I glanced again in the mirror and then down onto the ferry. The boat, nearly loaded, would leave the dock soon. I had to go. I had no other choice. I slipped the keys from the ignition and dropped them into the beverage holder.

As the baby continued to nurse, I eased my car door open. I ducked, holding RJ with one hand, and slipped from my seat onto the pavement. In a crouch, I walked around the front of the car to the sliding door of Susan's van. RJ continued nursing happily. I knew better than to take him off the breast. His howling would draw attention. With my sweater draped over him, I held the back of his head gently in place. From the passenger side, I could no longer be seen, but I watched Russ through Susan's tinted windows. I urged Leah from the car, and together we slipped beside the car in front of us. "Be very quiet, Leah," I coaxed. "We're playing hide-and-seek today." Miraculously, she obeyed without question.

Stealthily, we progressed from car to car toward the waiting ferry. The loading ramp rested in the down position, though the water around the car deck boiled from the engine's propellers. We ducked under the security gate and continued toward the churning water.

The attendant, one hand on the ramp control, shouted as we began to run. "Stop," he cried. "That ferry is leaving. You can't board now!"

"Leah, listen," I said, slowing in order to speak directly to her. I stopped and bent, placing my face directly in front with hers. "We are going to take a big jump onto that boat. It'll be fun, honey." I took her hand again. The ramp began to move upward. Suddenly I felt her grip harden, her body pull back. Only steps from the end of the ramp, she stood immobile. Too late I realized I had only one hand free to hold RJ. Was it over? Was I caught?

With the attendant running toward us from behind and the ferry slipping away from the dock, I dragged Leah forward, running the last few steps. Freedom called. Without hesitation I wrapped my entire forearm around the baby, gripped Leah's arm fiercely, and threw myself into the air above the moving car deck.

We landed with a mighty thud on the grooved metal decking. Leah must have been too stunned to speak. Only momentarily distracted by our crash landing, RJ latched on and continued nursing with satisfied sighs and gurgles. Behind us, unaware, Scott and Russ continued their car-to-car search. They never saw us. The ferry picked up speed, and soon a large stretch of churning wake separated us from Russell Koehler and Serenity Bay.

I began to giggle as the absurdity of it all suddenly struck me. Only a mother fleeing for her life could leap onto a moving ferry while dragging one child and nursing another. My giggles grew as I slid over onto my back, flat on the car deck, oblivious to the stares of the other passengers, and gave myself up to unchecked laughter.

Freedom. At last we were safe.

"May I help you, ma'am?"

I rolled onto my side and looked up. Standing very near my face, I saw the polished black shoes and dark green pant legs of a Washington State ferry employee.

Fifteen

"SHE HAS NO TICKET, CAPTAIN." The blond officer, whose shoes caught my attention on the car deck, nodded in my direction.

With his mouth just inches from a chocolate-covered bismarck, the captain paused with the sweet roll still in the air. Cream filling dripped on the cafeteria table. "So take care of it, Larson. Can't you see I'm taking a break here?"

Larson hesitated, embarrassed, and looked back at me.

We stood in the dining room on the super ferry's top deck, surrounded by enormous viewing windows. Bushy island vistas floated by as the ferry headed north. North. The wrong direction. I'd managed to jump ship onto a boat headed for Canada. The room buzzed with tourists, whose noisy conversation augmented the drone of the ship's engines. The floor vibrated, and the sound of ringing cash registers, cashiers counting change, and families collecting napkins, straws, and flatware filled the air.

"I would, sir, but, well"—he stepped slightly closer the table and lowered his voice—"I think you'd better speak to her, sir."

With obvious irritation, the captain placed his roll carefully onto a napkin. After licking his fingers, one at a time, he wiped his face with another napkin. Then for the first time, he looked at me—all of me—and I was glad that I had dressed with care. He observed Leah with equal curiosity. Certainly I didn't look homeless, dressed in Liz Claiborne slacks and a dyed-to-match cotton sweater. I felt him scan my wedding ring, stopping at the diamond hanging from the fragile chain around my neck, and again at the newborn I held in one arm. I tried to meet his eyes, but the threat of tears forced me to stare hard at the bismarck sitting in front of him.

"Larson, take the little girl on a ship's tour."

"Yes, sir." Larson held his hand out to Leah, who looked at me for reassurance. I nodded and managed a weak smile. Leah's eyes fixed unflinchingly on me while the stranger towed her away.

The captain gestured to the seat opposite him, and without speaking I sat, nestling RJ into my elbow. Oblivious to our adventure, he slept, his mouth working in dreamy sucking motions, his tiny fists curled against his face.

"So what exactly is going on here?" From this position, I read his identification badge clearly now. McDonald—Captain James McDonald. The picture on the ID portrayed a much younger man. The short man in front of me had a full head of salt-and-pepper hair. His eyes were grayer than they were blue, and he wore the largest hook I had ever seen on a nose.

"I don't have any money, sir. I left my purse in the car."

"I take it your car isn't with you?"

"No, sir. It's on the dock on Cummins Island."

His eyebrows drew together, leaving his forehead a mass of furrows. Puzzlement seemed to flood his face. "I'm missing something here. The purser tells me you jumped on board with no ticket, no possessions, and now you tell me you don't even have any money?"

I nodded, focusing stubbornly on the rim of his coffee cup.

"Care to tell me about it?" His voice grew softer, gentler. I glanced into his eyes and felt the sting of fresh tears. I blinked hard to hold them back. Today's carefully laid plans did not include explaining a bad marriage to a total stranger. "I had to leave suddenly. Very suddenly. I just didn't have time to grab my purse."

"You know we have a radio on board. I could call the sheriff and have you arrested when we dock." Calmly, he lifted the roll to his lips and licked at the cream filling. "I'll need more story than that."

My tears overflowed, and I brushed them away. Glancing out the window, I watched Leah climb on the railing, visiting with the purser. With one hand she held the deck rail, with the other she clutched her beloved book. Leah had gotten out with more than I had. She talked animatedly with the purser, probably telling him everything. Oh well. I would throw myself on the mercy of Captain McDonald.

When I finished my story, he sat quietly stirring his coffee. "I have a daughter," he began. More stirring. More silence. My stomach churned. Would he send me back?

"And a granddaughter, just about her age." His gray head nodded absently toward Leah and the purser. He put the spoon down on the table and rested his chin in his right hand, staring somewhere off behind me. "I can't say I know where you've been. I have no idea what kind of man would do the things you describe. But if anyone did that to my daughter, I'd kill him myself." He looked directly into my eyes. I saw kindness there, in spite of his threatening words. "You go get your daughter, and I'll clear this up."

"Thank you," I said, too overcome to say more.

Three hours later, I waited in the purser's office while Captain McDonald conferred with Canadian customs officials. Leah had gone with Larson to watch the giant ferry dock. Stretched out on his tummy, RJ enjoyed a long morning nap on the purser's desk. His bed, the lining of some unsuspecting crewman's jacket, barely softened the hard metal surface. After another thirty minutes, my stomach began to roll again. What could take so long? I tried to calm myself. But I had nothing to do, nothing with which to occupy myself. The tiny office held a desk and a chair, nothing more. I wondered if submarines had more space.

"Well, it's all taken care of," Captain McDonald said, entering the tiny office. He wore a small, tight smile.

"Great. Thank you so much."

"It will take us about an hour to unload and reload the car deck. In another four hours, you'll be docking at Twalleson, right where you meant to be."

"Four hours?" I sensed something terribly wrong.

"Yeah, sorry about that. The morning boat to Canada stops at all the islands on the way back, so the trip home takes a little longer."

"No. I can't!" Panic, first in my stomach, then in my voice. "I can't go that way."

He looked completely confused.

"Don't you see? Russ will figure out which ferry I boarded. He'll find my stuff in Susan's car. If I come back by the same ferry—especially if it docks at Serenity Bay—don't you see?"

Clearly Captain McDonald didn't see.

"Russ will be waiting. He'll take us home. I can't go home. Not now. Not ever." Panic changed my voice, and it sounded unreal even to me. I paced the office, as if in a cage. McDonald backed out of my way.

Framed by the doorway, he stood with one hand on his hip and the other fingering his mustache. "I see," he said slowly. "I see."

I continued to pace. Back and forth, pivoting through every other step. What could I do? Where could I go now?

He reached out and put a gentle hand on my shoulder. I jumped. "All right, I've got it," he said. "We have a state ferry that runs from Victoria to the Washington peninsula. I think I can get you back via that route. It will take some unofficial travel. But I think I can manage it. No one will be able to trace you that way. What do you think?"

Fifteen minutes later, Larson reappeared with Leah in tow. She skipped along the deck to the office doorway. "Mrs. Koehler, the captain wants me to escort you down to the customs office."

I scooped up RJ, taking the crewman's jacket with me, and we followed the purser down the inside stairway at the bow of the boat. When we reached the car deck, I found it empty. The engines rumbled, and the water around the ramp bubbled. I saw Leah freeze. Larson felt it too, and without hesitating, he bent over to pick her up. "Don't worry, Leah, we only allow our passengers to jump the ramp once a day." He smiled broadly at her frightened face. "This time you get to walk—just like normal people." She tightened her grasp around his neck, clutching her cast with her healthy hand.

Larson didn't speak again until we entered the customs build-ing. "You'll have to stay in a fairly confined place. Since you don't have identification, you're kind of a non-citizen. But John here— he's the man who arranged it—he'll take good care of you."

"I can't thank you enough," I began, not knowing quite what to say. "I promise, when things are settled, I'll get your ticket money to you."

"Not necessary, ma'am." He held a glass door for us. "Captain McDonald paid your fare. It's all taken care of." We went through the doorway into another, larger, waiting room. Just as I turned back, Larson thrust an envelope into my hand. "The captain said to give you this." He gazed at the linoleum floor and shifted his weight with the discomfort of a teenage boy asking for his first date. "The captain says you are to feed the children with it." I smiled my thanks, and with a gentle wave, he left us. In the envelope, I found a crisp twenty-dollar bill.

Just as we were promised, John drove us to the Victoria terminal, where three hours later he escorted us on board a ferry bound for Port Angeles.

It was 9 P.M. by the time we docked. Darkness had fallen. Though I had all day to think about my plans, none came to mind. I moved about in a cloud, like some kind of unexplainable shock. Exhausted, wrung out. All of my exquisitely laid plans still sat on the passenger seat of Susan's car. I had no one to call, only a bit of money left, no job, and no place to stay. Leah had grown very sleepy, and her temper was short. So was mine.

I guided Leah toward the brightly lit terminal building. In all the years I'd lived in Washington, I'd never been in this town, never seen this building. Just outside what appeared to be the lobby en-trance, I saw a pay phone with a telephone book hanging by a chain. I stood under a bare streetlight and turned to the yellow pages. I put some of the captain's money in the slot and dialed.

"Hello. Domestic Violence Hotline," an overly cheerful female voice answered.

"Uh . . ." I nearly hung up. "I need help," I whispered.

"You'll have to speak up." Her voice took on a commanding tone.

"I need some help," I repeated.

"Ma'am, are you in danger? If you are, you need to hang up and dial 9–1–1."

"No, no danger." I drew a deep breath. "I left home. I don't have anything, no money, nowhere to go. I . . ." I felt tears again and heard my voice tremble.

"It's all right, honey. I'm right here." The tone changed. The voice became gentle, understanding. "Where are you now?"

"The ferry terminal, in Port Angeles."

"All right. Can you get to a shelter?"

"No. I don't have any transportation. I don't know where to go."

"Do you have children with you?"

"Yes, an eight-year-old and a baby."

"Do you need a doctor?"

Her questions felt like an inquisition. "No. Right now we're fine. We just need a place to stay. Only for a while, really."

"All right. I'm going to have a woman come pick you up. We're about thirteen miles from you. So, say, in thirty minutes we'll be there. Do you think you'll be safe where you are for thirty minutes?"

"I think so." It never occurred to me that Russ might be looking for me here, at night, at the ferry terminal. I shivered and glanced uneasily around the darkened parking lot. "Please hurry."

"We'll have someone there as soon as we can."

Thirty-eight minutes later a tall woman with gray hair twisted into a French roll entered the terminal building. She stopped just inside the doors and scanned the room carefully.

We sat in the corner of the lobby behind a silk fig tree. Leah was asleep in the chair beside me. The woman moved toward us with long awkward strides. She wore a navy blue skirt, gray nylons, and black tennis shoes. She'd knotted a red chiffon scarf with gold print around her waist.

"So there you are. Not hard to spot you." She smiled, like a grandmother accompanying preschoolers on a field trip. "I'm Doris. Let's get you out of here." She took the baby from my arms and looked around the terminal. "Any trouble?"

I shook my head.

She turned abruptly and led the way out of the building. I realized I hadn't given her our names. At the end of the sidewalk waited a gray station wagon with the engine running. It was an import, almost like the one my mother owned when I was in high school. A hole, surrounded by rust, filled most of the lower half of the front passenger door, which Doris held open. As I started to get in, she stopped me.

"No, let's put the little girl in the front seat."

I stepped out of the way, confused.

"I don't have a baby seat," she explained, taking Leah's hand. "I think you'll be safer holding the baby in the back." After she buckled Leah's seat belt, she opened the back door. "Do you have anything else?" she asked, looking around again.

"No, nothing," I said. "Nothing else."

The engine in the little station wagon sounded like a jet. We tried shouting at each other over the seat but gave up after only a few sentences. I had no idea where we were going, but it didn't matter. I had no choice, no other options. My whole future rested in the hands of this strange-looking woman.

After a short ride, we arrived at our destination. Leah had again fallen asleep in her seat. The building, a simple brick square, looked more like a nursing home than a shelter to me. I saw no sign in front, and I realized that even though I was here, I had no idea where "here" was. The woman, who introduced herself only as Doris, parked in the breezeway and turned off the car.

"It's been a busy night." She turned in her seat to face me. "I haven't had a chance to phone for availability. So I don't know if they have space for you here." She turned back to her rearview mirror and adjusted stray strands of hair into purple plastic combs. "Why don't you just wait here while I check." She opened her door and unfolded herself onto the pavement.

Through the glass doorway, I saw clearly into the lobby of the building. Doris greeted a woman at the reception counter with some familiarity. They chatted back and forth before Doris gestured toward the car. The receptionist, a heavyset woman in a white crocheted sweater, looked tired and uninterested. She shook her head, and Doris leaned over the counter with her head on her hand. Together, they focused on something out of sight. Then the woman picked up a telephone.

After a long delay, Doris returned to the car. "Well, this place is all filled up," she said as she landed heavily in her seat. "But we made a few calls and found a spot for you. It isn't as nice as this, but you should be safe." She started the car and pulled back into the street.

We left Port Angeles and headed south, winding through tiny towns and forested two-lane highways until I finally fell asleep myself. Eventually the sound of the car turning onto a gravel driveway woke me.

Blinking and rubbing my eyes, I read the alarm clock glued onto Doris's dashboard. If accurate, we'd been traveling for more than an hour. Doris slid out of the car again and walked up wooden steps to the covered porch of an old dilapidated Victorian. Even in the dark, I saw shingles missing from the siding and paint peeling from the porch rail. Though the outside lights were on, the house itself was dark, with only one light visible from what must be a living room window. As soon as Doris knocked, the front door opened. She spoke with someone inside for a moment and then turned to the car, vigorously gesturing for us to come in. I struggled with my seat belt and the baby and scooted out of the car. Leah slept on.

As I climbed the steps holding RJ protectively, a woman emerged from the front door. All I could see of her were her teeth, which gleamed even in the semidarkness—beautifully white and perfectly even. The porch light reflecting off her face told me she wore glasses. As I sized her up, she engulfed RJ and me in an enormous hug. "Welcome, Patricia," she said, patting my shoulder while she held me tightly. "I'm Oleda. Come in now, honey. You'll be safe here." From over her shoulder, I saw Doris smiling.

"I'll bring Leah in," Doris said and started back down the stairs.

The black woman wrapped her large arm around my shoulder and squeezed, pulling my head into her generous bosom. "Come right in," she said again. And like a lost child coming home, I went into the old house.

The place smelled of bread baking, and with a pang I realized that I hadn't eaten since the meal on the ferry. Hunger squeezed my stomach. Inside, I noticed dark wooden stairs, which ended exactly to the left of the front door, and a long narrow hallway leading from the stairway through the entire depth of the house. Two rose-colored barrel chairs sat on either side of the dark hallway.

Oleda guided me to one of these chairs, and I sat gratefully. Her enormous bulk made the space inside the doorway smaller. She reminded me of Mammy from *Gone with the Wind*, only smaller, with no clear accent. She bustled around my chair, turning on lights. Just as I sat, Doris entered and deposited a sleeping Leah into the seat of the opposite chair.

The black woman hugged Doris with the same enthusiasm I'd experienced and patted her firmly on the shoulder as she exited the front door. With some sadness, I heard the jet engine of Doris's station wagon fade as she drove away. Though unusual, Doris was at least familiar. Alone again, I faced a strange new place.

"Excuse me for just a minute, honey," Oleda said and disappeared into a small office just off the front door.

From the next room, I heard metal file drawers opening and closing while someone slid back and forth in a rolling office chair. I wondered, sitting exhausted in my little chair in the hall, what I had done to myself. What would come of me here in this dark, depressing place? Dark carpet. Dark wood. Old wallpaper. I thought of my sunny kitchen overlooking the ocean. Hopelessness grew.

Then a more urgent need focused my attention. I needed a bathroom. Oleda came back into the hallway, and I noticed that she wore red, the kind of drapey, shapeless dress that very large women often wore. She carried a manila file in one hand, a pen in the other. Just as she began to speak, I interrupted.

"I need a bathroom," I said simply. Where had my manners gone?

"Oh, certainly. Here, let me hold the baby while you do that." She put her file and pen on the hall table and held out soft fleshy arms. "I so miss holdin' babies," she said, smiling into RJ's face. She made clicking noises with her tongue. "My grandbaby lives in Texas," she said, leading the way to the tiny bathroom she indicated.

Inside the room, bare shelves exposed an eclectic collection of towels and sheets. Not a single sheet matched another. Frayed edges of towels dangled from the shelves. This clearly was not the world of Ralph Lauren or Martha Stewart. The room was so small that I could wash my hands without ever leaving the toilet seat. I'd spent today in one tiny space after another. I'd left home and entered the land of the munchkins. My heart sank further.

When I returned to the hallway, I found Oleda rocking RJ in the barrel chair. With large swaying motions of her whole body, she hummed a tune I only faintly recognized.

"There you are." She smiled, gently handing him to me. "Such a beautiful baby. Here, let's go into my office, so we don't disturb your little one." She gestured to the door. "We can keep an eye on her from my office."

Her "office" was a transformed living room, holding a large old desk and two Queen Anne style chairs. As I chose the one nearest her desk, I noticed that my palms were wet, my fingers very cold.

"Now, honey. As I said, my name is Oleda. I'm an R.N. and I run this place. You're completely safe here." She sat down in the chair behind the desk and picked up a delicate gold pen. "So you just relax, and we'll go through the particulars before I show you to your room."

She spent the next fifteen minutes going through what she referred to as an "intake packet." Through exhaustion and bewilderment, I heard almost none of what she said. That is, until she got to the house rules.

"Now, everyone here has to share a room. At least we do these days. We're full up most of the time. Tonight I have an opening in the third floor suite. It's for two mothers and two children. No one is in there tonight, but I assure you," she sighed, "I'll have a woman sharing it with you soon."

Pausing, she glanced back over her paper work. "So tonight it's all yours. We all work here. We share chores and cooking and child care. I'll be putting your name on the chore list by the end of the week. We don't allow no liquor or drugs. And we have a ten o'clock curfew. For your safety, we don't allow no one to contact a spouse from here. If you want to talk to your man, you gotta do it from somewhere else."

She pushed her glasses up on her nose. "It's my job to keep these womens safe, and I can't do it if some angry man knows where we are. You understand?"

I nodded meekly and felt my lips begin to tremble. I bit my lower lip until I tasted blood, fighting a flood of tears. Oleda noticed. She stood abruptly and said, "Now let me put you to bed. You'll feel lots better in the morning."

I followed her up two flights of stairs, her carrying RJ and I carrying Leah. On the third floor, three doors opened off the landing. There, she paused, panting from the exercise. She passed the doorways on either side and crossed the hall. I followed her into a large room directly opposite the stairs.

The "suite" consisted of an attic room with two twin beds and a single bunk bed. Fifty-year-old floral wallpaper surrounded an ancient Persian carpet resting on a pine floor. I smelled dust in the carpet. Oleda placed RJ, now awake, gently onto one of the twin beds. Leah perched on the edge of the same bed, her eyes wide with fear.

"Now, this here is all ready for you. I'll just excuse myself and go find you some night things. We have women coming all the time without clothes. I'm sure I have something for you all." She started out the door, turning to close it behind her.

"Wait," I said, both embarrassed and desperate. "I haven't changed RJ since this morning."

"Oh, sure. I keep diapers, baby clothes, and such. I'll be right back, honey." The door closed. I sat down next to Leah.

"Mamma, where are we?" she asked in a tiny, frightened voice.

"We're safe, Leah." I said again to convince myself. "We're safe."

When Oleda returned, she carried clothes for all of us and a tray of hot water, tea bags, and freshly baked white bread. We ate with the eagerness of escapees from a concentration camp. After we'd changed, I helped Leah in the bathroom and tucked RJ into a small bassinet Oleda brought. Then I led Leah to the bottom bed of the bunk. As I pulled back the covers, she began to cry.

"What is it, honey?" *Please, Leah, let's just get some rest.*

"I don't want to sleep in this bed, Mamma. Please, not here," she whined.

"All right, tonight you can sleep with me." I led her back and tucked her into one of the twin beds. By the time I reached the switch for the overhead light, Leah snored loudly. Pulling back the blankets, I fit myself into the space around Leah. I thought of my king-sized bed on Cummins Island, the deep bedroom carpet, our whirlpool tub, and the sound of Russell breathing deeply beside me. I remembered my living room overlooking the Sound. I thought of the whales. And I fell asleep crying.

Sixteen

I WOKE TO GENTLE KNOCKING.

"Morning, Patricia," a woman's voice called through the door. "Breakfast in half an hour."

Sunlight, slipping through slats in the venetian blinds, made a pattern of bright stripes on the dark pine floor. For the first time, lying on my back, I noticed the details of the large old bedroom. I found it oddly shaped, with a portion of it protruding toward the front of the house. In this protrusion rested the single bed I shared with Leah. An identical bed occupied the wall opposite ours. A door, which must have led to a closet, stood near the end of the other bed. I hadn't opened that door. As of this morning, I had nothing to store in a closet.

Another portion of the room extended beyond a gently rounded archway, forming a small alcove. In this space, a simple wooden bunk bed rested against the far wall. Beside me, yellowing cabbage roses floated on fading pink wallpaper. Near the ceiling a wide strip of dark pine trimmed every wall. A serious leak dribbled a dark stain down the wallpaper below the molding in one corner. Along the floor, a matching molding strip, badly scarred, trimmed the floors.

I felt a small foot kick against my thigh as Leah stirred, and I realized with surprise that both Leah and the baby had slept through the night. Normally, any change affected both children. In spite of yesterday's tension and misadventure, I felt rested, refreshed. I slipped out of bed and made a trip to the bathroom.

When I returned, I found Leah wide-awake. Her face wore a sleepy, peaceful expression, instead of the fear I expected to find there. Her dark hair framed her small head like a curly wreath, bright eyes smiling up at me.

"Mamma, can you see it?" She pointed into the sunlight while she stifled a lazy yawn with her other hand.

"See what, Leah?" I bent over the bassinet and picked up RJ. I had just enough time to nurse him before breakfast. There were no chairs in the room, so I sat next to Leah on the bed, nestling RJ's tiny head in my elbow.

"The sunlight is dancing. See it?"

I looked beyond Leah's index finger. Sure enough, against the bright background of intense sunlight the dust tumbled and fell, then rose again in the moving air. "Yes, baby, I see it. You're right. It is beautiful." Oh, the eyes of a child.

When RJ had finished, we went downstairs a little tentatively, not quite certain what to expect. We heard voices and smelled wonderful aromas of bacon and coffee. My hunger came back with a rage. My nose would find the dining room without any help from anyone.

At the bottom of the stairs, we distinguished the voices of women among the sounds of children, dishes, and laughter. Imagine, in a place like this, that someone might laugh. The dining room seemed to be near the back of the big old house. We followed the long hallway from the stairs to a large room at the very back of the house. From the hallway, double glass doors opened into the dining room.

A massive oak table, laden with mismatched dishes and silver and surrounded by oddly mismatched chairs, sat in the center of the room. Three high chairs stood in a corner. Long narrow windows of beveled glass were evenly spaced along the length of the opposite wall, dressed simply with sheer fabric gathered onto rods midway from the sill. As Leah and I paused in the doorway, we were nearly knocked over by a woman carrying two bowls heaped with scrambled eggs.

"Oh, excuse me," she apologized as she slid by. "I wasn't looking where I was going." She giggled and set a bowl on each end of the table. "You'd have to cook with Diane to understand." She giggled again. "Sit down. Anywhere." We didn't move.

She wiped her hands on her apron. "I'm Maria," she said, holding out her right hand.

The name fit her. Olive skin, dark eyes, and miles of dark straight hair tied into a looping ponytail, she had a Hispanic air. Her face was round, as were her pudgy fingers.

"I'm Patricia. Patty, really." I shook her hand. Leah backed up until her body pressed against my legs, one small arm clutched tightly around my knee. "And this is Leah." I patted the top of her head.

Maria bent forward to look Leah straight in the eye. "Welcome, Leah. And who is your baby?"

"RJ," she whispered as she ducked behind my leg.

"A baby brother? You're so lucky." Maria touched the baby's hand with her index finger, and then drew her attention back to Leah. "Tell me, Leah, are you hungry?"

Leah nodded slowly and looked at the table laden with food.

"Then let's find you a seat. Where would you like to sit?" Maria's gesture took in the entire room. "You can sit right next to your mom, anywhere you like."

Leah chose the chair nearest the hall doorway. I pulled it out with one hand while I balanced RJ against my waist with my other. Maria brought a baby seat from the corner. "Here you go. This should be just right for the baby." Shoving a place setting out of her way, she put the seat on the table and helped me wrestle RJ into the safety straps. He seemed to grin at our efforts. "So beautiful," she sighed. "You're so lucky to have children."

I liked Maria already.

As we settled into our chairs, three more women entered the dining room, followed by eager and enthusiastic children. Chairs scraped against the wooden floor. Laughing children contended for their favorite seats. Their mothers, engaged in serious conversation of their own, paused only long enough to observe our presence.

One, a tall redheaded woman with long curly hair, gave me a shy smile. I noticed the fading green of bruises under her left eye. She noticed that I noticed, and her hand slid up to cover her cheekbone.

"Excuse me," Maria said. "Everyone, this is Patty, and this is Leah, and this is . . . uh-oh. I don't remember the baby's name."

"It's RJ," I said quietly, suddenly feeling shy.

"Well, welcome." She glanced around the room. "Has anyone seen Oleda yet this morning?" She sighed loudly. Maria muttered something in Spanish and turned to leave. As she started out the door I heard her complain, "I'd like just once to serve breakfast before it freezes on the table." Her stout figure disappeared into what I assumed must be the kitchen. Maria had not introduced the other women. I avoided eye contact by playing with RJ. He rewarded my attention with bright baby smiles. Leah sat staring at the other children. Five more women straggled into the room. Without speaking, each chose a seat.

Just as the silence in the huge room grew painful, Oleda, in flowing purple rayon waltzed into the dining room. "Good morning, ladies." She addressed everyone at once.

"Good morning, Patricia. Did you sleep well?" She smiled at me, and I noticed again her beautiful teeth.

"Yes, thank you." I heard relief and gratitude in my own voice.

She nodded approvingly. "Just what the doctor ordered." Conversation around the table resumed.

Oleda walked slowly around the room, patting shoulders, tousling hair, greeting the women and children by name. Beside each chair, she asked some personal, pertinent question and gave her undivided attention until she was satisfied with the answer. The children smiled and laughed freely with her.

When she came around again to us, she squatted near Leah's chair. "Hello, Leah. My name is Oleda. You were asleep when you arrived last night, so I didn't get to meet you officially." Again she smiled her disarming smile.

I tensed, wondering how Leah might react. As far as I knew, Leah had never spoken with an African-American before. I desperately hoped she'd remember the manners I had tried to teach her.

"Hello," Leah said simply. "I like your teeth." The women around the table chuckled.

"Good," Oleda answered. "Those teeth cost me lots of money, and I hoped you'd like them." She patted Leah's shoulder.

Maria returned with another woman, whom I assumed to be Diane. She had beautiful skin, as perfectly milky as porcelain china. A bright rosy spot crowned the center of each cheek, giving her the air of having just gone for a brisk walk on a winter morning. Diane wore no makeup, and I realized that her cheeks were as genuinely rosy as her eyes were genuinely blue.

"How nice of you to join us." Oleda smiled. Maria rolled her black eyes. "Shall we begin?" Oleda chose a seat near us and, standing behind the chair, grasped the hands of the women sitting on either side of her.

One by one, the women and children held hands as Oleda began to pray.

"Lord, we thank you for this day and for the womens gathered around this table. We thank you for your love and provision for us. Thank you for today's sunshine and good food. Thank you, Lord, for these friends and for the circumstances that bring them here to us. Lord, we thank you too for our new friends Patricia and Leah and RJ." She spoke each name deliberately, tenderly. "Help us to grow in love for you and for one another. Thank you, Lord. We give you glory."

She paused and everyone around the table joined her with "Amen."

Breakfast never tasted so good. We had sliced pineapple, toast, eggs, bacon, coffee, and juice. Deliberately, Oleda carefully included everyone around the table in light conversation. The redhead said little, and I noticed that when she rested her face in her hand, she kept her fingers stretched ever so slightly as to cover the bruise.

When breakfast drew to a close and women began to push their plates away, Oleda stood and tapped her water glass with a spoon. The *thud* of pressed glass startled me. I expected the tinkle of crystal. The women stopped their conversation immediately and looked expectantly toward her.

"Ladies, I'd like to officially introduce you to Patricia. She joined us late last night. I know you'll all help to make her and her family feel welcome." She smiled and nodded at us. Would she tell them about us? Did I want these strangers to know about my past, about Russell?

Oleda proceeded around the table introducing the women and children. With each name, she managed to include some interesting personal tidbit. "Now for this morning's announcements." Oleda continued. The women shifted in their chairs. "Please don't forget that I expect each of you to check the chore list every day for changes. Chores are to be done in a timely manner. Also, I have had some complaints from the second floor about the bathroom. Remember, womens"—she looked into each face—"you are to leave the bathroom as though it had been cared for by a cleanin' lady. Nobody likes an untidy toilet, do we?" She smiled through a slight pause. "I do hope I don't have to mention it again."

I heard a general clearing of throats and a slight murmur.

"Now, today's schedule is on the bulletin board. I expect each of you at tonight's Bible study in the downstairs lounge. Pastor May-field's wife will be teaching. I know you'll enjoy it."

She paused and looked down at her clipboard. Her glasses, dangling from the end of a pearl chain, clicked against her necklaces as she raised them to her face. "Ah, that's better."

The women smiled.

"Now, the intake group for those of you who are new will meet in my office in . . ." She paused and lifted her watch to focus the numbers in her reading glasses. ". . . exactly fifteen minutes. Be on time, ladies. Oh yes, today is linen day. Be sure to strip your beds and have them to the laundry room by ten." She looked around the room again. "That's it for now. You womens have a nice day." Oleda bent to speak to the red-haired woman on the other side of her.

Chairs scraped against the floor while everyone stood. They seemed to be clearing the table, but I had no idea about their traditions. Leah looked at me questioningly. I could offer no help.

What should Leah do while I went to the intake meeting? So many new things.

A square-framed woman with long straight hair entered from the hallway and came directly to us. "Hello," she said smiling. "My name is Jolette. I teach the preschoolers here."

I stood, and we shook hands. I introduced her to my children. She asked Leah if anyone had shown her the toy porch.

"No, ma'am," Leah answered politely.

"Well, then, I think we should take care of that." She reached down and began stacking our breakfast dishes. "First, I'll show you how we clear the table." I took our water glasses and followed her across the hall to a little window where a faceless pair of gloved hands received our dishes.

Jolette spoke directly to Leah. "Now shall we check things out? Your mamma has to go to a very boring meeting. We can have some fun in the meantime. What do you think?"

I nodded my approval, and they headed for a glass door at the end of the hall. I heard Oleda's voice booming from another room. I picked up RJ and followed the sound of her laughter.

Oleda's office occupied one half of what must have been the living room of this old Victorian home. She had squeezed furniture into every nook and cranny. In the bright sunlight of a new day, I saw the office in ways I had not noticed the night before. The enormous wooden desk sat perpendicular to bay windows. It still faced the Queen Anne chairs, though odd dining room chairs had been placed in a semicircle near her desk. I squeezed between two of these and tried to find a safe, inconspicuous place to sit. Other women filed in, visiting back and forth. I felt awkward, encumbered by my own shyness.

Though safe from Russell, I found myself with a new kind of fear. I'd landed in a religious place—that much was very clear. Susan would find my presence here a delightful irony. This woman had the same kind of religion that Susan had. Thinking of my old friend brought a stab of pain. I'd been gone only twenty-four hours, and I missed Susan already. How I wished I could talk with her, ask her how to cope in this strange new place. Nuns I could manage. But this? What did these people expect of me? What had I gotten myself into? I swallowed hard, trying to look both confident and happy, feeling neither.

Oleda joined us, and by shutting the door, called our meeting to order. After a lengthy prayer in which she mentioned each of us by name, she distributed manila envelopes to everyone. Inside, I found a variety of forms and information. We spent the first forty minutes going over four typed, double-spaced pages of rules.

"No alcohol or drugs of any kind are allowed on the premises.

"The front doors will be locked daily at 10 P.M.

"Weekly urinalysis will be given to every resident. Every resident will be tested for HIV. Random alcohol testing will be given when deemed necessary by the staff. Random searches of private rooms shall occur at the discretion of the resident supervisor.

"Every resident will apply for emergency welfare from the state. Your rent payment will be deducted from your welfare check.

"Every resident will donate eighty percent of your monthly food stamps to the house for the purchase of meals.

"No personal items of any kind are allowed downstairs.

"No grooming is to be done downstairs.

"No male visitors will be allowed on the premises. And for everyone's safety, every resident is required to keep our location in strictest confidence. Our mail is addressed to a post office box. This box number will be used in all correspondence, official and personal."

The rules went on and on until I began to think that perhaps living with Russell had not been so bad. A part of me rebelled. Though Russell was controlling, I'd never lived with these kinds of rules. This woman gave us less freedom than I gave my kindergarten class.

"All residents will do their chores immediately and thoroughly.

"Residents who have not completed a GED or a vocational program are required to finish one."

Finally, Oleda read rule number sixty-five. "All residents of Dorcas House will be required to know the rules and abide by them.

Insubordination is grounds for immediate eviction.

"Remember," she said, "the average resident stays here for about eighteen months before transitioning to a place of her own. You may be here longer, or you may leave more quickly." She paused and sipped coffee from a brightly painted mug. "But whenever and however you leave, what you decide to get from your time here is up to you." She looked around at each of us. I realized that we had not looked at one another. The four of us stared only at Oleda's animated face.

Her speech removed all doubt. Living here would be no picnic. Could I survive? How long would it be before I could find a safe way to leave Dorcas House behind? I had jumped squarely from Russell's control into Oleda's.

"Now," she continued, smiling, "you four womens are the new ladies on this block." She gestured toward us absently. "What I want to do is to have you introduce yourself and share with us the answer to one question." She paused again, dropping her reading glasses onto the chain around her neck. "Tell us, if you can, what exactly is your goal for your stay at Dorcas House." A lengthy silence followed her question.

She looked at a woman to my right and asked, "Valerie, tell me, what do you want to accomplish here?"

Valerie squirmed in her seat and pushed long dark hair out of her face. "I don't really know, Oleda. I guess I want to learn to be okay on my own. I want to live by myself and know I can be safe." Valerie spoke in a quiet voice, and I clearly heard fear in it. When she looked directly toward me, I recognized an Audrey Hepburn nose and lovely turquoise eyes. I felt a horrible stab of longing. Her eyes reminded me of Russell.

"That's an honorable goal and one I know you can reach," Oleda encouraged. "How 'bout you, Jill?"

The tall redhead with the bruised cheek sat between Valerie and me. She held her hands clasped tightly in her lap. The fingers rolled and played with each other. "Really?" she questioned and took a deep breath. "I want to be able to get a job, a real job—not just a job at some hamburger joint." She paused and I thought she had finished. Then suddenly she pulled the scrunchie from her red ringlets and shook out her hair. "And, I want to make sure that David never, ever comes near me again."

Oleda laughed. "Well, that's a goal." She jotted notes on her clipboard. "Jill, do you know that the woman who runs our other shelter has a college degree now? When she came here, she hadn't finished high school. With God's help, there is no limit to what you can accomplish." Her eyes held Jill's for a long moment.

"It's your turn, Patricia." She looked toward me expectantly.

I took a deep breath. "I don't know what I want. I guess I just want to be able to keep my children. I'm afraid that when Russ figures out where we are, he will take them from me." Unconsciously, I held RJ so tightly that he began to whimper. Surprised, I looked down and loosened my hold. Fear held me as tightly as I held RJ.

Oleda took notes and then spoke. "I understand that fear. When powerful men make threats and then back them up with violence, we turn into very frightened and desperate people." She smiled. "I felt the same way myself at one time." She turned to the last member of the intake group.

"And, Rochelle, what about you?"

Relieved that attention had been directed to someone else, I stole a glance at the woman sitting on my left. I saw tears trickle down her cheeks. "I want to stop using drugs," she whispered simply.

Nearly an hour later, Leah and I climbed the stairs to our room. We planned to read a children's book before lunch.

"What do you think of our new home, Leah?" I asked as we started up the last flight of stairs.

"I miss my dolls," she answered sadly.

Turning to face her, I sat down on the wooden stairs. She cuddled up beside me, and I hugged her, pulling her close. "I know, honey. I miss my things too." I paused, and for a minute we sat silently together on the stairs. There could be no way to explain the sense of loss I felt leaving behind everything and everyone I loved. Perhaps it was like being the only survivor of a plane crash. "But we're safe here," I said at last, squeezing her gently. "For now, that's the important thing." I took her hand, and we stood, starting up the stairs again.

But there was something more, something I couldn't put my finger on. Yes, we'd lost everything. Leah her dolls. RJ his father. I'd lost my closest friend and all the security I believed I could not live without. I had no home. No family. No money. The loss left me feeling heavy. Dead. Leaden. But I felt something more than loss. What was it?

Just as we arrived on the third floor, it hit me. This place was scary and confining, unlike any place I'd ever lived before. Still, I felt stronger here. Much stronger. As I stood on the landing, I think I realized that we would find a way. This was the difference. Hope was the difference.

Seventeen

WE LIVED THREE WEEKS in Dorcas House before I began to consider the little third floor room our home. Leah made the transition more easily. She joined a small group of elementary students who rode to school every day in a dilapidated minivan driven by Jolette. Soon after we arrived, we had her cast removed at a local health clinic, which pleased her very much. She had friends, a household routine, and school. Though she complained occasionally about missing her daddy, she smiled freely and talked incessantly. Leah came to terms with our new situation far more quickly than I.

Strangely enough, I knew I'd finally come to appreciate Dorcas House only after our new roommate moved in. Annaleigh, a slim beautiful black woman with lovely almond-shaped eyes, came to live with us after being beaten unconscious by her boyfriend. She was pregnant, though still in the becomingly padded stage. Annaleigh's perfect skin and beautiful hair, which she wore in miniature braids cut to a perfect bob, gave her the look of a fashion model. Leah loved her, and Annaleigh became "Auntie Lee" long before the end of her first week in our suite.

Annaleigh had no other children, and she freely expressed her fear of babies. I encouraged her whenever I could and let her practice her mothering skills on RJ. At first she picked him up with the gentle reverence of an archeological artifact ready to disintegrate with the slightest jostling. With time, she grew into the easy grace that becomes motherhood.

Though Annaleigh's boyfriend put her in the intensive care unit, she resented Dorcas House. Before long, she took every private opportunity to belittle the rules, the house, and the women who lived there. Especially critical of Oleda, she rarely missed a chance to berate her. "Have you ever seen such a fat woman?" she whispered one evening in our room. "And really, so much jewelry. A hippo would know better than to wear all that stuff hanging everywhere."

I tried to be tolerant of Annaleigh's criticism, but when it came to Oleda, I could not. I refused to let her badmouth the woman who had become my beloved friend. "No one is perfect," I answered Annaleigh. "Oleda loves food."

"That's much more than love, honey. That is adoration."

"Well, maybe her body is a little big, but so is her heart," I said, growing angry. "She works hard here. She gives us every bit of energy she's got." I slapped a diaper onto my bed and shifted RJ into my other arm. "You should be grateful for who she is—not what she looks like." I changed RJ's diaper roughly.

"Well, excuse me," Annaleigh said. "I didn't realize you were her personal defender."

"I'm not." I walked to the door. "I just thought since you're only alive because of Oleda, you might be more grateful." I left the room, closing the door with exaggerated care. I needed time to cool off. By the time I reached the bottom stair, I realized for myself how much I appreciated our new home. This place had saved me physically, of course, but more than that, I'd begun to find my first glimmer of hope here. Hope that I could survive. Hope that I could be a whole person, even without Russell. Hope that I could make a happy life for myself in spite of the terrible things I'd been through. Life hadn't ended for me, and I had Oleda to thank for drilling that into my consciousness.

I participated in house activities, though reluctantly at first. I went to Bible studies, to group sessions, and to private sessions with Oleda. I tried hard to do my homework, to read the items assigned.

The whole environment included much soul searching. As to the issues of violence, I participated enthusiastically. As to issues of a religious nature, I tolerated them. I did not want to experience God. Not now. I had been through too much pain. I felt overwhelmed and exhausted. I was putting all my energy into getting well, caring for the children, and planning for a future outside of Dorcas. I'd come this far. I would never go back.

As I listened and read, I discovered how many clues I'd overlooked in the early days of my relationship with Russ. I should have seen his love for his mother for what it was—not devotion, but a peculiar derangement. I recognized his transferring medical schools to be close to her, his dressing me for his mother's party— things I saw at the time as sweet—were truly warnings of an unhealthy relationship. And I remembered the early signs of control and jealousy—choosing my food for me at restaurants, his outburst when he found the symphony conductor at the house. More than anything, these memories made me feel horribly foolish, as though I had wanted to see Russell as Prince Charming, when he was something far different. The signs were there for all to see, but I'd been blind to the truth. I felt stupid and angry with myself for being so easily fooled.

One of our studies centered on the issue of forgiveness. My anger with Russell burned like an ulcer through my every waking moment. Not only had he hurt me physically and forced me to leave everything I valued behind, but he had conned me. The Russell I fell in love with was nothing like the man I lived with. I could never forgive his deliberate deception. Not ever.

I think too that part of me feared the issue of forgiveness. If I forgave Russell, then what? Constant resentment, bitterness, and anger provided the energy that drew me through the day. My anger gave me strength, fight. If I let go, what then? I feared forgiveness for another reason as well. I think I believed that forgiveness meant getting back together. Living with Russell cost too much to try it again.

For my required house chore, I chose to help in the kitchen, preparing the noon and evening meals. I functioned as a sort of ancillary cook, making salads, slicing fruit, or preparing sandwiches. Being part of the kitchen crew helped me to "belong" to this oddly mismatched group. No longer just the woman on the third floor, I became part of a team, and the team worked together with the precision of—well, not water ballet, certainly—perhaps rugby. Every time we served a meal, we felt we'd won a tournament.

Eventually I decided to apply for welfare, a very difficult step for me. I'd never received anything from the government, and I battled with my own pride as I faced the Department of Social and Health Services with Oleda. On a stormy Tuesday morning, Oleda and RJ and I drove into town in her little green Honda. She promised to stick with me through every step of the whole procedure.

Parking the car, she said, "Now, honey, I've been here a thousand times before. It won't be so bad." She got out and walked around the front of the car. I took a deep breath and followed. Oleda wore a black wool cape that billowed in the wind like a giant flag. On her head perched a handsome black fedora, which she held smashed down with a gloved hand. Oleda leaned heavily into gusting wind and gestured to me to follow along. I joined her just as she opened the glass door into an air lock. Inside, we smoothed our windblown clothes, took a deep breath, and entered the lobby.

Immediately we faced an electronic sign directing us to "Take a Number." I found the button labeled New Applicants, punched the knob, and pulled a piece of paper from the machine. Checking the number "Now Being Served," I realized that seventeen applicants already preceded me. How lucky. We found seats in the black wire chairs lining the room.

Oleda unwrapped herself from her cape, sat down, and opened her Day-Timer. Picking up an enormous black Bible, she began to work on her own study. I tried to focus on a four-year-old *People* magazine while RJ dozed in my arms. Every so often, Oleda leaned back, took off her reading glasses, and massaged her brows and forehead. At these moments she mumbled to herself in deep, reverent tones. Nearly always after this lengthy chain of events, Oleda would suddenly remember me, reach over, and pat my knee.

"Gonna be jus' fine, sweetie," Oleda crooned before disappearing again into her big black book. She continued to read and write, oblivious to the stares of others.

Try as I might, I couldn't focus on my magazine. Mostly, I watched people. I observed all kinds of clients, including some who matched my own stereotypical ideas about welfare recipients. Too many children. Poor education. Unclean. When I heard the call of my own number, I realized with burning heat in my cheeks just how far my own prejudice ran. I nudged Oleda and handed RJ, now awake, to her. No longer could I view these people as "those welfare people." Now one of them, my pride dropped several notches before I ever reached the man at the counter.

Impersonally, he directed me to a large room where rows of desks held social workers typing furiously at computer keyboards. I followed my host to an old laminate-topped metal desk, behind which sat a young man who looked to be fresh from college. From behind his desk, he motioned me to a folding chair beside him. With a Tweety Bird tie and denim shirt, he wore his hair parted down the middle, gelled into slick submission.

"Name," he demanded without looking up. I answered, slowly spelling Koehler for him.

"Address." His was not a question but a statement. A demand. I gave him the post office box of Dorcas House. He typed the information into his keyboard with the speed of a turtle sunbathing on a beach, using only his index fingers.

His questioning continued for several minutes, then he stated in a dispassionate monotone, "Marital status."

"Married."

For the first time, he stopped and looked up at me as though he had not heard. "Married?"

"Yes, but separated."

He nodded, typed a letter or two, and hit the Enter key several times. "Husband's name."

Alarms rang in my brain. Wait a minute! Why did he need to know my husband's name? Where was all this information going anyway? Suddenly I realized—a computer! Anyone can find anything on a computer, couldn't they? Could Russ use this information to find us?

"I can't tell you."

"Excuse me?" It seemed Tweety had never been refused.

"You see . . ." I hesitated, looking around cautiously. Could someone overhear us? I dropped my voice to a whisper. "I am living at a safe house so that my husband can't find us." I lowered my eyes, filled with shame. "He's violent."

The young man sighed, though not a compassionate sigh. It sounded more like, "Oh man, here we go again." Pushing his chair away from the desk, he crossed one foot over his other knee. Without speaking he tugged at his white athletic sock, then leaned back to lace his fingers together across his lap.

"Well, I guess it's up to you. But in order to provide benefits for your children, we must have information about their father." He shrugged to indicate his own helplessness in the situation. "The state retains the right to pursue paternal responsibility where necessary."

After a pause, he used his long fingers to pull himself back to his desk. "Of course, in cases like yours, they almost always respect the need for secrecy. Naturally, none of the information you relay will be given to your husband."

Fear still held me, clutching at my heart, squeezing my stomach. What if Russ found a way to access this information? He could. Russell was very clever. He was rich. He had more resources than I could ever access. My body moved into panic mode, beginning with the telltale pain in my gut.

"There is one other alternative." The social worker held up an index finger. "If I had an order of protection, we could enter your name by code into the computer. We use an alias. It would provide an additional measure of privacy and virtually insure that your husband could never access you via these files."

"But I don't have an attorney."

"You don't need one for a protection order. You can start the process at the county courthouse." He picked up a small manual filled with laminated pages. "I'll write down the phone number.

They have trained counselors to deal with these kinds of situations." For the first time he looked into my eyes. "Then when you come back to see me, I can virtually guarantee your complete privacy."

"Thank you." I stood and took the card from his hand.

"You're welcome." He smiled and stuck out his hand in an uncomfortable attempt at closure. "I'll store your information in my own system until I see you again." We shook hands. "I hope I've helped you—at least a little."

I turned to go. "Wait, Mrs. Koehler," he said. Surprised, I faced him again. "I just want to warn you," he said quietly. "In cases like this, if you really suspect that you are in danger—and only you can tell—be very careful." I nodded. He pointed at the parking lot. "These men can be very clever, very devious. We've even had them stake out our parking lot, watching for wives and girlfriends. More than once we've had to call the police to get them off our property." He smiled again, this time with genuine concern. "Please be careful."

"So how'd it go?" Oleda asked as she pulled out of the parking lot. I didn't answer immediately. I'd begun to imagine a new and horrifying scenario. While we waited at the intersection in front of the welfare office, I carefully examined every car in the lot. Did one of them belong to an informant? Was Russell watching me now— even here?

"All right." I counted the cars in the lot. "I didn't apply for benefits."

Oleda stole a quick surprised glance and changed gears. "Why not, honey?"

"He told me he couldn't code my name in the computer unless I had a protection order."

"But we talked about that. You refused to get one."

"I know. All I ever wanted was to disappear. I just hoped I could be safe until he forgets us."

"And now?" Between shifting gears and watching traffic, Oleda kept one eye on my face, studying my expressions.

"I think Russell has become an enemy I have to face. A ghost who won't go away until I face him. Until I tell the truth." I sighed, choking back a rush of tears.

She patted my knee, her own eyes shining.

"Oleda, on that first night I came to Dorcas, you said I had to apply for welfare and that I had to turn the money over to the house."

"Right."

"What if I don't go on welfare? How long can I stay before you have to throw me out?"

"I don't think 'throw you out' is the way we want to put it."

"You know what I mean," I answered with impatience. "You can't have me freeloading. How long before I run out of time?"

"Four more weeks. I have emergency authority for eight weeks. Our board of directors has given me very clear rules. After eight weeks, my hands are tied."

"Four weeks isn't very long. But I have a college degree. I ought to be able to get a job."

"As a teacher?"

"Never as a teacher. Too many people would know where I am—all the kids and their parents, administration, faculty. Way too many people to keep quiet." I thought for a moment. "No, nothing with children. That would be the first place Russ would look for me. No, I have to find something else." I thought hard, chewing on the end of my thumb, oblivious to passing traffic. "Then, with any luck at all, I can get out on my own."

"That frightens me." She paused to negotiate a difficult inter-section. "I don't know if you're ready to be on your own yet."

"I have to be. I don't have time to coddle myself."

"All right. You think some more, and I'll pray mighty hard on it. I'll help you where I can. That's my job." She changed lanes, moving deftly around a stalled truck. "But listen to me, Patricia. There's lots more to living alone than supporting yourself. You've been through more than physical abuse—your soul is wounded, honey. And it takes time, lots of time, for soul wounds to heal. In fact"—she glanced at my face again—"I think those are the hardest wounds to heal. Do you understand me, honey?"

"I'm going to need an attorney. I can't fight Russell without help."

"I don't think you're listenin'." She slammed on the brakes as a traffic light turned yellow.

"Of course I am. I just don't have time to worry about the inside. I've got to get on my feet. I have to make it on my own."

"We have some attorney fellas who work with the womens at the house," she suggested.

"But I can't afford one—not someone who could beat Russell."

"These guys give away their work." She paused, then asked, "He'd really try to do you in?"

How could I explain Russell to this woman? Who could possibly understand the cool, calculated, and unswervingly determined man he was? "He'll want to crush me." My voice revealed a certain, restrained dread. I knew what lay ahead, knew with as much certainty as a woman who faces her sixth childbirth.

Yes. Russell, who loved with such absolute abandon, would certainly want to completely annihilate me.

"Well, then, we'd better go back to the house and make a phone call or two." Oleda laughed. "You're the first girl we've ever had at the house who could make a decent salad. I don't want nothin' to happen to you."

We rode to the house in silence.

At home I went upstairs with RJ, determined to nurse him and let him enjoy a nap in his own bed. My poor boy had been shuffled around all morning, and his fatigue manifested itself in inconsolable crying. I felt exhausted too. Perhaps I could do my group lesson while he napped. Or better, I might take a little nap myself.

As I opened the door to our suite, I knew immediately something was wrong. Someone had stripped Annaleigh's bed, folding the blankets and bedspread neatly over her pillow. The closet door stood open, exposing the bare shelf where she kept her books and personal items. Panicked, I looked under the bed and searched the bathroom. Everything—slippers, toothbrush, makeup, shampoo— had disappeared. While we were in town, Annaleigh moved out.

Grabbing a fresh diaper for RJ, I threw him against my hip and ran downstairs to Oleda's office. The door to the outer office stood ajar, though Jolette seemed to have gone home. I slipped through the passageway into Oleda's office and found her sitting behind her desk, her shoulders sagging from behind. I knocked gently on the doorframe.

"Come in." Discouragement hung heavy in her voice.

I tiptoed in and sat quietly on the same Queen Anne chair I had chosen on my first night. Oleda stared out the window, her chin resting on one hand, the long fingernails of the other absently drumming on the desk. Her eyes told me she had gone very far away.

"Oleda," I began quietly.

"I know, honey," she said to the window. Her fingers flicked a small piece of paper across the desk. I picked up the paper, sick with dread, knowing without reading what it said. I recognized the bold artistic scrawl of Annaleigh's handwriting.

> *Dear Dorcas House,*
>
> *Thank you for allowing me to live with you over the past two weeks. I appreciate all your help. However, I cannot stay. I love Jamahl, and I have to go back. He says it will never happen again, and I have to believe him. I have to try.*
>
> > *Love,*
> > *Annaleigh*

I looked up to find Oleda, shoulders slumped, eyes wet with unshed tears, still staring out the window.

"Maybe she'll come back," I suggested hopefully.

"Maybe." Oleda shrugged. "Maybe not."

Eighteen

UNDER THE LOOMING DEADLINE imposed by the board of Dorcas House, I spent every day of the following week combing the want ads. I needed a job that assured both privacy and security. Because I would not teach, my college degree didn't count for much, but even a minimum-wage job would get me started. I planned to contribute my paycheck to Dorcas House and live there as long as they would allow. After making what seemed like an endless line of phone calls, I decided the time had come to begin interviewing in person.

Oleda brought me an interview outfit. Unfortunately, her selection came from the closet of a woman slightly taller than I, though about the same circumference. The resulting effect was that of clothes suspended on a slightly shrunken frame. On Monday morning while I dressed in this unknown woman's hand-me-downs, I fought with my wandering mind. I missed the lovely garments in my closet on Cummins Island. Beautiful wool suits, tailored silk pants and jackets—all manner of suitable clothes for interviewing hung there. But that was then. This was now. I forced my thoughts back to the present.

I borrowed Oleda's Honda and drove into town. I began with a law firm that, regrettably, had filled their vacancy. I progressed to a research firm, but they wanted someone with experience to answer their phones. One office after another turned me down, either because the job had been filled or because my experience was inappropriate. Most of the interviewers were gracious. Noting that I'd finished college, they asked boldly why I chose not to teach. Hearing my answer, they promptly refused to give me a job. My most amazing refusal came from a company whose personnel manager told me that the company did not hire persons "living in a group home." I didn't bother to respond to that one.

Exhausted, I returned empty-handed to Dorcas House. That evening I carefully hand washed the blouse I'd worn and hung it to dry. I would find a job, I told myself firmly. Given enough time, I could make it happen. But did I have enough time?

The next day I borrowed Oleda's Honda again. "Honey," Oleda called as I turned to leave her office, "that car needs gas." She reached under her desk and pulled a battered vinyl handbag into her lap. "Would you do me the favor of fillin' it, please? And while you're at it, fill yourself up. You missed lunch yesterday, I noticed. And, honey, you aren't big enough to miss many lunches." She chuckled at her own joke.

Gratefully I accepted her money. "Do you want me to buy gas some place special?"

"Nah. That ol' thing'll run on anything." She waved her hand at me. "Just be sure to put real food in you, though. None o' that cheap stuff."

I thanked her and headed for the front door. On my second day out, I went through all the same motions. Unfortunately, I had the same results. I began losing hope, wondering if perhaps I couldn't do this. Maybe I shouldn't try. Though I knew I would never go back to Russell, perhaps I should just give up on keeping my location a secret. Maybe I should use my own resources and do the best I could to safeguard my children and myself. I decided to look into a protection order.

Just after noon I drove to the parking lot behind the County-City building. After walking through a metal detector, submitting to a weapons inspection and a search of my purse, I spent the rest of the afternoon wandering through the various offices in the department of Domestic Violence.

I'd never been inside the courthouse before, and I was unprepared for the immensity of the building and the vast numbers of people there—some obviously lawyers, others obviously criminals, and hundreds of people who fell somewhere in between. At every desk I waited in line. I presented myself with as much decorum as I could muster under the circumstances, but I couldn't shake the feeling that Patricia Koehler had become just another case. Another woman with a jerk husband. Please take a number.

On a large poster, the legal advisor at the Domestic Violence office boasted free appointments. Her schedule, posted outside the office door, consisted of a sheet of notebook paper neatly divided into fifteen-minute slots. Twenty-four handwritten names, in diverse colors and shapes, completely filled the schedule. Women, some with children, some children themselves, waited with varying shades of patience in secondary school desks lining the outside hallway. The legal aid counselor, completely booked until the following afternoon, had no time for me.

In the Domestic Violence Advocate Office, I stood at the counter while a chubby-faced man in jeans and Birkenstocks ignored me for nearly ten minutes. After he made notes to himself, answered the phone, spoke to a co-worker, filed his papers, and walked to his desk to retrieve his coffee cup, he finally spoke to me. "May I help you?"

Not in this lifetime. "Yes, I'd like to speak to someone about filing for a protection order."

He nodded. "Sure, I'll get an advocate to speak with you." He turned to face a doorway behind him and began entering a security code on an oversized digital pad. Suddenly he turned back to me. "Take a seat. She'll be right out." Before I turned away, I noticed that he blocked the security pad from my view while he finished punching in the code. A light over the door turned green. With a shove on the handle, he opened the door and disappeared.

I scanned the waiting area and chose a desk in the corner farthest from the counter. *Calm down*, I told myself. *Russell isn't here. He isn't going to find you here. You haven't done anything yet. Asking questions isn't illegal.* Still, my hands grew damp and my breathing quickened until I felt that terrifying feeling of being in a room without air. Panic hit full force. Just as I was about to flee, a thick security door opened into the waiting room. A young woman stuck her platform shoe under the door, propping it open, while she addressed me matter-of-factly, "Are you waiting to see me?"

"I don't really know," I stuttered, looking around the room. Other women studied me curiously. She hadn't addressed me by name. I spoke softly, "I wanted to see about a restraining thing." My growing insecurity killed the proper terms in my brain before they could reach my lips.

She smiled encouragingly. "Come in." Still blocking the door with one shoe, she moved slightly and waved me toward the inner chamber. Fear nearly froze me to my chair. What was I doing here? Was this the right thing? Who was this woman? Could I trust her?

I passed in front of her murmuring, "Thank you." Beyond the door, I found myself inside a vaultlike room, in which every wall was lined by bookcases filled with color-coded files, much like the patient files in Russell's office. I stepped aside, so she could again take the lead, and followed her down a hallway to an office so small that it held only one desk and two chairs. She maneuvered around the extra chair to her own and sat down. She waited until I was comfortably seated before she nodded almost imperceptibly at the door. Responding to the unspoken cue, I closed the door behind me without moving from my chair.

"Well," she began, lacing her fingers together above the desk. "Tell me why you've come to see me."

No introduction. No warm-up. She went right to work, this woman.

I read her name tag. *Denise Sherrington*. Denise, with soft white skin. *So, Denise, am I just another victim to you?*

"I need to file papers," I said, faking confidence, determined not to blunder in front of her. "I need to keep my husband away from us."

"Away from us?" Her eyebrows rose ever so slightly behind her glasses. She crossed her legs, leaned back in her chair, and removed the lid from a water bottle. She took a long swig of springwater.

"From all of us. My children and me."

"I see. Tell me why you think you need legal protection." She picked up a ball-point pen and began taking notes on a yellow legal pad. Occasionally she stopped long enough to drink more water, each time unscrewing and replacing the plastic cap. "You don't mind if I drink while we visit? I had an early workout at the gym this morning."

Why didn't she just drink the thing and get it over with?

I nodded politely and continued my story, working hard to omit unnecessary details—to appear logical, unemotional. When I'd finished, she placed the cap on her pen and leaned back in her chair.

"Now, Mrs. Koehler, I know this is hard to talk about." She pushed her glasses up the bridge of her nose. "But at this point, I need to ask a few difficult questions. You must answer me as honestly as you can. I can only help if you answer with complete candor." She pointed her skinny index finger at me. "Is that all right?"

I nodded.

"You say that during the last episode, your husband's beating sent your daughter to the hospital."

I nodded again.

"Did you seek treatment for your own injuries at this time?"

"No."

"Did you tell anyone at the hospital that your husband caused your daughter's injuries?"

"No, I didn't."

"Why not?" she asked quietly, peering at me through the thick lenses of her glasses, her eyes tiny and distant. "Why didn't you tell the truth?"

"I was afraid. I thought that the authorities would take the children away from me." Suddenly shame and fear washed over me with the same intensity I'd felt on that day at the hospital.

"But, Mrs. Koehler, if your husband was the perpetrator, why would the authorities take the children from you?"

"I don't know. I thought they might blame me for being with him." I wiped tears from my cheeks. She lifted a Kleenex box from her desk and held it for me. "Thank you."

"Did anyone take pictures of the injuries?"

"There were X rays."

"No, I mean of you. Of the bruises you say he gave you."

"I don't think so." I blew my nose softly. "No. I mean, no." I took a deep breath. Why did I feel so guilty? "One woman, a nurse, listened to the baby's heartbeat." My stomach wrenched with nervous acid. "She told the doctor she saw bruises. At least that's what the surgeon said."

"But to your knowledge, no one wrote it down. No one took pictures. And you never reported any other incident?"

"No. You don't understand. Serenity Bay is a small place. No one would believe me."

"I do understand," she said firmly. "The 'good ol' boys' club is alive and well in many parts of the country." She sighed and swiveled back to face her legal pad. "Well, all right. This certainly makes things harder. But I'll help you fill out the paper work. If you still want to do so, we'll file for the protection order. I don't think it will be a problem."

"When will it happen?"

"Well, it could be served some time in the next two days. I have two deputies who work for our department. The important thing, though, is that you file your copy with the police department closest to your current residence so that you are certain they know the order is in effect."

"All right."

"There is one other thing you need to know." She finished writing and looked directly at me. "When these kinds of papers are served, sometimes guys go a little berserk. Some of them come after their wives in anger. Others decide that they can make the whole thing go away by trying to win the lady back." She took another drink from her water bottle. "You need to be prepared for anything. Stay alert. Never travel anywhere alone—at least for the next week or so." She stood, apparently finished with our interview. "If you don't want him to find you, then assume that he is everywhere. Pay attention to every detail. You'll be fine." She nodded again, took some notes. "Do you have any questions?"

"Yes. Just one." I had not stood, and reluctantly she sat again. "I need to know. How can I keep him from taking the children?"

"That's a question for the legal advocate. Have you seen her yet?" She pointed through the wall as though we could see the legal aide at work.

"Not yet. She's all booked up."

Denise raised her chin slightly, acknowledging the aide's impossible schedule. "Well, I can tell you this. Most of the time, a protection order has no effect on the issue of child custody, at least in and of itself. That is another battle you'll have to face." She put her pen down for a moment. "All I can say is that you can't fight about that fairly if you live under the constant threat of his attack. A protection order is the first step. Then you can move on from there."

The thought of losing the children took my breath away, and I sat there, unable to move, almost gasping for air, as though I'd been kicked in the chest.

Denise Sherrington nodded again toward the door.

I stood and obediently opened her door, knowing the process was finished. She stuck out her hand. "I'll call you when I hear the papers have been served." It was the most personal thing she said.

Safely inside Oleda's car I checked the digital clock she'd hot-glued onto her dashboard. Only three o'clock. Funny. It seemed as though weeks had passed in the advocate's office. After living on an emotional edge through the whole day, I felt completely drained. I decided to stop for coffee on the way home. I needed a break, some time by myself before I went home to face my daughter, a house full of women, and Oleda.

I parked near a dilapidated storefront café and went in to find a seat. An old, worn-out woman, whose hair looked like a cheap wig from the Salvation Army, showed me to a seat in a window booth.

"No, not here," I objected, perhaps too loudly, though I saw no other customers.

"All right." She drew out the words, putting one hand on her bony hip. Speaking cynically, as if I'd declared her choice unclean, she asked, "Which one, then?" She gestured to the room of empty tables.

I hesitated, looked around, and sized up the tiny restaurant. To the left of the cash register, wooden stairs ascended into black emptiness above. Tucked between the stairs and the wall, in the relative obscurity of a corner, stood a small one-customer table on which a tiny table lamp rested. From there I could watch the exit, yet remain invisible to the sidewalk. Denise's warning had already taken hold.

"There," I pointed. "That one would be fine."

She shrugged and slapped a worn plastic-coated menu onto the little table. The lampshade jiggled in protest. Embarrassed, I realized that I'd angered the old lady. I sat down and opened the menu, but the words swirled out of focus. Tears obscured my vision.

This whole day had been too much for me. Too much rejection. Too much honesty. Too much fear. I'd planned to live happily ever after. I'd never envisioned myself hiding in some hole-in-the-wall restaurant, with no job, no home, and no prospects. The old woman returned, wiping her greasy hands on a kitchen towel tied around her waist. "Coffee?"

I nodded and looked away. I couldn't bear any more.

She brought a cup and saucer in one hand, a carafe in the other. Filling the cup to the brim with dark rich coffee, she set it in front of me. As she turned to go, she put her bony hand on my shoulder and patted gently. This small token of affection became the hole in my emotional dam. Pushing the saucer away, I laid my face on my forearms and began to weep, letting go completely. After all, who would ever witness this small act of complete surrender? Why should I care what the old woman thought? I had come to my own end, to complete and utter humiliation.

I don't know how long I cried like that, but eventually the grief seemed to work its way out, and whether by exhaustion or cleansing, I came at last to the end of my tears. I didn't move, though. Still facing the wall, my head on my arms, I breathed the long shuddering breaths of the broken. At last I sat up, brushed the tears from my face, and blew my nose—hard—into the table napkin. It was quite a honk. When I lifted cold coffee to my lips, I saw her.

The old woman sat at a table across from me with knees crossed,

smoking a cigarette, waiting patiently. She caught my eye, stubbed
out her cigarette, and asked simply, "Are you finished now?"

I nodded, feeling my face burn, and wondered how long she'd
been there waiting silently like that. She took my coffee cup and
returned immediately with another, this time steaming hot. She
pulled a chair up to the table.

"So tell me about it," she said. Not really an invitation, the
woman issued a command.

"I can't." I took a swig of the coffee. It burned my mouth, my
throat, my stomach. I winced.

"It's hot, honey. Be careful." She lit another cigarette and
pulled an ashtray from behind the napkin dispenser. "You think I
haven't heard everything working here?" She gestured, dripping
ashes across the table.

Of course she had. My story wasn't special. If nothing else, I had
learned that lesson today. There were so many other stupid wives
out there that one solitary legal advocate couldn't see them all. Certainly this ancient woman had known her share of foolish females.
I started, slowly at first, and then with growing momentum, I confessed everything. My Prince Charming had become Jekyll and
Hyde, and one of the two wanted to kill me.

She let me wander through my story without interruption.
While I talked, she smoked, brushed away ashes, and smoked some
more. Normally smoke bothers me, but here, in the midst of my
own confession, it seemed appropriate—like penance for my own
simple-minded foolishness. I accepted the acrid punishment without objection.

"So what'll you do now?"

"I don't know." I blew my nose. "I still have to find a job. Then,
when I can, I have to move out of the house. And I have to decide
whether or not to apply for welfare." I shrugged, the gesture of the
completely defeated. "I have to live my own life. Whatever it takes,
I have to survive on my own."

She listened, then gazed back through the storefront window to
the sidewalk. Workers heading home for the evening hurried by un-
concerned. She sat watching the sidewalk in the fading afternoon

sunlight until I thought she might have forgotten me. Then without warning she stubbed out her cigarette and looked directly at me. Her expression grew intense, the lines in her worn face deepened.

"I need a waitress here," she said simply, "but I can't afford to pay . . . even minimum wage." She lit another cigarette, and when it was glowing satisfactorily, she pointed the glowing tip at me. "I have a one-bedroom apartment upstairs. Furnished, sort of." She puffed. "If you'll take that as payment for a forty-hour week, you can keep your tips."

I didn't know how to respond. The tumbledown restaurant had not had one customer the entire time I'd been there. No one could live on those kinds of tips.

Reading my mind, she said, "Not many people in here during the afternoon. But I do a land office breakfast shift. Turn tables like falling leaves." Her excitement over her own proposal grew. She reached up and vigorously scratched a flat place where her gray hair swirled around a cowlick. "I get real busy in the late afternoon too. Single fellas eat here instead of going home to frozen dinners. They'd be happy to tip a pretty little thing like you."

Was this my answer? Had I stumbled into this decrepit place to find my salvation? Could I trust this crusty old woman? Would she keep the grand promises she'd made?

"I'd like to see the apartment," I answered simply.

Nineteen

BY THE TIME I RETURNED to Dorcas House, the sun had set. But my preoccupation with the potential for work and a life out of the safe house kept me from paying attention to the time. I hadn't called Oleda.

When I turned off the main highway onto the gravel, I spotted a police cruiser parked in our driveway. Suddenly I wished I'd phoned. Oleda had obviously called the police to report me as a missing person. I parked quickly and rushed inside, expecting to be met by Oleda's warm hug and loving chastening.

Instead, I found the front hall cold and empty. None of the usual sounds or smells of dinner came from the kitchen. The women of the house seemed hidden, with a strange quiet echoing through the lower floors. I knew instantly that something was very wrong. Hearing voices in Oleda's office, I stepped to the door and raised my hand to knock. Before my fist struck the wood, I recognized Oleda sitting with her back to me, crying heavily. Husky deep sobs escaped her throat as she gasped for air.

"Oleda, I'm home!" I expected my announcement to end her tears immediately. When she looked up, instead of relief I saw distress in every feature and tears streaming down her face.

"Oh, Patricia," she said, and added almost as an afterthought, "thank you for checking in."

"What is it? What's happened?"

Two uniformed officers occupied the chairs across from her desk. They shifted slightly and glanced out the window, apparently uncomfortable with Oleda's unrestrained expression of sorrow. "What's happening?" My voice rose to panic. Leah? Had something happened to my children?

Oleda stood, clutching an embroidered hankie in her right hand, and stepped toward me, folding me into her scented embrace. "Patricia, these men came to ask about Annaleigh. They say she's dead." Oleda locked me in her arms, rocking ever so slightly as she cried. "They found her body this afternoon." Ignoring the men, we both dissolved into tears.

The officers had come, they said, to ask me a few questions. Since I had been Annaleigh's roommate, they thought I might have information they needed. Just a simple gathering of facts and background. Yes, Oleda could stay with me.

I sat in a heavy wooden chair near Oleda's desk, her hand lightly covering mine as I spoke. Somehow I managed to survive the interview, answering their questions as though from a distant country. No, she hadn't argued with anyone here. Yes, she did say her boyfriend had beaten her. Yes, she told me the baby was his. No, I didn't know of any other enemies. No, I'd never met the boyfriend. Yes, I'd seen his picture. Yes, that was him.

When it was over, I rescued RJ from Maria's loving embrace and went upstairs to nurse him. Having been gone all day, my breasts were full, hard and aching, beginning to leak. I needed the baby, not just to nurse him, but to hold him. I needed to be near life, to be needed.

We nestled in the pillows on my bed, the two of us, in quiet collaboration. Again I cried. Would grief never end? My eyes swelled beyond the help of cucumber chips, more than any herbal mask could rectify. I sat there nursing in the dark, tears dripping onto my baby's tiny face, wondering what would become of me. In that dark hour I thought of Annaleigh, of her beautiful eyes and hair. I thought of her love, her potential, all wasted by unrestrained anger. I thought of Russell, of his fury, and I realized that my own journey had only just begun.

Over the next few days, laughter temporarily left Dorcas House. Heavy with sorrow, a dense silence filled every room, every hallway, as though with the policemen's visit, the place had been transformed into a mausoleum.

Everyone felt it—that vague sense of guilt—knowing that any one of us, like Annaleigh, might have been murdered. Somehow, though, we'd survived. Every resident knew firsthand the rage that so easily becomes murder. We didn't have to guess or wonder what her last moments were like. We'd all lived through them—or moments very nearly like them.

At first I couldn't bring myself to tell Leah. But I knew the moment would come when I must. How do you explain death to a child?

In the quiet days before the funeral, while Leah was still at school, I slipped out, taking the baby with me. Back and forth I went, visiting the marble courthouse, meeting the legal advocate for domestic violence. I went so often that the police officer at the south entrance began to greet me with familiar words about the weather or the news.

Often afterward I went to the restaurant for coffee, observing the customers and my new boss, cementing my commitment to work there. I kept my plans from Oleda until after Annaleigh's funeral. Only then did I carefully outline my strategy to file for divorce and for full custody of the children. I told her that my protection order had been served, that the police near the café had copies of the filed papers, and that I had a job which would support me, at least minimally, until I could get Russell out of my life completely.

I'd explored my options with a fine-tooth comb, covering every eventuality. I hoped that my arrangements would prove my own worthiness to leave her beloved but encumbered safety.

"Well, Patricia," she said, shaking her head and leaning back in the chair. "I must say, you've done your homework." She paused, pushing aside the papers on her desk. "You've really changed since you came to us." I thought I heard a catch in her voice.

"I hope so." I blushed, thinking back to the utterly hopeless, defeated woman who'd been delivered to her doorstep just weeks ago. "When I came here, I was despondent, beaten down. I guess I should say beaten up." I released a small chuckle at my own joke. "But now I'm determined to win. I have to. I can't let my fear of Russell control the rest of my life."

"It won't be easy, honey," she said. Her long nails began their drumbeat on the desk.

"I know."

She sighed, heavy with resignation. "The worst is still to come."

"How can anything be worse than what we've been through?"

"I can't say what will be worse. I can only guess." She spun the ring on her index finger. "But I think the Lord has a bigger work still to do in you, Patricia."

"There you go again with that 'Lord' stuff," I said, frustrated. Who could argue with God? Besides, if God had such great plans for me, why didn't He get down here and let me know what they were? So far, I hadn't been able to see His loving hand in any of my circumstances. "Oleda, I want you to wish me luck. To hope for the best. I need your support, not your dire predictions of gloom."

"Patricia," she said, suddenly looking straight into my eyes, "I will do far better than 'hope for the best.' I will pray for you. Every day. God doesn't need luck." She poked the desktop for emphasis with her long artificial nails. "Nothing is luck with God," she concluded. "I know He has plans for you. I can't tell you how I know. I just do." She rubbed her forehead. "I don't say that about all the womens who come here."

I decided to interpret her words as a forecast of success.

Until the end of May, I worked at the little restaurant three days a week, learning the ropes, getting used to the customers. Mildred, the old lady with the polyester-looking hair, rewarded my first hours on the job by instructing me to call her Millie. "That's the name my friends use," she said, scraping grease away from the grill.

Millie turned out to be the owner of the little café, as well as the cook, hostess, bookkeeper, menu planner, purchaser, and maker of all the homemade pies. She worked tirelessly from four in the morning to closing, six days a week. Until I joined her, she had no wait staff, her last waitress having quit nearly six months before I came to work.

Millie's husband, whose only dream had been to make a go of a "Mom and Pop" restaurant, died two winters earlier while flipping pancakes. His earnings barely cleared expenses, and he died leaving Millie penniless, her survival completely dependent on a no-name diner, located between warehouses in an area of town long since abandoned by the aristocracy for latte shops and bagel franchises.

Millie lived upstairs too, in the second of two apartments over the restaurant. The upstairs hallway led from the front of the building to the rear with a stairway at each end. Millie's apartment door perched beside the landing to the dark stairway at the back.

These rear stairs opened by way of a heavy metal door onto a deserted alley. With noisy, rusty hinges, the dark green door was tucked unobtrusively into an alcove and always kept locked from the inside. Only Millie and I owned keys. The longer I worked with Millie, the more I trusted her. Though she was unkempt, smoky, and sometimes crude, she knew what I needed to survive, and she took me under her wing. She had complete confidence in me.

On the first weekend of June, Oleda herself helped me move my things into the apartment above the café. She donated sheets and loaned me enough cash to buy clothes of my own. These pieces, purchased from an estate sale near Dorcas House, looked to be the clothes of an eighty-year-old, who must have died in the midst of a Caribbean cruise. I bought the lot—white polyester pants, navy blazer, blue and white striped blouse, long baggy shorts, banded sweatshirts with appliqued flowers—for only fifteen dollars. The dead woman's daughter seemed delighted to see the stuff go. She even helped us pack it into boxes. At least the clothes fit, and in an ironic sort of way, I matched Millie. She had polyester hair, and I wore polyester clothes.

On the day I moved, Oleda stayed long enough to help make my bed and to set up the crib she bought for RJ.

"Hand me that screwdriver, honey," she said, lying on her back under the bed frame. Her large tummy barely cleared the space below the frame.

"Oleda, I didn't know you were so handy."

"Why, Patricia, you have no idea what I can do," she laughed. While I held the crib ends, Oleda screwed the sides in place. Slowly the crib took shape. At last we put a sheet on the mattress and dropped it into place on the springs.

I ran my fingers along the chipped paint at the top of the side rail. I knew Oleda purchased the crib with funds from her own hard-earned paycheck. Her gift came from her heart with much sacrifice, and I felt more grateful than I ever had been for any of Russell's extravagant gifts. "It's beautiful, Oleda."

When the time came for her to leave, Oleda wrapped me once more in her enormous embrace, as she had so many times before, and I felt her chest shudder with tears. I hugged back, squeezing hard. It hurt me to cause her pain. But I reminded myself that this mother role—of loving, guiding, and letting go—had been her choice. Still, I knew instinctively that letting go must be a constant source of anguish for Oleda.

Without another word she pressed a piece of paper into my palm and swept out the front door of the café. I looked down to find twenty dollars folded into a note. *I pray God's best for you. You can always come back. Love, Oleda.*

I would never go back. Whatever happened, I would make it by myself.

It saddened Leah to say good-bye to the other children at Dorcas House. As surrogate mother to the toddlers who lived there, Leah believed they wouldn't survive without her. The Dorcas children were far more fun than her sleepy, and as yet uninteresting, brother. She filled many hours reading to them, playing with them, and supervising their wanderings about the play porch.

Fortunately, only Leah's living arrangements changed with our move. Leah caught a bus from behind the café to attend the same school she'd attended from the safe house. The adventure of living above a real restaurant and Millie's constant friendship made the move easier for her.

By the time we settled into the apartment, only fifteen school days remained before the beginning of summer vacation. I planned to limp my way into summer and then allow Leah to help care for RJ from our apartment directly above the restaurant. I didn't know what would happen once school started again, but I refused to worry about that ahead of time. *One day at a time*, I thought.

In those days I sounded a lot like Scarlett O'Hara.

More than cooperative, Millie split my workday into small parts. In this way, she had help all through the day, especially during those hours she needed my help the most. She arranged to let me work the very early breakfast rush while RJ and Leah slept upstairs. I finished serving breakfast in time to scoot Leah out the door to catch the school bus. Then, after nursing the baby, I lugged the crib mattress downstairs, squashed it between the candy counter and the kitchen wall, and put RJ down for his morning nap. While he slept, I served the lunch crowd. Then I reset the dining room tables and took the baby back upstairs. By the time Leah came home from school, I had my own chores finished and a few moments to enjoy with her.

"Mommy, read me the book." She meant the book from Susan.

"Leah, you can read that book yourself." I sighed. "Why don't I read a chapter book with you? How about *Charlotte's Web*?"

"No, we can read that after the book."

"Why do you like this book so much?"

"I like the rhyme."

So every day after school we read the rhyming book that Susan had given Leah in the hospital. And all through the book, Leah joined in on the last line of every stanza.

> And if I lived down in the sea,
> God will live right there with me.

Or the next section:

> If I could live high in a tree,
> God would live right there with me.

Millie and I developed a system of sorts for watching the children. Whenever the action in the dining room slowed for a moment, one of us dashed upstairs to check on the kids. That was the whole system. Not exactly the ideal way to raise children, but we felt safe, and we were making it.

Leah declared that she would call Millie "Nannie," since Leah had no contact with Russell's mother. Millie responded by pampering both kids and worrying endlessly about me. Before long, she announced quite firmly that feeding us should be her responsibility. Millie definitely lost money on me.

In the meantime I proceeded to file for divorce. I knew I would never marry again, but I needed to finally and completely resolve the issue of custody. Without divorce proceedings, I knew I would forever fear the unknown. What might Russell do? When would he suddenly reappear? I desperately needed closure, and I was foolish enough to equate closure with safety. A certificate of divorce represented the finish line at the end of a long miserable race. Though the race left me exhausted and near burnout, I stubbornly reached for the finish line.

At the same time, I hoped that dissolution would end some of the financial struggle I faced. I believed the court would order Russell to pay child support. And, with any luck at all, I hoped the court would entitle me to some of our joint property.

Living above the restaurant, I actively fought against my own bitterness, though not because of Oleda's frequent warnings about the poisoning of my soul. I fought for a more practical reason. Early on, I realized that bitterness represented a waste of my most valuable resource—energy. And I had precious little energy to waste.

Over and over again I told myself that we had made it. We had a place to live and food to eat, though not much beyond that. I scrimped wherever I could, even growing out my hair to save funds. No matter how difficult things were, our survival—even just barely—took all the effort I could muster. Too tired to worry about the future and too exhausted to dwell on the past, I had enough challenge remembering which of my customers preferred decaffeinated coffee. Before I realized it, plodding through day after day like this, five more weeks passed, the weather warmed, and our summer routine had come together nicely. Leah, home for vacation, loved her role as surrogate mother.

On the second of July, Millie surprised us with an unusual announcement. "We're closing on the Fourth," she said abruptly.

"Oh?" I unscrewed the lid on a sugar container. "That's a good idea. You should take more time off."

"I thought we should all take a day off."

I nearly dropped the sugar canister. "Off?" I sat down on the bench. "Off?" I repeated blankly. "What did you have in mind?"

"Going down to the waterfront. The city plans a whole collection of old-fashioned Fourth of July activities. The place will be hopping with people and music and games. The kids'll love it. And you could use some sunshine yourself."

Her invitation delighted Leah, and on an especially beautiful summer morning, we boarded a city bus for the ride into town. We sat in long cool grass and listened to symphony music from the bandstand. We meandered among artists' booths, enjoying the work of local craftspeople. We watched men gorge themselves in a pie-eating contest. After our picnic, Leah and I listened to bluegrass bands. An especially gifted family of five played a medley of string pieces together. Just as I noticed a look of sadness slip onto Leah's features, she suddenly wanted to go buy cotton candy.

After sunset we spread Millie's quilts on the grass and sprawled out on our backs to watch fireworks. The air cooled quickly in the darkness, and we drew blankets over us, cuddling together to drive away the chill. I nursed a sleepy baby while we shivered and "oohed" and "aahed," marveling at the colorful display filling the air above us. Leah had never seen a fireworks display before, and the presentation mesmerized her. When it was all over, we wearily boarded a city bus for the long ride back to the apartment.

"Thanks, Millie," I said as we climbed the back stairs. "It was a spectacular day."

"Oh, don't thank me," she said, sounding very shy. "Pete never did like crowds. We didn't go out much. Would've missed it without you." She waited outside my door while I fished for my keys. She patted RJ's tiny diapered bottom as he slept soundly on her shoulder.

"Well, it was wonderful." I shifted Leah to my other hip and felt the key turn in the lock. I let myself in. Millie followed, turning on the light behind me. "Would you stay for tea?" I asked.

"No, dear, it's past my bedtime." She rocked the baby on her shoulder. "Just show me where I can find the baby's night things, and I'll help you put the kids to bed. You sure don't need them to wake up now."

Grateful, I led her to the little stand where I kept diapers. She slid the baby onto the table and coaxed his tiny feet from the sleeper. In the meantime, I stuffed an uncooperative Leah into her pajamas. In only a few minutes, we stood again in the hallway saying goodnight. Millie reached out and, in her bony, self-conscious way, hugged me. For once I didn't mind the smell of cigarette smoke that seemed to seep from her skin. "Sleep tight, kid," she said and waved as she disappeared down the hall.

I closed the door quietly. Tea sounded good to me, so I turned on the burner of my hot plate. While the water heated, I put on my own pajamas and brushed my teeth. I checked on the kids, and just as I tied the belt of my robe, I heard the old kettle whistle. With my tea and a book I'd found at a thrift store, I settled into the one comfortable chair in my living room. Determined to read and unwind, I opened the book. Suddenly the sound of knocking jerked me back to awareness, and I spilled cold tea onto my bathrobe. I listened, fully alert. Millie never had company. What had I heard? Was it my imagination?

No, steps. I'd heard steps and then a gentle knocking on my own door. I glanced at my wrist, wondering what time it was, and remembered I'd left my watch on the bathroom counter. Must be Millie. Millie must have forgotten something. I put my cup aside, went to the door, and opened it, expecting to see her trademark gray hair standing away from her head.

Instead, I looked squarely into Russell's aqua blue eyes.

"Hello, Pet," he said.

"Russell!" I wrapped my robe around my waist, tying the belt as tightly as I could. "What are you doing here?"

"I came to surprise you."

"Well, it's a surprise, all right." I pulled cool air in through my teeth, trying in vain to calm my racing heart. "How did you find us?"

"Aren't you going to invite me in?"

I chose not to answer. "Russell, you aren't supposed to be here." I stepped into the hallway, quietly pulling the door closed behind me. In the light of the single bare bulb, I noticed that Russell had lost weight. His face, marked by deep creases, had aged. Dark circles hung below his lovely eyes. With a pang, I realized I'd done this to him. "How did you find us?"

"Patty, aren't you glad to see me? Even a little?" His voice sounded hurt. Wounded. Childlike.

"No. I mean . . ." I drew a bigger, deeper breath. *Think, Patricia. Stay on top of this.* "Russ. You aren't supposed to contact me. I filed papers."

"I know about the papers," he said, the volume of his voice rising. "Don't you think I know about the papers? You had them served in my office. In front of everyone." He stepped back, looking wildly around the hall, running his hand through his disheveled hair. "Everyone heard him say I wasn't to contact you. The whole island thinks I'm violent, Patty. That I beat you." He moved closer, his voice suddenly threateningly soft. "How could you do that?"

This was not the cold, controlled Russell I knew. Something was different. Broken. Frightening.

"Do what, Russ?" I felt my anger rise and tried to check it. "I didn't do anything to your precious reputation. You did it yourself."

"How can you say that?" He seemed incredulous, completely baffled, as surprised as if I had declared that water ran uphill. "I love you, Patty. That's all I ever did. Of course we fought. Everyone does. You know there are no perfect marriages—"

"Be quiet, Russ," I broke in. "Don't wake the children." I stepped away from the door. "You know that ours was more than an imperfect marriage. It was dangerous." I knew that I could never win this discussion. I stopped myself and chose another tack. "Now I'm going to ask you to leave. If you don't, I'm going to go inside and call the police."

He looked surprised, wounded. "You wouldn't do that. You love me, Patty, as much as I love you. We were meant to be together." He stepped close. Menacingly close. What could I do? My fear escalated. His proclamation of love could easily end in pain, as it had many times before. I glanced around the hallway, realizing that I had nothing here to protect myself.

Russell took my shoulders in his hands, clutching hard at the muscles of my upper arms. "Patty, you have to take me back. You must." He stepped closer. Closer.

"You'd better back off, mister," Millie's gravel voice echoed off the concrete blocks of the hallway.

Still holding me, he glanced toward her. I saw him evaluate her and dismiss the threat. Still holding me, he stepped closer.

"Get out of here!" she shouted, moving forward.

"Millie, don't," I called to her from behind Russell.

"Stay out of this, old woman," Russell retorted.

I saw the flash before I registered the explosion. A bullet splintered the doorframe just inches from Russell's head. Not ten inches from mine.

Russell let go quickly, stepping back, hands high in the air. His eyes betrayed his new assessment of the old woman.

"I said, 'Get out of here,' mister," she repeated deliberately, "and I mean it."

Millie moved into the glaring light of the single bulb, and for the first time, I really saw her. She stood completely relaxed in a worn chenille bathrobe and feet bare. Funny how in moments of crisis you notice things you hadn't before. Millie wore dentures, and in the excitement of the moment, she had come into the hallway without them. Her lips sank into her jaw where her teeth should have been. In the dim light, I recognized the glint of metal. Though she hadn't remembered her teeth, she had remembered her gun.

It took Russell a few moments to realize how serious Millie was. I saw the moment of recognition and watched as a familiar hardness came over his features. "All right," he said, politely, quietly. "Patricia"—he turned to face me—"I won't give up. If you want a fight, then I'll give you a fight. I'll take you. You don't have a chance against me. I'll take the kids. I'll take everything." His voice became cold tempered steel. "I swear, I'll make you pay for this."

"Mister," Millie spoke, stepping toward us again. "I hate to point this out, but I do have a gun, and it seems to me that you are threatening this woman." She held the gun in both hands out in front of her, arms stiff, like a television cop. "Do I need to use this again?" Russell looked at her and back at me. He shook his head and calmly walked away.

As he approached the landing, Millie kept her gun aimed squarely at his head. He bounded down the stairs and through the metal door into the alley.

When I heard the door slam behind him, I slid down the door-frame in a heap.

Twenty

I SPENT THE REST OF THE WEEKEND stewing about Russell's frightening threat. Were his words simply an expression of wounded pride? *"I'll take you,"* he had said. *"I'll take the kids."* What did he mean?

The words rang over and over again in my mind. I tried not to magnify the venom I'd heard in his voice. But my imagination got the better of me. Did Russell really mean to harm me? His attorney, one from Serenity Bay, had already answered my petition for divorce. No, his was not a legal threat. This was personal. Very personal.

Russell's finding us shot my prior confidence completely, and my mind ran wild with worry. I could not sleep. Once again, I lived on antacids. I could do nothing more. I decided to play things safe. Leah and I could stay inside for a few days. We would not give Russell any opportunity to harm us.

On Monday morning I went to work downstairs as usual, though I felt jumpy and preoccupied. The bell on the front door rang as it opened and closed—just like usual. But today it seemed louder, even threatening. The regular crowd came and went for breakfast. Once, midmorning, Leah came downstairs for lemonade, and I sent her back up with the pitcher rather than have her be seen by anyone in the dining room. The real scare came during the Monday lunch rush when I stood at the end of a window booth serving a group of warehousemen. A crowd of regulars, they arrived every day in flannel shirts and work jeans, ready with teasing and laughter. I faced them, my right arm loaded to the elbow with lunch plates.

"Here's the club and soup for you, Stan." I leaned into the window seat. "And the Reuben for you, Rich. And the meatloaf . . ." I said, sliding a plate across the table. "And chili for you, Doug." I paused, wiping perspiring hands on my apron. "I'll be right back with more coffee." I turned away.

"Bring some ketchup when you come back, Patty." Rich always had ketchup with double fries for lunch. My tension expressed itself in absentmindedness. I'd forgotten to drop the bottle into my apron pocket.

"Sure, Rich." I turned back to the kitchen and nearly ran into a heavyset, gray-haired man standing at my elbow. He wore a navy twill shirt over jeans. No tie. No jacket. Only a Yankees baseball cap separated him from the customers I served every day. I'd never seen this man before.

"Excuse me, Mrs. Koehler?" His words startled me. No one in this part of town called me that.

"Yes?"

"I have some papers here for you," he said quietly, stepping back.

I must have looked frightened. Behind me, the warehousemen's boisterous conversation fell ominously silent. Their eyes skipped from me to the gray-haired stranger and back again. My heart began to pound relentlessly, viscously. When I reached out to accept the flat manila envelope he held forward, my hand trembled visibly.

"Thank you," I said weakly, feeling suddenly very dizzy.

"You all right, Pat?" The bulky longshoreman in the aisle seat made a move to stand, as if to defend my honor. The gesture warmed me, and I put a hand on his shoulder.

"Fine, Doug." I smiled. Taking a deep breath, I bit my lower lip to stop the quivering. "Everything is fine," I whispered. My eyes filled with tears.

Something in the deliveryman's features relaxed when I spoke to Doug. He tipped his navy blue cap and smiled sympathetically, relieved that I had not made a scene. "Sorry, ma'am," he said gently. Turning, he walked briskly toward the door and left, leaving only the bell above the door ringing behind him.

Mechanically I went to the counter and retrieved a ketchup bottle. Still clutching the envelope, I delivered ketchup to the table. Without a word, I smiled and nodded. My mind focused only on the feel of the packet in my hand.

I went to the same small table where I'd sat when I first met Millie and fell trembling into the empty seat. With shaking fingers I tried to open the envelope clasp. The package had been sealed, and I slipped my fingers underneath the flap. Tugging mightily, the envelope gave way with a ragged tear.

Inside I found legal papers and scanned them lightly, eagerly, anxiously. I could read carefully some other time. For now, I needed to know what the latest fight would be. What now? What horror had Russell conjured up now?

I didn't need a lawyer to explain these papers. Russell had upped the ante. Not only had he countered my action, Russell wanted sole custody of the children. Suddenly dizzy, I dropped my head onto the table.

"What is going on out there, Patty?" Millie called over the serving counter. "I got lunches ready to go out. You gettin' lazy on me?"

I didn't answer.

"You okay?" A gray cloud of hair appeared around the corner of the kitchen bar.

"No," I said quietly. "I've just been kicked in the teeth."

She came quickly to the table and, leaning over me, asked, "What is it? What has he done now?" She massaged my shoulders.

I stood and wiped the tears from my cheeks. Squeezing her forearm lightly, I said, "We have lunch to finish. Then we can talk."

In spite of my own emotional turmoil, I managed to continue serving lunch, making salads, and pouring coffee. My face ached with the effort of a frozen smile. When the restaurant finally emptied again, Millie insisted I go speak with the legal advocate at the

County-City building. "You need to understand all of this balder-dash." She lit a cigarette and took a long puff. "Now, you go on down there, and I'll watch RJ and Leah." She shook the glowing stick at me, dripping ashes. "You wait there until you talk to some-one and don't you take no for an answer." Another drag. "I'll watch the babies. No one will take them from here." Blue smoke hung in clouds around her head. Remembering the episode with the gun, I agreed. Russell had met his match in Millie.

I rode the bus downtown, gazing out the window but seeing nothing of the passing scenery. Over and over, I envisioned Rus-sell's angry face, his drawn, lined expression. My mind replayed his threat like an old record album stuck on a bad scratch. *"I'll take you. I'll take the kids. I'll take everything."* My heart continued to beat wildly, and the palms of my hands sweat profusely.

At the County-City building the security checkpoints seemed to take far longer than usual. I fought my way through the crowd at the elevator only to give up and run up the stairs to the Domestic Violence offices. Though I had no appointment, I was prepared to beg or weep—whichever was necessary—to get help. I waited in the same little lobby surrounded by school desks, first pacing, then sit-ting, then pacing again, for nearly two full hours.

Finally Julie, my legal advisor, escorted me into her office, look-ing frazzled and worn. "So what is so urgent that you need to talk about it this afternoon?" she asked, collapsing into her chair. "You know it's better to make an appointment."

"This," I said, shoving the envelope filled with papers across her desk. She took a moment to look through the packet, shuffling back and forth between copies. She read them slowly, rubbing her index finger over her lips as she did.

"Tell me, Mrs. Koehler," she began tentatively, "how much does your husband make every year?"

Embarrassed, I realized I had no idea. I'd never seen a bank statement. He'd carefully left me out of the exact state of our finan-cial affairs. "I don't know," I admitted. "He didn't want me to spend money. He said I wasn't very good with it."

"Did you ever sign an income tax form?"

I thought back, wondering. Had I? "I don't know," I admitted.

"What kind of car does your husband drive?" she asked.

"A Jag." I answered.

"New?"

"Well, it was new two years ago." Truthfully, I'd always wondered about Russell's double standard when it came to money, but I knew better than to ask. A professional designer decorated his office. He drove a new car. He wore custom suits. Truthfully, I didn't want to ask about these details. Whatever the explanation might be, I felt certain that it came with bruises. I didn't need to understand that much.

"Did he buy it on time or pay cash?"

"The car?" I paused to think. "I don't know."

"Mrs. Koehler, I'm going to be very honest with you." Julie paused, placing her pen on the desktop. "It seems that taken together—your husband's profession, his family's finances, and his behavior—all indications are that Russell Koehler may have a great many assets which total a very substantial estate. I know that it has never been your intention to punish him or to bankrupt him. However," she paused with a slow exhale and looked at me with an unsettling directness, "you must weigh your own ability to wage a battle against these kinds of resources." She gestured to the clinic area. "My job is to represent indigent women in this community—women who have nothing to lose but their lives." She removed her wire glasses and rubbed her eyes slowly before she continued. "They have nothing, but neither do their husbands. The truth is, Mrs. Koehler, your husband is about to bring out some really big guns." She held both hands palm up, one higher than the other, like an unbalanced scale. "And you can't win a war under these circumstances—not with publicly appointed legal advice."

"Are you saying he could take the children?" I asked, terrified of her answer.

"Absolutely." She nodded solemnly. "Our state is not prejudiced with regard to which parent may have sole custody of the children. He only needs to present you as unstable, unpredictable, or in this state, highly unwilling to cooperate with his visitation rights.

If it goes to trial, he'll use everything at his disposal."

My tears spilled over, coursing down my cheeks. "My children are all I have."

She nodded again, looking away. "There is another way, though." She paused, and her voice took on a conspiratorial tone. I felt hope rise again. "I believe it's time to retain another attorney."

"But it takes money to hire an attorney." I heard desperation in my voice. "I don't have money. I left everything to get away from him."

"You only need enough money to retain an attorney. After that, a good attorney will ask for temporary support, and in the process acquire enough to put you and your husband on more equal legal footing." She brushed imaginary crumbs off the lap of her skirt. "The thing is, hiring someone to go after it diminishes the total value of the estate you are trying to divide—the estate you are legally entitled to. So the assets have to be valuable enough to support the cost of an additional attorney." She jotted a note to herself. "Otherwise it wouldn't be worth the trouble. In this case, it just may be worth the risk. Even if you end up exhausting the estate's assets, it might be the only way to protect your children."

"I don't know. I'm too tired to fight. I don't want to battle."

"No one does. And normally I avoid them myself." She opened a drawer and rifled through it before pulling out a business card. "This woman specializes in cases like yours. I'd do some checking about your husband's assets, if I were you. And if you'd like, I'll give her a call."

The entire afternoon had been one long wild-goose chase. Now, instead of feeling comforted, I felt threatened. If this woman was correct, Russell could take the one thing I valued more than my own life—my children. How like him to take the things most precious to me, leaving me feeling useless and spent. Feeling the heaviness of milk in my breasts, I hesitated only a moment. "Call her, please. I'd like to see her as soon as possible."

Three days later I had my wish. Standing in the lobby of the Moyer Lake Professional Building, I paused, looking over the building directory. Behind me, three glistening brass elevators waited for passengers. I looked down at the business card in my hand and back to the white letters of the sign. I found Judy Barton's office on the eleventh floor. Taking a deep breath, I turned to the elevators and pushed the Up button. The ride seemed very, very long.

The doors opened into a large reception area, dominated by a glossy black U-shaped desk, at which a young redhead sat. She wore an earphone tucked conspicuously into her left ear. Typing furiously, she paused only long enough to answer a large console telephone. I introduced myself.

"Please have a seat, Mrs. Koehler. Ms. Barton will be with you shortly."

The attorney herself came to the waiting area, which surprised me. She wore a dark wool suit with a blouse of maroon silk. Her long thin legs made an almost comic contrast to her broad shoulders and heavy bust. The front of her jacket did not quite close over her ample chest. The entire effect was that of a frog about to leap. After brief introductions, she led the way to her office. "Follow me," she said cheerfully, glancing back over her shoulder. "Would you like coffee?"

"Yes, please."

"Gina, please bring in a tray." Her voice had a confident, authoritative tone.

"Yes, ma'am," the redhead responded. Her typing continued without interruption.

Judy escorted me into a large office where delicate roses floated on soft peach carpet. Pale marble floors trimmed the edges of the room, and recessed lighting filled the area with warm soft light. "Sit down, Mrs. Koehler," she said, indicating a couch upholstered in white leather. She sat in a tapestry club chair and took a legal pad from the glass coffee table before her. In the center of the table a black marble sculpture of mother and infant stood as a silent testimony to her passion.

I'd come a long way from legal help for the indigent.

"Now," she said casually, "why don't you tell me a bit about yourself."

"Well . . ." I hesitated, suddenly feeling very shy, very outclassed in all of this obvious luxury. How should I begin the story of the battle which now threatened to annihilate me? "What do you want to know?"

She stood and crossed the room lightly. Standing before a bookshelf, she brought down a photograph of three older children. "Let me start then," she said, with a soothing low voice. "These are my grandchildren." She brought the photo to me. "Thirty-two years ago I married a man who beat me for entertainment. He liked to hear me beg for mercy."

She sat down again, tucking her skirt carefully around her knees. "I didn't have anyone to turn to. There were no agencies. No therapists. No attorneys for situations like mine. But I loved my kids enough to want to give them a normal life." She took the photograph again. "My husband eventually died of liver failure. He drank. And I . . . well, I raised my kids alone and went to law school." Running her finger tenderly over the glass, she seemed lost in her memories. She took a deep breath and continued. "I decided that if it were up to me, I would make a difference for women trapped in violent homes." She looked at me intently. "Mind you, I don't think every situation is irreparable. Some can be helped with counseling. And, where there are no real assets and no children involved, my help isn't necessary. The state has finally made sure of that. I can't solve everything, but some women deserve the kind of help I can provide. And I intend to be there for them." She smiled again.

This woman knew. She understood. Once the ice was broken, our camaraderie established, I poured out my story. Just as I wound down, I heard a gentle knock at the office door. Gina entered, carrying a tray with a white insulated coffee server, two porcelain mugs, and a plate of shortbread. The scent of fresh coffee entered the room with her.

"Thank you, Gina."

With a nod and a faint smile, Gina disappeared.

"Julie tells me you need my help." The attorney poured coffee for two.

"I need someone's help," I answered, a little desperately.

"Are you quite sure that your relationship with your husband cannot be saved?"

"I would never go back. I'm afraid I won't survive his next temper tantrum."

Judy lifted her cup, considering. "Well, it won't be easy. It may involve a trial, and that takes a great deal of both time and money." She spoke quietly, thoughtfully. "But your case does seem to be one that precludes an arbitrator. And the estate does seem to have grown at your expense." She paused again, setting the cup down. "The only thing is, we'll almost certainly have to compromise in the area of visitation."

I drew in my breath sharply. "But after what he did to Leah, I'm afraid for the children."

"Are you afraid for them, my dear?" she asked quietly. "Or are you afraid for yourself?"

It shamed me that she saw through me so clearly. "Both," I agreed.

"Well, there are ways to get around it all." She looked out her windows over the vast concrete cityscape far below. I thought I'd lost her again when suddenly she tugged at a stray hair near her face, sweeping it back behind one ear.

"All right. We have much work to do." She stood abruptly and crossed the room to a mahogany credenza beside her dark granite desk. Pulling open lower doors, she retrieved a packet of papers, which she carried to me. "You must fill out these papers as carefully as you know how." I took them from her, glancing over the first page. "Some of the information you may not have, such as bank numbers and so forth. In the meantime, I want you out of your apartment in the next four weeks. Find a nice place. Contract with reasonable day-care services, and get a job that uses your education."

"But, Russ, what if he . . ."

"You are not to worry about Russ. You must let me worry about him." From the top of her desk, Judy picked up a pair of reading glasses and put them on. "I want you to keep a detailed list of your daily expenses. And get some new clothes." She looked down at her papers, and then at me. "Clothes that fit." She smiled. "And get some decent clothes for the children."

"I don't have any money to do all of this." I stood and walked to her desk.

"Can you borrow some?"

"Maybe." For a moment I considered contacting my brother for help. I felt my face redden, anticipating the shame of asking for help. I'd told Steve in a letter that I was leaving Russell, but I'd never explained why. In fact, I hadn't contacted him at all in the three months since I'd left the island.

"Do it," she answered abruptly. "If you want to keep those kids, we'll have to show that you live in a stable, comfortable environment, that you are gainfully employed, and that you have reliable care for the children."

"But what about Russ? What about his . . . his violence?" I spit the word out, unable to think of another way to phrase it.

"We will try to establish his pattern of violence toward you," she said with confidence. "But it won't be easy. And it may not make a difference when it comes to the children."

My mouth dropped open. How could Russell's violence not make a difference?

"Remember, worry is my job." She patted my shoulder. "And one last thing. Find a job no more than thirty miles from Russell's home. I'd suggest a school that will let you enroll Leah in the same building."

"Why?"

"We want to show that you left the marital home because of his violence, but you are open to supporting the relationship of father and child. By being no more than thirty miles away, and by being completely up front about your intentions, you present a much better picture to the court."

"And while I do all this, what will you do?"

"I'll try to get a temporary order for support. Of course, your husband will oppose the amount I suggest, in which case I'll be able to subpoena his financial records in discovery. I'll have an expert review the business and tax statements." She made more notes. "I'll try to establish custody of the kids as a temporary measure, with supervised visitation only—if I can." She slapped her tablet onto the desk and sat heavily in her chair. "The temporary order will probably require a hearing. And you must understand. There are no guarantees when it comes to contested divorce.

"Remember, in only a few minutes we're asking a judge to review years of records and testimonies and make a very important decision. It could go either way." She sighed. "So . . ." She scratched another shorter note to herself and stuck the paper onto the corner of her file.

The buzz of her intercom made me jump. I recognized Gina's voice as she spoke.

"Ms. Barton, the prosecutor's office is on line three."

"Thanks. I'll be right with him." She stood and gently put an arm around my back, guiding me toward the door. "Now, Patricia, I'll call you at the diner if I need you. In the meantime, you take care of the things I've instructed you to do." She opened her office door. "One more thing, and this is the most important thing I have to tell you." I stepped through the door into the hallway. "Don't worry."

Easy for her to say. She'd never met Russell.

Over the next seven weeks, Judy Barton did as she promised. She managed to convince a judge to order temporary support. However, the same judge also ordered supervised visitation of the children. Judy explained the hearing results over the telephone. "The judge declared his decision 'without prejudice.' " She sounded quiet, almost exhausted.

"What exactly does that mean?"

"The order can be changed by a new motion." Her disappointment came through clearly, even over the telephone. "I had hoped to restrict him to supervised visits until the divorce trial. But for now, at least, we've done the best we can do."

"What do you mean, changed?"

"It means that Russell can seek a hearing to modify the order. It could happen at any time. We need to be ready. I'm going to start seeking proof on the violence issue."

For the millionth time, I wished that I'd told the truth in the hospital.

Twenty-One

ACCORDING TO THE JUDGE'S DECREE, once each week either a representative of the court or a mutually satisfactory individual would accompany Russell to a public place where they would pick up the children for a five-hour visit. The supervisor, ordered to stay for the entire time, would then accompany Russell to return the children to me.

Russell lost no time demanding his court-appointed visitation rights. Within three days of the judge's decision, Russell called my attorney to arrange a day with the children. Russell suggested Belinda, his receptionist, as our mutually agreeable representative. Reluctantly I agreed. I trusted Belinda with the children. She adored them. But at the same time, I feared Russell's control over her. Belinda had always done exactly as Russell instructed. My nervousness left me sleepless.

On the day RJ turned six months old, I agreed to meet Russell and Belinda in a nearby coffee shop to transfer the children. As we waited for Russ, I bought hot chocolate for Leah and a latte for myself. We chose high stools facing the counter, sipped our drinks, and visited about her school projects. Leah, now ten, had a book report due, and for her presentation we discussed the relative merits of a shadow box over a poster. I had difficulty staying with the conversation.

The prospect of seeing Russell made me so anxious that even

the slightest movement or noise distracted me from Leah's words. *We are safe*, I repeated to myself. *We are in public.* I forced myself to focus on Leah, trying to measure her feelings about the outing. As far as I could tell, Leah had completely forgiven Russell for the violin incident. She still loved her daddy, and she told me this frequently. I wondered how she might translate her words into actions once he came through the coffee shop door.

Russell arrived thirty minutes late, carrying a large gift-wrapped box. *Ever the Sugar Daddy*, I thought.

Belinda, in jeans and tennis shoes, slipped in behind him. "There you are," Russ said to Leah. "Had an emergency and missed the ferry."

Leah took the box he offered her and looked inquisitively at me. "Should I open it?"

"Sure. Fine." I sipped coffee and looked absently out the window, as though the gift made no difference to me.

She removed the silver foil wrapping carefully, and inside found an Obermeyer ski jacket. "Oh, Daddy, it's beautiful." She held it up, fawning over the gift. From her hands hung an iridescent purple jacket, trimmed in black nylon, with black fur on the collar and hood. It appeared to be dyed fox. She petted the fur tenderly.

"I'm glad you like it," he said, obviously pleased with himself. "I think it's about time you learned to ski." He gave her a squeeze about the shoulders. "Now, where is that son of mine?" He bent over the car seat and eagerly unfastened the buckles holding RJ inside. Tenderly, without waking him, he scooped RJ into his arms. "Oh, he's grown so much," he said in a soft voice.

"Babies grow," I answered, sliding off my stool. "Well, I'll be off." I bent over and kissed Leah's cheek. "Be good for Daddy," I whispered. "I'll be here at six tonight to meet you." She smiled, softly, bravely.

I kissed RJ and handed Russ the diaper bag. From my pocket I retrieved a carefully lettered instruction sheet. He tucked it into his jacket without reading it, which irritated me.

"The milk is frozen breast milk," I said. "The stuff is hard to come up with, so don't waste it. Keep it frozen." I tousled Leah's hair and kissed her cheek. "See you tonight." Stepping in front of Belinda, I left without looking back.

I'd made a lengthy list of promises to my attorney. I would not keep the kids from Russell. I would transfer the kids only in a public place. I would not betray my fear of him in word or in action. I would not allow him to contact me by phone or in person. I would not speak to his attorney without the presence of my own. But of all of these, I found my promise to be brave around Russell by far the most difficult to keep. I thought about it constantly. "Calm down, Patricia," I repeated out loud. "Be reasonable, Patricia. The children are safe with him, Patricia." These words I repeated again as I unlocked the door of my car.

My biggest fear was that Russell might disappear with them on one of these weekends, and I lost no time in telling Judy Barton of my fear. She reminded me of all he stood to lose should he decide to run. "He has a lucrative business, Patricia, and a medical license," she reassured me. "Most important of all, this man really cares about his public image. He won't do anything to tarnish that." She chuckled as she spoke. "He may try to look like the poor, mistreated, falsely accused father, but he won't jeopardize his reputation with anything illegal."

So if Judy Barton felt confident, I would be too. I drove straight home and busied myself preparing for a classroom full of kindergartners.

Yielding to her advice, I had obtained a teaching position in a small school district near the mainland ferry terminal and had taken a lease on a three-bedroom tract house in a middle-class development not far from the school. The hardest part of these changes involved leaving Millie and the restaurant. I no longer saw Millie as a strange and smelly old woman. She'd grown into a good and dependable friend. I hated to move. She made it easier though.

One evening, two days after seeing Judy Barton, Millie announced, "You know, that Oleda woman called me this week. She wants to know if I'll take in another one of her ladies after you leave." Millie took a long drag on a fresh cigarette. "I don't know what makes that woman think I want to coddle all her little misfits back to health."

In spite of myself, I smiled. "But you'll have all the help you need. What a wonderful idea, Millie!" I leaned over and kissed her sueded cheek. She couldn't have looked more startled if I'd slapped her.

Officially, the school district hired me as a part-time teacher after an exceptionally high number of new kindergartners registered for fall. I supplemented that salary by substituting in the afternoon. The hours were just right, and with Russell's support payments, I finally was able to make ends meet.

Most of my neighbors were either single parents or working couples. Our identical ramblers stood only about ten feet from one another. In spite of our physical proximity, the families in our development were too tired to connect emotionally. Each of us lived an encapsulated life, struggling in our own efforts to survive. I did not know my neighbors' names. I'd never even spoken to any of them.

In order to make these changes, I'd been forced to swallow my pride and call my brother. He expressed outrage with Russell, feeling the kind of anger many men feel when they are helpless to undo damage already done. But more than that, Steve felt horrified that he had not been around when I needed him. He berated himself for not having sensed that something was seriously wrong.

"You couldn't have known," I said. "You lived clear across the country. I didn't tell anyone. I didn't think anyone would believe me. Besides, for a long time, I thought it was all my fault. Who wants to tell anyone what a bad job they're doing in their marriage? Even our neighbors didn't know what was going on."

"What can I do, Patty? What do you need?"

"My attorney says the biggest battle is still to come. She managed to get an order for protection and for support. But she says I need to move." I explained as carefully as I could the need to look cooperative to the court.

"I can help," he told me. "The company did really well this year. I put my bonus away for the kids' college. It's yours. All of it.

You'll have plenty of time to get it back to me." He sent a cashier's check two days after I called.

The divorce, and all of the negotiations involved, seemed to sap energy from my life, like water on a sandy beach. Daily activity required enormous effort. I slept little and ate less.

I never realized how hard burying a life, ending a relationship might be. Whoever said divorce was an easy option, lied. Life contains no easy options.

After a long and anxious day without the children, I drove back to the coffee shop in the little car Russell bought when we first moved to the island. Coming out of hiding brought some positive rewards. I could now contact friends and begin to reassemble the tiny parts of my life that I'd left behind. The best part of my past returned to bless me. Whenever she could, Susan came to visit. She'd taken it upon herself to reclaim my clothes and treasures from Russell's possession. Soon after I moved, she and David brought the car I'd left at her house—and of course, the envelope of money I'd left on the seat at the ferry terminal. I never drove the car without thinking of her, remembering her enduring friendship.

I arrived at the coffee shop just before six and sat at a small corner table reading the Sunday paper. At ten after the hour, a college student waiting tables nearby asked if I needed anything. At six thirty, he mentioned that he would close in half an hour. Still no Russell. Nerves folded my stomach in half. I ate two Rolaids.

Ten minutes later, Leah struggled to open the glass door. I rushed to greet her and found myself face-to-face with Russell. He held the car seat and the diaper bag. Belinda was not to be seen.

"Russ, you're late."

"Let's talk."

"No." My response was abrupt. I tried again. "I mean, Russell"—I glanced around the deserted store—"you know we aren't supposed to be together like this. And where is Belinda? She's supposed to be with you all the time." My frustration and fear mingled together, rising with the acid in my stomach. Together, these emotions threatened to steal what little self-control I had.

With false gaiety, Russell broke in, "Leah, choose a table." She glanced around the dining room and pulled out a chair very close to the bar. Russ held his palm flat, in front of his tummy, and with a bow pointed me to my seat.

"No," I objected. "No!" The volume of my voice surprised me. The waiter glanced over at us. I grabbed Leah's hand, yanking her off the chair. "It's late." I took another ragged breath, trying again to sound pleasant and in control. "Leah, don't forget, you have your poster to finish coloring." I bent, reaching for the handle of the car seat. "Thanks for getting the kids back, Russ."

As I lifted the baby, Russell's fist closed over the handle at the same time. I tugged. He pulled back, bringing my face very near to his. "It isn't over, Patricia," he murmured. "It won't ever be over."

I yanked the seat away from his hand, jarring the sleeping child inside. "It is over, Russell. It's all over." I didn't care that I might wake the baby. Russell frightened me, and I needed to get away.

Hurriedly, with palpitating heart, I nearly burst through the swinging door, dragging a surprised Leah into the parking lot. "Mommy," she objected, "it hurts." My hand squeezed hers, holding tight. I could not let go, not until I had her safely belted into my car.

The look in Russell's eyes when he brought the children back frightened me. That, combined with the fact that his supervisor for visitation hadn't made it through the day, all added up to trouble. I expected it. Even before I got the phone call, I knew Russell would soon try something. Within one week, Russell brought a motion for regular unsupervised visitation.

"Can we stop him?" I questioned Judy Barton over the phone.

"We can try, but it won't be easy. There will be a hearing," she answered calmly. "I've been looking into the violence issue. Your medical records are clean."

"I know. I told you. I've never told anyone what happened."

"Well, I looked. Sometimes they document it anyway. In this case, it isn't there."

"What about the doctor? He said he knew."

"I'm checking into that. The doctor you saw has left the state."

"Left the state?"

"Yes. Moved, joined a practice in Missouri."

I heard steely determination in her voice. In spite of her tenaciousness, I felt hope closing down. I dropped my forehead into my free hand. "So what do we do?"

"Remember, this battle is just for unsupervised visitation. If we want to win in the long run, we have to stay on the offensive."

"And that means . . . ?"

"It means we have to fly to Missouri to depose Dr. Becker," she answered calmly. "The only good thing is that a deposition will be as much hassle for Russell and his attorney as it is for us. At least it should scare him."

Miraculously, Judy located the orthopedist and arranged for a deposition to be taken two weeks later.

───

Nine long weeks passed before our hearing with Judge Henry Ingram. On a Tuesday morning, two days before Thanksgiving, we met in a long, narrow courtroom, surrounded by cheap paneling and green commercial carpet. I shivered constantly, from both chill and fear, waiting for our case to be called.

Russell and his attorney, a thin man whose gray hair made a fuzzy circle around the shiny surface of his balding head, sat at a solid wooden table to the right of the courtroom. I sat on Judy's left, wearing a plain wool suit in navy blue. Before the judge even entered the courtroom, fear turned my chill into hypothermia, and I clenched my teeth together to keep them from chattering.

Susan sat on the bench behind me wearing a long blue maternity dress and boots. In the midst of my personal misery, Susan had discovered her own wonderful surprise. She and David now expected their third child, due before Christmas. Susan's happiness over her own good fortune had been tempered by her anguish over mine. I turned to smile at her and caught her gently rubbing the fullness of baby in her tummy. She made a face and smiled back at me. Though I knew she felt nervous about testifying, only her hands fiddling in her lap betrayed her anxiety.

Russell had shaved his mustache for the occasion and cut his hair very short. He looked especially professional in a navy sport coat and gray slacks. Clearly, he came to win.

"Is the matter of Koehler versus Koehler, case number 762341, ready?" the judge asked.

"The matter is ready, Your Honor," Russell's lawyer responded.

"And the defense is ready?"

"We are, Your Honor," Judy answered.

The next thirty minutes passed in a blur of documents, depositions, and affidavits. Russell's attorney hotly contested our deposition of Dr. Becker. "If the physician in question did not see fit to record his observations on the medical record, why then," the attorney asked, "should he claim to remember now, nearly nine months later? How can he identify the cause of injuries he did not document in the first place?"

Judy Barton called Susan to testify. "Can you tell me about your relationship with Patricia Koehler?"

Susan swallowed hard, tried to speak, then cleared her throat, trying again. "Yes, we have been close friends for the past eight years."

"And in that time, would you say that Patricia Koehler confided in you?"

"Yes, she did."

"Did you trust her?"

"Yes. Absolutely."

"Did she ever, on any occasion, lie to you?"

"Not that I am aware of."

"Did she ever volunteer information about her relationship with her husband?"

"Not really. In fact, she didn't talk about him much."

"What did you observe when the two of them were together?"

"They seemed tense."

"Objection." Russell's lawyer stood. "The witness is being asked to make an evaluation."

"Sustained," the judge said. "Move along here, Ms. Barton. This is not a murder trial."

"Yes, Your Honor." Judy moved back to our table, picked up her notes, and began again. "Then I will come to a very specific date. Mrs. Addison, can you tell me about the first time you came to understand that the Koehlers' marriage was not what it appeared to be?"

"Yes."

"Tell us about that visit."

"Well, I was going to bring some cookies I'd made. I stood on the front porch about to knock when I heard yelling inside. I heard Pat and then Russell. It sounded pretty intense, so I decided to leave and come back another time. Then I heard glass break, and Leah started screaming. I didn't know what to do. I was so afraid someone might be hurt. I pounded on the door and rang the bell." Susan waited for the next question, fidgeting with her cuticles.

"And did someone answer the door?"

"Yes, Patty did."

"And what did she look like?"

"She had a fresh bruise on her cheek. Very blue."

"Did she ask you in?"

"No, not at first. At first we cried. We stood on the porch and cried." Susan's voice trembled, and her eyes filled with tears. "Then she asked me in."

"Did she tell you what had happened?"

"She didn't have to. I knew Russ had hit her. We talked about Russell's hitting her in the past."

"Objection. Hearsay." Russell's attorney didn't even stand this time.

"Overruled. Counselors, our job is to get to the truth here." The judge made a note with his pen. "Continue, please."

"Were there other occasions when you knew Mrs. Koehler had been beaten?"

"Yes. She occasionally had other bruises. And when that happened, I knew. We didn't talk too much because she didn't want to. But the last time, the time before she left him, that was the worst."

"Can you tell us about that time?"

"I went to the house to take them to the hospital."

"Who had been injured?"

"Leah had broken ribs and a broken wrist."

"And Mrs. Koehler?"

"She had bruises. Most were in places she covered with her clothes."

"Did you see the bruises?"

"Yes, I helped her dress for the hospital."

"Did you see other damage at the time of the hospital visit?"

"Yes, her cello. He broke it—destroyed it," Susan's voice broke. "He completely destroyed it," she whispered through tears.

"Objection. Whether or not the cello was damaged is irrelevant to this procedure, Your Honor." Russell's attorney sounded bored.

"Sustained. Please contain yourself to questions about the children or Mrs. Koehler, Council."

"Your Honor, it is proven in cases of violence that the perpetrator often destroys items of value in order to threaten the victim." Judy took a relaxed stance, a gentle note of appeal in her voice.

"I am not here to argue the issues of domestic violence, Council," the judge answered. "This is a case of visitation rights. We will confine ourselves to these issues."

Judy shrugged slightly, looked directly at me, and put on her glasses. Glancing down at her notes, she began again. "Mrs. Addison, did Mrs. Koehler tell you how the injuries she and Leah sustained occurred?"

"Yes. She told me that Russell had done it. He beat her."

"Thank you, Mrs. Addison. Your witness, Council."

"Mrs. Addison. Did you at any time ever witness the accused, Dr. Koehler, strike his wife?"

"No."

"Did you ever see him strike his children?"

"No."

"Now, thinking about what you have observed directly, how would you characterize Dr. Koehler's parenting of the Koehler children?"

"He was okay."

I smiled at Susan's determination not to give Russell credit for anything.

"He was a good father, then? Never struck them? Did he raise his voice?"

"Not that I observed."

"Didn't Dr. Koehler take his children to Sunday school every week?" I noticed that his lawyer referred to Russell only as Dr. Koehler. "And didn't you yourself observe this caring behavior?"

"Yes, he did take Leah to Sunday school."

"So the fact is, you are testifying about abuse that you never saw happen directly. Is that correct?"

"Yes," Susan said very quietly.

"I'm through, Your Honor."

"The witness is excused."

In less than two hours, the judge's gavel slammed onto his desk declaring his decision. "The court acknowledges the presentation of evidence regarding the violence of Russell Koehler toward his wife, Patricia Koehler. However, the court has not seen sufficient evidence to warrant continued supervised visitation of Russell Koehler with his minor children. Therefore, I order that the petitioner, Russell Koehler be hereby granted unsupervised visitation with his minor children under such conditions as guarantee the continued health and safety of Patricia Koehler. The court orders that these visits will be expanded to include one weekend every other weekend and that all transfers of said children shall continue to occur in public places. Mr. Koehler, do you understand the decision of this court?"

"I most certainly understand, Your Honor."

"Mrs. Koehler, I will not tolerate the use of children as weapons in dissolution proceedings. Do you understand that?"

"Yes, sir."

"That having been said, I also want to make one thing very clear. I will not tolerate any infraction of the order which prevents contact, harassment, or physical injury of Mrs. Koehler by Mr. Koehler." The judge glanced down at his papers, made a note on something, and continued. "I promise that should such an incident occur, I will use every tool in my power to make sure that it is the last such incident. Do you understand this clearly, Mr. Koehler?"

"Of course, Your Honor."

"Decision rendered. Next case?"

I slumped back in my chair. Beside me, Russell exchanged hearty congratulations with his attorney, shaking hands, slapping him on the shoulder.

My mind swirled. *So this is it? After all he's done? He can be a violent husband and a good father at the same time? Where is the justice in that?* With one decision, the judge had changed my life forever. Nothing could ever be safe again.

"Come on, Patricia." I heard Susan's gentle voice beside me, her hand resting lightly on my shoulder. "Let's go have coffee."

MY DISAPPOINTMENT over the results of our hearing lasted only ten days. On the morning of the eleventh day, I received a phone call from Susan. "Guess what?" she asked.

"You had a baby!"

"We did!" Susan betrayed no hint of fatigue. Excitement bubbled from her voice. "At six-thirty this morning. A beautiful girl. We named her Mandy."

I promised Susan I would come to visit as soon as Christmas vacation began. "Stay with me on the island," she insisted. "You don't have to spend Christmas by yourself. Bring the kids, and you can help me with the baby."

"I don't think bringing my kids would be much help."

"Having you here would be a help," she answered. "Please come."

Spending Christmas on the island with Susan and David and the kids gave my mind a wonderful vacation from what I came to term "Russell-Worry," a worry that almost always ended in antacids.

————

After the New Year, I checked in with Judy Barton by telephone. To my surprise, she extracted yet another promise. I promised her that I would read everything I could find about domestic violence. I kept that promise. I went to the library and checked out every

book, pamphlet, and article I could find on domestic violence and
divorce recovery. All through January, after I put the children to
bed, I ended nearly every evening reading. Often I kept at it until
well past midnight. I found myself on those pages. I found Russell
there as well, his manipulation, his rage, and his constant need for
control. I discovered something I already knew but had not yet admitted. I was not the only woman who had lived through this nightmare, and I would not be the last. My late-night reading sessions
left me exhausted, both from lack of sleep and from the roller
coaster of emotions I felt during the learning process.

One morning after a long night of reading, I woke feeling slug-
gish. I decided a shower might help me perk up. I stood under the
water for a long time, letting the stream massage my tired body.
After I turned off the water, I reached down with a squeegee to wipe
the water from the tiles behind the faucet. The edge of the rubber
blade caught behind the hot water handle and somehow, though
I'm not sure how, a single four-inch tile dropped into the bathtub
and shattered. "Shoot. Just what I need." I bumped my knee stepping out of the tub.

Our tract house had only one bathroom, and I couldn't afford
to lose the shower. I dried off and decided to investigate. Trying to
determine if other tiles were loose, I poked the wall behind the
handle. Surprisingly, the wall itself yielded to my touch like the surface of three-day-old Cream of Wheat. Another tile dropped into
the tub.

What did I expect from a tract house? I made a mental note to
call my landlord from school.

During lunch, the teachers' lounge echoed with noisy voices. I
spent my lunch hour huddled over a telephone in the corner, trying to locate the owner of our house. It proved to be a difficult task.
Sitting on a vinyl couch, I placed the telephone in my lap and dialed clumsily. How long had it been since I'd used a phone with an
actual dial? Like all the equipment in our building, this phone had
been installed as part of the original equipment. Nothing had been
replaced, not even the telephone.

I discovered my landlord's business number busy, his cell phone refused to answer, and his home phone was in the loving care of a machine. After four tries I finally reached the secretary at his accounting firm, who informed me that Dennis had left for a Caribbean cruise and would not be available for another three weeks, give or take.

"But I have a problem in my bathroom!" I shouted over the noise around me.

"I'm sorry. I'm not authorized to help you with that," she answered. Her voice betrayed no trace of sorrow.

"What?" The noise level in the lounge suddenly rose, something about the firing of a college football coach. "I'm sorry, you'll have to speak up. I can't hear you."

"I can't help," she shouted back, enunciating every word. "You're on your own." Even in the noisy lounge, I recognized the click on the other end of the phone. *Now what?* I placed the phone in the cradle with deliberate care.

"What's up with your bathroom?" Vera Walters folded herself softly into the seat beside me. As our building principal, Vera managed to be everywhere and nowhere at the same time. A tall woman with graying hair and unusually graceful hands, Vera considered herself overseer, mother, and friend to her entire staff. She was an old-fashioned administrator.

"I don't know," I answered, sighing. "I just noticed that the wall behind my shower feels like finger Jell-O, the tiles are falling off, and my landlord is on vacation."

"Not a good thing." She laughed.

"I agree. But it's our only bathroom. I don't have the option of not using it."

"You know, I'll bet you could fix it yourself and save a bunch of money."

"Why would I do that? It's the landlord's responsibility."

"Because the money you save him becomes yours," she smiled again.

"I doubt I could repair it anyway." I sighed. "I've never been any good at fixing stuff. I don't know which end of the hammer to hang on to."

"Well, how about if I send Ken over to have a look?"

"Ken?"

"My husband." She answered lightly. "The consummate handyman. He might be able to give you some advice as to what to do next."

I'd met Ken only once. A retired pipe fitter, he'd hosted his wife's employees at a barbecue just after school started. "Would he?" I remembered him as a friendly, fatherly type, but I didn't believe she should volunteer him for such duties.

"Of course. He loves to help. He especially likes to rescue damsels in distress." She patted my knee as she stood up. "I'll have him give you a call."

True to her promise, Vera's husband called Monday night and arranged to look at the shower the following evening after dinner. On Tuesday, just as I fastened the pin on RJ's diaper, the doorbell rang.

"Leah, let Mr. Walters in, please." I called from the bedroom.

I heard the front door open and voices in the hallway.

"I'll just be another minute," I called, snapping the sleeper closed. "I'm putting the baby to bed." I heard the phone ring. *Oh brother, I could use about four more pairs of hands.* "Would you answer the phone, Leah?"

It rang again, and I repeated myself, this time with irritation. Then in mid-ring, someone answered. I kissed the baby, turned out the light, and closed the bedroom door. As I entered the living room, I found Mr. Walters hanging up the phone with a puzzled expression on his face.

"Who was that?" I asked.

"I'm not sure," he answered. "Your daughter went into the bathroom just before the phone rang, so I answered it." He shook his head. "I said, 'Hello,' and some guy just started shouting, 'Who is this?' I tried to explain that you were in the bedroom, but he never let me finish. He just hung up."

I shuddered. I knew exactly whom Ken had spoken with. Russell. So quick to misunderstand.

I offered Ken coffee, but he refused and we went directly into the bathroom, which Leah had abandoned for the television set. He stood in the shower, poking the wall with his finger. "Yep. Dry rot." He nodded, poked, and pulled away the tile near the faucet. "See here?" He pointed. "Whoever built this house should have used waterproof wallboard behind these tiles. But this stuff—why, it's soaked clean through. Needs to be replaced. All of it."

I'd hoped for a less serious diagnosis. "So what do I do now? My landlord is out of town."

"Well, it isn't a huge job. I'd say, you should have someone rip down the wall and put up new tile backer. Then you replace the tile."

"Tile. Isn't tile expensive?" My face must have shown my bewilderment, because as Ken Walters climbed out of my shower, he launched into a detailed explanation of how and when he planned to remove the existing walls. Vera's wonder husband.

Three days later, Ken had stripped the walls and replaced the wallboard. I'd purchased new tile, adhesive, and grout and stacked it all neatly in the bathroom. Leah and RJ were scheduled to spend the weekend with Russell. I planned to spend my weekend replacing the tile. Enough bathing in the kitchen sink, I would finish my bathroom or die trying. Even if I had to go without sleep, I'd finish by Monday morning.

We met Russell at the coffee shop. He was late as usual, and I noticed that he seemed detached, distant. "Russell," I asked, "are you all right?"

"Fine. Fine."

"Rough day?" I asked gently.

"Why would you care?"

"Daddy, what are we going to do this weekend?" Leah interrupted. Sensing the tension between us, she glanced anxiously from my face to Russell's and back.

"We're going to spend the weekend at Grandma's." He bent down and lifted her, draping her tenderly over his hip. "Would my favorite girl like that?"

"Will we get to swim?"

"Absolutely. The heater is already on. I called ahead."

Though I had not heard that Russell and his parents had reconciled, I should not have been surprised. They abhorred me, not Russell. With me out of the picture, Russell's deviant relationship with his mother could pick up exactly where he'd left it. At that moment, I realized he probably already had.

As I gave him the diaper bag, I repeated my instructions. "RJ is just starting solids—there's rice cereal in the bag. Mix it with formula. The can is in there. He's drinking formula from a bottle now. It's all in there. A schedule, the instructions. Everything." I leaned over to kiss Leah on the cheek. "See you Sunday night, baby." I bent to caress RJ's soft skin with my index finger. Happy and full, his brown eyes crinkled into a grin, his fat face revealing bare gums. "Bye, sweetie. Don't give your ol' dad too much trouble, hey?"

"What will you be doing this weekend?" he asked, a hint of suspicion in his voice.

"I'm working on the house. Have to replace all the tile around the tub." I smiled and threw my purse over my shoulder. "Well, see you all Sunday night. Please, Russ, try to be on time. It's a school night."

As I went out the door, I saw him standing there, holding Leah, with a haunted expression on his lined, gaunt face.

The weekend proved to be long and exhausting. When I insisted on doing the tile myself, I had no idea what the job involved. Whether I liked it or not, I was a perfectionist. The same musician who insisted on precisely tied sixteenth notes also insisted on perfectly straight plumb lines and exactly parallel grout lines. When I finally gave up on Saturday afternoon, I had tile adhesive rubbed through my hair and even in the recesses of one ear. I'd only managed to tile halfway up the wall at the end of the tub, far less than I'd planned. When Ken arrived around five to inspect my work, I'd grown irritable, exhausted, and ready for bear.

"Not half bad," he said, nodding smugly. "In another year or so, you should have the whole thing finished."

"Not funny."

"Sorry. I never said it'd be easy—just cheap."

"Thanks for the clarification."

He stepped out of the tub. "I think tomorrow you should just concentrate on the wall above the tub, go up ten or twelve inches. Then at least you can use the bathtub until the whole thing is finished."

I nodded. "Good idea. But could you show me how this tile cutter thing works?"

He sat the cutter on the counter near the sink, drew a line across a corner of a tile, and deftly scored the mark. The tile broke crisply along his line. "Nothin' to it. Just practice on a few before you expect too much." He threw the corner in my trash can. "Now, how 'bout dinner?"

"No thanks, I'm going straight to bed."

"Ah, come on. Vera and I are going out for teriyaki. You should come along. You'll need sustenance if you're ever going to finish this." He gestured toward the disaster surrounding my tub.

I thought for a minute and looked at my watch. It was still early. If I went out for dinner, I'd get some much-needed company and still have time to fall into bed before nine. "All right. I'd love to come." Being with Vera and kindhearted Ken might take the loneliness out of a weekend without the kids.

In bed by nine-thirty, I had just drifted off to sleep when the scream of a passing siren shook me awake. A moment of fear—unreasonable, unexplainable fear—passed through me like an electric current. How I hated having them gone. I had no concrete reason for this breathtaking fear every time Russell took the children. I decided to read, hoping fatigue would eventually have its way.

The next day I fought again with tiles in the bathroom. At one in the afternoon, my doorbell rang. I stood up, feeling an enormous ache along the length of my back. I'd been squatting in one place far too long. I paused to wipe my hands and went out to answer the door.

There stood Ken, in white overalls, holding a tool bucket. "Thought you might need some help," he announced smiling. Vera came up the walk behind him carrying a casserole dish between oven mitts.

"If you're going to borrow my husband, the least you can do is feed him," she grinned. "He eats like a horse. Where shall I put this?"

"In the kitchen," I said, pointing.

Ken, already in the bathroom, called out from the shower. "Get in here, Patty. I'm here to help, not take over."

When I entered the room, I found he'd moved aside my tools and clutter. In a matter of moments, he changed the process into an organized, efficient system. Tile after tile went onto the wall in perfectly aligned rows. Eventually, he sat on the tub rim, placing the tiles as I handed them to him. I prepared adhesive and handed him tools. When the walls were nearly covered, we reversed places. He took the position at the bathroom counter, cutting tiles into precise angles and handing them to me. I placed them, like the last pieces of a jigsaw puzzle, into the final empty slots. At nearly six in the evening we finally put the last of the grout onto the walls. Finished at last.

I looked at my watch. "Oh no! The kids. I have to pick up the kids."

Vera, who sat in the hallway alternately reading a novel and offering unsolicited advice, chimed in, "You go on out. We'll clean up here."

Ken glared at her, and she scowled back. "Sure, you go on ahead," he agreed with less enthusiasm.

I glanced at the reflection in the mirror, appalled. "I'd better at least wash my face and change clothes." I hurried down the hall to the bedroom.

"Don't worry, dear," Vera called. "We'll be gone by the time you get back."

When I left, they were busy washing the grout off the bathroom floor. I pulled into the coffee shop parking lot just as the dashboard clock turned to 6:38.

Tired and disheveled, I'd arrived eight minutes late. I looked over the lot and noticed the absence of Russell's new cream-colored sport-utility vehicle. Great. I could order coffee and read the Sunday paper while I waited. I needed a minute to catch my breath before full-fledged motherhood began again.

I ordered a double-tall decaf and spread the day's newspaper across one of the round glass tables. Warm and relaxing, the coffee let me sink deep into the magazine section before I thought again to check the time. Seven-fifteen. With a pang of irritation, I realized Russell had ignored my plea to bring the children home on time. I glanced outside. It was overcast, raining lightly, a gentle breeze blowing. The weather hadn't kept him. I began to think about the chores left to complete before school. I had laundry to do, some lesson plans to finish, and who knows what schoolwork Leah had left to the last minute. My stomach churned. I deliberately forced my attention back to the paper.

A few customers came and went that evening. With every ring of the bell over the doorway, I looked up, checked my watch, and fought irritation, which rapidly transformed itself to anxiety.

Later the kid running the counter asked me if I needed anything. "No, I just planned to meet someone here," I explained lamely. "Do you have the time? Maybe my watch is wrong."

"Nine-thirty," he replied. "I'll have to close soon."

"All right." I stood and dug into the depths of my purse, looking for change. Only a quarter. "Could you change a bill for me? I think I'll call and see what's holding them up."

With a pocket full of quarters and dimes and a head full of angry thoughts, I called my own answering machine first. I listened to Vera explain that Ken had left a tool, and would I please bring it to school on Monday. I heard Leah's little friend invite her to a birthday party. But my machine had no messages from Russell.

I called his parents' house in the city. No answer. I called our house on the island. No answer. Where was he? I went back to the coffee shop where the young employee assured me that no one had come in while I was away. I swallowed the last of my drink and turned to leave. "If anyone comes with two little kids, would you tell them I went home? Tell him to bring the kids straight home."

"Sure, lady."

I drove home, confused, and more than a little frightened. Had there been an accident? Why was he late? Were the children safe? I checked the answering machine again and dug out my old personal telephone book. I began making random, slightly desperate, phone calls. First Susan. I asked her to check the house on the island. Perhaps they'd gone home for the weekend. Why they hadn't answered the phone was beyond me. She agreed to check and call me back.

I called Russell's office and left a message, not a very polite one, on his private line. I even managed to find his receptionist's home phone number. I'm sure Belinda thought I'd lost my marbles, but perhaps he'd said something to her.

I turned up nothing. Desperation grew. If the kids were with Russell at his parents' home, why didn't someone answer the phone?

I decided to call the police.

The emergency dispatcher offered no help at all. "I'm sorry, ma'am. What you're describing is a custody issue. Truthfully, it happens all the time. One parent doesn't bring the kids home on time just to jangle your chain. The best thing you can do is to sit tight. They'll be home soon."

"Can you tell me if there's been a car accident?"

"No, ma'am. I only take calls for emergency help. If you like, I can have an officer get in touch with you."

"Yes, please. Please have someone give me a call." I gave the dispatcher my home number and then began to pace the living room floor in front of the phone.

At 10:45 the phone rang. "Patty, I've been out to the house." Susan's voice betrayed her fear. "Everything is buttoned up tight there. No sign that anyone has been there all weekend."

"Nothing?"

"No. I went by the office too. There isn't anyone there. I even called the hospital in Twalleson and asked the operator if Russ had been seeing patients this weekend. He hasn't checked in on the physician system since Friday morning."

"Who's covering for him?" At least I could call the other doctor and find out what Russell might have told him. Perhaps I'd misunderstood the whole plan.

"That's the funny part." Susan covered the phone, and I heard her speak to someone nearby. "Sorry—my husband—anyway, the operator says that the nurse in emergency told her no one is covering."

"No one?" Strange. Russ never left his patients without coverage. Above all, Russell prided himself on his responsibility. His patients had always been his first priority. Something about this latest finding frightened me even more.

"I'd better get off the phone," I said. "I'm waiting for a call from the police."

"What do you think is going on?"

"I'm too frightened to guess."

"Patty, it's time to pray," Susan whispered. "Right now."

I took a deep breath and uttered agreement.

"Oh, Father," she began, "I know that you are everywhere. Right now you are with Leah and RJ. You're holding them in your loving arms. You are not confused or lost. We ask that you keep them safe, Father. And, God, give us wisdom. We really need it. Show us how to find them. Lead us to them, Lord. And, Father, please give us peace. Take away our racing hearts and anxious thoughts. Help us to think clearly. Help us to trust you with what looks so horribly frightening. Right now I place our fear in your hands, and I ask you to replace it with your overwhelming, absolute peace."

"Thanks," I breathed.

I hung up and waited another twenty minutes before the phone rang again. This time I spoke at length with an officer familiar with these kinds of events. He tried to reassure me that things were probably fine. No, there had been no accidents. No. No one had hospitalized any children who sounded like mine.

"So what should I do?" I asked.

"I think you should try to get some sleep. They'll probably be pounding on your door first thing in the morning."

I thanked him, hung up, and paced the floor again. I'd used all my options. I had no idea how to track them down. I could only outwait them. I read myself to sleep sitting on the living room couch.

With the first rays of sunlight peeking through my front windows, my terror returned instantly. Wide awake, I looked around the room in startled horror. Where were those slow, lazy wake-ups I'd read about in novels? I glanced at the wall clock—ten minutes to six. I began the round of phone calls again, with no response. This time I let Susan sleep. She'd done all she could.

I tried to believe the officer I'd spoken to. If Russell did bring the kids home soon, I'd need to hustle to get everyone to school on time. *All right. I'll get ready.* I drew a bath in my new bathtub, careful not to let any water splash on the curing grout. Sleeping on the couch had put kinks in my neck and soreness in every limb. I took a long hot bath. I dressed for school, put on makeup, made coffee, and waited in the living room. I knew better than to try to eat. My stomach was in no condition for visitors. I sat on the couch watching the minute hand make a slow sweep of the clockface.

Eight-fifteen. Enough. I decided to leave a note and drive to Russell's parents' myself. Something had gone horribly wrong, though I still did not understand quite what. Everyone at our police station made light of my concerns. "We don't operate on feelings, ma'am," the desk sergeant droned.

If they refused to check, I'd have to find out for myself.

I called the school to say I couldn't come in, left a note on the front door, packed my purse for the day, and finally got in the car. It's a wonder I made it into Seattle alive. I spent the entire trip focused on oncoming traffic, scanning every car, watching for Russell, looking for Leah. I listened to News Radio and heard nothing. My mouth was dry, my hands damp, and my stomach cramped painfully.

When I arrived at the house, it appeared deserted. The closed drapes and locked doors gave the impression that no one had been there in days. I decided to walk around the house. I knocked at the door to the breakfast nook. Perhaps I could rouse someone inside. No answer.

When I stepped onto the front porch, I noticed a Sunday paper resting off to the side of the porch, nearly hidden under the branch of an overgrown juniper. As I walked toward it, I noticed something else as well—something I hadn't noticed before. The porch light was on. In the broad light of day, both the porch light and chandelier inside the entry hall were still on.

Frightened by this discovery, I went around the house again to the side of the detached garage. There were no windows on this side. I kept walking. Around the back on the corner, I found a rectangular window up high, too high for me to see in. I needed help, and glancing around, I spotted a garbage can behind the back door, obscured by a privacy fence. I ran to it and dragged it to the rear wall of the garage. Placing it under the window, I climbed on, and just as I raised myself onto my feet, the garbage pail tipped over, spilling me into the junipers below. I climbed carefully from the prickly bush and realized that the uneven ground would not support my weight on top of the lid. I looked around desperately. What could I put under the can?

I tore off the lid and pulled out a garbage bag. Squishing it onto the ground away from the wall, I built a berm of garbage to support the can. I put the lid on and tried again. It worked. This time the can stood evenly. I peered into the high window. Inside, I could just make out the shape of the room. What I could see was empty. I cleaned the window with my shirt sleeve and stretched higher to view the entire garage.

There, just below the window, was Russell's new sport-utility vehicle! Russell had been here! Was he still?

I climbed down from my perch and ran stumbling to my car. I needed help. Now they would listen. The police had to help now. How I wished I owned a cell phone. I backed out of the long concrete driveway and headed for the nearest public phone booth. Overwrought, I know I ran at least one stop sign. I grew more agitated with each passing block. By the time I dialed 9–1–1, I'd grown nearly incoherent with fear. Somehow the dispatcher managed to figure out where I was and promised to send an officer.

By the time he arrived, I'd worked hard to calm myself, taking deep breaths, pacing through the parking lot of the gas station. I needed to appear reasonable, reliable. I answered the officer's questions in short perfunctory sentences. It seemed he wanted all the details. Where were the kids? How old were the kids? When were they due home? Why did I suspect trouble?

I knew that I had his attention when the gentle concern in his eyes changed to a barely perceptible frown, forcing a crease across his forehead. I felt certain of it when he called for backup and asked me if I felt well enough to lead him to Russell's family home.

When we arrived, Officer McDonald retraced my steps. He saw the paper, the lights, and even stood on the same garbage can I had. By the time the second patrol car arrived, McDonald was on the phone to his supervisor.

"We're going to try to get permission to break in," he said when he came back to the porch. "I need to have my patrol supervisor make that decision. The only reason we are considering it is because of the age of your baby."

"Why do we have to wait? My kids may be alone in there." My hands were cold—frozen, really—and I clutched them trembling, the fingernail of my thumb between my lips. Tears began again, and rather than receive comfort from the officer's concern, I'd instead grown an enormous terrifying fear.

"I know it looks like exaggerated care, Mrs. Koehler," he explained gently, "but actually, we are responsible for the home if we break in. We only do it under very extreme circumstances. Normally a simple custody dispute doesn't qualify. But with the situation here, plus the welfare of an infant—well, I need his permission to continue."

We waited in his patrol car for the supervisor to arrive. When he came, he slipped into the backseat with me. Again the questions. All of them repeated. More added. The supervisor looked at me with intense brown eyes. Who had I called? Were there others who might know where he was? Had I called Russell's business office?

"Not today. I called last night and left a message."

"Well, if we call the office and find out that he hasn't come to work, then we'll go in." The supervisor got out of the car. "I'll be back as soon as I know."

Again, more waiting. Hours—though it seemed days—later, he returned. "Okay, we go in," he said without further explanation. Officer McDonald slid out from behind the steering wheel, saying,

"Mrs. Koehler, you'll have to wait outside."

"No . . . my babies!"

"I'm sorry, but we don't know what's inside. Could be anything. We can't have you along. I'm going to have you sit with Officer Anderson in her car while we go in."

Officer Anderson, a soft-spoken woman, had arrived in another patrol car just after we called the supervisor. I slipped into the backseat of her squad car and waited. She sat without comment in the seat in front of me. I watched her in the rearview mirror as her eyes repeatedly darted to the scene behind our car. She had parked at the end of the Koehler driveway, and through the rearview mirror her eyes watched the street behind us with the intensity of a stakeout.

While she watched the street, I watched the house, hoping against hope to see Leah run down the steps to the car. Again, time slowed to a crawl. As I waited, I found myself pleading, begging God. *Please, let me have my children.* Silently, I flung my prayers heavenward.

Eventually the front door opened. Officer McDonald and his supervisor came down the front steps toward the car. Searching their faces, I saw only tight-lipped, carefully frozen expressions. McDonald came toward our car while his supervisor walked to his own and climbed in. Before Officer McDonald settled into the seat beside me, the supervisor had driven away.

"I'm sorry," he said softly. "The house is clean. Your kids aren't there."

"But the car in the garage."

"I'm sorry," he said without emotion. "They just aren't here. In fact, I can't see any evidence that they've ever been inside."

"Perhaps you've made a mistake," Anderson added sympathetically from the front seat. She turned to face us. "Maybe you misunderstood the arrangements."

"I know my husband's car. He picked them up in that car Friday night."

"Look, lady, this happens all the time," McDonald added. "We get called out to a house with some hysterical mother sitting around, and the lady is certain her husband has skipped town with the kids. Usually it just doesn't pan out."

"But where are they?" I asked, my voice trembling.

McDonald answered, "Well, wherever they are, they aren't here. The place is clean."

Twenty-Three

I HAD NO CHOICE but to return home.

When I arrived, I called everyone all over again, finding little in the way of new information. However, I did discover that Russell had scheduled a full day of patients, most of whom waited in his office for hours before they gave up and went home. His staff, including Belinda, could not explain the oversight, and I heard apprehension in her normally confident voice as she told me this bit of news.

I called the local police. After several transfers, I spoke with the duty officer. "Believe me, Mrs. Koehler," he said with exaggerated patience, "this happens all the time."

"But never to me. Russell has never just failed to show. Something is wrong."

"You may be right. But let me explain it this way. Last month alone we took six calls exactly like yours. In every single one of those, the missing parent turned up with some excuse for forgetting or misunderstanding the arrangements."

"So are you saying I have to wait?"

"Yes, I'm sorry. But, Mrs. Koehler, if your kids don't show up in the next twenty-four hours, then you come in and file a missing child report. Then I promise you, I'll assign a detective to the case."

"What do I do in the meantime?"

"You keep asking. Keep calling around. See what you can find out on your own. Tomorrow morning we'll have more to go on. This really isn't a criminal matter as of yet."

Not a criminal matter? My children were missing. Innocent kids, taken from their mother. And this is not a criminal matter? I called Susan again. She answered before the first ring had ended.

"What did you find out?" she asked, concern in her voice.

"Nothing. They won't do anything."

"I don't understand that. The court says you're supposed to have the kids, but you don't. Tell me, what isn't criminal about that?"

In spite of the horror, I smiled. No wonder I liked Susan. She said things I only dared to think.

"Do you want me to come over? I could stay with you awhile."

"No. Not yet. Your kids need you. You need your rest."

"Okay. But I promise to pray. And will you do me this favor?"

"What?"

"Call your brother. You need to let him know what is happening."

"I'll think about it. In the meantime I'm just going to crawl through the hours until the police can help me. They'll do something. I'll be okay."

I decided to wash the kitchen floor. Then I washed the walls in the living room. I washed all the windows inside the house, careful always to remain within earshot of the telephone. At seven Susan called again to ask if I'd heard anything more. Susan, who spent the whole day on the phone making inquiries, had no new clues.

I called my principal. Vera assured me that she would have a substitute for me as long as I needed it. "But, Patty, what is your gut feeling?" she asked. "Would Russell really just disappear with the kids?"

In the instant before I answered, all the voices of the past months swirled through my head. I heard Judy proclaim that Russell had too much to lose. I heard Oleda warn us that men were not to know the location of the safe house. I heard Russell yelling, just as he had on the day of my final beating. I heard again his final warning on the Fourth of July.

"I don't know," I answered her, defeated. "I don't know anything for sure anymore."

I stayed up until nearly midnight, frantic with worry, cleaning everything in sight—drawers, closets, kitchen shelves—trying in vain to distract myself from the anguish I felt. Then I decided to take a warm shower and attempt to express some of the milk which filled my breasts. Though RJ nursed only in the morning and before bedtime, my breasts were now swollen and painful with unused milk. I hadn't nursed all weekend, and now another day had passed. *Forget the grout.* Letting the warm water slip over my back, I tried to gently coax the unneeded milk from my body. Every motion hurt. Every squeeze reminded me that my baby was missing. Still crying, I slipped exhausted into bed, an ice pack wrapped firmly around my chest. I could not sleep. In the morning, I would call Steve. I needed him.

At five-thirty, I woke to the sound of a neighbor's car starting. The ancient car coughed while the starter screeched and coached the reluctant engine into motion. A normal sound on a normal day. But not for me. Sliding my feet over the edge of the bed, I reached for my robe and headed for the kitchen. I must have slept some, but my head felt as though I'd been run over by a cement truck. My swollen eyes refused to open wider than the tiniest slit. I needed coffee, and I needed it badly.

With my coffee mug filled, I sat down to call Steve. He had been the financial support I needed when I began the legal war with Russell. Now, with the children missing, I needed him for emotional support. Though I hated to be the dependant baby sister, I had nowhere else to turn.

"Hello," Christine answered the phone.

"Hi, Chris," I said and heard my own voice break.

"Patricia, what is it?"

"Is Steve home?"

"Yes, he is. He just came down for breakfast," she said. "I'll get him, Patty." I heard her put the phone down on the counter.

"Hi, Patty." Steve picked up an extension. "What're you on the phone for? It's my turn to call."

"Steve," I whispered hoarsely, trying in vain to control the trembling in my hands. Tears filled my eyes and spilled down my cheeks.

"Patty, what is it? What's happened?"

"It's Russell." I wiped my nose with the back of my hand.

"What happened?"

"He's gone," I blurted. "He's taken the kids." My emotions finally won, and I broke into choking sobs. Until now, until this moment, I had not spoken this truth even to myself. Now, with my brother, I dared to say it out loud. The reality of it struck me with the severity of a fatal plane crash.

Our conversation didn't last long. I had so little to report. Yes, I'd called the police. Yes, we searched his parents' house. No, I hadn't spoken with his parents. They were out of town. Steve made me promise to call as soon as I filed the missing child report, or sooner if I heard anything new. Then, if I needed him, he would fly out to be with me.

I tried to force myself to eat a piece of toast, but it tasted wooden, and I threw it in the trash. I finished my coffee and watched the clock. At eight, I planned to go to the police station to file my report. Until then, I had to stay calm, keep busy, and hope for the best. It seemed more than I could do. I went into the bedroom, threw myself across the bed, and sobbed.

At the police station I found a woman sitting behind a thick glass partition wearing a royal blue polo shirt with a police emblem at the chest. She wore a headset, with a tiny microphone-tipped wire in front of her mouth. Through a hole the size of a Styrofoam cup, she asked, "Good morning. What can I do for you?"

"I'd like to see a police officer," I answered. "I need to fill out a missing child report."

She gave no visible response other than nodding slightly. Her countenance suggested I had come to report a missing tricycle. "Just one minute, ma'am," she said. "I'll call a police officer out to take the report. Please take a seat in the lobby." Without lifting her eyes, she touched a button on the console before her and continued speaking, "City police. How may I direct your call?"

I turned from the glass to face a lobby full of low-slung padded chairs covered in blue upholstery. A single metal and Formica end table supporting a plastic plant occupied a corner near a window. In the center of the room, a wire stand held pamphlets designed to inform citizens about security and police programs for neighborhood watch groups. I chose a seat and sat forward, my elbows on my knees, watching the door to the area behind the desk. I waited anxiously for the officer who would bring my children back to me.

About twenty minutes later a slim, small man came through the door into the lobby. He too wore a blue polo shirt—like the woman in the reception area—and below them navy blue chinos. "Hello. Are you wishing to speak with an officer?"

"Yes, sir," I said, offering my hand. "I was told, uh . . ." My eyes filled with tears. "I spoke to someone yesterday. They told me to come in today and fill out some paper work."

His eyes squinted slightly at the corners as he smiled gently. "Why don't we sit in this room over here," he said, gesturing forward with one arm. "I think we can get more done where we won't be disturbed." With his other hand, he guided me into a small room off the lobby. He flipped on bright fluorescent lights and gestured again toward a metal chair. He took another and opened a notebook. Pulling a pen from inside, he began, "First, let me introduce myself." He smiled. "I am Officer Terry Reichle. And you are?"

"Patricia Koehler."

"And why are you here, Ms. Koehler?"

"My children have been taken. I told the duty officer yesterday, and I told the woman at the desk. Doesn't anyone talk to anyone around here?" My curt response surprised me. "Sorry," I murmured.

He said, "Tell me. Who is missing?"

"Leah Koehler and Russell James Koehler."

"Your children?"

"Yes."

"And how old are they?"

"Leah is ten, and RJ is ten months old."

"Do you have pictures?" Using his left hand, he wrote notes on

the pad as I spoke. I sat to his right, and though I tried to read what
he wrote, he held the pad at a peculiar slant, which made his notes
undistinguishable. He noticed me watching and reminded me gently, "The pictures?"

"Yes. I brought them." I took my shoulder bag from the floor
and tossed the flap back. Bringing out the manila envelope that I
packed the night before, I pulled out pictures. Leah walking on the
beach, and RJ snuggled in Oleda's arms.

He took them from me and laid them carefully across the table
at the top of his notebook. "When did you last see the children?"

"My husband took them for the weekend."

"And what arrangements did he make to return them to you?"

"We always make the exchange at a little coffee shop over on
Waller."

"Not at your home?"

"No. It's a condition set by the judge." I hesitated, trying to
control my frustration and emotion. "My husband was violent. He
made threats."

The officer squinted in concentration, making more notes. "Are
you and your husband divorced?"

"Not yet. We're in the process."

"Has someone been granted custody by the court?"

"Yes. I am the custodial parent. Russell has them every other
weekend."

"Do you have that custody order with you?" I don't know why,
but I had thought clearly enough to bring the papers. Somehow I
knew that the divorce and custody issue might make this a difficult
situation, though I had no experience in this kind of thing. I pulled
the papers from the envelope and handed them to Officer Reichle.

He unfolded the papers gently, made note of the case numbers,
and read through them quickly. "I'll need to make copies of these,"
he said, laying them aside. "Have you any evidence that your husband may have left the county with the children?"

"Yes, I think so. My husband is a doctor, and I called his office
yesterday. Belinda said he scheduled patients but never came in to
see them."

"And Belinda is . . . ?"

"His receptionist. Even she is worried."

"Hmm," he mused for a moment, rubbing the tip of his finger over his lip. "Did you bring a picture of your husband with you?"

A moment of panic broke through my thoughts. I hadn't brought a picture of Russell. Of course they would need one to look for him. How else could they possibly find the children? What a stupid mistake! "No. I'm sorry. I didn't think of it."

"Well, we have time. You'll need to drop a picture of your husband by the station, and I'll put it into the files."

Our interview continued for well over an hour, and as the time passed I became more and more frustrated. If only he would stop asking these stupid questions and find the children. They were out there somewhere, wondering why I hadn't come to get them. Would Russell care for them? What had he told them about me? Where had he taken my babies?

At last Officer Reichle stood and offered his hand again. "You'll be hearing from the detective assigned to the case sometime in the next day or so."

"Detective? You mean you won't be looking for my children?"

"No, Mrs. Koehler. My job is to take the report." He shrugged the notebook into his other hand and slid his right into his trouser pocket. "Then our desk sergeant—he's the one who does the assignments—will give it to a detective to follow up."

"But what about now? Who will keep Russell from leaving with the kids now?"

"We immediately file the case with the Center for Missing and Exploited Children. We'll also order a 'Be on the Lookout'—it's kind of like what you see on television. They call them an 'All Points Bulletin.' That will help the police force to watch for him." He shook his head. "Other than that, there isn't much we can do right now. But thanks for coming in. I'll get this right into our computer."

Terry Reichle walked me through the lobby to the main doors of the precinct. "Try to stay hopeful, Mrs. Koehler," he said. "Most of these guys show up with the kids in a few days." He shook my hand and walked through the locked door behind the receptionist.

As soon as I got home, I called Grand Forks. Chris answered the phone. "I need Steve," I said.

"Then he'll be on the first plane out of here."

Twenty-Four

I DON'T KNOW HOW I MADE IT through the next twenty-four hours. Susan called frequently to report the results of her self-imposed investigation on the island. She turned up nothing new. Every time Susan phoned, she asked if I needed her with me, and though I told her not to come, she arrived on my doorstep at noon the next day, carrying a tin of cookies and herbal tea in one arm, a car seat holding her newborn in the other. She set down the baby and pulled me into a long, wordless hug. Then she held me stiffly in front of her, fingers tightly clutching my arms. "How long has it been since you've slept?"

"How long have the kids been gone?" I answered, smiling weakly. "Come inside. I'll put on some water." In spite of our light banter, I felt safer somehow, just having her with me.

Susan followed me into my kitchen, where she plunked herself down at the table. She unbuckled Mandy and lifted her from the seat, asking, "When is Steve coming in?"

"Tomorrow morning, around ten." I handed her a mug of steaming raspberry tea.

"Have you heard from the guy who is going to investigate?"

"The detective? Not yet."

Carefully she placed her mug on the table beside her. "I've been doing some research, Patty," she said, her voice serious, determined. "This situation could be much worse than we originally thought. Right now, Russell can have as much as four—maybe five—days head start on the police. Unless he is stopped for some crazy fluke like speeding or"—she threw her hand in the air, gesturing wildly—"failing to yield to a yellow light, they don't have much chance of finding him." Her voice intensified. "There are organizations out there who deal with this kind of thing. We need some real help."

"Not yet. The police will find Russell," I said stubbornly. "They have to. I have custody. I have all the papers. I have a lawyer." I stood and paced the room in front of her. "Besides, as crazy as Russell is, he wouldn't just disappear with the kids—not forever. He stands to lose his medical license, his reputation, his practice. He wouldn't throw all that away—just to hurt me."

"It never bothered Russ to hurt you before."

"But this isn't hitting me."

"I'm just saying that maybe we should be more proactive."

Stopping suddenly, I turned to face her. "What do you mean?"

"I think we should go see your lawyer."

"Why?"

"Because from what I've read, Patty, this whole thing may come down to finding the kids by ourselves. If the police won't—or maybe they can't—do it, well, then, we're going to have to do it ourselves."

"It shouldn't come to that—to me finding them by myself. How could I do that?"

"Well, it just may. Can't we at least call your attorney?" Susan leaned forward, reaching for the plate of cookies on the table in front of her. As she lifted a macaroon from the plate, the phone rang, and we both jumped a little. I felt my mouth go dry and my heart race as I hurried to the wall phone in the kitchen. Police detective James Alder introduced himself over the telephone. I slid down the side of the cabinet to sit cross-legged on the kitchen floor. Susan, watching from the dining table, flashed a question mark with her eyes. I pointed to the phone with one hand.

"Yes, Detective Alder. I'm so relieved to hear from you." I took a slow deep breath.

"Mrs. Koehler, I am the detective assigned to investigate your missing children. I just called to ask, are the children still missing?"

"Yes, of course." His question stunned me.

"All right. Well, then, I'll go ahead with the investigation." It sounded as though he might hang up.

"Wait! Detective, I don't understand. I would have let you know if the children were home."

"You'd think so, Mrs. Koehler. But actually, about nine out of ten of these missing kids come home without any help at all. And you'd be surprised how many parents forget to let us know. I never start the official work until I am certain the children haven't already been brought home."

"I understand." I rubbed my forehead with the fingers of my free hand, trying to control the anger I felt. Every moment seemed so important, and yet Detective Alder had yet to start the investigation. "What happens now?"

"Not so fast. I have one more important question. Do you have a certified copy of a custody determination in your possession?"

"Yes, of course. I gave it to the police officer who took the report. He put a copy in the file." I heard frustration in my voice and stopped to take a deep calming breath. I ran my hand through my hair and continued more calmly. "We went to court this fall. It's a temporary order, but yes, I have it."

Through the phone, I heard him shuffling papers. "Oh yes, I do have a copy here." A pause. "And do you have proof that your husband is fully aware of the decree?"

"He was in the room when the judge issued the order."

"Good, the records should say so. One more question, have you followed the conditions of the order explicitly?"

"I think so."

"Think so?" He sounded irritated. "Either you have or you haven't."

"I'd have to think about it," I answered, remembering Russell's phone call to the house, the numerous times he had been late bringing the children home. I remembered Russell's violation of the supervised visitation. I didn't want to lie, but I really didn't know what constituted violations of the order.

"Because if you have changed the determination in any way," he continued matter-of-factly, "either verbally or implied by mutual action, you have effectively nullified the custody determination."

"All right," I answered, unsure of what I should say, afraid that a wrong answer would keep him from helping me. In my current emotional state, I had difficulty following his thoughts.

"Now, this is the hard one, Mrs. Koehler. I have one more issue to mention. You must determine if you want to have your husband charged with the crime of custodial interference."

"What does that mean?"

"As the name implies, it has to do with disobeying enforceable custody determinations. The parent must have full understanding of the determination. Then, the severity of the crime is determined by where your husband has gone."

"What do you mean by 'where'?"

"If Dr. Koehler has left the state, he can be charged with a felony. If he still resides inside the state, his crime is a misdemeanor. It's that simple."

It didn't sound simple to me. The detective's words reeled in my mind as I imagined the consequences. Felony. Misdemeanor. Starting over. Left the state. Fragments of his words floated around in my head, each clamoring for my attention.

His voice interrupted my thoughts. "You can think about it for now. But I'll have to know soon. I'll contact the prosecutor's office for direction as well."

"What will you do next?" I asked.

"Well, I can do a lot from right here—from the phone on my desk," he continued confidently. "The first task is to find out where Dr. Koehler has taken the kids. I'll start by having the school district flag Leah's records. If he really means to start over somewhere else, there is usually a request for records by the new school. These days you can't get into a school without them. We'll know immediately."

With a sinking feeling I realized that this might be how Russell had found us. "But that could be days . . . or even months from now."

"True, but we can still nose around in the meantime. I'll also check the passport office to see if we can find anything there."

"The passport office?"

"The children would both need one if he decides to flee the country." The police officer took a deep breath. "Really, Mrs. Koehler, I don't mean to discourage you. But until we know where he is, there isn't much we can do to get the kids back. The best thing you can do is to try and figure out where he might have gone. Question the relatives. Ask his friends. I'll need your help if we're ever going to find him."

"All right. I'll . . . uh . . . I'll see what I can find out."

"Well, then, that's it for now," he said as though he were about to dismiss me.

"Wait," I said. "When will I hear from you again? How do I contact you?"

"Oh yes. I'll give you the number of my voice mail. You can reach me anytime at this number, and I'll be in touch with you every couple of days."

"Days?"

"Yes." He sighed heavily into the phone. "Mrs. Koehler, don't forget that these things take time. I am also assigned to other criminal investigations. I'll do the best I can. But you must be patient." I wrote down the number he gave me. With a polite exit, he hung up. I rolled over onto the floor, overwhelmed with discouragement. My knight in shining armor had other crimes to investigate. Things far more serious than Leah and RJ. He would do what he could from his desk. Tears filled my eyes, and I covered my face, rolled into a ball on the floor, and wept.

Susan let me cry. Sitting beside me on the kitchen floor, she rubbed my back and listened to my sobs. I felt her presence, her commitment, and through it, I recognized her love. Somehow it comforted me. When my weeping slowed to trickling tears, I sat up and tried to fill her in on the detective's instructions.

"I know," she answered gently, "I figured most of it out by hearing your end of the conversation." She sat quietly. Handing me a tissue, she asked, "Where do we start?"

"I have no idea." I blew my nose. "The detective said he needed my help in finding Russell, and I have no idea where to start." My voice, mostly air, spoke the words punctuated by little hiccups and squeaks of breath.

"All right. Then we'll figure it out." She slid onto her knees. "I've always wanted to be a cop. This is my big chance. But first I think we need to make two phone calls."

"What?"

"First I want to call your doctor," she answered. "I think you need some help. If you don't get some sleep, you'll be no help to us at all. Then we need to call Judy Barton."

"I don't really have a doctor."

"You leave that to me. I'll call the lawyer too." She stood, poured a tall glass of water, and handed it to me. "Here, drink this," she said. "You're going to get dehydrated the way you lose tears." Patting my knee, she smiled.

I did sleep better, thanks to the over-the-counter medication the Urgent Care Clinic recommended. Susan made a three o'clock appointment with my attorney and drove me to the airport in her white minivan. I knew I would feel better when Steve arrived.

I didn't know how much better until I saw him walking up the gateway from the airplane. "Oh, Patty," he said, holding me tightly. "I'm so sorry about all of this."

I fought tears. "Thanks for coming," I whispered into his chest.

"We'll get it straightened out." He patted my back lightly.

Together the three of us went to lunch. I picked at my food while Steve and Susan made a vain attempt at light conversation. I heard their voices through a thick fog of deep sadness. My body no longer made breast milk. RJ's long absence had convinced my breasts that he no longer needed me. Only my mind refused to cooperate. My baby needed me. My daughter needed me. I needed them. And here we were, eating lunch.

At promptly 2:50 we stepped out of the elevator onto the thick carpet in Judy Barton's waiting area. Steve guided me to a chair and then announced us to the secretary. The fog refused to lift, and I saw everything through a vague and distant lens—as though I weren't really present but rather watched the events through a camera.

We sat together in the leather furniture around her glass table—Steve closest to Judy, Susan in the opposite chair holding Mandy. Steve, with his sequential and logical thinking, actively followed Judy's instructions, interrupting her frequently for questions and clarification, all the while taking copious notes.

Judy had little to offer. As I understood it, she promised to call the prosecutor on our behalf. She gave us a booklet on parental abduction produced by some group of missing children's advocates. She filled a legal pad with notes of her own.

"Now, let's go through the assignments." She turned back to her first page of notes. "We need to file a certified copy of the custody decree in the San Juan County courthouse. This afternoon I'll call the prosecutor's office and see if I can light a fire under the criminal side of this mess. Then I'll call the detective involved and press for an active investigation. It can't hurt." She checked off the items on her list as she spoke. "Patty, do you know if the children have been entered into the NCIC computer?"

"NCIC?"

"National Crime Information Center, the Missing Persons file."

"Oh, I . . . I don't really remember."

"Okay, I'll check on that for you," Judy said, making a note to herself.

Steve said, "One thing we haven't covered is the expenses. This whole thing is going to cost money. Lots of money. How do we manage that?"

"That's something we can't worry about now. We'll just have to come up with the money. Eventually, when we find Russell and the kids, we'll petition the court to enforce our custody decree. Then the police can go in and get the kids for us." She carefully laid her tablet on the table in front of her. "When we do that—go for enforcement—we'll ask the judge to have Russell pay all of our expenses for search and recovery. Judges often order abducting parents to pay. But," she sighed, "it only works when the parent has money." She put her reading glasses back on. Patiently she continued where she left off. "The next question is—do Russell's parents know where he is?"

Steve and Susan both looked at me. "He told me they were out of town."

"Where?"

"I think the Caribbean somewhere."

"I want you to find out where and contact them. I will send a copy of the custody decree with a very strongly worded letter directly to their home address."

"What will it say?" Steve asked.

"I will remind them that they may be held liable in a civil court for failing to reveal what they know about their son's whereabouts."

"But," Susan broke in, "couldn't they be angered if you threaten them? Then they might be even less help."

"True. I will keep that in mind. However, they need to understand that if sufficient evidence exists to prove that they helped Russell, they could face criminal charges as accomplices. It doesn't hurt for them to have every possible consequence carefully explained," Judy said, smiling as if she'd hidden a diamond in her coat pocket. "I'm only bringing their attention to the law as it now reads. That's what attorneys do, you know." She turned the page. "I'd suggest you have a second phone line installed at the house. That way, you can do your homework on one phone and keep a line open in case Leah calls home." She glanced down at her notes, fingering the lines as she read to herself. "Now, Patty, do you know if the police have issued a Be on the Lookout bulletin?"

"I think the police officer told me he would."

"I'll check on that as well," she said. "I can also press for search warrants to see if he left any clues at the house or with the bank or even at his business office. If we find evidence that Russell has fled the state, we have grounds for a felony arrest warrant." She paused and looked at each of us in turn. "That will win him a warrant on federal charges—Unlawful Flight to Avoid Prosecution. We'll look at that later. The most important thing to do now is to find him. Of course, the sooner we find him, the better. In all likelihood, the three of you have all the resources you need to figure out where he has gone. Use them. The big action really starts after we find Russell."

Susan reached out and patted my hand. "Did you hear that, Patty?" she asked gently. "Judy said 'after' we find them, not if. We'll find them, Pat. We'll get the kids back."

Susan's words did not register. I sat staring vacantly at the pattern of a rose on a corner of her office carpet. Something bothered me. What was it? "The detective—his name was Alder—said something about passports. What did he mean?"

"Good point." Judy Barton made a short note to herself. "Russell could make a living anywhere. Perhaps he does plan to flee the country."

"Then what do we do?" Susan asked, baffled.

"We make sure he can't get the children out of the United States. I ask for a court order restraining the removal of the children from this country. When I get that, I file it with the passport office."

That one thought—that Russell might leave the country—made me shudder violently. All the way home, I wrestled to drive out a horrible sense of dread that threatened to send me crashing into despair.

We'd been home from Judy Barton's office about an hour when the phone rang again. Susan answered it in the kitchen, where we sat at the table trying to make plans to find Russell. Handing it to me, she mouthed the word "Police."

"This is Detective Alder," he began in a businesslike tone. "I have some bad news, Mrs. Koehler."

I steeled myself to his words and leaned heavily onto the counter.

"I spoke with the school district today," he said. "They checked the records. I found that Dr. Koehler requested Leah's school records two weeks ago—before he even took the children." He paused. "So that avenue is closed."

"Now what?" I said, my voice trembling.

"Well, like I said before—we try to find him." I heard him sigh. "He hasn't disappeared. He's just made finding him a little harder, that's all. I just thought you'd want to know. It makes your work more urgent."

I went back to the table with a new sense of desperation. This game of hide-and-seek gambled with the highest stakes: my children. I fought despair in order to concentrate. I had to find Russell. I had to get the children back.

After several hours of work, Steve decided to fix dinner. He boiled spaghetti noodles, browned hamburger, and opened a can of premade sauce. Soon the kitchen filled with warm condensation from the boiling pots. Italian aromas floated through the air as Susan broiled cheap white bread brushed with butter and garlic. I almost felt hungry by the time the phone rang again. I picked it up.

"Hello, Patty." I heard Russell's unmistakable voice.

Desperately fighting an entire convocation of emotions, I answered tightly, "Russell, where are you?"

I heard him laugh. "You think I'm going to tell you that?" He paused, and I thought for the tiniest moment that I heard the gurgles of a baby in the background. "Listen, Patty, I just called to tell you to call off the search. You'll never find me."

"Russell, please—"

"No." He yelled the word. "This whole thing is your fault, Patty. If you hadn't left, you'd be holding the baby right now. Instead, I have him. You have only yourself to blame. I would never have done this—except you forced me." He waited, apparently expecting me to answer. I said nothing. "Give it up. I just called to tell you . . ." He paused. "You're never going to see the kids again." The line went dead. My appetite vanished.

The three of us talked long into the night, exhaustion preying on all of us. Russell's call angered Steve, and he grew more furious as he thought about it. Susan, on the other hand, sank into one of her quiet, introspective moods. She made a phone call to the island and joined us again seeming somehow lighter. I guessed that she called home. As soon as she sat down, she announced that she would stay the night.

I didn't care where Susan slept. I felt like a woman who had just spent hours swimming upstream. I could hear Niagara Falls just below my feet. No matter how hard I tried, the falls were always there, waiting to swallow me whole.

Russell was right. If I hadn't left, this would never have happened. What I wanted most in the world—to be a mother and a wife—had been irretrievably stolen from me. Just a family—that was all I ever wanted. What should I have done? Why couldn't I have found another way? How could I live without the kids? Russell was right in more than one way. I would never find the children. I would never play music with Leah. I would never know RJ as a toddler. I would never dress him for his first day of school. After all that fighting, Russell had won. And he'd won everything that really counted. I sank into the most complete despair I had ever known. Though Susan and Steve continued to talk, I slipped further and further away from them. The accusations I brought against myself became more and more severe until at last I brought down my own gavel. Guilty as charged. I'd failed my children. I didn't deserve to find them.

As I prepared for bed that night, I carefully executed each step of my normal routine. I brushed my teeth, washed my face, and put on hand cream. Then I slipped into bed. I reached for the package of sleeping pills on the bedside table. Carefully, I punched all of the remaining pills from their individual packets.

Then, holding a large glass of water in one hand, I swallowed them all.

Twenty-Five

FACES AND IMAGES FLOATED PAST my mind's eye. Close to my breast, RJ nestled in and, with eager panting, turned toward me, rooting lustily. I bared myself to his request, happy to be so wanted. He latched on, and with satisfied sounds, he nursed. Milk began to flow and I pressed my fullness away from his tiny nose. Satisfied sighs and noisy swallows filled the air, wrapping me in the enormous warmth and satisfaction only a nursing mother can feel. From somewhere I heard music, and I turned to see Leah playing a violin. I heard the soft vibrato of the notes coming from the almost imperceptible movement of her left hand. I experienced intense pride as she played a particularly difficult passage. I felt her loving gaze and met her eyes, holding them with an intense, almost painful love. She ran to me, and we hugged. I squeezed until I thought I had driven the breath from her tiny frame. No, no. She only fainted. As she collapsed, I called to her. "Leah, Leah! Mommy is here. Don't go. Don't leave me." I struggled to bring her back, shaking her, blowing air into her mouth. As I worked frantically, almost violently, she faded from my view, escaping my grip like a phantom. She faded . . . faded. At last she vanished. I heard voices calling me away from her. "Patty," they called. No. No. I must save Leah. She needs me. She needs me. . . .

"Patty. Wake up, Patty." I heard the voice again and suddenly became aware of an intense heaviness in my body. Somehow I'd become encased in concrete. I heard but could not respond. Though I tried, my mouth would not open.

Again, the voices. I called to the voice. "I'm here. I'm trying, but the words won't come." I felt crisp cotton sheets under my fingertips and became slowly aware of other sounds. Unidentifiable sounds. Beeps. Bells. I could not move my hands. More voices. At last I opened my eyes, lifting slow, heavy lids and saw Susan through the chrome bars of a hospital bed. She sat in a chair beside my bed. Her right hand rested on the sheets. I tried to turn my head but could not manage even the simplest of motion. So heavy.

She sensed the movement. Immediately she stood, bending over the rail. "There you are. About time you woke up." She smiled a relieved grin. "You scared the living daylights out of us," she reproved. "Don't ever do that again." Leaning closer, she said, "I just want you to know that if you do, I'm gonna make it really hurt. I don't ever want to be scared like that again." She turned to pour water into a glass, adjusted the straw and lifted it gently to my lips. I noticed that her hand trembled. "Seriously, I don't know what I would do without you. How you feeling?"

"Heavy," I answered. "So heavy."

"You are a very lucky girl," she said. "Steve went into your room to check on you before he went to bed. He found you only moments before it would have been too late."

"Where am—?"

"Valley Hospital."

"How long have I been asleep?"

"You've been sleeping on and off for a couple of days."

"The kids? Have you heard about the kids?"

"Nothing yet. But we do have news."

"News? What news?"

"We don't know where they are. Not that much. But little things. I'll tell you more later, when you're feeling better." She turned to put the glass back on the nightstand. "In the meantime, the doctor said you need to drink lots of water. And rest. He says you need to sleep this off."

I nodded, too tired to argue.

By the next morning I'd progressed enough to be discharged from the hospital. In truth, I didn't want to leave. I didn't care. Even now, nothing had changed. Though they'd saved my body, they had not rescued my soul.

Though no one said it out loud, I knew it was nearly time for Steve to return home. Steve's family needed him. I knew it, but I hated it. I hated the thought of his leaving. Susan promised him that she would care for me at her home until I was completely well again. Steve and Susan packed clothes and picked me up at the hospital for the trip to the islands.

I tried not to care that Steve had to leave. He couldn't help anyway. No one could. I rode silently in the middle seat of Susan's minivan, watching the scenery speed by without seeing anything. I rode the ferry without getting out of the car. Susan went up to the snack bar for coffee. I accepted the Styrofoam cup she offered but never drank, never spoke. Putting the cup aside, I fell asleep and slept until we pulled into Susan's driveway.

I woke to Susan's gentle tugging at my shoulder. "Patty, I think you've had enough sleep." Her voice betrayed her smile. "Come inside, kiddo."

I sat up, rubbing my face heavily. Still fighting an overwhelming sense of disorientation, I glanced at the cars in her driveway and felt panic. "The cars. Why are so many cars here? I don't want to see anyone."

"You'll find out. If you'll just get out of the car. Come inside and you'll find out all kinds of things you didn't know before." She smiled and offered me a hand. I tumbled like a drunk out of her car.

Beside the minivan someone had parked a red Suburban. Beside that, several other varieties of minivans mingled with trucks, big and small. An old station wagon had parked on the street, flanked on both ends by a nearly endless variety of sedans. Who were they? Why had they come? Fatigue dragged at my arms and legs. I couldn't face a house full of people. "Susan, I can't. I can't face these people. Not now. Not after all I've done." I tried to resist her shepherding embrace.

"You don't have to face anyone, Patty. These people want to encourage you—not judge you. Believe me, you're safe here."

I felt tears sting at my eyes, and I hated myself for being so weak, so helpless. And I hated that I could not refuse Susan's love. I allowed her to lead me to her front door.

In the entry hall, Steve helped me out of my coat and led me to the living room, where I found every available chair filled by the people of Serenity Bay. When I entered, their quiet conversation stopped, and they turned to smile a warm welcome. I nodded politely and stood gazing but not speaking. While I stood completely baffled, Steve strode into the room and dropped into a chair near the window. Beside him, my dentist sat on the fireplace hearth. The school librarian sat in a folding chair near the dining room. The Walking Women, as Russell referred to them, sat together at the dining room table. I saw faces of people from the stores and offices I had visited nearly every day I'd lived on the island. As my gaze wandered around the perimeter of the room, the clearing of a throat caught my attention. In the opposite corner, Oleda, in flowing turquoise, perched on an ottoman.

"Hello, Patricia," she said softly. Her lovely smile flooded her face and brightened the room.

"Oleda!" Surprised, confused, overwhelmed, I could not understand the meaning of this gathering. From the post office, the hardware store, the Stock 'n Save, even the waitress who'd first waited on us the day we'd come to see Nana's property. The manager of our bank was there along with his wife, a teacher at the island school. Susan's pastor and another man stood looking out the living room window.

All these faces, most familiar, many unrecognized, smiled back at me. I glanced at Susan, who came to stand beside me quietly. "Well, everyone. Now that we're here, we can get started." She ran the palms of her hands together as if she were about to begin an exciting board game.

I wanted to ask what we were starting when Scott, the sheriff I knew to be Russell's friend, jumped out of his chair, saying, "Here, Pat. You sit here. You must be tired, and you'll want to hear everything we have to say."

I felt my heart beat rapidly and my hands grow moist. I ran one hand through my hair, then sat in the chair with as much grace as any completely stupefied victim could manage. "Thank you," I murmured simply. What was all this about?

Susan, framed by the archway to the entry hall, began to speak. "Well, thanks for coming, everyone. Patty doesn't yet know what we're up to. I haven't told her anything. First, let me introduce Steve, Patty's brother." Steve gave a little celebrity wave, which started a ripple of laughter through the room. He winked at me, and I glared back. Susan continued. "Okay, now, Patty, the short of it is that these people have decided to join forces to help us find the kids. Everyone in this room has taken some part of the job— and it's a big job—but together, there's a chance we can pull it off." Still speaking, she walked into the room and took a folding chair for herself. "I took the liberty of starting this whole thing. But actually it's Joe's ball game now. So, Joe, why don't you tell us what is happening."

Joseph West, Susan's pastor, moved to Serenity Bay the year after Russell and I. Locals viewed him with a peculiar mixture of mistrust and awe—mistrust because of his profession and because he had not been born to island life, and awe because of his uncanny ability to win their loyalty by his genuine concern for others. Joe and his family had been Russ's patients, so I had many opportunities to form my own opinions. I noticed whenever he came to the office that he spoke kindly to everyone he encountered. When his son came in for an ear infection, he asked our nurse about her sick puppy, a detail he remembered from a previous visit. Once I saw him chat with another patient about an ill spouse. The conversation lasted for so long that Joe asked me to give his turn with the doctor to another patient so that they could finish talking. These kinds of things led the locals who did not attend Susan's church into a camp of unspoken loyalty. Though they themselves did not attend, they would not tolerate disrespect toward this loving and gentle—though completely human—man.

I'd come to know Joe personally when Leah attended Susan's Sunday school class. He'd driven out to the house to call on us, and though Russell wasn't home at the time, I'd poured lemonade and talked with him on the front porch. He expressed a genuine interest in my answers to his questions, and I found him neither pushy nor offensive—qualities I had expected from Protestant pastors.

This same Joe West now stood in Susan's living room drinking coffee from a mug I myself had used. From his place near the windows, he brought the meeting to order. "Well, actually I can't take credit for much. When Susan called, I knew I wanted to help. But I had no idea how." He smiled and gestured to Scott. "So I called Scott, and Susan called Oleda."

Susan perked up. "Oleda tells me she's had lots of experience with parental abduction."

"More than I like," Oleda agreed.

"And she's even snatched a few." Susan grinned. "Kids, I mean. That's experience we may be able to use."

"Anyway," Pastor Joe continued, slightly amused at the interruption, "Scott helped me get things started. From there, the whole plan just sort of started rolling."

"Enough self-depreciation," Susan said, and the room giggled behind her. "Patty needs to know what we've already done."

"All right. Sorry." Smiling lightly, he bowed and picked a clipboard up from the coffee table beside him. "This is what we've discovered so far. We started at the local bank. And"—he gestured at the bank manager—"as Mike Dempsy will tell you, much of that information is a matter of public record. Why don't you fill us in, Mike?"

"Well, it seems that on the Friday before he took the children, Russ closed the family bank account, which is perfectly legal. Either spouse may close an account. He took the account balance in cash, so we won't be able to use that to track his present location. The good news—" he paused with a light tone in his voice—"is that on the day Russell closed the checking account, the savings account was empty, or nearly so. For whatever reason, he did not close the savings. However, on the fifteenth of every month, his business makes an automatic deposit into his savings. It seems that Russ didn't take that into consideration—or maybe he forgot." Mike smiled outright. "So we have two aces in our possession." Holding up his fingers he illustrated. "One, we have money to help Patty through this until we have some resolution to the crisis. Her name is on both the business and the savings accounts. That means the balance is as much hers as it is his." He paused to let that sink in. "And two, Russell will eventually remember the savings account. He'll probably make some move to get hold of it. We have plenty of time to get a subpoena so that we can use any information he gives us to help find him." Mike Dempsy gave a smile of satisfaction like that of a plumber who has found and explained a leak.

"Good report, Mike." Pastor Joe read the notes on his sheet and then looked directly toward me. "Patty, you need to contact Mike while you are here this week. In the midst of gathering this 'public information,' we've discovered a few things that Russell may have done without your knowledge." I expelled a small bitter laugh. There had been so much I didn't know. "We've discovered that Russ also paid off the island house and managed to subdivide the property with the county. It seems he was in the midst of planning something that he never quite managed to finish. We've put those details in the speculation pile to deal with later."

"At this rate there never will be a later," a voice said peevishly. "Could we pick up the pace here?"

"Right. We do have an agenda. Sorry, folks." Joe looked down at the list. "All right, let's have the poster group go next. Donna?"

One of the walking women stood, holding a large roll of paper. "Great," she began. "Well, Patty, Susan got us pictures, and while you were in the hospital, we came up with this." She held the paper high overhead with one hand and unrolled it to its full size. The poster, divided into evenly spaced quarters had a large bold title, PARENTAL ABDUCTION. Underneath the words stared the smiling face of Leah and a current snapshot of RJ. Beneath both pictures she had printed detailed descriptions of the children and the abduction itself. Below the children, Donna had centered a recent snapshot of Russell. Details of his physical description, profession, and disappearance were placed below his face.

"Now," she began as she held the poster high in the air, "this is the large size. We made an early run of two hundred. The ladies from church have already put them up. We have them all over the island and on all the ferry terminals out of the San Juan's. We have several thousand of the smaller version." With this she paused and lifted an essentially identical copy printed on a notebook-sized sheet of paper. Holding it high enough for everyone to see, she continued, "We've had quite a lot of success with the small one. We have it in all of the employees' lounges at the airport, thanks to a friend of a friend. We have faxed one to every border crossing in the three nearest states and to the corporate offices of several major chains of day-care centers. In fact, the local wholesale grocery distributor has agreed to send it out to every store it supplies. Our early success depends on blanket coverage, and later, as clues come in, we'll focus more specifically on an area where we think Russell actually may have been." She continued speaking, though I no longer listened to her words. I saw only the faces of my children staring back from the poster before me. Tears came again, filling my eyes for the thousandth time and trickling down my cheeks. Susan noticed and came over to sit on the footrest near my chair. "You okay?" she whispered, patting my feet.

"No, I'm not okay," I said out loud. "I don't understand this. Why are you all here?" I slipped my feet off the rest, away from Susan. Though Donna stopped speaking, her mouth froze in mid-speech, her eyes wide with surprise. She sat stiffly, her mouth still hanging uselessly open, and turned to Pastor Joe.

Joe took the question with grace. "Patty, what question are you really asking?" He looked hard at me, though still with kindness. "I mean, we could give you a superficial answer—about caring or something. But there is a real answer, a good one." He paused. "I'm just not sure you really want the whole story."

"Of course I do." I choked back sobs and dragged my sleeve at the tears still flooding my cheeks and dripping onto my sweat shirt.

"I have just spent ten days begging for help. But could I get anyone to help me—even the police? No. I gave up. I mean, I really gave up. And now this. You're asking me to hope again. To believe that somehow all of us—actually you—can find the kids. I'm no good to anyone." I dropped my face into my hands and cried. "Everything I ever did caused more pain and misery. I don't want to hope. If I can't have my children, I don't want hope." My words made no sense, even to me. But neither did my feelings. Susan patted my shoulder and let me cry. The room fell into a long uneasy silence. Agonizing moments passed.

I heard Joe clear his throat before he started to speak. "Well, Patty, I guess now that you ask, I don't quite know where to begin." He rubbed his face with one hand. "I guess I'll start with Leah. Because, to be truthful, I don't think I'd be here if it weren't for Leah. I got to know her when she started coming to our Sunday school. I make it my habit to visit all of the elementary classes a couple of times over the course of a year, and I was in Leah's class just a couple of weeks before she went to the hospital."

By now my crying had eased some, and I wiped my nose on the sleeve of my sweat shirt and looked up to find the eyes of everyone focused intently on Joe. He planted one hand in the pocket of his jeans.

"That Sunday, I got to teach the lesson about Jonah and the Whale, which is pretty easy, because all kids love that story. Anyway"—Pastor Joe gestured casually—"in Leah's classroom, the kids chose to read the story themselves. Of course most of us know that it is the story about a servant of God who decides to run away from his assignment for God. And I remember we were talking that day about how many jobs we'd all like to run away from. Some kids mentioned homework, and some mentioned chores. But Leah was very quiet that morning. And I noticed, so I asked her, 'Leah, what part of this story do you like the best?' And her answer startled me. It was very perceptive for a nine-year-old. She said, 'I like that God met Jonah in the whale.'" Joe paused and looked around the room. "I guess I'd never thought of that myself. But Leah was right. God did meet Jonah inside the whale. By the time that class was over, I understood two things as clearly as I see you all today. I understood that Leah Alice Koehler believed in a living, caring God. And the second thing I saw that morning was that children have some amazing insights about what God is doing around them." He paused again. "So when Susan called to tell me she was going down to the city to stay a few days with you, I knew. I knew we had to do what we could to help."

Gesturing to the papers he had spread over the table beside him, he continued. "All this work is not about being nice. It isn't about choosing sides. We must do this to help Leah. Leah is a member of our church family because she belongs to Jesus. We care about her and about the baby. We know that having the children with you is both morally and legally right. They deserve a safe home. They deserve to grow up without hiding, to attend school, and to be part of a church that cares for them." He looked straight into my eyes. "We want to help you, Patty, because it's the right thing to do. Leah decided to become part of our church family. It's part of our identity to bear one another's burdens. But also"—he shook his head—"we want to help because we care about you. And that is going to be very hard for you to believe right now." He allowed a long pause to fill the air of Susan's living room. "So will you let us?" he asked. "Will you let us help you?"

I gave him the tiniest of nods. "Yes," I whispered.

The meeting continued for another full hour. This group had done their homework. They covered every aspect of the assignments already given, and still they managed to give out more work. They thought of new ideas for obtaining information and clues about Russell. Together, they constituted a formidable bunch. Each person in the room represented endless friends and contacts who were, they declared, eager to help. Exhausted, I had difficulty following it all. I had to trust the notes Pastor Joe made. For the first time since Russell took the children, I dared to entertain the potential for hope.

When they finished, they surprised me by ending in prayer. Joe asked Susan to pray. And though I cried through most of the prayer, this is what I remember of her words: "Father, here we are. Some of us have chosen to belong to you, and some of us haven't. But you know us. You know each and every one of us, inside and out. You made us. And nothing is hidden from you. Right now, you know exactly where Leah and RJ and Russell are. Though we want them back, we know that you are caring for them right where they are. You are with them. You promised"—her voice trailed to a whisper—"that you would never leave us or forsake us. That's a promise you made to Leah, Lord. And right now, more than any time before, we are hanging on that very promise. Care for her. Keep them, Lord. Care for RJ. Meet his every physical and emotional need." Susan took a long shuddering breath. "And I ask too that you would keep us. Help us, Father. We have no idea where to look or what work to do. But you can lead us through every step. Keep us focused. Keep us working well together. And most of all we ask—" she paused and wiped her nose with her fingertips—"that you keep Patty. Father, give her reason to hope. Give her a reason to look forward to tomorrow. We love you, Lord," she concluded, "so very much."

And everyone added "Amen."

Twenty-Six

WE FILLED THE NEXT TWO DAYS with busy activity. Steve bought a fax machine and plugged it into an additional telephone line he had installed in Susan's home. The fax enabled us to keep in touch with the various agencies looking for the kids. It also served to get court documents, pictures, and information instantaneously to the authorities helping us as well. We had the National Center for Missing Children hotline phone number on all of our posters. They too could contact us via fax, to confirm the identity of any suspicious children reported to them.

Steve also had the phone company arrange to forward all of my calls to Susan's house. One dream remained—that somehow Leah could get to a telephone and contact us. Whenever the phone rang, I trembled.

We combed Russell's island house for clues and spent an entire morning going through his trash piece by piece. The next evening, we searched Russell's business office. We didn't want to offend Belinda, so we went in after they closed up. It felt a little like being a member of a *Mission Impossible* team.

By my third day on the island, it became apparent to Russell's clinic staff that he did not intend to return. Their loyalty was taxed beyond endurance. The absence of future paychecks drove most of them to resign, which they called me to do. Only Belinda, his receptionist, continued to go to work every day. I couldn't understand what she was thinking. Did she really believe that he would suddenly reappear?

We interviewed all of the locals who might have spoken to Russell in the days before he left. For the most part, they sympathized with my anguish. Many confessed that they "never really liked him" anyway. I took a perverse pleasure in their confession.

The attorney who attended the meeting at Susan's house agreed to give us free legal advice so that Judy Barton could be used as sparingly as possible. This promised to keep our legal costs down. His immediate concern involved selling Russell's practice while it still had patient records to sell—an extensive legal difficulty, made only slightly easier by the fact that Russell was missing and suspected of felony custodial interference.

Steve designed a plan to hire a private detective. It included a contract that effectively limited the detective's hours and expenses. The investigator would work on tasks as we assigned him and submit only preapproved expenses.

Eventually, though we tried to avoid thinking about it, Steve had to return home. He'd been gone from his work and family for nine days. He reluctantly made arrangements to catch a shuttle to Lake Washington from Serenity Bay. Soon Steve would be on his way home to Grand Forks.

In the late afternoon of his tenth day in the Northwest, we loaded Susan's minivan with Steve's things and drove to the docks. He carried his bags down the steep ramp, and in silence we waited for the floatplane to arrive. Eventually it landed with a roar and taxied into place, blowing water all over the dock. The pilot jumped out, tied the plane down, and threw Steve's two suitcases into the tail. A dock employee loaded boxes from the island and gassed the plane.

Steve gave me a long tight hug. "Good-bye, Pet. I love you."

"Good-bye, Steve. Thanks for coming." The tears flowed. You'd think a person would run out. The pilot stood behind us with one foot on the dock and one on the pontoon. He tried to appear patient, but over Steve's shoulder, I noticed he checked his watch.

"Don't forget, I promise I'll keep working on that lawyer thing from home." I understood that he meant selling Russell's practice. The engine noise made conversation difficult. "And, Pet, please come out to see us. The kids miss their auntie."

Slowly, he let go of my shoulders. He reached out to shake Susan's hand, but instead, they gave one another a long embrace.

"Thanks for coming," Susan said. "We needed you here."

Steve smiled and turned to climb into the plane. I covered my trembling lips with one hand and waved meekly with the other. Susan put her arm around my shoulder.

The pilot released the tie-downs and climbed into his seat. When his seat belt was fastened, the attendant slammed the pilot's side door and pushed the floatplane away with his foot. With a deafening roar and the finest of salt spray, the plane taxied away from the dock. Reaching the far end of the harbor, it turned to face the wind, powered up the engines, and started across the harbor, building speed as it went. We watched as though mesmerized. Lifting off, the plane climbed the hill behind the ferry landing and circled the bay before turning south. I thought for a moment that I saw Steve waving from his seat behind the pilot. Then, through a blur of tears, I watched the little plane disappear.

I never felt more alone than I did watching the six-seater fly out over the bay. It was late, nearly five, and though the sun had officially set, in that lengthy glow that persists over the western horizon, it was still light enough to see. The afternoon had been warm, but by the time Susan and I walked back to her car, the evening air had turned very cold.

"It's going to frost again," she said, unlocking the minivan with her automatic lock. The bleep of the electronic security system startled me back to reality. Could I make it through this now that Steve had flown home?

"What? I'm sorry. What did you say?"

"Nothing." She smiled at me over the roof of the car, and we got in.

We rode back to her house in deepening darkness and complete silence.

We drove into the garage and entered through the mud room,

where Brittany, almost twelve, greeted Susan enthusiastically, throwing both arms around her waist.

Taylor came through the dining room holding Mandy—Susan's surprise baby—dressed in an aqua sleeper and slung over her hip, facing away. At the same time, with one ear cocked slightly, Taylor held conversation on a cordless phone pressed against her shoulder. On seeing Susan, Mandy's round, bright face broke into a huge infant smile, her arms and legs kicking and pushing like a puppy in a swimming pool. Susan rolled her eyes at me before rescuing her baby. I felt a stab of horrible grief and turned away. "I need to use your powder room."

"Sure," Susan said. "I'll finish feeding the baby."

In the bathroom I sat on the floor and sobbed with hoarse, throaty sounds. I felt sick, nauseous. Depression threatened to engulf me once again. There were no tissues, so I unrolled great lengths of toilet paper and stuffed them into my jeans pockets. Would I ever again be able to function in a world where children lived? I realized, even as my mind asked the question, I didn't care if the answer was no. Without Leah and RJ, I had no reason to function. No reason to resist the horrible dark cloud of grief threatening to swallow me whole. No reason to live.

I rinsed my face with cold water and dried it with Susan's initialed guest towel. As I reached for the bathroom door, I took one last look in the mirror. The face staring back at me was horrifying. Saltwater and wind, kicked up by the seaplane propeller, had curled my dark hair into ringlets, cementing them into pieces and leaving them standing straight up at odd angles. Bags dragged at my lower lids, my makeup long lost to tears. Splotchy redness on my cheeks betrayed the constant stress and pain of overwhelming emotions. I didn't resemble anyone I recognized. No wonder Russell never loved me. Who could love a face like that?

Odd, how you observe yourself in times like this, seeing yourself clearly yet unable to alter the course of your own thoughts. I heard Susan call from the living room, and turning out the lights, I opened the door to leave. I'd seen all I wanted to see.

"Mandy needs her bottle," she said, plunking down into a chair, "but Taylor has managed to burn spaghetti noodles." She shifted her weight so that Mandy's head rested on the arm of the chair. "That's better. She's getting so heavy."

I dropped into the matching swivel rocker.

"Patty, I wonder, could you help Taylor with that mess in the kitchen? Tell her I said she's been on the phone long enough. I don't think Brittany has even had dinner yet." As Susan spoke, she did not look at me but rather gazed into Mandy's dark eyes. From across the room, I heard Mandy's satisfied swallowing. I had known that mother love. So long ago.

I stood to do her bidding, wondering if Susan knew how hard the task would be. Did she realize what she was asking? I shook myself. Susan had done so much for me, had been with me through so much. The least I could do was to make sure her children had dinner.

A short time later I returned to the living room as Susan snapped Mandy into her sleeper. "I've been thinking," she said, offering the baby the rest of the bottle. "What about a letter?"

"What letter?" I asked, sitting heavily in the chair.

"I think you should write a letter to Leah," she said, without looking up.

"Are you crazy?" My voice rose. "Why would I write a letter she will never read?"

"Never?"

I began to cry again.

"I'm not saying," she continued, "that Leah will read it tomorrow. But someday she may need to know what you are feeling tonight. She may need to hear how much you loved her and missed her. How hard we tried to find her."

"Why are you asking me to do this?"

"Because, from what I've read, when a parent abducts his children, he lies to them. He tells the kids that their mom is dead or that she doesn't want them anymore."

I blew my nose. It seemed that every time I stopped to consider my situation, things slid further into a whirlpool of hopelessness. How much more could I take?

Susan stood, lifting Mandy gently to her shoulder. "I'm going to put the baby to bed. You think about it, and I'll get some stationery."

Moments later, I held stationery in one hand and a pen in the other. How could I possibly write all that was in my heart?

————

It seemed as though many days had passed since we put Steve on the plane, but the chiming of the hall clock shook me from my memories. I glanced up to find Susan entering with a tray. She had placed glasses, napkins, and cookies around a tiny crystal vase holding a single rose. Did she know that Russell used to do the same? She set the tray on the coffee table and put my latte on a coaster in front of me.

"Here, let me take that paper. It doesn't look like writing was a very good idea. I'm sorry." She reached for the paper.

I looked at her blankly. My mind seemed to have developed a delay between hearing and recognition. I struggled to follow her sentence. She put the paper on the table beside us and reached for her own mug as she sat again in her rocker. I felt a wave of restless anxiety swelling in my chest. My heart beat faster. This was the moment, I knew from somewhere deep inside me. If ever I ask, it must be now.

"Susan," I began quietly, almost in a whisper. Tears made my voice quiver. "Remember at the meeting when Joe told the story about Leah and your class?"

"Sure. I remember."

"Well, I can't get it out of my mind." I concentrated on every word, wanting desperately to make sense. "Joe said so many things that I don't understand. Some I do—I mean like God being everywhere. That was what that little book was trying to say, right?"

"Yes," Susan answered. "That day in Sunday school was the reason I chose that book for Leah. I figured the hospital is a pretty scary place and the book would be comforting for her. She needed to remember that God was with her there." Susan paused, looking out her windows. "I never thought about her needing that kind of comfort now."

"I've been thinking." I saw her nod gently, encouragingly. "When I married Russell, what I really wanted was family. I was desperate for it. The reason I stayed so long may have been partly because I couldn't give that up." Tears fell again. I wiped my nose, then leaned over to pull another tissue from the table near me. "Now I think I finally get it. You've been trying to offer me family this whole time."

Susan nodded and bit her lip, as if to suppress an enormous laughing smile, while at the same time tears spilled down her cheeks.

"But I didn't understand." I took another sip from the cup and continued. "On the day of the meeting, Pastor Joe said that Leah believed in a living, caring God. I'd like to believe in the same kind of God. I think I'm sitting inside the whale, Susan. It's dark and scary, and I'm so alone. I know I have you. And I have all those people who are helping us. But I need God. I need Him to meet me here." I gave in to quiet weeping. "If He is with Leah, wherever she is, I need Him here with me too."

Susan drew her trembling lips into a tight line and suddenly let go. A smile flooded her face. "That can easily be arranged," she answered. "I thought you'd never ask."

Epilogue

WELL, THAT IS MY STORY.

For a long time I thought that it might be the only story I would ever have to tell. But I have learned this remarkable thing about God in my short time with Him. Just when one thinks the ending credits should roll, God begins a new story.

For months after that night at Susan's house, I hung suspended like a spider web in a gale force wind, blowing back and forth between terrifying fear and tentative trust, between forgiveness and horrible anger, between growth and rebellion. We worked endlessly to find the children. All the while I wondered if I would ever see them again. Then, catching myself in my own disbelief, I would rebuke myself soundly and make an agonizing attempt to believe what others told me—that God loved me and would someday bring this horror into focus. Many nights I cried myself to sleep. Others, I rested completely in what seemed to be a sea of unexplainable trust—a shelter protecting me from the terrifying loss I experienced.

I'd love to tell you that I figured it all out, but I didn't. It would have been nice to have a wise, faith-filled person explain it all to me, but no one could. I had to live believing without evidence and trusting without resolution that God could get me through it. And He did. Day by day. Hour by hour. Often, minute by trembling minute.

I made it through the end of the school year and then resigned from my teaching job. I needed to be back on the island. I needed Susan and my pastor and my church family. Without the threat of Russell's violence, the island seemed suddenly changed. It became home. How I wanted to go home!

Because Russell had been charged with felony custodial interference, finances no longer proved to be an obstacle. The court granted me an uncontested divorce and awarded me full custody of the children and all of the marital assets. What was left of them, anyway.

I sold the big house on the island and moved into Nana's old home. With the kindness of a telephone company representative named Carla and a significant investment of money, we managed to keep my old phone number in the process. We wanted to be certain that if Leah ever had an opportunity to call, she would get me—not a message. We even linked my cell phone to the house phone number so that the cell would ring first. There were times—terrible, lonely, painful times—when I sat crying and holding my cell phone, willing it to ring. It never did.

God did not seem surprised at my anger. He never hit me with lightning. Instead, He gave me Susan's comforting arms, Joe's constant encouragement, and a new job as the receptionist at Dr. John Severin's dental clinic. Just as I had at Russ's office, I scheduled appointments, billed insurance companies, and ordered supplies. The job was the same, but the boss was very different. Dr. John exuded kindness and gratitude. For the first time in many years, I lived and worked outside of fear.

Ten months after the children disappeared, we had our first glimmer of hope. Leo, our private detective, called me at work. "Patty, do you have a minute to talk?"

"Of course, Leo. What is it? Have you heard something?"

"I'm not sure. But I may have some news." He cleared his throat. "Now, Patty, I'm calling because I want your permission to check this out. I don't really know what I have, but I can't find out without getting closer."

"Leo, cut it out. Tell me what you know!"

"Okay. Here it is. I've been doing some internet research lately—lots of it. I've been watching for new physicians' offices opening, for new medical licenses being issued in other states—"

"Leo, I know all this. What did you find?"

"I checked last night and found an interesting little article in a Florida newspaper, quite by accident, really."

An older woman stood opposite my desk, waiting for me to schedule an appointment to seat her gold crown. Impatiently, she tapped her fingers on the counter. I made a desperate face, covered the phone with one hand, and hissed, "Just a minute." I pointed at the phone. "I'll be right with you." I swiveled away from her.

Leo continued without a pause. "It turns out that someone had a heart attack at Disney World last week. Right in the middle of the Magic Kingdom." Leo chuckled. "Anyway, a physician traveling with two children managed to save the guy's life."

"But it could have been anyone," I objected. It sounded too remote, too desperate, to connect the incident to Russell.

"I thought so too," Leo agreed. "But then I noticed that the guy refused to give his name to the reporter who wrote the article. So on a hunch, I called the newspaper and had them fax the picture that went with the column."

"What did you see?"

"Well, behind the ambulance guys, in the back corner of the picture, I found a little girl with dark eyes and curly dark hair."

"Oh, dear God, please," I breathed.

"Now, don't get your hopes up. She's older, but it sure looks like your Leah to me. But I can't tell if it's really her. That area of the picture is out of focus. And even if it is, they may have just been visiting, in which case they'd be long gone by now." Leo's voice sounded very determined. "But Russell might have settled there. And if I go nosing around, I might be able to get a lead on them. At least the heart attack happened in public. A lot of people might be able to identify them."

"I can't believe it."

"Don't relax yet. I don't know for sure. What I'm asking is, can I go to Florida and check it out?"

"How soon can you be on a plane?"

────

Leo called from Florida three days later. "I've got good news and bad news," he began.

My heart sank like an unchecked elevator. "What is it?"

"Well, the people here at the park gave me a positive ID on your husband. They recognized Russ's picture right off. The bad news is, I haven't been able to talk to the victim or his family. They've already left the hospital."

"Have you figured out whether Russ is in Florida permanently or not?"

"Not yet. That's going to take some time. I plan to visit every major hospital in the state to see if he's on staff anywhere. It isn't a sure thing. Maybe he isn't practicing medicine. Maybe he's changed his name."

"Then what will you do?"

"I'll cross that bridge when I come to it. He has to be supporting the kids somehow. If he's still in the state, he's working at something. We'll see."

I hung up feeling more anxious than ever. What if we were really close to finding Russell? What if we just missed him? What if he runs again? My stomach churned, and I cried. This time I was wise enough to call Susan. She came over and we talked it through. Susan's presence didn't change anything. It never had. But I could count on her love. She believed that God would see us through, and somehow, in my terror, she managed to transmit her trust to me.

────

More than a week later while I heated canned soup for dinner, Leo called again. This time from Pensacola. Without so much as a hello, he began. "I've got him!" His voice rang with triumph.

"Where?"

"He's working for an insurance company as a doctor who approves patient treatment plans."

"How did you find him?"

"A doctor at one of the hospitals recognized him from a conflict he'd had with the insurance company. The guy was delighted to turn Russ in."

"The kids?"

"I haven't seen them."

"What do you mean?"

"I just found his house. A little joint on the outskirts of town. Homes are far enough apart that the neighbors can't be too nosey."

"Do you think the kids are there?"

"I'm certain of it. I saw an old woman go in the house yesterday just before he drove off for work. He must have her come in to watch the kids."

"What next?"

"I'm going to watch for a couple days and confirm everything. In the meantime, you'd better talk to your lawyer." Leo gave me a number to contact him.

Not two minutes after talking with Leo, I had Judy Barton on the phone. "Leo thinks he's got them," I said without introduction.

I heard Judy land in her chair. "Thank God," she said simply. "When will he know for sure?"

"He says it may take a couple of days."

"Where are they?"

"Outside of Pensacola."

"All right. Here's what we do. I'll arrange to file with the court there. Unless Russ has done some fancy legal footwork, they'll honor our custody decree. When that's done, we'll have the police pick Russ up and snatch the kids."

"How? When?"

"Patience, Patty. When we're this close to finding them, we need more patience than ever before."

———

Two agonizing weeks after that last phone call, nearly eleven months since Russell disappeared with the children, we obtained a decree to enforce custody from a Florida court. Police officers waited patiently for us to arrive in Florida, holding an arrest warrant for Dr. Russell Koehler. They planned to snatch the kids as soon as we arrived.

Susan and I booked tickets aboard American Airlines Flight 432.

────────

At last today is the day. After settling in our seats, I gaze out the window, watching baggage handlers throw bag after bag onto the ramp moving into the belly of the airplane. My heart pounds like a runner going uphill. *Take off,* my brain demands. *Finish it, and take off.* I strain to see my own bag, unaware of the cabin attendant walking through the aisles checking seat backs and tray tables.

"Excuse me," she says to the woman on the aisle, "could you bring your seat forward for takeoff?" The cabin attendant smiles and waits for the chair to move up, then moves on. Susan, sitting next to me, leans over and gives me a thumbs-up. Then she pulls the seat belt tighter around her waist. I smile back, trying to appear confident. Inside, violent trembling threatens to stop my breathing. The baggage vehicle moves away, and moments later our plane shudders and backs away from the gate.

We taxi slowly, watching Seattle pass by the window. It begins to feel as though we will drive to Florida, when eventually we come to the end of the runway and turn to face the wind. Then, in a rush and a shrieking roar, the plane rises from the ground. Susan sits calmly reading *Bon Appétit,* hardly seeming to notice. I clutch the arms of my seat, inadvertently pushing the call bell. When the cabin attendant returns looking perturbed, I blush.

I would like to ask for some courage on-the-rocks.

Ten minutes later, when the pilot turns off the Fasten Seat Belt sign, I lean forward to pull the black nylon carryon from its cubby in front of my feet. I know what I want. Know exactly where I've hidden it. I brought it with me, wanting to revel in the wonder of this moment. Wanting to feel again what I felt when I wrote it and relish the wonder of my changed circumstance. I let my mind wander back to the night that Susan asked me to write this letter. How hard I tried to write but could not. Then later, after Susan and I talked, I began writing and could not stop.

I open the zipper and pull the envelope from the front pocket. The letter has waited there, in the very same envelope, for eleven long months. With fresh tears I suddenly realize that today I will read the letter to Leah.

Carefully, I slip the stationery from the envelope. My mouth is dry. My eyes ache with more unshed tears. Hands trembling, I unfold the letter. Beside me I feel Susan watching, and I notice her eyes glistening with tears. She reaches up to brush a straggler from her cheek and smiles.

Reading again, I treasure the words written on tear-stained stationery. Words written long ago.

Dear Leah,

I don't know if you will ever read this, but I must try to write to you. Susan says I must—that writing this will help me. One day, she says, reading it will help you, though I don't know how. At this moment I can't believe that anything will ever help me. But because Susan is my friend, I will try.

I want you to know that I pray for you every day. I ask God to keep you safe and happy. I ask that you live a wonderful life, full of peace and security. I pray that you are not living hidden, inside, away from other children, away from school. I pray that your little brother is well, and that he is growing up to be as wonderful as you are.

I want you to know, Leah, that I have come to know the same Jesus you know. He is my Savior now too. I have made many mistakes, and I hope that you can forgive me for them all. I am learning, just like you, how to please Jesus. In the meantime, I know He is able to keep you, and I must trust that He is writing a story in your life, as He is in mine.

I want you to know that I never wanted to leave you. Without you, I have been miserable. Every day, every child I see reminds me of you. Every smile, every voice, every laugh, every store window reminds me that you are gone. I have pictures of you and RJ all over my bedroom. I look for you in crowds, on the television, on busses, in all the strangest places—hoping against hope that your smile will beam back at me from some unexpected place.

I will never stop looking for you. Never stop doing whatever it takes to find you and bring you home. Please tell RJ about me. Tell him how much I love him. Tell him what I look like, how we played together, how we laughed. Remind him of the songs we sang, of the books we read, and of the stories we shared. Try to keep me alive for him, and in the telling, for you also.

And most of all, Leah, never give up hope. We will be together again, honey. I promise.

Love,
Mommy

When I finish, I fold the letter and carefully replace it in the envelope. Susan takes my hand and gives a gentle squeeze. I lean toward her and whisper directly into her ear. "I'm going to hold my babies today."

We laugh.

Acknowledgments

I wish to thank the many people who have helped to supply advice in the writing and researching of *Serenity Bay*. My most sincere appreciation to Mary East, R.N. of Phoebe House (a rescue house for victims of domestic violence), Tom Neuman of Cedar River Counseling and Nancy Murphy of Northwest Family Life (both therapists specializing in the field), Drs. Neil Jacobson and John Gottman of the University of Washington, Rebecca at the Pierce County Domestic Violence Advocates Office, and Steve Holmes (detective, Tacoma Police Department). My thanks also to Karl Zeiger and Mark Howard, who willingly gave hours helping me wade through the legal issues involved in this story. Without these experts, *Serenity Bay* would not be what it is. Thanks, guys. May God richly bless your willingness to share your experiences.

My special appreciation goes to Andrea Gjeldum, the designer who created the perfect cover. And to Barb Lilland, the world's best editor, who saw a better end in a rocky beginning, my deepest thanks. You've both made dreams come true.